CONTAINMENT

Also by Caryn Lix

Sanctuary

A SANCTUARY NOVEL

CONTA

NMENT

CARYN LIX

SIMON PULSE
NEW YORK   LONDON   TORONTO   SYDNEY   NEW DELHI

SIMON PULSE

An imprint of Simon & Schuster Children's Publishing Division

1230 Avenue of the Americas, New York, New York 10020

First Simon Pulse hardcover edition August 2019

Text copyright © 2019 by Caryn Lix

Front cover art copyright © 2019 by Jacey

Jacket art on spine, back cover, and flaps copyright © 2019 by Thinkstock

All rights reserved, including the right of reproduction in whole or in part in any form.

SIMON PULSE and colophon are registered trademarks of Simon & Schuster, Inc.

For information about special discounts for bulk purchases, please contact

Simon & Schuster Special Sales at 1-866-506-1949 or business@simonandschuster.com.

The Simon & Schuster Speakers Bureau can bring authors to your live event.

For more information or to book an event contact the Simon & Schuster Speakers Bureau

at 1-866-248-3049 or visit our website at www.simonspeakers.com.

Jacket designed by Sarah Creech | Interior designed by Mike Rosamilia

The text of this book was set in Adobe Garamond Pro.

Manufactured in the United States of America

10 9 8 7 6 5 4 3 2 1

Library of Congress Cataloging-in-Publication Data

Names: Lix, Caryn, author.

Title: Containment / by Caryn Lix.

Description: First Simon Pulse hardcover edition. | New York : Simon Pulse, 2019. |

Summary: Kenzie and her friends learn that more aliens are headed to Earth,

and it is up to them to stop the invastion at all costs.

Identifiers: LCCN 2018035878 (print) | LCCN 2018042137 (eBook) |

ISBN 9781534405387 (eBook) | ISBN 9781534405363 (hc)

Subjects: | CYAC: Adventure and adventurers—Fiction. | Extraterrestrial beings—Fiction. |

Supervillains—Fiction. | Science fiction.

Classification: LCC PZ7.1.L5853 (eBook) |

LCC PZ7.1.L5853 Con 2019 (print) | DDC [Fic]—dc23

LC record available at https://lccn.loc.gov/2018035878

To all the people who read
and loved SANCTUARY, especially
my friends, my family, my students.
There is no book without readers,
and there is no future for Kenzie
without you.

From darkness comes the signal. From light the dark. From dark the shine, the ripple of death ricocheting through the collective.

Minds awaken. Consciousness perks.

And the death ripple tears through them like a storm, coarse, and fear and pain and rage, above all rage, as the collectors are harvested.

The mind releases.

The assault begins.

ONE

MY BARE FEET POUNDED THE BLACK FLOORS, my breath coming in short, sharp gasps. Strings of flickering lights illuminated my way, and I jumped over a piece of something unrecognizable lying in the middle of the corridor. By now, on my twelfth loop, it was a conditioned response.

A thin sheen of sweat covered my body, one I wouldn't be able to rinse away, and my foot throbbed slightly. Reed, our resident healer, had fixed my earlier injury, but either he hadn't managed it completely, or I was experiencing ghost pain. Life on this alien ship had made me soft. No exercise regimen, no training sessions, nothing but sitting around worrying and ignoring increasingly frantic messages from my dad on Earth until my comm ran out of battery. I couldn't afford to lose my edge. And so I ran, around and around the ship until I collapsed from exhaustion.

Cage kept pace beside me, bare arms gleaming, muscles sharp and defined even with our recent enforced inactivity. I scowled and put on a burst of speed, but even without using his powers, he easily kept pace. *With* his abilities, of course, he could have lapped me a dozen times before I blinked.

Like everyone else on this alien ship, Cage was an anomaly, a superpowered teen recently escaped from the orbital prison Sanctuary. Of course, even though I was an anomaly too, I'd worked as a guard before being taken hostage by the prisoners. I'd only banded together with them to survive an attack from vicious alien creatures, all while discovering my *own* lurking powers, which gave me much more in common with the prisoners than with Omnistellar, the company I had once devoted my life to. By capturing this alien ship on a wing and a prayer, we'd barely avoided the aliens hell-bent on assimilating us, and for some stupid reason, I'd thought that now things would calm down a little. Sure, we still had Omnistellar to deal with, and we were all criminals on the run, but the combination of freedom and a near-death experience had to count for something, right?

Not so much. Not living in the very pit of the vipers who'd tried to kill us. Taking the alien ship had been a victory. It was the only reason we'd survived their attack on Sanctuary and escaped with our lives. But every time we turned around, we faced alien technology, alien architecture. The ship didn't want us here. We'd taken it, but it wasn't ours. And nobody forgot that for a second.

As if constant prickling unease weren't enough to keep me busy, I had my dad back on Earth probably thinking I was dead. I'd ignored his messages at first because I didn't know what to say, how to tell him about Mom's death or confront him with my knowledge that he'd implanted the power-controlling chip in me when I was young. As time went by, things only got worse, and now my comm battery was dead, so I couldn't talk to him even if I wanted to. Add another layer of guilt, please.

And I wasn't the only one who'd lost people. With so many friends and family members vanished from our lives, living with the perpetual shadow of the things we'd done to survive, it was no wonder our escape hadn't proved an easy solution.

Some of us seemed to be able to live with those things more easily than others, of course. Cage jogged to a casual halt in front of me, leaning his hands on his knees and casting me the boyish grin that always made my lips twitch in return. Our current workout seemed to absorb every bit of his attention without a hint of the relentless stress in the back of my mind. Cage set the mood for the others, and I knew he took that role seriously. But even with me, he hadn't offered any indication that his past decisions cost him a moment of sleep. "I give up," he gasped now. "Mercy."

"It's not a competition," I said, although it totally was, and I had totally just won—the test of stamina, anyway. Cage had more than matched my speed.

Cage pulled a bottle of water out of one of the supply bags

we'd strung along the walls and passed it to me. Our fingers brushed, more contact than we'd had in two weeks, and I tried to keep my face impassive as I cracked it open. "Thanks," I said, draining half the bottle in a single gulp.

He grabbed a bottle of his own and sank to the floor. I sat across from him, and we gazed at each other. The tips of our toes were almost touching, but the space felt wider with all the words and fears unspoken between us. Something had happened after Sanctuary. The night we'd escaped, I'd huddled against Cage and we'd clung to each other like a lifeline. But as the days passed and reality intruded, those touches, those shared jokes, those moments of peace and refuge vanished beneath the mountain of things we'd done to make those small moments possible.

I glanced both ways to make sure no one was in earshot and said, "I've been thinking . . ." *About Matt. About what happened back on Sanctuary, that terrifying, horrible moment when the gun jerked in my hand. The shot I thought would save him, which ended up being the shot that ended him.*

"Did it hurt?"

I rolled my eyes. "That's a joke my dad would tell."

Cage smiled, although the effort never quite made it past his lips. "That's what I'm known for. What are you thinking about?"

Everything. The moment he'd argued in favor of killing the aliens on this ship, and how little the thought of genocide seemed to bother him. Rune shouting at her brother, desperate to prevent him from murdering an entire race of creatures, Cage's furious response, his desperation to eliminate the creatures before they awoke and came after us again. The way every sound in every corner made me freeze in terror as if an alien might leap from behind a wall. The tension on the ship, so thick you could almost bathe in it. I settled for the thing most frequently on my mind: "Matt." Matt. My friend, Cage's friend, everyone's friend, really. He'd been one of the only prisoners to treat me with respect from day one. And then the alien had attacked him, and I'd been the one with the gun.

I'd shot, of course. Who wouldn't? To save a friend?

But I'd missed. In the wake of that horror, of Matt lying breathless and sightless on the floor, it had been Cage who'd dragged the body away, Cage who'd convinced me to lie, to say the alien killed him. And I'd been lying ever since.

A cloud settled over his face. "Kenzie, we've talked about this."

My stomach twisted and scuttled for cover. So much easier not to discuss these things, to laugh and change the subject. But I'd been searching for the opportunity for days. "I know. And you were right, at first. Back on Sanctuary, we couldn't tell anyone what I'd done." The prisoners on Sanctuary had already viewed me with suspicion and hatred. If they'd known that I shot their friend, even accidentally, they never would have followed me off the ship. The truth would have killed us all. But now . . . "We're all stuck together. I've gotten to know people better. They trust me, or I think they do."

"They do." He leaned forward, fixing me with his earnest gaze. "Or they're coming to. But what do you think will happen to that trust if they find out you've been lying to them for weeks?"

That tore through me. "*I've* been lying to them?"

"*We've* been lying to them," he amended quickly. "But that's not how they'll see it. And even if they do, I have history with them. They'll forgive me before they forgive you."

I closed my eyes, took another swallow of water, and thought about how I'd react if I found out Rune had been lying to me all along, that she'd secretly jettisoned the aliens herself despite arguing against it. Cage knew these people better than me. They were just coming to trust me as Kenzie, instead of the Omnistellar guard representing all their fears. I supposed there might be a few other corporate citizens on this ship, but most of them were probably government kids who'd grown up with only the most basic supports. Even if I hadn't been a guard, I was still a representation of corporate citizenship and all the benefits and privileges that came with it, especially in a huge corp like Omnistellar. It was only natural that they viewed me with suspicion and resentment.

Now, finally, I was getting past that surface, convincing them to see me for who I was and not what I represented. If I threw that away, if they turned on me, I couldn't protect myself, not even with Cage's support.

But that meant I had to carry the burden of what I'd done

all by myself, see my guilt reflected in the growing trust of my friends. Feel it widening the gulf between Cage and me with every word we didn't say. "Look," I tried again, searching for the words to change his mind, or maybe my own. "I don't . . ."

Voices rose in the distance. Our eyes met, and as one, we heaved ourselves to our feet and jogged in their direction. Tensions ran high on this ship. If we didn't break arguments up before they got out of hand, they tended to escalate in a hurry.

But by the time we got there, the situation was under control, thanks to Reed. He stood in one of the waist-high crevices scattered across the alien ship, only the tip of his dark hair visible as his voice echoed through the corridor. "I'm not kidding," he said, his voice somehow teasing and yet carrying a hint of authority. "If the two of you get into any more fistfights, I'm not patching you up."

Cage groaned inaudibly at the word "fistfight," and we both quickened our step.

A boy sat on the floor of the crevice with Reed crouched over him, fingers against his temples. The boy twisted his head to scowl at us, revealing blood caked along his face, but before my eyes his nose twitched, repositioning itself, knitting back into shape.

"Again?" said Cage irritably. I bit my lip against a similar response. At least Reed had the presence of mind to pull them into a more isolated area. More fights were not going to help the already tense mood on board this ship.

The boy—what was his name? John? Jason? Something with a J—scowled. "Tell Keith to stay away from my boyfriend and we won't have a problem."

"I'm not telling anyone anything, and you need to figure out how to solve your problems without punching each other."

Reed finished his healing and the boy launched himself to his feet, dragging himself out of the crevice and shoving past us. "You're one to talk," he tossed over his shoulder as he stormed down the corridor. "How did you deal with the aliens?"

"That was Mia," Cage said crossly to the kid's retreating back. "And also, bloodthirsty aliens. So, you know, not the same thing."

Reed flopped back in the crevice and stared up at us, shaking his head. "This is getting worse, you know. More fights. More stupid little arguments. People waking up screaming because someone passed them on the way to the bathroom in the night. The original plan, the drifting through space to freedom thing? That's not going to work unless we get a whole team of psychiatrists in here with us." He looked thoughtful. "Think Omnistellar would sponsor us? It'd make a hell of a live vid series. Watch the Anomaly Kids of Sanctuary deal with their alien-induced PTSD, on the aliens' ship, no less! Live and in color!"

Cage stared at him blankly. "In color? What else would it be in, shades of green?"

"You really need to learn your history," Reed sighed.

I jumped in before he could launch into a lecture. Reed was usually about the best-natured among us, but get him going on spaceships, or racing, or technological history, or anything, really, with an electronic focus, and you'd be there the rest of your life. "Thanks, Reed. We'll keep an eye on things." I caught Cage's sleeve and dragged him in the opposite direction.

Once I had him around the corner, though, I glanced both ways and met his gaze steadily. "He's not wrong. People are starting to freak out. We're living on an alien ship, Cage. Every inch of it reminds us of those things."

"If you have another plan, I'm all ears."

I shrugged helplessly, and once again that tension built between us. Cage and I had been together every step of this journey, from the moment the aliens attacked Sanctuary, through our devastating near misses, discovering the chip that meant I had powers of my own, escaping the station . . . We hadn't known each other that long, but the sheer breadth of our shared experiences made it feel much longer. We slept side by side in the same crevice at night, worked out together during the day, argued over the best course of action.

And yet . . . every day, we seemed to grow further apart. Lying about me killing Matt? Cage's idea. Venting the aliens into space? Ditto. And he kept doing it, every moment of every day. I couldn't help but wonder . . . was he doing it to me, too?

"Hey," he said, reaching out. For a moment it seemed like he might take my hand, and my skin tingled in anticipation, but his fingers fluttered softly back to his side. "You all right? You vanished again."

Heat rushed to my cheeks. I was used to being the strong one, always on guard against any sign of weakness. But even I had to admit the alien ship was taking its toll. "I don't want to be here anymore," I confessed. The lights we'd strung across the corridor flickered, illuminating the smooth, blocky alien architecture, a constant reminder that we weren't home. We weren't anywhere humans were meant to be. "And no, I don't have anything better to suggest at the moment. The second we're spotted, Omnistellar will descend on us. We'll all end up back in prison—if we're lucky. If we stay here, we eventually run out of supplies, or we all kill each other due to stress. I don't see a way out."

He grinned bleakly. "You'd think escaping the most secure prison in the solar system would be the challenge, huh? Or the vicious aliens. Not keeping everyone's heads together in the aftermath."

I examined his eyes, warm and dark and sparkling and yet with a layer over them that kept anyone from seeing his true self, even me. "Don't *you* feel it?" I demanded, fighting the nervous tremble in my voice. "You're always so . . . so calm. Don't you feel fear? Remorse? Worry? Does any of it touch you?"

For a moment that veil dropped, and turmoil raced behind his eyes. "Kenzie, you have no idea."

And I didn't. Because he didn't tell me. Didn't *trust* me.

The silence between us grew taut and cold, and at last I forced a smile. "Our course was going to take us near Mars today. I'm going to check in with Rune, make sure we're outside the range of their sensors. I'll see you later."

"Kenzie, wait."

"What?" I faced him, arching an eyebrow, affecting an annoyed demeanor even as I hoped he *would* have something to say, some way to make things better. To alleviate the guilt. The fear. The pain.

But he only sighed. "Right. See you later," he said.

"Yeah." And with bitterness gnawing at my heart, I stalked across the corridor and out of sight.

TWO

USUALLY ONLY RUNE HUNG OUT IN THE COMMAND
center, fiddling with technology, trying to force a bond with the
computer, but even she had taken a break from her usual perch.
A nest in the corner marked where she slept, a smattering of dirty
clothes, electronic parts she'd pilfered from God knew where,
and nutrient bars. Just the sight of them made my stomach turn
over. We'd survived on nothing else for about three weeks now.
The sickly sweet smell permeated the entire ship.

A series of raised symbols filled the fluid comm board, and
I ran my fingers over them. I'd grown increasingly familiar
with the alien language over the last few weeks, but not familiar
enough to sight-read it. Like everyone else, I had my own set of
powers, a "gift" from the aliens who'd sought to harvest us as
hosts for their own reproduction. Rune bonded with computer
systems. Me? I understood languages. I could communicate

easily with Rune and her brother Cage in Mandarin, or with our friend Alexei in Russian.

The alien language, though, that was something else, utterly nonverbal and completely intuitive. It took all my focus to make heads or tails of it. I let it wash over me now, struggling to decipher system updates. Otherwise, there simply wasn't much of interest. The alien system didn't match anything I'd ever encountered, full of technical specs and coordinates and not much else. I hadn't found anything approximating a culture, a religion, or even a comic book. And man, did I miss comic books. Without my connection to Earth, I hadn't even downloaded the latest issue of *Robo Mecha Dream Girl 5*. And I'd never finished the issue before that.

Something tingled at the edge of my consciousness, but I couldn't quite catch it. I chased the meaning, but it fled from my amped-up emotions. I had the best success with my power when I was calm and centered. I hadn't managed that in weeks, and my argument with Cage had left my heart racing. The fresh helping of guilt about Matt didn't help either.

Sighing, I stepped back from the console. I should probably try to figure out the new glitch in the system, but last time I'd noticed something off, I'd spent an hour working on it and had given myself a blinding migraine only to realize it was the computer telling me about a minor course adjustment. This new glitch was probably nothing. And I needed to calm down before it would make any sense.

Something clattered behind me.

Every muscle in my body froze, steel slamming into my spine. My heart rate jackhammered as a surge of terror enveloped me. *Claws scrambling against metal . . . the long slow rattle of alien breath . . .*

Goddamn it, there were no aliens on this ship. Mia had seen to that.

Mia. Of course. "Mia," I said sharply, pivoting in place. "Is that you?"

She shimmered into view, appearing disappointed. Her hair hung in greasy clumps around her pale skin, and she gave me a wicked smile. "I tripped."

"Isn't everyone on edge enough?" I snapped, fighting to hide my irritation. "Do you have to sneak up on people just to prove you can?"

She shrugged. "Sorry," she said, not sounding apologetic at all. "Just curious to see what you were up to." She drew close to me and leaned against the wall, resting her sore leg. Reed had fixed her as best he could, but the alien's claws had done some serious damage to her muscles, and there were limits to his power.

"Since when?" I demanded suspiciously. Mia had never displayed the least interest in what Rune and I were up to in the control room.

She scowled. "Okay, I was bored. So, what are you doing?"

"Where's Alexei?" I countered. I rarely saw Mia without her massive shadow.

"He was driving me crazy, so I turned invisible and gave him the slip. He seems to think that if I lie still long enough my leg will heal. If Reed couldn't fix me, bed rest isn't going to do it either."

I blinked, startled. That was probably more raw honesty than I'd ever gotten from Mia in a single statement, and it showed that she wasn't any more immune to the stress permeating the ship than the rest of us. In a way, it made me feel warmer toward her. I'd come to appreciate her strength and determination. But she was still volatile and unpredictable, and I didn't dare count her a friend yet.

"I was just checking in on our location," I replied honestly. "We're near Mars, and I want to make sure we don't get inside their sensor range." Omnistellar didn't have a presence on Mars. That was Mars Mining's domain. But Omnistellar was the most powerful corp in the solar system, and any other organization, especially an up-and-coming group like Mars Mining, would jump at the chance to curry some favor by arresting us.

"Can sensors even pick up this ship? I thought Sanctuary couldn't."

"It didn't seem to, but . . ." I shrugged. "Why take chances?"

Mia nodded, glancing around, pacing back and forth with the grace and danger of a caged tiger. I'd seen her do it before, stalking the ship's corridors. I remembered Alexei telling me that Mia hated confined spaces. The words hovered on my lips—*Are you okay?*—but I didn't think Mia would appreciate them, so I only said, "Reed broke up another fight just now."

"Reed's good at that." She examined a console as if she could understand it if she stared at it long enough. "People don't get offended when he tells them off. He does it with a wink, and they walk away laughing."

"You could try that," I offered, raising an eyebrow to show I was kidding.

Mia laughed. "Diplomacy might not be my strong suit." She hesitated. "Look, I've been meaning to say . . . everything that happened back on Sanctuary? I didn't trust you, not for a long time, but you came through. We wouldn't be here if not for you. I was . . . maybe a bit hasty judging you. Anyway. Thanks."

A sudden burst of some unidentifiable feeling choked me. This was the closest I'd ever heard to an apology from Mia, ever. And I didn't deserve it. Not her apology. Not her gratitude. Yeah, I'd saved a few of the prisoners on Sanctuary. But I'd been part of the company that imprisoned them in the first place, and worst of all, Matt was dead because of me.

But I couldn't tell Mia any of that, so I forced a smile. "Thanks," I said. "But I don't think I did that much. You were the one who—"

Mia waved me aside as if I was boring her. "Let's not do that."

This time I grinned for real. Mia might be dangerous, but she was genuine. You didn't have to play games or guess with her. "All right. Then just thank you."

She nodded, glanced at the console once more, and suddenly disappeared. Her boots scuffed loudly against the floor as she retreated from the console room, a courtesy, I knew, because Mia could move as silently as a snake when she wanted.

The exchange left me bewildered, although not unpleasantly so. I'd made progress with Mia over the last few weeks. I'd hoped the shared experience, the terror of escaping the aliens, might bring everyone together, and it had for a while. Some of us felt it more than others: Mia and Cage and Rune and Alexei, who had faced the nightmare themselves, who had seen friends die around them, and me and Imani . . . Imani, who we'd found dangling from chains on the alien ship, who'd healed herself too late to help her sister.

As the space between Cage and me grew, I'd started spending more time with Imani. We didn't talk about it much, but we'd both lost family in that attack: Imani lost her sister, and me . . . I lost my mom. When I hung out with her, we talked about anything *but* our families: reality vids, VR games, our favorite video bloggers. Imani seemed to have a thing for beauty bloggers and could rattle off names I'd never heard of, the so-called beauty belles and their incredibly popular channels. I listened in fascination as she explained exactly what I needed to do to my eyebrows to maximize my features. Maybe I would even try it if I ever got off this ship.

Hanging out with Imani was nice. She was the only person who never brought up the aliens, the deaths, our current circumstances. She had never once turned to me and said, *What do we do now?* Like me, she just wanted a few minutes to forget, and sometimes we could find that together. I wished she were here now. I could use a few minutes of forgetfulness. I contemplated going to find her, asking her a question guaranteed to engage her interest—*So what did you say was the key to a successful online presence?*—but a sudden burst of exhaustion overwhelmed me.

I sank down against the wall, staring at Rune's corner, and stroked my fingers over the smooth silver of my wrist comm, trying not to dwell on how much I missed my dad, no matter how furious I still was. The silence of the control room settled over me. It had been a long time since I'd been alone. Unbidden, memories surfaced: feeling my way around this room in the dark, every sound a potential alien waking from its slumber. I winced, wrapping my arms around my knees, a wave of nausea threatening, and I allowed myself just one moment of weakness, my limbs trembling, my heart racing, my breath coming in short gasps, before I pulled myself together. I couldn't let anyone see me like this. I had to . . . what? There was nothing to do. Nothing I could do. I stared miserably at the tangled nest of blankets.

And then footsteps raced along the hall. My head shot up, and I jerked to my feet, shaking off my lethargy just as Rune charged through the door and straight into me. We collapsed in a tangle of limbs and Mandarin cursing. Her elbow jammed into my ribs, sending pain spiking into my lungs. "Rune!" I exclaimed, rolling over and clutching my arm. "What the hell?"

"Sorry!" Rune caught my hand and yanked me to my feet with surprising strength, then pulled me toward the console. "Take a look at something."

"What's going on?"

"That's what I'm hoping you can tell me." A muscle in Rune's jaw twitched. "I sensed something wrong in the system, and it's only getting worse. But the computer won't talk to me, it won't . . . you haven't noticed anything, have you?" She turned her wide eyes on me, frantic and imploring, and with a guilty start, I remembered the strange blip I'd noticed a few moments ago.

"Let me take a look," I said.

"Wait." Rune closed her eyes, frowning. She ran her fingers over the console, dipping them in and out of the surface, a quirk of her power that had terrified me at first but now seemed as normal as breathing. "It's clearer here, in the control room. Kenzie, I think . . . it's a communication!"

"A communication from *outside*? Like from another ship?" My brain caught up, and Rune's urgency infected me. If that was true, this was the first signal we'd had from anyone in three weeks.

I swallowed hard, forcing myself to be calm. But no communication from outside could be good. It might be Omnistellar on our tails. At best, it was a merchant vessel wanting to know what the hell we were, and that was a question we'd have trouble answering. At worst, it was someone out for blood: an Omnistellar bounty hunter, maybe, someone who'd figured out that we'd survived Sanctuary, who'd come after us to track us down and drag us home.

Still, a tiny part of me hoped that maybe, just maybe, my dad was on the other end of that comm. When he didn't hear from me, would he have gone to the lengths of hunting me down? Did Dad love me enough to go against Omnistellar for me? Or . . . my fingers trembled on the edge of the console. What if it *was* Dad, but instead of setting out to find me for my own sake, he'd done it *for* Omnistellar?

But one look at the actual language dispelled any such illusion. Words washed over me, or not words, precisely, but meaning, and that meaning made my blood run cold. All at once it came rushing back, every second on Sanctuary: the aliens stalking us through the corridors, their unseeing eyes milky and ghastly as their claws ripped into people I cared about; Tyler, my friend, floating into space; Rita, closer than a sister, soaked in her own blood; and of course, Mom, her lifeless body cradled in my arms.

These weren't words, but they had meaning. Concepts, alien and foreign and yet somehow teasing the borders of my brain with significance.

The aliens were searching for their ship. And if another

ship found us, if more aliens were on the way . . . if, God help us, they realized that Mia had ejected hundreds of their unconscious siblings into space . . .

It took every ounce of my decade of Omnistellar training not to run from the room in terror. I'd recoiled from the board when the first wash of meaning hit me, and I felt Rune's gaze boring into me. I used an old trick my dad had taught me and stared at a spot on the floor until the world stopped spinning, set my jaw, and returned to my task. My fingers found the raised symbols and I closed my eyes, striving for stillness around the rampage of my heartbeat. Doing this came easier now, as I grew more familiar with my power, but I didn't think the alien language would ever feel natural, even for me.

I brushed the symbols and their significance washed over me, simultaneously benign, almost routine, and yet menacing enough to send a chill down my spine. There was no mistake.

The aliens were coming.

I'd known they would. I'd known it. But I hadn't let myself consider the idea with any seriousness. I'd hoped we had time, time to plan and think and figure out what to do next. Now, only weeks after we'd escaped Sanctuary, here they were. And if they responded this quickly, who knew what they planned? What sort of firepower they had? What they would do to us?

My eyes fluttered open and found Rune's anxious gaze. "We have to get off this ship."

. . .

Ten minutes later we huddled in the control room with what I'd come to think of as our core group. Reed watched with his characteristic quiet wit dancing in his eyes, like he was sketching each of us from the sidelines. Mia paced. Nearby, Alexei folded his huge form against a wall and monitored her with growing concern. Imani sat on the floor near Rune, working her fingers through her long braids. Like Reed, Imani had healing powers, but hers were the mirror image of his. Reed could heal anyone except himself, and Imani could heal *only* herself. Now, she frowned at her fingers and wiggled them. "Hangnail," she explained to no one in particular. She caught my eye and winked. I think I was the only one who saw through Imani's cheerful demeanor. Understanding passed between us, unspoken but never unfelt.

And of course, Cage, his presence simultaneously reassuring and threatening as he stood at my back, Rune as far away as she could manage. She still hadn't forgiven him for arguing in favor of venting the aliens into space. I wasn't sure I had either. He might have been right to do it, and we'd reached an uncomfortable truce in the matter. But I couldn't help remembering how *easy* the decision had been for him. And there was the way he'd turned on Rune: *It's not the first time I've had to kill someone to keep you safe.* I'd let it go. I mean, we'd been in the aftershock of an alien attack. But for three weeks, we'd had nothing but time to talk, and I still hadn't brought it up, still hadn't asked the questions hovering on my lips. Every day I didn't, it got a little bit harder, and the space between us got a little bit wider.

He looked to me for support. He wanted answers, but I didn't have any. I wasn't sure how I felt myself. Cage was my lifeline on Sanctuary. We'd saved each other half a dozen times, not only physically, but mentally. In a short time, I'd drawn closer to him than to almost anyone else I'd ever met. But the last three weeks had driven home how little we knew each other. I liked Cage. I liked his humor, his level-headedness, his charisma. But even after a month, I didn't *know* him. Did anyone, really?

Every eye landed on me. I met Cage's gaze and nodded. How could he make me feel so confused, so uncertain, and yet so secure at the same time? "The aliens are looking for their own," I announced without preamble. That brought all movement in the room to a standstill. I spoke quietly; we hadn't dared close the door for fear of creating too much curiosity in the other prisoners. I didn't want them to hear what I said, not yet. They were too volatile, too recently released from their cells, and some of them for very real crimes. The last thing we needed was a panic in an enclosed environment.

I allowed myself a small smile. I was thinking like a guard again. Omnistellar would be proud. Too bad I wanted nothing to do with my former corporation ever again.

Mia snapped her fingers an inch from my face, and I

recoiled in spite of myself. She smirked. "Wanna explain that, sunshine?"

I counted to ten before I answered, grinding my teeth in irritation, managing to keep my voice level. So much for our moment in the control room. "We received a message. It's nothing important, a basic call for information, I think. It looks like they're telling us where they are and asking for our location in return. The good news is, their position seems pretty far off. But it means there are other aliens, and they're tracking us."

Cage folded his arms, frowning. As usual, his mind processed information at the speed of light, calculating and planning while everyone else struggled to absorb what they'd heard. "Could we send a response?" he suggested. "Fake coordinates, maybe? Buy ourselves some time?"

I shook my head. "I'm nowhere near comfortable enough with the language to risk that. The second they got my message, if I could even figure out how to send it, they'd double their speed. Rune's already attempted to disable the signal with no success. We have to get off this ship."

"We have to *destroy* this ship," said Alexei in his soft, barely accented English, so at odds with his massive bulk. "Otherwise they will track it no matter what we do and head straight here."

"They're already coming," I said bluntly. A chill raced down my spine. Cage moved as if to take my hand but must have thought better of it. Because the others were watching? Or . . . ? I shook my head and pressed on. "Rune's picked up two more messages since then. The aliens are getting closer with each one. We have some time, but . . ."

"But we have to decide what to do," Cage agreed. The others regarded him with a deference they never showed me, and I stifled a wave of annoyance. He'd led them for a long time, after all. It made sense that they trusted a fellow prisoner more than a guard who'd oppressed them, even if I *had* turned out to be more like them than I'd ever guessed—or been willing to admit. Still, I'd saved everyone's lives on Sanctuary. The least they could do was give me the same attention they offered Cage. "Alexei's right," he continued. "The only way to throw them off our trail is to destroy this ship, and we don't have the means to do that, do we?" He turned to Rune, clearly addressing his question to her, but she folded her arms and glared at the wall.

I sighed internally. The last thing I needed right now was to referee a game of chicken between angry siblings. "Rune?" I demanded.

She addressed her response to me, not Cage. "I checked for any kind of self-destruct mechanism as soon as I got us moving. I couldn't find anything. Even if all the aliens die, the ship continues. As soon as it goes a few days without manual input, it veers off and returns to wherever the aliens came from. And it carries a full record of everything that's happened to it."

Once again, I closed my eyes. Everyone knew what Rune's words meant, but no one wanted to admit it. I pictured the other kids on this ship. Some of them were your basic teenagers. One was barely more than a child. But some of them, more than enough, were unpredictable. They were criminals before their arrest, and years of imprisonment on Sanctuary had done nothing to improve their self-control or social skills. The alien attack, and the following weeks of what was essentially another prison, hadn't helped either. When they learned about this, I had no idea what they'd do or if we could control them.

Well, no one else was going to say it. As much as I'd tried to leave the guard behind, I kept embracing that role. Someone had to think responsibly. "So, we either keep going with this ship broadcasting our signal, not to mention our solar system's, to the aliens, or . . ." A sinking feeling rose in my chest, and I fought it down. After everything we'd been through, after our daring escape . . . "Or we find a way to destroy it from outside."

Cage nodded, his thoughts already mirroring mine. "And the only way we can do that . . ."

"Is to turn ourselves in."

THREE

TURNING OURSELVES IN TO OMNISTELLAR WAS a true nightmare. For the rest of the kids on the ship, it meant going right back to the hellhole they'd escaped, a lifetime of imprisonment for no reason other than their powers or, as Mia pointed out, worse, since they'd proven they could escape a high-security prison once. For me, though . . . I was a corporate traitor. That was the lowest of the low. Sure, people could, and did, switch corporations, leaving one behind for another, but that only happened rarely and with the possibility of advancement. There were policies to follow, rules to obey. Actually betraying your corporation, turning on it, was almost unheard of, and I would be lucky if imprisonment was the worst I faced.

Predictably, Mia didn't take the news very well, shouting and ranting until Alexei quietly asked, "Would you rather bring the aliens here?"

That shut her up. Because even Mia, with all her bravado, knew better. At Alexei's words, a stillness settled over us as everyone relived the horror of those moments on Sanctuary: tails slithering, claws lashing, speed and blood and the high, hissing rattle that meant you'd been found.

No. We couldn't go through that again. And we certainly couldn't bring them to Earth.

But that didn't make anyone happy with our choices.

The hours following Rune's discovery passed in a blur of action, Cage insisting on speed. "We need to move fast," he said. "Not give anyone too much time to think." As usual, he was right about that stuff. People fell into line out of simple relief that someone else was taking charge, and no one asked too many questions. Cage was always able to predict how the others would react. It was only me he couldn't seem to figure out.

"I can't believe we're doing this," he muttered now. He leaned against the console, fists braced on its edge, as if the symbols in front of him might start to resolve into English, or maybe just helpfully tell him what they said.

"That makes two of us." Mia unfolded herself from where she leaned against the doorframe. "You guys sure?"

I nodded and met her eyes, searching for stability, reliability, something to trust. "We're counting on you if things go bad."

"Oh, don't worry about that." She strung her fingers together and cracked her hands, rolling her shoulders. A shiver of fear raced through me. Given the chance for freedom, would Mia return to rescue us? After a few weeks with the girl, I still didn't get her. She seemed loyal to Cage and Alexei, but she also hated confinement more than anyone I'd ever known. If she got a taste of freedom, could I even blame her if she didn't risk recapture to save our skins?

I looked from person to person, hoping for another plan to materialize, preferably one that relied less on Mia's altruism. Nothing came to mind. I glanced at Cage, but he obviously didn't share my concerns. He'd trusted Mia from day one. I sighed. I didn't have much choice but to trust her too. "Everyone's okay with the plan?"

Reed ducked into the room behind Mia, a grin playing on his lips. "You mean your batshit idea where you walk into the arms of interstellar law enforcement? Not sure I'd call that a *plan*. And 'okay' might be a bit strong. Do you have any idea—?"

"Reed," said Cage dryly, "if anyone knows what we're getting ourselves into, it's Kenzie."

Well, he was right about that. I'd grown up in Omnistellar's ranks, and I knew the company inside and out. It didn't take failure lightly. Traitors were quietly executed. Or maybe not that quietly, because the details always seemed to circulate. Mom and Dad chalked that up to corporate leaks, but Omnistellar definitely wouldn't let information disperse if they wanted it blocked. Mom and Dad had to have known that, too. Something else they'd lied about.

Regardless, Omnistellar had a formidable reputation for efficiency and ruthlessness. Not even Mars Mining Incorporated, a pretty lax corporation in the grand scheme of things, would risk their wrath. We were taking on the biggest, best-organized corporation in the solar system. *My* corporation. My former family. The place I'd thought I'd spend my life.

But what was the alternative? Lead a horde of vicious aliens to Earth? I squared my shoulders, meeting everyone's gaze in turn. "Get in position," I ordered.

Reed backed through the door, but Mia hesitated. "Not too late to send Rune with us," she pointed out.

Cage winced. Mia had hit his weak spot. But before he answered, Rune spoke, determination lacing her voice. "No one else can land this thing, and I'm not going to risk everyone else's escape for my own safety. I'm not a child, Mia. I can take care of myself."

Mia and Cage simultaneously exchanged glances calling that statement into question, but I shot her a quick smile over the console. Rune and I had worked together nonstop for the last twenty days, and I'd come to appreciate the independent core she usually kept hidden. Rune *could* take care of herself. She'd just never been given a chance to prove it.

Cage and Mia, of course, might never see it that way. But it didn't matter: Rune was the only one who could land the ship. We didn't have time to get her to safety once we touched down. Bad enough that the three of us were marching into enemy hands; no point risking the rest of our crew. Besides, we needed people on the outside if things went wrong.

That must have settled the matter, because Mia gave a slight nod and left us on our own. Cage, Rune, and I inspected one another, Rune apparently forgetting to be angry at her twin in the heat of the moment. "All right," I said. "Are we doing this?"

Cage flashed me that smile of his, the all-teeth one that simultaneously gave him a dangerously wolfish edge and made me go weak in the knees. "No sense delaying," he said. I found myself smiling in return. I loved this about Cage, this willingness to plunge headfirst into whatever ridiculous scheme he'd concocted, so bizarre to my strict Omnistellar upbringing. His everyday was my forbidden. In this moment, we could almost have been on Sanctuary again, fighting side by side in a last-ditch attempt for survival. All we'd been through together—huddling under the bed, clutching each other for safety, saving each other's lives—all of it losing the edge of panic and taking on an almost romantic allure until more painful memories intruded.

Claws hoisting Cage in the air, hurling him across the room.

The gun bucking in my hand, Matt's scream in the distance.

Standing in total silence, trembling with effort, as aliens prowled a heartbeat away.

Rune cleared her throat. "Kenzie," she said.

Right. The plan. I shook off the memories of Sanctuary. Some of my Omnistellar lessons needed reinforcing. If we wanted to survive, I had to stop letting the aliens terrorize me from beyond the grave. We might have vented them off their own ship, but that hadn't exorcised them from my mind.

Rune and I approached the console. She closed her eyes, focusing, and plunged her arms elbow deep in electronics. Her shoulders relaxed as she melded with the circuitry, which she always seemed to embrace like a long-lost friend.

"Found comms," she announced after a moment. "Kenzie, you ready? I'm going to put it on speaker because that's all I know how to do. Cage, once I do, keep your mouth shut. Kenzie knows the protocols. You don't."

I looked over my shoulder in time to see him blink back an expression of mingled surprise and hurt, but he only muttered, "Understood."

A moment later a voice cut through the room as clearly as if its owner stood beside us. We had no visuals, which felt strange and wrong for ground-to-ship communications, and would definitely set off warning bells on Mars if their sensors weren't already going crazy.

"Unidentified spacecraft," came a sharp male voice with an unfamiliar accent. "You are in the space of Mars Mining Incorporated and approaching weapons range. If you do not identify yourselves at once, we'll be forced to open fire."

"Please don't do that," I said, surprising myself with how calm I sounded. But as I'd recently learned, I was pretty good at submerging my anxiety and fear until they were a gnawing, raging monster in the pit of my belly, completely invisible to anyone on the surface. "My name is Kenzie Cord, and until a few weeks ago, I was a citizen of Omnistellar Concepts. I can hold my position while you look it up."

A few seconds passed before he spoke again, this time with a touch of suspicion. "Kenzie Cord. You're listed as deceased, you know that?"

"I'm not surprised. I was on the space prison Sanctuary, which was destroyed last month."

"Yeah, it's all over the network at the moment," he agreed, sarcasm creeping into his tone. "And here you are drifting into my space in . . . what the hell *is* that thing?"

"That thing is the reason we're here," I replied, struggling to keep my voice mild. "I'm on board with the Hu twins, former prisoners on Sanctuary. The three of us escaped before the prison was destroyed, and we stole an alien ship to—"

"I'm sorry, you're going to need to repeat that. Did you say an alien ship?"

I closed my eyes and ground my teeth. "Look, do you want us to turn ourselves in or not?"

A long pause followed. "Yeah," came the voice at last. "Yeah, I'd like that a lot. Somehow, I don't think you're offering unconditional surrender, though."

"You're right about that. We have one condition, and one only: after you have us in custody, you destroy this ship. If you don't have the authority to make that deal, connect me to someone who does."

Another long pause as he considered. I glanced at Cage, who shrugged. Impossible to tell if my negotiations were working. Maybe we *should* have let Cage do the talking. But his charisma tended to vanish when dealing with authority figures, and belligerence wouldn't get us anywhere.

When the voice returned, it had shed its lackadaisical tone. "Now why would I agree to something like that? You're flying around in what you claim is an alien ship, something the likes of which we've never seen before. Do you have any idea how much that thing is worth to the scientific community? Not to mention the price it'd fetch on the open market."

"I'm not asking for my own entertainment," I growled. "Right now, this ship is broadcasting a signal to what may be an alien fleet. Those creatures are terrifying and deadly. They can rip you and your armor to shreds, and you do *not* want them descending on Mars. If you give me your word you'll destroy this ship, we'll turn ourselves in. Otherwise, well . . . I'm sure we can find another corporation willing to deal."

The man sighed. "Give me a minute to verify what you're saying." He disconnected the signal, and I flew into action, pacing the confined space.

"You sure we can trust him, even if he agrees?" asked Rune dubiously. "He doesn't seem like the most—"

"I'm not sure of anything," I snapped, then raised my hand in apology as she frowned. "Sorry. I know this is a risk. But our options are limited. It's Mars Mining, the criminal underground, or Omnistellar Concepts. The criminal underground will almost certainly steal the ship out from under us *and* turn us in if they don't kill us, and I have no idea what Omnistellar will do anymore." Whatever it was, it wouldn't give anyone else the chance to escape. I'd lied and said there were only three of us on board, hoping Rune's confidence in the ship's shielding was justified. "Mars Mining is our best—"

"All right, Kenzie," the man's voice interrupted me, and I winced, shooting an accusing glance at Rune. She'd left the channel open? Hopefully I hadn't said anything incriminating. "Land that ship, turn yourselves in, and we'll blow it into dust."

My throat constricted. I swallowed around the sudden lump and said, "You've got yourself a deal."

"I'm trying to send you landing coordinates, but the message doesn't seem to be going through."

"Yeah, we're dealing with an unfamiliar system here. You'll have to tell us verbally."

The man sighed as if I'd deliberately used alien technology to annoy him, but he did give us the information. Rune nodded, confirming she was locked onto the landing zone, and we cut the comms.

We had absolutely no idea what to expect when this ship landed. We'd already warned the other twenty-one survivors of Sanctuary to lock in and hold tight. Once we reached the surface, they'd be in Alexei's and Mia's hands. If Mars Mining broke their word, hopefully Mia would rally some of them to our aid. I didn't kid myself. Most of them would make a break for it, and I couldn't blame them.

"Okay, here we go," said Rune. Cage moved to a corner and readied himself as best he could, since the ship didn't seem to have straps or belts or anything that might actually keep us safe in the event of a rough landing. We were taking a lot on faith and relying pretty heavily on Rune's power. Who knew if this ship was even designed to break atmosphere? Then again, if it crashed in the landing and took all of us with it, I guess I didn't have to worry about the aliens tracking our signal.

I closed my eyes and braced myself, ready to interpret any information Rune couldn't glean directly from the AI. My hands trembled, and I locked them around the console's edge to hide my fear. I had to hold things together. Rune and Cage relied on my knowledge and experience. If I let them see how terrified I was, all the possible ways this might blow up in our faces, they might back down. And that wasn't an option. Not if we wanted to save Earth. Not for the first time, I wished for my commanding officer, my *mom*, to tell me what to do. But there was no one else. Just me and my friends and the weight of the solar system on our shoulders.

Rune glanced at me and Cage. Cage looked like he wanted to say something, whether to her or me I wasn't sure. I locked eyes with him and silently willed him to speak. To explain. To say something to restore the feeling on Sanctuary when he'd taken me in his arms, that split second when I'd been completely safe and protected.

But he only bit his lip and smiled, and Rune and I returned to the console. She glanced at me and tilted her head. "Okay. Here we go." Squaring her shoulders, she plunged her arms into the circuitry.

The entire room lurched, driving Rune and me forward. Her chin smashed against the panel, but she didn't open her eyes, didn't even squeak in pain as blood trickled from the corner of her lips. I threw my hands up to brace myself, narrowly avoiding a similar injury.

The ship heaved violently, information spasming against my fingers in protest. This ship was obviously *not* designed to land. I didn't know much about the aliens. I'd gathered that they did have some sort of homeworld, but the way this thing protested, it had never breached atmosphere before.

Once more the ship tipped and heaved, like it was trying to expel us into space. Rune's face slammed into the console again. With her arms sunk into the electronics, she couldn't protect herself. I wasn't sure she even felt her injuries. Throwing caution to the wind, I jumped toward her. At the same moment the ship jerked and twisted, pitching us to a forty-five-degree angle. I caught the edge of the console to keep from plummeting backward and dragged myself toward Rune, my fingers curling and my booted feet scrambling for purchase.

"Kenzie, hang on!" Cage shouted. "I'm coming over there!"

"No! Stay where you are! Another person flying around the room won't help!"

I reached Rune just as the ship gave a massive shudder. Wrapping my arms around her, I tried to simultaneously protect her face from any more impacts and lock us in place, preventing the ship from bucking us across the room.

"Kenzie!" Cage roared. I turned toward him, but the ship pitched, and it took all my energy to hold Rune. "What's happening?"

"She's okay!" I called. "Are you?"

"Hanging on! Are we going to make it?"

I shook my head, knowing he couldn't see me. I didn't have the time or focus to interpret the alien language right now. Rune was too far immersed in the system to answer questions, and we had no windows to see outside. I had exactly as much information as Cage.

The ship's spin increased in speed, giving me the sense of being on a sickening VR carnival ride. I tightened my grip on Rune as the centrifugal force threatened to tear us apart. At least she wasn't in danger of hitting her face again, but the combined force of the ship's spiral and my hold might dislocate her shoulders. I managed to shift my grip to her middle. I wasn't even protecting her anymore, merely holding on for dear life, because at this point, if I let go, I would smash headfirst into a wall.

As suddenly as it had started, the ship ground to a halt. Rune flew forward and took me with her. Just in time, I jerked my hands around her so her head collided with my palms instead of the console. Pain shot through me at the impact, and the recoil threw me to my knees.

I braced for the next assault, but we weren't moving.

And neither was Rune.

FOUR

"RUNE!" I SHOUTED. CAGE WAS AT MY SIDE IN
an instant. Rune slumped over the console. Together, Cage and
I half lifted her, but her arms remained embedded in the circuitry. I pulled on her waist, but I didn't see any give, and I was
afraid I'd hurt her if I kept tugging. She threw her head back
against my shoulder and moaned around a mouthful of blood.

"Rune," I repeated, this time in relief. She was alive. "Can
you hear me?"

"*Meimei.*" Cage caught her chin and gently turned her face,
examining her for injuries. "Open your eyes."

She groaned, louder this time, and shifted, taking her own
weight. As her eyes fluttered open, a familiar voice crackled over
the comms, that obnoxious sarcastic inflection back in place:
"That was quite the landing."

Lord, give me strength. "Strangely enough, our alien ship

didn't come with an instruction manual. Our deal still in place?"

"Affirmative. You surrender yourselves and we destroy your ship. I'm sending an armed contingent to meet you now. I don't suppose I have to tell you they're prepared to use lethal force if you deviate from our arrangement?"

"I assumed as much." The other corporations might not have Omnistellar's total dedication to the idea of anomalies as monsters, but no one in the solar system viewed us with much trust.

Us. That still sounded strange. After seventeen years of regarding myself as an elite prison guard ready to take down dangerous anomalies at the drop of a hat, shifting allegiances so quickly hadn't caught up to me. It still kept surprising me at inopportune moments—like this one. I glanced down over my tattered guard uniform and zipped my hoodie, hiding the shame of my former identity.

We met everyone near the airlock. Alexei, Mia, and Reed were near the front, their expressions determined. "Where's Anya?" I asked. I wanted to make sure our youngest charge was well back from danger.

"Imani has her. She'll make sure she gets to safety."

I glanced over the assembled faces, all weaker and more exhausted than three weeks ago, but somehow livelier, too, as if their taste of freedom strengthened their resolve. Even Kristin, Rune's old cellmate and not my biggest fan, forbore giving me her usual disdainful glare. "All right," I said, raising my voice.

"You all know the plan. Rune, Cage, and I will give ourselves up. While we have the guards' attention, Alexei and Mia will create a distraction. Reed is familiar with Mars, so follow him. He'll get you off the station and to safety. Anyone willing to risk recapture to make sure this ship gets destroyed, stick with Reed. The rest of you scatter. Go to ground and don't come out."

It wasn't much of a plan. Most of them probably didn't have contacts on Mars, and they didn't have credit chips or anything else on which to survive. I knew all of that. But it was the best chance I could offer, and no one disputed it.

I returned to the front as Mia shimmered out of existence. I winced. I'd never get used to her habit of turning invisible whenever the urge struck her, even if, as now, it was planned. "I can't think of any more excuses to delay," I said to Cage.

He examined my face, pulling in his bottom lip. "We'll be fine," he said. Did he feel as assured as he sounded? I envied his confidence. "I trust Mia and Alexei. They've got our backs."

Alexei nodded, giving me one of his rare smiles, and flexed the muscles along his shoulders. "See you soon."

I faced the smooth black plastic of the ship's exit. Even though the ship had provided us with refuge after we'd escaped Sanctuary, it had never felt like home. It was too alien, too bizarre. I wasn't sorry to see it go, even if it meant turning myself over to the authorities. The ship had never been a destination. It was a place between permanence, even between identities. I still hadn't found my next home, but this certainly wasn't it.

"Here goes nothing," I said, and jammed a screwdriver into the exit slot.

The black material shimmered and flowed, re-forming itself into an opening about ten feet above our heads. Earlier, Imani and Cage had rigged a rope ladder to make it easy to vacate the ship. But over twenty people needed to escape behind us. Mia and Alexei had been vague on the details of how exactly they planned to accomplish that, and when pressed, Mia muttered something about playing it by ear and creating a distraction. I just hoped it would be big enough to give them the time they needed.

I waited for Mia to exit the ship ahead of me. The ladder swayed with her movement. Once it stilled, I caught a rung, a makeshift plastic bar I hoped would support Alexei's weight, and crawled after her.

I emerged on top of the alien ship and got my first view of Mars. My eyebrows shot up in amazement, and in spite of the situation, I took a moment to stop and stare. My family had lived all over Earth before we moved to Sanctuary, and we'd vacationed once or twice on a luxury star cruiser. But I'd never set foot on another planet. I'd never admitted it to anyone, but Mars had always fascinated me. It had the same allure as *Robo Mecha Dream Girl 5*: someplace with mystery and danger left to uncover. Humans had walked the surface of Earth for millennia. We'd only colonized Mars in the last fifty years, and aside from a few scattered mining camps, there was only one real settlement: Mars City, with its strange mix of tourist attractions, mining homes, and corporate research facilities.

We were on an exterior landing pad, an invisible bubble trapping oxygen and atmosphere in the space beside the huge gunmetal-gray building. To my left and right, Mars stretched away, red dust billowing as far as the eye could see. Behind the building lay Mars City: a labyrinthine complex of flashing lights and dark shadows, high-priced hotels and metal lean-tos. I drank it in, my imagination filling in the city with back-alley deals and the desert with unexplored caverns.

But between me and adventure stood twelve heavily armed soldiers, all bearing the logo of Mars Mining Incorporated. I couldn't see the guards' expressions through their mirrored faceplates. Somehow, I doubted they were friendly. Their firearms might be primitive compared to Omnistellar's arsenal, but they were plenty lethal. I raised my hands to show I posed no threat and picked my way across the ship.

One of the soldiers gestured. As Cage emerged behind me, an automated staircase rolled toward us. It wasn't quite tall enough or the right shape to reach me, but it only left a gap of about a foot, and I cleared it easily. I kept my arms spread wide, as the Mars soldiers looked edgy, fingers twitching on triggers, and I didn't want to give them an excuse to open fire. My heart skipped at the sight of all those guns, and for a moment I almost froze. No one knew like I did how easily you could hit the wrong target. Staring down the business end of the rifles sent a tremor through me, and I had to force my feet to resume their climb.

Behind me, Cage and Rune scrambled onto the staircase. I didn't hear Mia land, but that meant nothing. Girl moved like a ghost.

We hurried to put as much distance between us and the ship as we could. My courage faltered as we approached our masked captors, and I was suddenly, powerfully grateful for my companions—Cage on my left, Rune on my right, keeping so close our arms brushed with each step. I resisted the urge to grab for their hands. If I'd learned anything in years of dealing with Omnistellar, it was never to show your fear.

As we drew near the soldiers, one of them stepped forward. "That's far enough," he said, and I recognized his voice from the comms. "Which of you is Kenzie Cord?"

"I am." I took a step ahead of the others, clenching my hands into fists. My hands often shook when I got nervous. I'd learned long ago that fists made me look stronger than trembling. "And we followed through with our side of the deal. Are you going to honor yours?"

"Of course," he said, a little too smoothly and quickly, but that didn't necessarily mean anything. Most corporate suits had a bit of sliminess to them. "But first, we have some business to take care of. I'm going to need the three of you to—"

At that moment, a massive explosion rocked the area. I smashed into the pavement and skidded, my ears ringing, spots dancing before my eyes. Skin tore from my wrists. Rune landed on top of me, and all the soldiers toppled despite their armor.

The world lurched in sickening heaves. Through the haze of disorientation, I was dimly aware of shouting and flames, utter chaos. Behind me, Cage stumbled to his feet and caught the nearest soldier, yelling about something—keeping his attention here, I assumed, because this had to be Mia and Alexei's version of a distraction. It was distracting, all right. I twisted, still not trusting myself to stand, and found a wall of flames not five feet in front of me. On the other side of the shimmering heat, a steady stream of teenagers scrambled over the ship and leaped for freedom.

I wasn't the only one to notice. Shouts rose around me as the soldiers took aim. I threw myself at the nearest armored goon, knocking their arm aside and sending their shot careening wildly into the barrier surrounding the landing platform. It absorbed the bullet's energy, leaving the bullet to ping to the ground, harmless. I got a gun hilt to the face for my trouble. Pain ricocheted through my skull, and the back of my head smacked the pavement.

The kids scattered, bolting through the Mars landscape toward the neighboring city, trusting in their powers or their own willpower to get them through the few seconds of vacuum separating the bubbles. The flames blocked the soldiers' pursuit. Some of them made to charge after the escaping prisoners, but their commander called a retreat. "Let them go!" he bellowed. "Make sure no one else is on that damn ship! We'll put out an APB. They can't leave the city, and they won't last long with a reward on their heads."

My heart sank. There was nowhere else to go, not without a passport or a Mars Mining pass. But the city was big and had a reputation for hosting a healthy horde of criminals as well as Mars Mining citizens. With luck the commander overestimated the city's love for his corporation.

I had my own problems to deal with, as the commander approached the three of us, tilting his faceplate back. He was older than his voice had led me to believe, with a grizzly white beard and flashing dark eyes. "I suppose you think you're clever," he snarled. The ringing in my ears was fading, but I still struggled to catch his words. Instinctively, I stepped between him and Rune, and Cage drew up beside me. Rune sighed heavily behind us, and I winced, remembering how she'd complained about Cage treating her like a child. Now *I* was doing it. Before I could apologize, though, the man continued. "How many murderous maniacs did you just turn loose in my city?"

"None," I replied sharply, forcing myself to stand straight and meet his eyes in spite of the fact that the world continued teetering, in spite of the agony where the skin had torn from my palms. I didn't know the background of every single kid I'd just turned loose on Mars, but I was willing to stand up for them regardless. "None of those kids are what you think."

He spit on the ground in disgust. "That's what I get for trusting an anomaly."

"We kept our word," Cage broke in. "The three of us surrendered in exchange for you destroying the ship. That's what you bargained for, and that's what you got."

"And you simply forgot to mention the other prisoners hiding in your hold, is that it?"

"No, we left it out intentionally. You didn't ask. We didn't tell. They weren't part of the bargain." Cage flashed him an unsettling grin. I watched him from the corner of my eye. Who else had seen that grin? For some, it might have been the last thing they ever did see. "So. Are you going to keep your word, or not?"

"Unfortunately, that's not up to him." Another soldier spoke, approaching us from the line behind the commander. She tipped her own faceplate back, revealing a surprisingly small woman with a sharply angled nose and eyes like deep-set obsidian. "I'm Commander Yang, the officer in charge of this outpost and official representative of Mars Mining Incorporated."

I closed my eyes. I should have known. "Your subordinate here made promises he couldn't follow through on," I said, laying emphasis on the word "subordinate" and glaring at the man, who showed me his teeth. "What about you, Commander Yang? Do you understand how dangerous this is? The situation we're in?"

"No, but I'll give you a chance to explain once we have you safely in custody." She gestured with her gun, making it clear we were to precede her into the station.

I exchanged glances with the twins. It wasn't like we had a

lot of choice. Cage might outrun these clowns, but I knew he wouldn't abandon me or Rune, and none of us stood a chance against this many armed soldiers. Besides, we'd made a bargain, and I had to at least try to convince Yang to follow through. According to Rune's calculations, we didn't have much time to destroy the ship before the aliens' course became irreversible. Still, the idea of walking into captivity . . . Not so long ago I'd stood on the opposite side of this equation. I clenched my fists again and swallowed a lump in my throat. We'd get through this somehow. The only thing that really mattered was destroying the ship. So many of us had died. I couldn't let it be in vain, couldn't let those monsters return for the rest of humanity.

I took in my surroundings: the Mars Mining soldiers, the unsuspecting city, the red dust leading to scattered mining camps. If the aliens followed our signal here, no one would survive. We'd made our way off Sanctuary through cunning, skill, and more luck than we ever should have managed. I didn't dare count on that sort of fortune again. At least on Sanctuary, we'd been able to contain the aliens to a limited space. Let them loose on Mars . . . A tremor shot down my spine. Give me Omnistellar. I'd take my former corporation, their wrath, even a death sentence before I faced one of those things ever again.

"All right," I said, bowing to the inevitable, and we followed Yang through the crowd of angry soldiers, returning to the one place we had fought at all costs to avoid: back into corporate custody.

FIVE

THE SECOND WE PASSED THROUGH THE HEAVY
metal doors, the guards slammed us against the wall. Still disoriented from the blast and the blow to the face, I couldn't even muster the energy to protest as they bound my hands behind me in huge, heavy cuffs. Some sort of padding forced my hands into involuntary fists as painfully tight bonds clamped over my wrists. My shoulders instantly ached, the weight of the cuffs dragging my arms down, pulling my elbows together. Out of the corner of my eye, I saw them do the same to Cage and Rune, jamming their hands into what looked like metal boxers' gloves. Cage's face locked in a mask of indifference, although the muscle twitching at the corner of his eye communicated volumes. Rune didn't even try to hide her distress, closing her eyes and breathing heavily as the manacles snapped into place. As awful as this was for me, it had to be a hundred times worse

for them. They'd only recently escaped five years of prison, and a few weeks later, they were voluntarily returning to a jail cell.

If Cage and Rune could handle this, so could I. At least that was what I told myself. But as the metal bit into my wrists and added what felt like ten pounds to the drag on my arms, ice-cold panic clawed at my chest, constricting my throat. I closed my eyes, tipped my head against the wall, and pretended I was in *Robo Mecha Dream Girl 5*. Yumiko was taken captive, on average, once a week. She always survived, and so would I.

The thought gave me just enough courage to keep my feet as the guard behind me tugged on my cuffs to make sure they were secure. He said something to Commander Yang. It sounded like Mandarin, a language I'd become pretty comfortable with between Cage and Rune. But I couldn't understand a word of it.

Power inhibitors, I realized numbly. Mars Mining didn't have Omnistellar's fancy inhibitor chips, so they'd found another way to cut off our abilities. The heavy metal cuffs suddenly seemed to double in weight even as my mind raced through corporate technology. Some sort of injection, probably. Temporary. I hadn't felt it, which meant the cuffs contained a numbing agent. That explained the lack of feeling in my wrists, which I'd attributed to the weight of the cuffs.

"You all right?" Cage muttered as the guard grabbed our elbows and propelled us forward.

I nodded. Cage glanced past me to Rune, but she stared

straight ahead, her chin jutting forward, her muscles tightly corded. I shook my head at him, telling him to leave her alone. She looked stronger than I felt. Let her get through this however she could.

At that moment, though, Rune glanced at us and gave me a small smile. She turned to include Cage, and he smiled back. It was the tiniest movement of her lips, the slightest quirk of his, but it went so far toward calming my panic. In this moment, all barriers among the three of us melted away. It's hard to focus on much else when you're fighting to keep your head above water.

Yang removed her gloves and helmet, passing them to a random underling. She scanned her thumb and the door connecting the corridor to the tarmac slid shut behind us. She opened the next passageway, and we stepped into the headquarters of Mars Mining Incorporated.

I'd never been in Omnistellar Concepts' headquarters in London, but I'd seen lots of other corporate facilities when my parents did intercorporate training missions. They'd led sessions for all the big security firms: New Earth, Sphinxhead, even the closest thing we had to a competitor, Surge Networks. Some, like Omnistellar and Surge, were immaculate, run by the book and according to strict regulations. Some were a lot laxer. But I'd never seen anything off planet before.

This was the city's central hub. We were in a huge open area, all exposed metal and hastily welded pipework. But it had been designed with something more professional in mind. Faux leather couches, worn and patched now but good quality, lined waiting areas, and huge windows revealed Mars's expanse on one side and the city's flashing lights on another. A thin layer of red dust covered everything. They might have sealed Mars City in an atmospheric bubble, but apparently that didn't stop the windstorms from doing their work.

Corridors branched off the main area in four directions. I scanned the signs overhead. They hadn't bothered labeling them in anything but English, so I didn't even need my powers to interpret TOURISM AND CORPORATE IMMIGRATION, MARS MINING AFFAIRS, MEDICAL, and SECURITY. Unsurprisingly, Yang led us and our escorts toward the last one. Dozens of people gathered in the main area, but none of them batted an eyelash at the sight of us. Obviously, arrests weren't uncommon here. I assumed no one had noticed the huge alien spaceship on the tarmac, not to mention the resulting explosion. There was a reason they'd directed us to a landing site at the rear of the facility.

The weight on my arms continued to grow, a steady ache spreading through my shoulders and neck. I focused on the echo of my heartbeat, battling a claustrophobic panic. Having my hands bound this way was like waiting for the air to drain from an airlock before a spacewalk combined with the sensation of first learning about my chip. I was completely and utterly trapped. I couldn't even reach for Cage or Rune for support. Even if our hands hadn't been bound, the guards kept us several feet away from one another. My family had never been very physical, but

I'd spent a lot of time with Rune over the last few weeks, and I'd gotten used to her quick hugs, the way she tipped her head into my shoulder or poked me in the arm when she wanted my attention. The physical separation felt strange and wrong.

But the second we passed through the doors to security, a sense of familiarity settled over me. Security was just as dusty and run-down here as everything else, but things ran with a greater sense of efficiency and purpose. In a strange way, it felt like coming home. I didn't want to consider what that said about me, that I found empty halls and blank faces more comforting than a sea of normal people. Omnistellar conditioning.

I bit my lip. How in the system, with all my love for *Robo Mecha Dream Girl 5*, had I never realized I was living in a corporate nightmare? That I had missed out on everything— friendship, freedom, agency—that made her life worth living? Or maybe I had realized it. Maybe that was why I loved the series so much: it reminded me of what I lacked.

Yang strode down a hall and deposited the three of us in a small room with a table and four chairs. "Wait here," she ordered.

"Hang on a second!" I cried, bounding after her. One of the guards drew a gun, and I skidded to a halt. "What about the ship?" I demanded, enunciating each word as carefully as possible, my eyes trained on his weapon. My mouth went dry, but I forced myself to continue. "Commander, that ship is broadcasting a signal to an alien race you do *not* want to meet."

"It only took a handful of those things to kill everyone on Sanctuary," Cage added softly. "Trust me. They'd destroy Mars in hours."

"I'll return shortly and hear what you have to say." Yang fixed each of us with a steady, penetrating stare. "Until then, the best thing you can do is wait patiently."

Cage started to speak, but I shook my head at him. I knew how corporations worked. There was no point arguing with red tape. As much as I wanted the ship destroyed, I didn't think a delay of an hour or two would make much of a difference.

At least I *hoped* it wouldn't.

The door closed. I sank onto a chair awkwardly, with my hands manacled behind me, and raised my eyebrows at Cage. "I should have known better than to trust Mia and Alexei's idea of a distraction."

He flashed me a smile, jumping onto the table and resting his feet on a nearby chair, quick even without his powers. Even without his hands. "When you ask Mia and Alexei for a distraction, their first instinct is fire. The bigger, the better. Everything okay, *meimei?*"

His tone was deceptively casual when he addressed Rune, but something in it caught my attention. I twisted to find her standing in a corner, staring at the ceiling with an expression of intense concentration on her face. She ignored Cage entirely, maybe hadn't heard him. Her gaze traveled across the ceiling, down the walls, sliding over us like we weren't even there.

Cage and I exchanged worried looks. "Rune?" I asked.

She shook her head as if waking from a dream. "Two cameras," she announced, gesturing with her chin. "One in the right corner, one in the left. They're almost certainly wired for sound, but there's a microphone under the table, too. Maybe more I can't see."

Of course. Even without her powers, Rune was a technological powerhouse. She'd been scouting for surveillance, exactly what I should have been doing. Instead, Cage and I had just given away Mia's and Alexei's names, and given Mars Mining usable evidence to prove we had planned the distraction. I kicked myself inwardly. *A few weeks out of Omnistellar and I'm already forgetting my training?* I expected more from myself.

I cut off the voice that followed—my mom's voice—telling me *Omnistellar* expected more. Omnistellar no longer mattered, and Mom . . . Mom was dead. The events of the last few weeks, losing my mom and Rita, the horrifying alien attacks, Sanctuary's destruction, still weighed on me. It felt nice to have the excuse to dwell on them, and that made me wary. I couldn't afford to indulge in nice feelings. Unless I wanted to spend my life in prison (and it would be a very short life, since the aliens would no doubt arrive to end it before long), I had to be at the absolute top of my game. I studied my scuffed boots, remembering how one of my camp trainers had yelled at me for failing to polish them. At least I'd never have that problem again.

We settled to wait in silence. Rune sank to the floor,

apparently exhausted, and stared straight ahead. Cage and I sat against the opposite wall. Part of me longed to drop my head on his shoulder or at least eliminate that last inch so our arms touched, but I didn't do it. There was no sense alerting anyone watching to the nature of our relationship. Whatever that was. Actually, maybe I *should* alert them. Maybe they could help me figure it out. A semihysterical giggle welled inside me, and I promptly swallowed it, putting iron in my spine and following Rune's example, fixing my gaze ahead. I forced myself to focus on the alien threat. I still had a father on Earth. I had to keep him safe. Him and the rest of humanity.

I spared a thought for the other kids. Had they escaped to Mars City safely? I particularly worried about Anya, the youngest member of the group. But Imani had taken charge of her, and if there was anyone I trusted to keep her safe, it was Imani. She had lost her little sister, who was about Anya's age. I knew she would protect Anya with her life. I just hoped it wouldn't come to that.

We didn't have to wait long after they realized we weren't going to drop any more information. Commander Yang returned in the red jacket and black pants favored by Mars Mining, their logo emblazoned on her left breast pocket. Like everything on Mars, her uniform had seen better days, but she wore it with pride. Three other guards in similar uniforms entered behind her. "Let's get you a little more comfortable," Yang said, taking one of the chairs. She nodded and one of the guards approached, recuffing our hands in front of us. The other two stood by the locked door, weapons trained, alert for any sign of movement, especially when they uncuffed Cage. They must have taken the time to look up our files.

"Can I get you anything?" Yang asked as the three of us settled into the chairs across from her and the guards took positions by the door.

"Yeah," said Cage. "Proof you destroyed that ship."

Her lips quirked into a thin smile. "I meant more like a glass of water. This might be a long conversation."

"We don't need anything," I said. "And you don't have time for a long conversation."

Yang examined us thoughtfully, then turned to Rune. "You're very quiet."

Rune shrugged. "If you won't listen to them, you're not going to listen to me."

"All right." Yang slid a security stick onto the table between us and set it to record. "Tell me everything."

There was no point arguing with corporate policies. She wasn't going to take any action without knowing the facts, and part of me understood corporations well enough not to blame her. As quickly as I could, with the occasional input from Cage, I told her what had happened on Sanctuary. As I described the events, my voice echoed back at me as if through a tunnel, hollow and disconnected. Everything made sense: the distress signal, Rita's absence, the prison break, the alien attack. But the words seemed devoid of life. Even as I recounted how the aliens tore through the station's hull like paper, even as I listed the dozens, the *hundreds* of dead, none of the fear and terror and urgency came through. It sounded like I was composing a story for a particularly boring English assignment.

Obviously, I didn't explain everything. I didn't mention my sense of betrayal at learning that my parents had chipped me to disguise my own powers. I didn't mention how many prisoners had survived to escape into Mars City. And I sure as hell didn't mention the moment when my shot went wide and killed Matt. The thoughts followed close on the words, though, threatening to break through the wall of detachment I'd created. I forced myself to turn to the problem at hand, which offered plenty of fuel for emotion all on its own. "Those things are on their way here right now. They're following that beacon, and it's going to lead them right to you."

"Of course, I understand your concerns," Yang said smoothly. "We'll do our very best to find and eliminate the signal."

Find and eliminate the signal . . . My heart plummeted right through my feet. My lips moved, forming soundless words until I realized I wasn't breathing and sucked in a gasp of air. "You're not going to destroy the ship," I managed, my voice little more than a whisper.

She smiled thinly. "Kenzie, be reasonable. That ship is unlike anything we've ever seen. It represents billions of credits on its own, not to mention the potential advances to weaponry and space travel. Do you really think the corporation would allow me to destroy it?"

Fear surged over the border into anger. "You lying little—"

"I suggest you don't finish that sentence." Steel entered her tone. "I promised you nothing. My subordinate had no authority to bargain, and I won't be held responsible for his words. And even if there was an agreement in place, you voided it with your stunt outside. Now tell me, Ms. Cord: Exactly how many anomalies are running loose in my city?"

Cage snorted. "I thought you were going to round them all up in a matter of minutes. Not as easy as you anticipated?"

She leaned forward, pushing the security stick aside and resting her elbows on the table. "Do you three understand exactly how much trouble you're in here? Omnistellar Concepts has been alerted to your presence, and they are *very* interested in speaking with you. Your crimes are going to warrant a lot worse than a cushy stint on a prison like Sanctuary. You have maybe twenty-four hours before they get an operative here, at which point it'll be beyond my power to help you. Think on that for a while." Abruptly, she pushed back and nodded to the guards. "Take them to their cells. We'll see how they feel in a few hours."

Reality settled over me like a blanket. She was leaving. She was going to walk out that door and not destroy the ship. It would keep broadcasting its signal, because if Rune couldn't find it, Yang and her team sure as hell wouldn't. I scrambled for words, but darkness descended around me, claws and screams and terror. "You have to destroy that ship!" I shouted, all of my carefully laid plans of earning her trust and convincing her vanishing in a surge of adrenaline. I had no idea how far away the aliens were or how fast they traveled. Memories assaulted me, the creatures screaming in triumph as they brandished Tyler's mutilated body, the thud of my own heart as I dodged their flashing claws. "They could be here before Omnistellar, do you understand? If they can destroy a space station, they can destroy a colony!"

"*If* you're telling the truth about what happened, and *if* these so-called aliens are on their way, a prepared Mars security force will be more of a match for them than a station full of unarmed teenage delinquents."

If only that were true. She didn't understand, and it was my fault. I couldn't communicate it. Even with my power, I couldn't have explained the terror of becoming prey, stalked on our own station, knowing that every step might lead to an alien shriek and a claw tearing through your flesh. And before I found the words to describe it, Yang turned her back and walked away.

"Yang!" I roared, lunging after her. I didn't know what I was going to do, only that I *had* to make her listen. We couldn't let what had happened on Sanctuary happen here. I'd die first. "Wait! There's more to—!"

The guard grabbed me and shoved me. I rebounded and

chased after her. The guard jerked his stun gun into play, aiming it straight at my chest. Agony tore through me as my muscles spasmed, sending me twitching to the floor, my teeth snapping shut on my tongue. A sea of blackness surged against me as two of the guards grabbed my elbows and hauled me to my feet. I struggled to speak, but my brain responded sluggishly, fighting the aftereffects of the stun.

Dragging me between them, they prodded Rune forward, leading us in one direction—and Cage in another.

The call is made. It is not answered. It is and it isn't and the mind is and isn't and rises and falls, and more awake, more arise, uncurling and unfurling and spreading.

There is no one. The hive is all. The hive is calling. A ripple tears through it. Pain and fear. Unfamiliar. Unpleasant. Unwelcome.

Follow. They have found it. They have set their sights.

Harvesters are gone.

Hunters awaken.

There will be no escape.

SIX

I NEVER ACTUALLY LOST CONSCIOUSNESS from the stun gun blast, but I must have come close. The world swam around me in a disorienting mess. The next thing I knew, I was huddled on a hard bench, Rune crouched beside me, terror in her eyes. "Kenzie!" she cried, her fingers sunk into my neck as she prodded for my pulse. "Come on, Kenz. Talk to me."

I swallowed painfully. "I'm okay," I said, or tried to. It felt like I had a mouthful of bloody cotton. A few years earlier, I'd had dental surgery. The laser seal went wrong, and they sliced part of my mouth. All the damage was repaired before I opened my eyes, of course, but they'd packed my cheeks with cotton to absorb any blood, and I'd awoken with this same awful sensation.

Rune vanished, reappearing momentarily with a glass of water. I fumbled for it, but my fingers were sluggish and clumsy, and she had to hold it to my lips. The first few swallows tasted of copper, and the taste didn't improve as the blood washed away, but at least the dry, swollen feeling dissipated. "Thanks," I said, sitting up. Rune caught my arms, helping me ease myself to the edge of the platform. I leaned against her, accepting her support even as her worry washed over me. My stomach gave a sickening lurch. Would Rune hold me like this, give me that gentle smile, if she ever found out what I'd done to Matt?

We were in a holding cell, even worse than the one on Sanctuary. There was only a single bench. An exposed toilet and sink sat at the back of the cramped space. Rune held a plastic tumbler. Clear reinforced bars separated us from a series of other cells, but I didn't see any guards, or any other prisoners. "Cage?" I asked. My voice sounded steady, but inside I reeled. This was my first time on this side of the prison bars. My hands trembled as I gulped the rest of the water.

Rune shook her head. "I tried calling for him and got no response. Either he can't hear me, or he can't answer."

I digested those possibilities. Rune leaped to her feet and paced back and forth across the room. "Your hands are free," I said, and in the same breath realized it was true of me, too.

She nodded toward the hallway outside our cell. "Massive dampeners in the ceiling. No one's powers will work in this area. Not even a comm device will function unless it's on a special channel. Standard security in a lot of prisons that don't have Omnistellar's fancy chips. It wouldn't be practical to keep prisoners cuffed indefinitely."

I dropped my head to my hands. This plan had failed abysmally. The ship was still broadcasting its signal, Yang didn't recognize the hell descending on her planet, and Cage, Rune, and I were all in prison. "Will Mia and Alexei come through?"

"I . . . yes. Yes, they will," said Rune.

My head shot up at the hesitation in her voice, and I winced as pain ricocheted through my skull. "But?"

"But how long will it take them to realize the corporation isn't following through on its word? And how long do we have?"

I closed my eyes, my worst fears surging to life. Every second of that hell on Sanctuary—I might have to live it again. And the chances of the exact circumstances that had allowed our survival happening again were almost nonexistent. "Even if the aliens don't get here before Mia, Omnistellar might. They'll have advanced weaponry, elite soldiers . . . Mia and Alexei will never get through them to free us. At best, they might destroy the ship. And that's *if* Omnistellar doesn't buy it and transport it off planet."

Rune climbed onto the bench beside me, drawing her knees to her chin and wrapping her arms around her legs. Once again, she fixed her gaze on her feet. "Do you think we activated that signal when Mia vented the aliens into space?"

I winced. I'd been avoiding that possibility. Mia and Cage had made the decision to send hundreds of sleeping aliens to their deaths. I hadn't agreed with them, but I'd understood their logic. Rune, on the other hand, considered their actions little better than murder. "Maybe," I allowed. "But maybe not. Maybe the ship activated the signal for some other reason. A remote call, for instance. Or it could activate automatically if the ship goes so long without checking in. We can't know."

Rune nodded. "I've never been mad at Cage for this long," she said softly. "I hate it."

I glanced at her out of the corner of my eye. The words I didn't want to say hovered on my lips: *Then why don't you just forgive him?* Then again, why couldn't I? I bit them off, but she heard them anyway. "It's not only that he was willing to kill them," she said, resting the side of her head against her knees to look at me. "It's the way he talked to me. The way he yelled at me. Like I was a child who couldn't understand what needed to be done. Cage has always been protective of me, but he's never treated me like an incompetent before."

I sighed and stared at my fingers, the skin dry and splintered after weeks in space. Rune gave me her confidence so easily, with such trust. Did I dare return the favor? I wanted, so badly, to tell her the truth about what had happened with Matt. If anyone was going to believe me, it would be Rune. She didn't have a vengeful bone in her body.

Or . . . did she? Cage knew his sister better than I did, and he thought she'd take it as a betrayal. There had been something between her and Matt, too, something more than friendship. I examined her out of the corner of my eye and made a decision. I *would* tell Rune the truth. She deserved it.

But I would wait until we could afford her anger, until a fight wouldn't tear us apart. And that meant getting out of here and stopping the aliens.

Still, I could at least try to patch things up between her and Cage. "I don't claim to know much about how Cage thinks, but I can say for sure that he does *not* think you're incompetent." I sighed. "He loves you, Rune. He wants to make things better, but he doesn't know how."

"I know." She forced a smile. "I do know that. But Cage, he . . . he's good, Kenz. He really is. But we grew up hard, and it took a toll on him. Sometimes he forgets how to be human. He gets so busy scheming and calculating, he forgets that he's dealing with people, not strategies."

I swallowed hard. That tallied perfectly with my worst fears about Cage. "That's probably true, and I'm not going to defend it. But he is your brother. Are you going to ignore him for the rest of your life?"

Resolve settled into her brow, and she nodded. "You're right. I'll talk to him. If, you know, I ever see him again."

At that moment, footsteps echoed in the corridor. Rune and I shot to our feet, me a bit unsteadily, and retreated to the rear of the cell. I clenched each of my muscles individually, loosening them, working feeling into my numbed extremities. My arms threaded into bands of steel, the strength of my posture belying the anxiety thudding through my heart. I had never experienced this kind of helplessness before: trapped in a cell, at the guards' mercy, knowing about the oncoming alien threat but powerless to stop it.

Two guards approached, weapons drawn. "Kenzie Cord," said one of them, holding the heavy metal cuffs they'd used to transport us here. "Come with us."

Rune's eyes narrowed. "Where are you taking her?" she demanded.

"None of your business, that's where." The guard slid the cell door open and nodded at me. "You going to cooperate, or do we have to stun you and drag you?"

Yeah, I wasn't eager to experience that again. Resistance wouldn't get me anywhere. Besides, maybe Yang had come to her senses and wanted to discuss destroying the damn ship. I swallowed the hope before it could spark too brightly. "I'll cooperate," I said. I forced a smile for Rune's benefit. "It's okay. I'll be back." I glanced at the guard. "Right?"

He sighed impatiently. Someone wants to talk to you. Drop the paranoia and come on."

I resisted the urge to point out that paranoia felt pretty justified given how they'd broken their agreement with us and shot me with a stun gun. Instead, I stepped forward and placed my hands in the metal cuffs. They resembled giant yellow mittens, and I suddenly remembered my dad tucking my hands into similar mittens when I was young and heading outside to play. My heart stuttered. I hadn't thought of that in years. Why did the memory have to resurface now?

I forced another smile for Rune as the guard took my elbow and led me away. Now that I was waiting for it, I felt the cool numbing gel on my arm, blocking the pinprick of the needle, and the tiny burn of some sort of power inhibitor flowing through my veins. It was temporary, of course. Not even Omnistellar had come up with a permanent solution to anomalous powers, unless you counted the chips.

The sensation faded almost as quickly as it came. As we proceeded along the corridor, I kept my eyes peeled for Cage, but I didn't see him in any of the cells. "What did you do with our friend?" I asked, struggling to keep my voice neutral, free of either accusation or panic. God, what would I do without Cage? No matter how confused things became between us, he kept me sane. The other prisoners only followed me because he did. Without him, would they even keep me around? Not if I told them the truth, that much was certain. And I had to tell them. I couldn't keep living a lie.

The guard ignored my question. "Through here," he directed, taking me down a narrow hall between two cells. They opened a door and ushered me into a minuscule room. It contained a single metal desk bolted to the wall and a matching chair. I glanced at the guards, who gestured for me to proceed. As soon as I stepped inside, they closed and locked the door.

Sighing, I sat at the desk. "Incoming call," announced a loud voice, making me jump.

I blinked. Well, they'd said someone wanted to talk to me.

"Okay," I said cautiously. When nothing happened, I tried a familiar phrase in dealing with AI: "Put it through."

My father's face shimmered into view in the frame above the desk, a rigid mask of fury. "*Kenzie Elaine Cord*," he bellowed, "what the hell is wrong with you?"

"Dad!" I cried. I leaped to my feet, instinctively putting distance between us as my heart struggled to escape my chest. A whole range of emotions assaulted me at the sight of him: fury at his betrayal, guilt at not contacting him sooner, love and anger and hurt all bound in the messiest package ever.

His image leaned forward as if he gripped the edge of the table, his face almost purple in rage. "You're alive," he snarled. "You're *alive*, and you didn't think to tell me? You didn't think that maybe, *maybe*, that was something I would want to know? You let me believe you'd been blown up on Sanctuary along with your mother and Rita, and instead you've been gallivanting around the solar system with a bunch of anomalous hoodlums? What in the name of Omnistellar were you *thinking*?"

I'd recovered my composure after my initial shock, or at least hidden it beneath my Omnistellar-trained exterior, but I'd never seen my father so angry before. My mom was always the disciplinarian, the set-in-her-ways Omnistellar soldier. My dad, while true to the company's beliefs and ideas, was content to sweep along in her wake, giving me the occasional wink or smile when her discipline became too rigid. They'd each had their roles, served Omnistellar in their own ways, and been content in the system. Or so I'd thought. A lot of things weren't as they'd seemed. After all, if Dad was so happy, why had he left in the first place?

I resisted the urge to shout that the only reason the prisoners' escape plan worked was because Dad wasn't on station. Deep down, I knew his presence wouldn't have changed anything, except maybe gotten him killed too. "My comm device ran out of batteries," I said, which wasn't exactly a lie. It currently sat dead in its hollow at my wrist. It had taken three days for that to happen, though. "How much do you know?" I continued, forcing my voice to be calm as I reclaimed my seat.

My composure seemed to startle him. I took a certain amount of vindictive pleasure in that. Even though part of me was so glad to see him I could cry, a lot of me burned with resentment and anger. I struggled not to let either side gain control. Right now, this wasn't my dad. It was an Omnistellar official. Destroying the alien beacon was my top priority. It had to be or getting answers from my father would suddenly become a moot point.

"Mars Mining contacted Omnistellar," he said at last, his voice slightly more modulated. "They told us everything."

Hope surged within me. "Then you know about the aliens," I said. "Dad. Listen to me. They have to destroy the alien ship. Whatever it takes. You have to convince them, convince Omnistellar—"

But he was already shaking his head. "Kenzie, that ship

might hold the answer to defeating those things if they make another appearance. Omnistellar is working with Silver Sun Maltech. They're the top scientists in the field. Silver Sun will shut down the signal. I promise."

"If Rune couldn't do it, no scientist will."

"Right." My father's face twisted into a scowl. "If the teenage delinquent can't do it, how could the professionals have a chance? What happened to your training, Kenzie? Your professionalism? Do you realize you've sacrificed your citizenship? It's going to be all I can do to keep you out of a mining prison, let alone give you any semblance of a life after this!"

"I was never going to have a normal life," I shot back. "I'm an *anomaly*. Was Omnistellar really going to let someone like that into their top tiers?"

His expression collapsed. "How . . . ?"

"I read my file," I said, throwing every word at him like a knife. He recoiled as if physically stung by their force. "I removed my chip. I know *everything*, Dad. Everything except why you and Mom did this to me."

He stared at his hands, not meeting my eyes, as my chest heaved with imaginary exertion. My throat constricted. This was the moment. If Dad had anything to say, anything to clear himself and Mom of my suspicions, make everything okay again, he would say it now. And even though I knew that wouldn't be the case, I couldn't help holding my breath in anticipation.

"Kenzie," Dad said at last, "this is more complicated than you can possibly imagine. And not something we should discuss over an unsecured line. I'll be there in less than twenty-four hours, and we can—"

"Wait." His words echoed inside my brain. "You'll be *here*? Dad. Where are you now?"

"On an Omnistellar ship bound for Mars."

I sank into the chair as my worst nightmares came true. Not only was I stuck in a prison broadcasting our location to a malevolent alien presence, my dad was on his way to join us. It was Sanctuary all over again. "Turn back," I snarled. "And tell Mars Mining to get off their asses and destroy that ship!"

"Kenzie!" Shock exploded over his face.

"*Do it!*" I shouted, rocketing to my feet so fast I sent the chair flying backward. "Do it now or we're all going to die! Don't you understand? Why won't anyone *listen*?"

The computer's flat monotone interrupted. "Prisoner heart rate is dangerously elevated. Please calm yourself at once."

I spit toward the camera in the wall and spun on Dad, my face so hot it felt like the blood would come surging from my cheeks. The door slammed open behind me and guards grabbed my arms. "Destroy it!" I screamed at my father, at the guards, at anyone who would listen. "You have no idea what you're doing! You have to destroy it!"

One of the guards brandished his stun gun, and I lunged at him, bringing the heavy metal cuff down on top of his wrists.

He shouted in pain and the gun clattered to the floor. I hurled myself at the comm screen. "Dad!" I pleaded. "If you love me at all, if you never listen to anything I say ever again, trust me on this. That ship has to be destroyed!"

He stared at me, his face an agony of indecision.

And then the stun gun blast hit me from behind, and I knew nothing.

SEVEN

WATER DRIBBLED ON MY FOREHEAD, AND I moaned in response. Two stun gun blasts in as many hours had left me disoriented and woozy. Slowly I blinked to find Cage bent over me, concern flooding his face as he let water drip from his fingers. "Hey," he said softly. "Welcome back."

"Cage!" I gasped, or tried to. I shot straight up, and the world lurched with me. If his strong arms hadn't come around me, I would have kept going right off the other side of the bench.

I struggled for words, questions, but my mouth still wasn't connecting to my brain. I closed my eyes and let my mind drift back to the conversation with Dad. That wasn't how I'd imagined our first encounter. I'd thought I'd have to tell him how Mom died and what happened on Sanctuary, but Mars Mining and Omnistellar had taken care of that for me, really the only thing I was grateful for. Everything else about the conversation was a total disaster. Instead of understanding, Dad had parroted the company line, just like Mom. And instead of being helpful, he'd yelled at me.

Still. He had a right to be angry. I'd let him think I was dead for three weeks.

Rage crested in my throat, so sudden and powerful it sent a wave of dizziness washing over me. Yeah, I'd let him think I was dead. My survival had come about no thanks to my parents. After all, they were the ones who'd chipped me, hid my power, and lied to me about anomalies my entire life. And for what? Dad hadn't exactly been forthcoming with answers.

And of course, none of that mattered if the aliens arrived to kill us. I groaned, pressing my hands into my eyes so lights burst behind my closed eyelids. I was starting to feel normal again, and I wasn't sure I welcomed the sensation. "Where's Rune?" I managed.

"Asleep." He tilted me gently so I could see her curled against the wall. "They finished questioning me and must have brought me back shortly after you left. She was out by then. She needed the rest. I don't think she's stopped in days."

"None of us have." I coughed, and Cage tilted the glass to my lips. A few swallows of water cleared the cobwebs, and I leaned against the wall, wrung out.

A tremor shot through my body, and the muscles along Cage's spine tensed. "What did they do to you?" he snapped.

I shook my head, sending a wave of nausea through me. "It's only a stun gun blast. I'll be fine."

"Another one? Too many of those are dangerous."

I glared at him. "Thanks for the heads-up."

A sudden grin spread across his face. "Yeah, I know. You're not doing it on purpose. Trouble just seems to follow you around."

I couldn't quite return his smile . . . or meet his eyes. "Cage, do you think the aliens are on their way because of what we did? Venting the creatures into space?" *What you and Mia did*, I amended silently.

He didn't answer for a long time, and then he sighed, long and heavy. "Kenzie . . ."

"Venting the aliens. Lying about Matt. Doesn't it ever bother you?" I asked quietly. "Deceiving everyone? Lying to your twin sister, the person who loves you most in the world?"

I could see the denial hovering on his lips, but he did me the courtesy of swallowing it. Sinking onto the opposite corner of the bench, he raked his hands through his hair. "You think I lie because I enjoy it?"

"No, of course not. But I do think you're pretty quick to decide who needs to know the truth and who doesn't. And I'm not sure what gives you the authority." More quietly, I added, "Or when you're lying to me."

His head shot up, his eyes flashing. "I've never lied to you. Not once."

"But you haven't told me everything, either."

He didn't deny it, and the knife in my chest twisted a little further. Cage moved restlessly, as if he could physically pluck an explanation from the air. "Kenzie . . . it's not that I don't want to tell you things. It's just . . . I'm so used to being careful. Sometimes it doesn't even occur to me to volunteer information, and I don't know if that will ever change. But I can promise you that if you ask me a question, you'll get the truth. It's the best I can offer."

I examined him thoughtfully. How far could I trust that promise? What happened if another situation arose, something like the moment I'd shot Matt, and Cage decided it was safer to keep me in the dark?

Well, he could prove himself to me at this moment, anyway. I'd been wondering what he'd meant when he said he'd killed to protect Rune before. He could at least explain that.

But before I could ask about what had been bothering me for weeks now, Rune shifted, moaning, and sat up. Cage and I pulled apart as if we'd been caught doing something wrong. Another broken moment, another missed opportunity.

Genuine happiness filled her eyes when she saw me. "Kenzie!" she cried, jumping to her feet. "I was worried. When they brought Cage in and not you . . ."

"Thanks," he interjected dryly.

She shook her head. "You know what I mean. I . . ." Her voice trailed off, and she tilted her head to the side like a curious bird. "You hear something?"

I couldn't hear anything over the ringing in my ears and said so. Rune shot to her feet and paced to the bars, craning her neck and pressing her face against them, tilting her head at what looked like an uncomfortable angle. "What is it?" I demanded. She didn't answer, just flapped her hand at me behind her back. I wasn't sure whether she was telling me to shut up or to come look. I chose the latter, struggling to my feet and crossing the room. My legs bore my weight, even if my muscles shook. Cage hovered behind me, ready to catch me if I collapsed, although he didn't move to support me. I appreciated both gestures.

We joined her at the bars, and I grasped them to keep myself upright, straining to hear around the ringing. I wasn't used to being out of the loop. In training, I'd always been on top of things, and as much as I was coming to hate Omnistellar, I missed that feeling. "Cage, do you hear it?"

He frowned. "Maybe. I don't—"

The exterior wall of the corridor flew apart in a deafening cascade of metal and wire. The three of us dove for cover instinctively, even though the destroyed wall was a good fifty feet away. We landed at the rear of the cell and stared in mutual disbelief at the resulting disaster.

Mia's face shimmered into view outside the bars. Rune yelped, and I swore. "Which way's the exit?" she demanded without preamble.

"Th-that way," stammered Rune, pointing.

Mia bolted down the corridor, leaving us still trapped. "Great," I called after her. "Thanks."

But the words had barely left my mouth before Alexei jogged into sight. "Rune, the cells are locked electronically. Open yours."

"The dampening field . . . ," I began before realizing I'd just seen Mia use her powers.

Rune seemed to catch on at the same moment. She shoved her hand through the cell door, and a moment later it popped open.

We ran into the hall to find Imani clutching a stun gun of her own. I resisted the urge to hug her, settling for a wide grin, which she returned. I'd known that whatever happened, Imani and probably Reed would return for us. I hadn't been certain about anyone else, not even Alexei, because if Mia decided to turn her back on us, nothing in the world would tear him from her side.

But Alexei was here and so was Mia, jammed against the far door as if she could keep it closed through sheer force of will. A tall, stocky boy I vaguely remembered from the ship stood beside her. He braced himself with his feet and arms spread wide, his hands directed toward the massive hole I assumed he'd blown in the wall. Now he held it shut with a mishmash of debris. "Quick!" he shouted when he saw Rune. "Disrupt the other locks before—"

The door at the end of the corridor flew open, sending Mia smashing to the floor. She flipped to her feet and into a fighting stance as three guards raced inside, weapons drawn. Imani raised her weapon, but before she could fire, Alexei pivoted and hit them with a blast of flames, driving them back. He dove after them and kicked the door shut, throwing his weight against it. "Rune!" he bellowed.

"Right!" She raced to his side and plunged her hand into the electronic lock. A moment later, something spluttered, and sparks flew around the door's edge. Alexei stepped away, revealing a long burn against his right arm. He must have superheated the metal door. I couldn't imagine how much pain he'd been in holding it shut.

Mia righted herself and nodded to Cage. "Let's go!" she ordered. "Jasper?"

The boy holding the wall in place grinned. "With pleasure," he said. He set his legs wide, closed his eyes, and pulled back his arms. As he thrust them forward, the wall exploded in the other direction. Shouts told me there had been guards on the opposite side.

I'd thrown up my arm instinctively to shield my face. When I dropped it, Mia was nowhere to be found. A second later, a guard screamed. Another cried: "What happened? Who's there?"

"That's our cue," sighed Cage. We peeked outside. Mia had chosen the spot well: an isolated area separated from the city only by a massive wall, through which someone—and I didn't have to think hard to guess who—had already blown a hole.

There were two guards on the ground. The remaining four searched frantically. As I watched, another dropped, presumably struck by Mia. The other three opened fire. I winced, but no telltale spots of blood appeared.

Alexei wound up and unleashed a blast of flame at the guards, apparently unconcerned with hitting Mia in the crossfire. Sure enough, she deftly dodged his blast. "Now!" he ordered.

I staggered a few steps, still unsteady from the stun gun blasts. Then Cage was there, sweeping me into his arms and whisking me dramatically to safety, or at least, to the other side of the wall. The others were only a few seconds behind. Jasper's eyes narrowed, and he reached for a conveniently placed metal sheet, telekinetically manipulating it over the hole. A blast from Alexei welded it into place. "That will buy us a few minutes at most," he said. "Let's go."

As much as I wanted to demand explanations, this wasn't the time. "I'm okay," I assured Cage, managing to stand on my own two feet. He braced his hands on my shoulders and examined my face, his own a mask of worry. My heart surged in spite of itself. This wasn't the first time he'd pulled me from danger. Maybe we were really only at our best when saving each other's lives. Did that mean we had nothing to fall back on when no one was trying to kill us?

I stepped out of Cage's grip, facing our rescuers. Imani holstered the stun gun at her waist and looked me over, her face unreadable beneath her makeshift hijab. She hadn't really recovered from losing Aliya, who'd died on the ship after the aliens injected her with whatever they used to transform us into creatures like them. Since then, she seemed to wear a mask of constant indifference. In unguarded seconds, though, glimpses of her abiding grief slid through: unshed tears, bitter anger. Her emotions mirrored my own, and I understood all too well what she was going through.

"We'd better get moving," she said at last. "Reed's waiting."

The others seemed to know where they were going, so we followed them. I hadn't been sure what to expect from Mars City. From a distance—and on all the movies and vids—it was a glamorous, exhilarating place, full of high-priced hotels and fancy casinos.

Wherever we were now, it definitely didn't resemble the fancy Mars City they showed on vidcasts. We made our way through narrow alleys of packed red dirt, corrugated metal huts on either side of us. Cloth draped the windows, and the place seemed deserted. Alexei ducked between two houses, turning sideways to accommodate his broad shoulders, and we followed in single file: Jasper and then Rune, Imani, me, and Cage. Presumably Mia was somewhere nearby. Who the hell knew?

Alexei led us through a series of twisting alleys that all looked the same. Subtle differences marked the homes: splashes of paint here, metal sculptures there, wind chimes fashioned from old cans, homemade rag mats flanking doors. Most of the residents of Mars worked for one of two corporations: Mars Mining or Tourism Rouge. This area clearly belonged to Mars Mining. The Tourism Rouge workers lived closer to the fancy area of Mars City, not in anything resembling the high-priced hotels, I was sure, but probably in dorms or hostels a lot nicer than these metal shacks. The only noncorporate citizens on Mars were criminals, and no one was entirely sure how they kept getting in—helping one another, probably. So far, we hadn't run into any of them, either.

I kept my eyes peeled, but I didn't see anyone, and there were no changes in the architecture until Alexei stopped by what looked like a large warehouse. "Here," he announced, shouldering open the door.

Mia appeared nearby, crouched on a dumpster. "I've been trailing you," she told us. "As far as I can tell, no one's following. The guards took a while to recover from our attack and they set off in the wrong direction."

Alexei's face relaxed and he smiled. I'd noticed before how he held himself tenser and tighter when Mia wasn't around, as if only her presence truly relaxed him. It might have been worry, but he'd never shown any indication that he didn't trust her to handle herself. I honestly thought he didn't feel completely himself without Mia by his side.

We entered the building, which was exactly what it looked like: a mining warehouse. Crates along one wall bore neat labels, ready for shipment back to Earth. A few offices and desks were scattered near the front. When Alexei flipped a switch, dim lights flickered around us, revealing a windowless interior caked in red dust.

Reed leaped off a crate, his face collapsing in relief. "Could you have taken any longer?" he demanded.

"You're the one who wanted to stay behind," Mia pointed out.

Reed scowled at her. "Yeah, Mia, it was totally a choice. I would have been incredibly useful in a fast-paced prison break." He met my gaze, shook his head ruefully, and indicated his left ankle. "I think I sprained it jumping off the ship. Ironically enough, I'm the only one I *can't* heal. Speaking of which . . ." He limped over and took my face in his hands, turning it with a frown. "Are you okay?"

"I'm not sure," I confessed. As the adrenaline of our escape wore off, the effects of the stun gun blasts returned: a general sense of dizziness, like my insides had been scrambled.

"You'd better sit down." Reed guided me to a nearby crate and settled me against it. He closed his hands over mine and shut his eyes. A moment later, a sense of warmth and well-being flowed through me, like a gentle finger running over the interior of my spine. A fog I hadn't even noticed lifted in the wake of his touch. I shifted my position, and no pain echoed through me as a result. Everything sharpened, coming into clearer focus.

Of course, with my physical pain dulled, the emotional toll only expanded. Dad's face swam in front of me, and Matt's, and even Tyler's, the soft-spoken boy who had forcibly read my mind on Sanctuary. I'd forgiven him for it by the end. I hoped he'd known that in the moment the aliens gored his stomach, tearing him to shreds.

If I could forgive that violation, why couldn't I forgive my dad, or Cage, or even myself? I knew shooting Matt had been an accident. I knew I couldn't change it. But it stayed on my shoulders, an omnipresent burden of fear and self-loathing. I had to get it out in the open sometime soon, because every moment I spent with my friends made that bundle of emotion a little heavier.

And that included right now, with Reed channeling healing energy through my battered limbs.

When he stepped back, I rolled my shoulders experimentally. Even the lingering pain from the weight of the cuffs had disappeared. "Thanks," I said, shoving my guilt aside for the moment. "That's better."

Mia tapped Reed's shoulder and nodded at Alexei. "Check out the tough guy over there."

Reed straightened, his head snapping in Alexei's direction like a homing beacon. He was the cheerful joker and prankster until he sensed an injury, and then . . . "What's wrong with Alexei?" he demanded.

Alexei waved his hand in dismissal. "*Nichego*." But he peeled off his shirt without argument to reveal his terrifyingly muscled body, marred by the angry scars running down his chest and the freshly burned skin all over his right arm. Reed muttered a curse and moved behind him, closing his eyes and setting to work.

I turned to Mia. "Thanks. That was fast." I didn't voice my earlier fears, that she'd arrive too late to help us—or abandon us altogether. The fact that she'd returned strengthened my trust in her, reaffirmed what Cage had always said: there was more to Mia than met the eye.

"Yeah well, somehow I didn't think we could trust a corporation to keep their word." Her face twisted in a scowl. "The ship's still broadcasting."

"Easier to deal with now that we're free," Cage pointed out. "Where's everyone else?"

Her scowl deepened. "Cowards. They scattered and took off. The only ones willing to come back with us were Reed, Imani, Jasper here, and Anya."

"Anya?" I demanded. Anya was a ten-year-old girl without a spare ounce of flesh on her birdlike bones. "Please tell me you didn't bring her into this mess."

Mia sniffed. "Don't be stupid. We said absolutely not and left her with someone Jasper knew. That's what took so long. We had to stash her safely before we moved."

I turned to Jasper. "I don't think I've said thank you."

He grinned, tucking his long, dark ponytail over one shoulder. "I spent every day on that ship wishing I'd been brave enough to cut out my chip and help you guys on Sanctuary. This was my chance to step up." I struggled to remember his file, but only recalled a few tidbits of information. Jasper Many Chiefs, sixteen, with a power something akin to telekinesis that only applied to inanimate objects.

Imani joined us. "I'm not sure what help I'll be, but I'm here for the long run. I'm not going to let what happened on Sanctuary happen to anyone else." She twisted her long, delicate fingers in front of her as if imagining an alien between them, and I knew she was picturing Aliya.

What I saw in that warehouse didn't fill me with hope. Imani was determined, but her ability to heal herself wouldn't be much use against Mars Mining or Omnistellar, not to mention the aliens. Rune, Cage, and I leaned against the walls in varying stages of exhaustion. Reed was almost finished healing Alexei, who slumped on the crate, wincing occasionally. Only Mia and Jasper seemed to be in good moods and ready for the next battle. "So, this is it," I said. "The eight of us against two major corporations and an entire race of pissed-off aliens."

Mia shrugged. "I've had worse odds."

Cage leveled a finger in her direction. "Name one time the odds have been worse than this."

She grinned. "I don't know. Maybe a few weeks ago, when we decided to break out of an inescapable prison in the middle of space?"

"Yeah, that didn't exactly go off flawlessly."

Mia glanced at Imani with what, for Mia, passed as guilt.

"I guess not. But we survived, and we're here, and we're going to survive this, too."

I nodded, letting her determination inflame my own. "You're right. This isn't the time to quit. Let's share what we know and—"

At that moment, a buzzer rang through the room. We all jerked upright as the front door rattled. "Hide!" Cage growled. He grabbed my arm and swept me along with him, raising a blast of dust as he pulled me behind the crates seconds before the door swung open.

EIGHT

CAGE SHOVED ME INTO A CORNER, PHYSICALLY
shielding me. Even in the tension of the moment, I registered
the strength of his body against mine, and an uncertain thrill
raced down my spine. Resolutely burying it, I peered around a
crate. Imani, Rune, and Jasper crouched behind a similar stack
opposite us. Alexei and Reed had ducked behind their own
crate, which barely hid Alexei's broad shoulders. Mia, of course,
was nowhere to be seen.

Loud voices reached us, and I winced. It wasn't the guards
from the prison, so that was something. But we were dealing
with at least three miners. Mars Mining wasn't the best corporation in the solar system. They didn't offer a ton of perks to
their citizens, and they weren't exactly a political powerhouse.
But they were on the map with their proprietary dome technology, the only reason cities even functioned on places like Mars

or Jupiter's moons. That meant that even without paying their citizens particularly well, they tended to attract people with ambition. My mom always said Mars Mining was a corporation to watch. They weren't much now, but she said if we gave them a decade unchecked, they'd rival Omnistellar in power, and people who saw the winds shifting that way were willing to put up with a lot to get in on the ground floor. Mars also attracted loyalists—not of the Omnistellar brand, which was its own unique type of fanatical, but loyalists all the same. The *corporation* might not bind their hearts, but the community did. People who lived on Mars viewed off-worlders as trouble, a perception Mars Mining didn't exactly discourage.

Which meant that when all was said and done, I'd rather not attract miner attention. We could take them down, of course. We had a stun gun on our side, not to mention Alexei, Jasper, and Mia. But I didn't know when they were expected to check in or who their disappearance might alert.

Now I prayed that Mia followed my thinking and waited them out. She was useful in a fight but completely unpredictable and unreliable outside one. My temples throbbed. I'd never had to deal with this kind of uncertainty before. Omnistellar had clear rules and regulations to govern any situation, and sometimes I really missed knowing exactly what to do. People like Cage and Mia, though, wouldn't have stuck to the rules even if they'd known they existed.

There was no sign of Mia as the miners advanced into the

warehouse, not giving any indication that they noticed any-thing amiss. Two men and a woman approached, joking and chatting, checking crates against something on their tablet. Cage's chest convulsed against me with each breath, and my fingers turned white as I clutched the edge of a box, frantically scanning for anything that might reveal our presence and com-ing up empty. We were safe—for now.

But what if they didn't leave? They wouldn't come in merely to check one crate. Whatever they were doing, they'd make their way through the whole warehouse, which meant sooner or later, they'd find us. I closed my eyes, fighting for a plan. I hadn't fled a secured prison only for some errant miners to capture me.

I gauged the distance to the doorway. If we stayed quiet, we could escape without alerting them and make our way to safety, wherever that might be.

I twisted in Cage's arms. "Hey," I whispered, and he turned, brushing his cheek against mine. "If we—"

A crack of electricity and a yelp of pain erupted from the other side of the crates. Without thinking, I shot to my feet in time to see the female miner pivot as her companion went down. Before she made a sound, a burst of stun gun fire, seeming to originate from nowhere, struck her in the back, and she collapsed too. The third miner met my eyes, his gaze wild. "What . . . ?" he managed before he joined his friends in the dirt.

"Mia!" I shouted, fury overwhelming common sense.

She appeared with a shimmer and arched an eyebrow in my direction. "Yes?" she asked.

"Where did you get that?"

"From Imani." She returned it to the other girl. "Here. Thanks."

"What the hell were you thinking?" I demanded.

Mia produced a revolver from her waistband. "You'd rather I used this?"

I closed my eyes against a wave of revulsion. "I thought we agreed to leave that on the ship."

"Why would we? It has seven shots yet. It's useful."

Useful for killing people. My hands clenched into fists at my sides. How was I supposed to explain my sudden, irrational terror of that gun? It was the gun I'd held in my hands as I targeted the alien, when my shot went wide. Matt's face suddenly appeared before me, his blond hair streaked with red, his eyes wide and staring. Because I'd missed. And I'd missed in the worst way possible.

"Kenz," said Cage softly, a hint of warning in his tone. He was the only one who knew about Matt, and the only one who could follow my thoughts at the sight of the gun.

Somehow, I managed to keep my voice calm and steady. "Mia, there had to have been a better way to deal with this situation."

"Sure there was. I could've killed them." She tossed her

head, her greasy dark hair reflecting the red of the dirt. "Are you seriously going to pussyfoot around this mess? We have one goal here: to destroy the alien ship. If we have to take out a few guards to do it, I'm not going to shed any tears."

"Those weren't guards," said Jasper coldly. "They were miners."

I tried to remember and drew a blank. "Jasper, did you grow up here?"

"I did." He leveled Mia with a dark, challenging glare.

She shrugged. "Friends of yours?"

"No."

"Do they need to be?" Reed demanded. "If we start killing people, we're exactly what the corporations say we are."

Mia ignored that, keeping her focus on Jasper. "You loyal to Mars Mining?"

"No. My family is part of Tourism Rouge."

"Then what does it matter?" she exploded, jabbing an accusatory finger in his direction. "Why are we even discussing this? I didn't kill them! They'll wake up in an hour with a headache like Kenzie's. Is that really such a bad thing? You guys better grow up. There's no way we're going to destroy the ship without hurting someone. Maybe even killing them."

"She has a point," said Imani softly.

My jaw dropped, and I spun on her. She shrugged uncomfortably. "I'm not on board with killing anyone. But if those *things* arrive, they're not going to share my scruples. I mean,

I know it sounds awful, but if it comes down to a few dead guards versus an entire planet?"

Rune and Reed both shook their heads, but the others went strangely silent. I drew another deep breath. I expected Alexei to follow Mia's lead, and I didn't really know Jasper. But it troubled me to see Imani and especially Cage yield to her logic. It troubled me even more that I kind of understood her point. "All right," I managed in a reasonable tone of voice. "I get what you're saying. I do. And if we have to knock out a few guards, that's fine. But can we *please* leave violence as a last resort? There are always unintended consequences. We don't know who's waiting for these people, or who will come looking for them. And when they regain consciousness with those headaches you mentioned, they're going to report us."

"We'll be long gone by then," Cage said. I spun to glare at him, and he held up his hands in surrender. "I'm not saying Mia was right. Hell, I'll be honest: I don't know what's right anymore. Not sure I ever did. But what's done is done, and we need to get out of here and destroy that ship. Fast."

The sense of his words registered. How far away were the aliens? How fast could they travel? Would they set off in immediate pursuit of the ship once they received the signal? Would they even receive it? There were too many questions and not enough answers, and no one, apparently not even my father, was going to listen. Whatever we did, we had to do ourselves.

That realization went a long way toward steadying me. I

took in the faces around me: Alexei introspective, gazing at the floor. Reed uncomfortable and obviously in some pain. Imani nervous and frightened, but resolute. Rune and Jasper thoughtful. Cage calculating. And Mia, of course, the picture of determination. I envied her single-minded sense of her own rightness. Mia never seemed to question anything. I might not agree with every action she took, but she did act. On some level, I respected that. "Cage is right," I heard myself say.

Mia rolled her eyes. "*Cage* is right?"

I grinned. "Okay, sorry. You're all right. Our primary focus right now is destroying the ship before Omnistellar shows up." *Or the aliens do.* But saying that wasn't going to help anyone. They were all thinking it already, and I didn't need mind-reading abilities to know it. "Jasper, you're most familiar with Mars. Any suggestions on where we can go?"

He sank his teeth into his bottom lip and stared into the corner, nodding absently. "Yeah. Yeah, I think I have an idea."

"Okay. Then for now, let's get somewhere safe. We can discuss a plan later."

Without another word, Jasper edged open the door, peered outside, and glanced over his shoulder. "It's clear. Let's move."

"I'll help you," Alexei offered, giving Reed his arm. Reed took it gratefully, his face a mask of pain. "Power or no, we should see to that. Mia mine, can you check for a first aid kit?"

Mia scrambled onto a stack of crates. Before my astonished eyes, she vaulted onto the balcony of the warehouse, her hand barely grazing the rail as she flipped over it. A moment later she reappeared carrying a small red case. "Found one," she said.

Alexei nodded. "Bring it with you, please. We'll help Reed when we reach safety." He glanced at the smaller boy. "Are you all right until then?"

"I've made it this far," said Reed with false bravado. Sympathy pains shot up my leg. I'd sprained my own ankle at a training camp when I was thirteen, and I didn't have fond memories of the experience. "Hopefully Jasper doesn't plan to have us walk too far."

Imani came to Reed's other side, offering him a rueful smile. "You only heal others, and I only heal myself. Between us, you're the only one we can't help."

"Life has a stupid sense of humor," Reed agreed succinctly. "You can let go now, Lex. I'll lean on the pretty girl instead."

Imani glanced away to hide her flush, and Alexei snickered quietly, heaving Reed more heavily against him as he started into the streets.

As we trailed Jasper, Cage drew up beside me, jamming his hands in his pockets and whistling tunelessly under his breath. The sun was setting, sending Mars into shadowy relief, strange half-light and shadows everywhere. In spite of myself, I paused a moment, spellbound. This was my first time on another planet. I'd been in plenty of ships, plenty of prisons, and just about every continent on Earth. But here I was standing on *Mars*.

Out of the corner of my eye, I caught Cage doing the same thing. He glanced at me and grinned. "Sorry," he said.

"Don't apologize. It's . . . beautiful." And it was. Even taking into account the shantytown and the metal and the dust and the dirt. Mars was raw in a way Earth wasn't. Sure, Mars City was pretty much the epitome of pillaging the land and debauchery, but the city only covered a very small area. The bulk of Mars remained unmined. Untouched. And even though right now I only saw the same teeming mass of humanity you'd find on Earth, I sensed Mars pressing in on all sides.

It was hard to get a reliable estimate of Mars's population. The criminal underworld kept sneaking people in, and Tourism Rouge tended to shuffle their people among their many destinations at will. Still, even with tourists and illegal inhabitants, there couldn't be more than a couple hundred thousand people on Mars, fewer than anywhere I'd ever lived—except, of course, Sanctuary.

"Mars City reminds me of Taipei, without all the water," Cage said softly, hands still in his pockets. "The very rich"—he nodded toward the gleaming lights of the tourist center ahead of us—"the very poor"—he indicated the shantytown surrounding us—"and the unseen."

Cage and Rune had been part of the unseen, the criminal element working below the surface. Exactly how strong was the criminal presence on Mars? According to the corporations, it was nonexistent, but we all knew that wasn't true. Even diehard company loyalists acknowledged that there was some crime on Mars, largely accepted by the miners because it benefited them—the criminals made sure it did—and ignored by the tourists because it never became dangerous enough to interfere with a wild vacation. Did Cage know more about it than I did?

I almost asked, but the look on his face—dreamy, calm, and almost boyishly enthusiastic—trapped the words in my throat. This was a side of Cage I didn't often see. And why would I, when we were constantly on the run from aliens or arguing about whether to tell the others that I'd murdered their friend?

That thought intruded on the peaceful moment, guilt bringing a lump to my throat and making me notice the others drifting ahead. "Hey," I said softly. "We should get moving."

Cage nodded and gave me a smile, some of his confidence settling into place even as the wide-eyed boy lingered behind it. And that moment left a warm feeling in my heart, a sense that maybe, just maybe, things would be okay after all.

Legion 1. Do you copy?

Copy, base. We are en route for intercept as planned.

Hold that, Legion 1. It may not be necessary.

With all due respect, we have a mission, and we plan to fulfill it. Or at the very least, we plan to be paid for fulfilling it.

You'll receive your due. But if they see you coming, it could spoil everything.

Laughter No worries, base. They won't see this *coming.*

NINE

JASPER LED US IN A SHUFFLING, SHAMBLING procession through the winding streets of Mars City. As night fell, people emerged: streaming from public transit, mingling in the alleys, opening doors and windows. The temperature, which had hovered in the midseventies, dropped about ten degrees in a matter of minutes. I knew the domes managed some temperature control; otherwise, Mars would be freezing. But obviously they left nature a certain amount of authority.

We stuck to the shadows, avoiding contact with anyone. The people of Mars were unpredictable. You had your ambitious and your loyalists, but mining was still a tough life, and very few chose it voluntarily. You had families with mouths to feed, people with no other options who couldn't get a job with a better corporation on Earth. Sometimes that meant they had no real loyalty to Mars Mining, which played somewhat fast and loose with its workers' safety and paid them a bare minimum: enough to keep them alive, but never enough to get off planet and seek employment somewhere better.

On the other hand, you had people who took the opposite approach, becoming fiercely loyal to the only corporation willing to hire them. Mars was tough, but things could be worse. You could travel months in stasis to Jupiter's moons, where the life expectancy was ten years due to hard working conditions and frequent breakages in water filtration. Or, worst of all, you could be a government citizen, scrambling for odd jobs and relying on charity for your next meal. We couldn't predict who we'd run into. Those who resented Mars Mining might help us. Those who worshiped them, though, well . . . I'd already seen what that looked like with my parents.

Lost in my train of thought, I followed Jasper around a corner. Suddenly, everything changed. Where once had been lean-tos and corrugated metal were now flashing lights and tall buildings of chrome and glass. I froze, not sure if we'd wandered into a different world. Well-dressed tourists lined the streets, talking, laughing, and drinking. This was the Mars I knew from vids: a world of high-class debauchery where Earth's rich and bored traveled to unwind away from corporate laws. We'd left Mars Mining Incorporated behind and ventured into the territory of Tourism Rouge. That didn't help us much, of course. Mars Mining policed the entire planet, since technically Tourism Rouge only operated with their permission. But hopefully they'd be reluctant to charge after us, guns blazing, in a crowded tourist district and incur the wrath of the only other corporation on the planet.

The others stopped too, gaping in openmouthed disbelief. A few steps ahead, Jasper realized we weren't following. "What's wrong?" he demanded.

Mia shook her head. "We don't exactly blend."

She had a point. Everyone here carried that corporate air. They weren't all dressed in finery, but even those in jeans had a well-tailored look, manicured nails, neatly styled hair. We all wore prison jumpsuits in various stages of disrepair—or in my case, an Omnistellar guard uniform. We hadn't showered in almost a month. We were filthy and incredibly conspicuous.

"All the more reason to get off the streets before we're noticed," Jasper explained patiently. "Come on. This way."

"Are these casinos?" I asked as we proceeded along a side street. Here, too, an air of holiday cheer suffused the space. People dined at outdoor tables or sipped drinks while they talked and laughed. Conversation faded in our wake, shocked murmurs trailing us. We had a few minutes at best before someone called security, and security on Mars meant Mars Mining. With a tourist invitation, they'd charge in here without provoking so much as a whisper from Tourism Rouge.

Jasper shook his head, gesturing vaguely behind us. "Casinos are that way. Mars law. Everything has its own district. The theaters are over there, the casinos behind us, the more, um, sketchy entertainment on our right. We're heading to the hotels." He glanced both ways and ducked behind a very fake row of bushes, gesturing for us to follow.

Cage peeled some of the plasticky branches back for me and Rune, who gave him a reluctant smile. "Thanks," she said softly. It was probably the first civil word she'd spoken to him since we'd left Sanctuary.

His expression betrayed his surprise, but a wide, genuine grin spread across his face. Catching my eye, he quirked an eyebrow, and I smiled involuntarily in response. It was hard not to smile at Cage when he beamed like that. He was the flip side of everything I'd grown up valuing. Was I attracted to him or to that? Did it even matter? I ran my fingers through my hair, wincing at the texture. Hey, if he could look at this without frowning . . .

The others followed us through. As soon as we left the streets, Mia vanished. I supposed I had to admire her restraint in not doing so in full view of the crowds of tourists. I'd sensed her twitchiness as we advanced, her desperation to escape the horde of watchful eyes.

We paused a moment to collect our breath in relative privacy. We were in a slightly tacky but still impressive park: fake grass surrounding a massive fountain where fish spit water to one another before it trickled down to a pond, complete with rubber lily pads. "Do I hear frogs?" I asked dubiously.

Jasper grinned and pointed. Following his finger, I saw a

cleverly camouflaged speaker tucked into the leaves of a fake palm tree. Rows of plastic hedges surrounded us. At either edge of the garden, gates flanked a stone path. Even here, Mars's telltale red dust settled over a good portion of the area, but robotic cleaners zipped around our feet, vacuuming it up quickly and silently. I could almost have been back on Earth.

Even as the thought crossed my mind, though, my gaze traveled up to where Phobos sat in the sky, a misshapen lump nothing like Earth's moon. Deimos drifted nearby, smaller and dimmer but unmistakably a second moon. Once again, my stomach clenched at the sight. I was on *Mars*. It didn't take away from the horror of what I'd been through, but it was a moment I could take in and enjoy just for what it was.

Something rattled in the bushes, and I jerked to attention, my heart slamming into my throat. Automatically I grabbed for a nonexistent stun gun, my knees dropping into a near crouch as I waited for something to charge through the greenery. I froze in place, terror ricocheting through my frozen heart, not moving a muscle.

A small robotic cleaner, painted green to blend with the grass, buzzed along instead. I closed my eyes, hoping no one had noticed my momentary panic. *Not an alien. Not a monster. Get it together, Kenzie.*

If anyone had noticed my flashback, they didn't say anything. The park absorbed their complete attention. "Where are we?" asked Reed wonderingly.

"The courtyard of the glamorous Spring Veil Resort," Jasper replied. "Ladies and gentlemen, if you'll follow me?"

"Hang on a minute," Imani said, raising her hand. "I need a minute to catch up. Why are we here exactly?"

"Oh, fine, ruin the surprise. This is my family's hotel."

"What?" Imani and I demanded in unison.

Even Alexei raised an eyebrow. "You told me your family ran a hotel on Mars," he said. "I didn't realize you meant Spring Veil."

"You've heard of it?" Rune asked.

"Everyone's heard of it," Alexei replied. Imani and I nodded in agreement, but no one else seemed to know the name. Alexei and I exchanged glances, neither of us finishing that sentence: everyone who grew up relatively wealthy had heard of it. I scrutinized Imani out of the corner of my eye, wondering what her background was, but she was too busy examining the fountain to notice my inspection.

"Spring Veil is one of Mars's more exclusive resorts," I said, filling the uncomfortable silence. "A lot of Omnistellar's upper brass like to vacation here, which makes it a terrible place for us to hide."

"Or it would," countered Jasper smoothly, "if we couldn't trust my family to cover for us. Look, we can spend the night in an alley in shantytown hoping no one stumbles over us and turns us in, or we can do our scheming in a luxury hotel suite. It's your call."

Well, when he put it that way . . . "You're sure your family won't freak out?" I asked, imagining my parents' reaction if I'd arrived on their doorstep with a bunch of escaped convicts in tow.

Of course, my dad had already managed to make his opinion of my antics clear, and my mom, well . . . she'd never get mad about anything ever again. I closed my eyes as grief threatened to break over me once more. I couldn't even mourn my mother properly. She'd turned on me, lied to me, tried to kill me. I couldn't bring her back to life, but I wanted to just miss her without the turmoil of anger and betrayal. Even that small comfort was denied me.

A tremor racked my limbs. I drew on all my training, forcing myself under control. *Do not break.* Words floated through the mist of grief, and I grabbed at them, latching on to Jasper's voice and using it to steady myself.

"I'm not saying they'll be *happy*, but they won't turn us in or anything." He shrugged expansively. "Look, you guys do what you want. Me, I've been on Sanctuary for over a year. I'm going home."

By mutual and unspoken consent, we fell into step behind him. "Jasper?" said Imani hesitantly. "How did you wind up on Sanctuary?"

A shocked hiss emerged from the emptiness beside me. Mia, presumably, but I still jumped a mile, immediately scanning for aliens. "*Stop. Doing. That,*" I growled.

Jasper must have heard her too, but he waved his hand.

"You mean, am I on Mars's most wanted list? No. It was an accident. When my power manifested, I accidentally blew out my family's kitchen. No one got hurt, and insurance covered the damage. Unfortunately, it was a pretty public display. Tourism reported me to Mars Mining, and a week later Omnistellar showed up to take me away." He swallowed. "My parents tried to resist, but Tourism Rouge made it clear: if they fought, I'd still go to prison, and they'd lose their license to operate on Mars. This hotel is all we have."

"So, your parents let you go," said Reed softly, sympathy in his voice. I wondered if they all had a story like that—all except Rune and Cage, who'd gone silent, perhaps remembering their own father. He had used them as virtual slaves until their escape.

But Jasper shook his head. "No, they still would have fought for me. I slipped out in the middle of the night and turned myself in. My family built Spring Veil from nothing. I wasn't going to be the one to take it away . . . more than I already had, I mean." He swallowed, slowed for a moment, and then resumed his determined trek. "Trust me when I say they'll take us in."

"Do you think they'll let us shower?" asked Reed hopefully. "Do you think they'll *feed* us?"

"There's always spare food around. And I think they'll insist on the showers." Jasper held up a hand in caution as we approached the far gate, then beckoned us forward. We followed him into a shadowed recess. In front of us loomed Spring Veil, a ten-story spectacle of neon lights, rounded chrome edges, and mirrored glass. Somehow it all came together to look impressive, more than the sum of its parts.

We followed Jasper through the passageway, not meeting a single guard or tourist, until we came to a closed metal door, one not nearly as fancy as the rest of the hotel. Jasper visibly steadied himself before knocking.

I glanced at him dubiously. "Maybe no one's home."

"They're in there." He knocked again, louder this time.

A moment later, the door flew open, almost knocking him over. "Yeah?" demanded a voice. I couldn't see its owner. "What do you . . . ?"

There was a long, tense silence, followed by an ear-shattering shriek. A girl, a couple of years older and a few inches shorter than me, flew through the door, launching herself into Jasper's arms. He staggered, managing to catch her before they went flying. "Easy, Nina!" he laughed, hugging her in return.

"Oh my God, Jasper, is it really you?" She stepped back and stared at him. She had Jasper's high cheekbones and dark hair, although hers was braided and coiled around her head, and the same arched, almost elven ears. She was dressed for kitchen work in a clean white apron, jeans, and a T-shirt. The rest of us watched awkwardly as tears flooded her cheeks. "The news said Sanctuary blew up. It said *no survivors*, you jackass! We had a funeral for you!"

"Nina, I'm sorry. I'll explain everything, I promise."

She withdrew, wrinkling her nose in disgust. "You stink."

"Tell me about it."

"Jasper, Mom and Dad are going to *freak out*. Not to mention Lita and Gabriel and . . . oh my God, Kiikaa. He cried for days."

Jasper winced. "None of this is as helpful as you might think."

"I'm not trying to *help* you! I'm trying to tell you how . . ." Her voice trailed off as she noticed the rest of us. "Jasper," she said, a dangerous note entering her voice, "who are these people?"

"It's a long story, but they're friends of mine. Can we find them a room, some clothes, some food?"

"Absolutely not. You're coming straight to Mom and Dad. You don't think they deserve to know you're alive?"

"I said them, not me. I'll do the family reunion thing." He sounded annoyed, but a pleased glimmer in his eyes belied his exterior.

Nina shook her head furiously, her beaded earrings jangling. "All right," she said. "But it's better if the kitchen staff don't see them. I'm guessing none of you are supposed to be here."

"You've got that right."

"Meet me at the family entrance. I'll be there as soon as I figure out which suites aren't being used tonight." She gave him another fierce hug, punched him in the arm for good measure, and slammed the door behind her.

"Um," said Jasper. "That was my big sister."

"We guessed," replied Cage dryly.

"Apparently, I have some explaining to do, and I suppose some of you do too. If you want to call your families from the room, you can. Get Rune to scramble the number. Just in case anyone is, you know, suspicious." I glanced around curiously. I didn't know anyone's family situation but Rune's and Cage's, but no one's face gave anything away.

Jasper led us down another narrow passageway, stopping outside a plain door. "This leads to my family's rooms, but it connects to the hotel, too. Come on in."

We found ourselves in a surprisingly low-key entrance. Framed family portraits lined sleek metal walls, dozens of shoes and jackets strewn about. Jasper's sister emerged from a door I hadn't noticed on the other side of the entry. "Okay, come on," she said. She led us up a dark, shadowy staircase, probably either a staff passage or a fire exit. After five flights of stairs, with Reed gasping all the way, she used her thumb to open a door and peered outside before gesturing for us to follow.

The corridor was the picture of elegance, in sharp contrast to the stairwell. Not a speck of Martian dust here. Soft lighting illuminated polished wood floors, which we tracked dirt over with every step. A whirring told me the busy robots would tidy here, too. Framed pictures of Martian landscapes graced the walls. Nina led us to a set of double doors between two pillars, the number 530 etched across them. "You're in luck," she said. "Only a few visitors on this floor right now. But don't stick your heads outside. I'll have some food sent up. Don't answer when they knock. I'll tell them to leave the cart. If you need something, call the front desk and ask for Nina." She glared at us as she scanned her thumb to open the doors. "Don't wreck anything. Jasper, you come with me."

"Yes ma'am," he said with a mock salute. "I'll be right back, guys. I hope."

Nina looked about three seconds from grabbing him by the ear and dragging him off, so we hurried into the room. Unable to help myself, I peered around the corner and watched Nina lead Jasper away. She stood a full foot shorter than him, but Jasper still cringed as she delivered what appeared to be a stinging lecture. I bit my twitching lips. At this moment, I would have given almost anything for that kind of reunion with my parents. Even if Mom were alive, though, and even if Dad weren't furious with me, that had never been our family dynamic. We were quick-hug-and-pleasant-smile people. It had never bothered me before. I'd always known love lay beneath. Now, though, I realized the truth. For my mom, at least, love of Omnistellar outweighed love of me.

What about Dad?

"Oh my God," gasped Rune. I turned and staggered.

This wasn't a room. It was some kind of luxury suite. We were standing in an entranceway leading into a spotless living room, four doors exiting to other areas. We gaped in silence for a moment and then all broke into a run at once. We threw doors open, finding bedrooms with king-sized beds, holovids, and best of all, their own private bathrooms.

"Dibs on the shower," announced Mia, materializing in the middle of us and bolting for the biggest room. Without a word, Alexei followed, slamming the door in our faces.

"Ow," muttered Reed, who'd been peering into the room behind Mia. He rubbed his nose.

"All right then," said Imani dryly. "Rune? Be my roommate? I'll let you have first shower."

Rune took her extended hand. "That's not a deal I can refuse." She glanced over her shoulder at Cage. "Um. We should maybe talk or something. You know, later."

"Later," he agreed with a smile.

Reed sighed heavily. "I guess that means Mia's *not* going to give me that first aid kit she found in the warehouse, huh?"

Cage gestured at the closed door. "Feel free to storm in there and demand it."

"Yeah, no. I think I'll go spend about three hours soaking in a tub." Reed's eyes twinkled. "Kenzie? What do you say? Roomies?"

Before I could answer, Cage gave him a shove in the direction of one of the rooms. "Get moving, smartass." He glanced at me, his expression awkward as Reed chuckled and limped toward the door. "Um. That does leave the two of us, but I'm not saying we have to share. I can easily sleep on the couch."

"Great," I said brightly. "That means I get the shower to myself, right?"

He leveled a finger in my direction. "That you have to share." Red suffused his cheeks as he realized what he'd said. "Wait. Not . . ."

I laughed in spite of myself, but quickly sobered as the awkwardness of being alone together settled in. We stared at each other. It wasn't the first time we'd been alone since Sanctuary, but someone always lurked around the corner. Now, as we stood in a closed space with little threat of interruption, tension wrapped us in its grip. "You and Rune aren't the only ones who need to talk," I said quietly.

He closed his eyes as if in pain but nodded. "I know."

"I think . . ." I shifted awkwardly. I'd been dodging the subject for weeks now. How did you ask someone if they were a murderer? Whether all the fears you'd held about them might be true? Especially when it was someone you cared about? "I think I need a shower," I blurted out.

Great. Fan-bloody-tastic, as Mia liked to say. Way to step up and face the music. I gritted my teeth and forced myself to continue, "But we can share the room. We've been sleeping beside each other for weeks anyway. And we do need to talk. Just . . . can we do it later?"

Cage passed his hand over his face and nodded. "Yeah. I

think we'll both think more clearly once we've cleaned up and eaten. Why don't you grab the shower first?"

I pivoted and ran for the bathroom, ignoring his chuckle. The dual opportunity of escaping this conversation and getting clean? I'd never wanted anything more in my entire life.

TEN

NOTHING HAD EVER FELT AS GOOD AS THAT
shower. I stood under the hot water, washing three weeks'
worth of filth, blood, and dirt down the drain. The hotel
provided abundant shampoos and soaps. I used an entire bar
scrubbing myself raw. Part of me screamed at the delay. We
should be destroying the alien ship right now, or at least making a plan. But we couldn't go much longer without rest. We
had a deadline: less than twenty-four hours until Omnistellar
arrived. I didn't think the aliens would show up before that. At
least, I hoped they wouldn't. If we took a few hours to bathe
and eat and recharge, well, was that so terrible? I'd never been
someone to put my personal well-being above my duty, but I'd
never faced challenges like this, either. Even in the brightly lit
bathroom, I had trouble closing the shower. I couldn't stand
not seeing the entire room. What if something lurked in the

corner, waiting for me, stalking? I knew I was safe. I knew that. And yet I left the shower door open.

At last I emerged and let the sonic beams brush me dry, my hair settling into a curly mess. I couldn't face the thought of putting on my filthy guard's uniform, maybe wouldn't have wanted to even if it had been clean. The Omnistellar logo was no longer a mark of pride but a symbol of my own gullibility. I'd accepted everything the corporation said without question. I'd toed the company line. My mom had drilled that into me. She'd been a true believer herself, and she'd molded me in her own image. In another thirty years, would I have sacrificed my own child for company regulations? I bunched up the uniform, shoved it into the garbage chute, washed my hands again, and wrapped myself in a thick robe.

I took a moment to stare at myself in the mirror. I'd turned my back on Omnistellar. Seventeen years of defining myself as a guard out the window. What did that make me now? Outlaw? Anomaly? Reject? All of that, yes. But maybe more: friend, fighter, planner. I brushed my hair behind my ears and nodded at myself.

My experience with the aliens had left marks on me. Physical marks, yes, but something deeper. I used to walk through the darkest silence without fear. Now, every muscle tensed, every nerve in my body constantly ready to flee. I'd faced a formidable enemy, one no amount of training or expertise or maybe even anomalous powers could defeat. If it returned . . .

Blood drained from my face, and I clutched the counter to keep from falling. Before Sanctuary, I would never have believed there existed a threat Omnistellar couldn't conquer. The rest of the corporation might believe that too. Dad seemed to. How did you argue against blind allegiance? No amount of facts would convince them of Omnistellar's fallibility, nothing but the sight of bodies torn to shreds.

I wouldn't let it come to that. I forced my face into a steely resolve. Robo Mecha Dream Girl would never allow a corporation to call aliens to our solar system. I'd always dreamed of being Yumiko anyway. Until I found my own identity in this new world, maybe I could rely on hers.

In the bedroom, I found a bag on the bed with my name written on it. I opened it to find two T-shirts, underwear, a pair of jeans, shoes, socks, even a toothbrush. I didn't know where it came from, but I dressed gratefully, combed my hair, brushed my teeth, and at last noticed what I'd somehow missed before: the smell of food wafting in from the other room.

I burst through the door to find Rune, Imani, and Reed attacking an assortment of dishes spread across the coffee table. They were all clean and dressed in new clothes. I lunged between Imani and Rune on the sofa, grabbed the nearest item, which happened to be a sticky pork bun, and shoved it into my mouth.

We hadn't starved on the ship, but we'd survived on pressed bars of protein, emergency rations pilfered from Sanctuary.

"Oh my God," I said, collapsing over the back of the sofa. "Is this as good as it tastes, or am I just desperate for real food?"

"Both," said Rune. "Get over here and try the clam chowder. And there's an amazing fruit salad. Nina didn't know what we liked, so she sent a bit of everything."

"And everything means everything." Reed grabbed a piece of cake and shoved it into his mouth with his bare hands. Rune uttered a cry of protest, and he grinned at her around smears of icing. "What? Who knows when we'll eat like this again? I'm taking advantage of it while I can."

"Take advantage of the forks." Imani tossed one at him. He snatched it out of midair and made a show of scraping the icing off his face, licking the fork clean between each swipe.

I grabbed a plate and loaded it with anything in reach—except the stuffed mushrooms, obviously. Who ate fungus?—before Reed could make me lose my appetite. Nina might not be thrilled that Jasper had dragged us home like stray dogs, but she'd come through with an abundance of food. I no longer had any doubts about Jasper's family. They could turn us in to Mars Mining for all I cared at this moment. "Where's everyone else?" I mumbled.

"Cage said you took too long and went to use our shower," Rune answered. I winced inwardly. Had I really spent twice as long in the shower as the other girls? But no one seemed too put out; Rune mentioned it in a casual tone and immediately moved on. "We haven't seen Mia or Alexei in a while. And I assume Jasper's still with his family." She glanced at Imani and Reed. "What about you two? Do you have family you want to contact? I can rig the comms so you can't be traced."

Reed fidgeted with the hem of his shirt. "I guess I should. My moms are probably worried. But . . . I'm not sure what to say to them, you know? This whole thing isn't over. We could still be killed. And soon. I don't know if I want to give them a bunch of hope and then . . ."

Imani nodded. "I see what you're saying. But I still want to call home. I should do it now, before I chicken out."

"Let's go." Rune swallowed a mouthful of chowder, wiped her hand across the back of her mouth, and led Imani into the other room, leaving me with Reed.

"How's your ankle?" I asked.

His face twisted in annoyance. "Sore. I'd really like to get my hands on that first aid kit."

We glanced at Mia and Alexei's closed door. After a moment I got to my feet, crossed to it, and knocked loudly. "There's food!" I called.

"Go away!" Mia bellowed.

I returned to Reed, shrugging. "I tried."

"My hero," he replied dryly, shaking his head and biting into an apple. "It's so ridiculous, you know? Here my power is healing, and I'm sidelined by a sprained ankle. I have a feeling I'm going to have to stay here while the rest of you take on the ship. I'll only slow you down."

"You're absolutely sure your power only works on other people?"

"Yeah." He made a face. "Learned that one the hard way. When my power first manifested, I cured my sister's broken arm. I assumed I was invincible. Then I fell off the roof of our house and cracked my skull. Wound up in the hospital for three weeks. That's how I learned I can't heal myself, and that my power only applies to injuries, not illnesses." His expression became distant, sad. Something had happened to cause that look. I was about to ask when the door burst open to admit Jasper, looking somewhat disgruntled, but clean and in new clothes. His seemed to fit better than ours, leading me to assume he'd raided his own closet.

"Thank God for Nina," he muttered when he saw the food, straddling a chair and reaching for plates, shoving things into his mouth without worrying about cutlery. Reed nodded approvingly.

"For your entire family," I said awkwardly. I barely knew Jasper, but I owed him a lot. "This . . . this is better than anything I could have imagined."

He shrugged. "Well, once Mom and Dad finished yelling at me, and my grandparents had a go, and my siblings got done, they turned me over to my cousin, who stood outside the shower swearing at me until I was ready to get dressed. So I figure I earned it."

I hated to ask, but I had to. "They won't turn us in?"

Jasper shook his head, seemingly unoffended. "Nah. They might be citizens of Tourism Rouge, but they're not the biggest fans of the corporations. Tourism Rouge is a pretty laid-back corp. It doesn't demand undying loyalty the way Mars Mining and Omnistellar do. And besides, my family would never turn their backs on each other."

A moment later, Rune and Imani returned from their room. Imani's eyes were suspiciously red, but she kept her head high as she settled on the couch, gnawing on a piece of garlic bread. "So," she said, "what do we do now?"

"We need to make a plan to destroy that ship," I replied immediately. As I spoke, Cage emerged from the girls' room. I glanced at him and he almost took my breath away. I'd damn near forgotten what he looked like clean and healthy, and I'd never seen him without his prison uniform. In his jeans and T-shirt, his hair tousled, a black hoodie slung carelessly around his shoulders, he looked more confident, stronger, more like someone you'd run into on the streets. He caught my eye and winked, and my cheeks grew warm. Actually warm, like a blushing anime schoolgirl. I wrenched my eyes away to hide my embarrassment. "As I was saying," I said, "we have to destroy that ship, and it has to be soon. Before Omnistellar gets here, for sure. Sooner if we can manage it."

Reed glared at Mia and Alexei's closed door. "We should have everyone here before we discuss this."

"Still?" Cage rolled his eyes, crossed to their door, and hammered on it. "Mia! Lex! Get out here!"

I couldn't hear the response, but Cage shouted in reply, "I don't care! We need you. Let's go."

He rejoined us on the couch and snagged a bowl of soup. "What?" he demanded as we stared at him.

"I don't . . ." I met Rune's gaze and shook my head. "Never mind." I still didn't understand Cage's relationship with Mia, or Alexei for that matter. But they seemed to more or less follow his orders. Not mine, evidently.

But at the same time . . . I realized that if I'd banged on that door shouting for help, both Mia and Alexei would have materialized in seconds. Alexei was easier to understand. He was soft-spoken, kind, protective, but with a metal core you couldn't tarnish. Mia, on the other hand . . . on some level I liked her and thought she liked me. But now, I realized I trusted her as well. Despite my initial worries, she'd come back for us at the Mars prison without any second thoughts. Whatever else happened between us, I knew Mia had my back.

Or at least would. As long as she never discovered I'd killed Matt. What would someone who gave her friendship so carefully and her loyalty so completely say about that?

Before I could follow that train of thought to its disturbing conclusion, they emerged from the room, clean and dressed. "Food!" said Mia brightly, as if I hadn't shouted that at her a few minutes before. She dove for the table and stacked items seemingly at random on a plate, Alexei right behind her.

"All right," I said, fighting to keep my voice calm and

unemotional, to put Matt and the aliens and my father behind me. "Now that everyone's here, can we please figure out how we're going to get into a Mars Mining facility and destroy an alien spaceship that everyone is watching?"

An hour later, I sat at the window in my darkened bedroom and stared at the bustle of tourists below. "We're all going to die," I said.

"Probably." Cage settled himself awkwardly beside me, and we gawked at Mars's bright lights. After a moment, he asked, "Have you ever been on another planet before?"

"No. You?"

"Once or twice. We worked some jobs on Mars."

That was a natural opening, but the words stuck in my throat. I wrapped my arms around my legs and leaned against the wall, staring out. Somehow, the sea of people below gave everything a distant feel, and I found the courage to say, "Cage. Back on the ship, you told Rune you'd killed for her before."

He was quiet for a long time. "Yeah," he said at last, very softly.

"What did . . . I mean . . ."

I watched his reflection as he sighed, raking his hands through his hair. "I don't know what to tell you, Kenz. Rune and I did dangerous operations for dangerous people. Sometimes guards came at me and the only way to keep myself safe, to keep *Rune* safe, was to take them out."

"How many?"

"I don't know."

I laughed, choking on the sound. "You're serious? You've killed so many people you can't even count them?"

"That's not what I meant." A sharp edge entered his voice, and he leaned into my field of vision. His face sank in shifting shadows, the tendons on his neck standing out with tension. Talking about this wasn't easy for him. "Real battles aren't like training. You don't always know what's going on. Everything's dark and chaotic. Sometimes I knew I'd killed someone. Sometimes I was sure I hadn't. Often I simply didn't know. I'd knock someone down and they'd bang their head and I could only hope they'd be all right. I didn't have time to stop and check. Not if I wanted to get myself and my sister out alive."

I retreated as far as the window seat allowed. Cage's words made sense, and I got it. I could understand how circumstances might make things difficult. But to not even notice that you'd flat-out killed another human being? "I might not have been in any *real* battles, but I'm pretty sure I'd notice if I killed someone." I heard the edge in my voice, raging just outside my control. I'd always reacted poorly to anything that felt like condescension. I didn't mean to do it now, but I couldn't seem to break the habit. And besides, it was *true*. I still remembered stumbling over to Matt, the blood soaking his shirt, his sightless, staring eyes.

After, I reminded myself. You noticed that *after* the alien died. At the time it had just been triggers and chaos and fear.

"I did notice, Kenzie. The first time. It gets easier." He stared outside, his face silhouetted and somehow mournful in the half-light. "God help me, but it does."

"When did the first time stop hurting so much?" I whispered, a bitter taste on the back of my tongue. "I still wake up every night with . . . with *his* blood on my hands. I still hear that gun in my dreams. I haven't gone a single day without thinking of Matt since Sanctuary."

Cage reached for me, his expression lost in shadows, but I shook my head and wrapped my arms more tightly around my legs. "We have to tell the others," I said flatly.

"We've had this conversation."

"No, I've had this conversation, and you've told me what to do." A tinge of bitterness entered my voice. I'd just left Omnistellar behind. For the first time in my life, I was free: no corporate rules, no parents monitoring my every step. Just Cage, and I didn't need his control any more than I needed anyone else's. "But I've made my choice. I'm going to be honest with them."

He sighed. "When? Tonight? That'll work out great, what with us planning to take on Mars Mining. We need everyone to trust us right now. We can't afford to have them second-guessing."

"Not tonight." I hated the truth in his words, but I accepted it. "Soon, though. They deserve the truth."

A long silence stretched between us. When Cage finally answered, he directed his gaze outside, and his voice was suspiciously even. "I can't stop you if that's what you've decided."

"No, you can't." I hoped he realized that. "I'm not your sister, and I'm not your subordinate. I'm your . . ." Your what? "Your friend," I settled on at last, and when he turned back to me, the quirk of his eyebrow visible even in the dim reflected light, a smile brushed my lips. "Maybe more," I allowed. "But either way, you can't make choices for me. You just can't."

"I don't mean to. But you said you didn't want me to lie to you, and I'm trying to be as honest as I can here. I think telling the others is a bad idea. Rune and Matt had something between them. I'm not sure what, but I know how deeply she feels. She'll be devastated by this. Mia, who knows how she'll react? And I don't want them blaming you. None of this was your fault. You saved our lives, Kenz. Saved them over and over again, and that stray shot was nothing but bad luck. It wasn't like my past, where I took people down knowing full well I might kill them. You were trying to save Matt's life." He sighed, standing his hair on edge again, threading his hands through it and leaving them there. "I guess . . . I see you beating yourself up over this every day and night. I don't think you need anyone adding to your guilt, that's all."

My heart melted slightly. "I appreciate that," I said softly. And I did. Cage was right. I blamed myself for Matt's death.

But was that any less than I deserved? Intentional or not, I had killed him. He might have survived the alien if not for me.

As for Cage's past, well . . . I had my answer. It wasn't as bad as it could have been, but it wasn't as innocuous as I'd hoped. I should ask for specifics. I should press him for details. "My dad's on the Omnistellar ship," I told him instead. It was the coward's way out, a safer topic, but still one I desperately wanted to discuss.

Cage blinked, surprised. "You talked to him?"

"At the prison. He called."

"You okay?"

I smiled without quite meaning to. Cage always cut through the noise and got to the heart of a problem. "I will be. It was weird. He was really angry. And so was I." Too angry, I realized. Or maybe not. I had a right to be angry. But I shouldn't have lost control before I got answers, not when so many questions lingered between us.

Speaking of angry . . . "Mia still has that gun," I said, thinking out loud. A shiver went through me. I'd fired guns so many times in my life, at training camps, at target practice. I'd never been fantastic at it, but it had always seemed like a game. I'd known on an intellectual level that guns were weapons, of course. Designed to kill and nothing else. But it didn't seem that way until Sanctuary. "Can you convince her to give it up?"

Cage hesitated. "Maybe," he said at last. "I think it's making her feel safe. Mia won't just get mad and shoot someone, Kenzie. And that gun might come in handy."

I sighed. "Fine. We'll let her keep it and just hope she doesn't kill anyone." *Like I did*. But Mia was a better shot than me. Hopefully she wouldn't screw up. And hopefully I'd never find myself in a position where I needed to take that gun. The thought sent a chill down my spine. Could I do it? If I had to grab that gun to defend myself or one of my friends, would I even be able to close my finger around the trigger? "Carrying that gun opens the possibility of someone dying. Or after killing countless people, does that not matter to you?"

Cage glared at me. "You asked for honesty, and I'm trying to give it. You're not helping."

He was right, but I didn't have an apology in me. A long, angry silence lingered between us, long enough for me to regret my words. "We should get some rest," he said at last. We'd decided to let the hunt for us die down for a few hours before we attacked, and I'd managed to recharge my comm device. Jasper reclaimed his from his sister too, so we had a way to communicate. We'd both set alarms for four a.m. We'd judged it the best time to attack. It also gave us a few hours to sleep, as we were all exhausted. No one had rested well on the alien ship, and I didn't exactly count my semiconsciousness after getting zapped with stun guns as restful.

Cage slid off the window seat and glanced at the bed. "Offer's still open. I can sleep on the couch."

I sighed. Part of me wanted that. Send him away. Use the time to reflect, to be by myself. But no matter how much we fought, Cage and I had always stretched out side by side on the alien ship, and even if we didn't touch, I appreciated his warmth, the reassurance of his presence.

"I don't know what's going on between us," I told him honestly.

He sighed. "Neither do I. For what it's worth, my feelings haven't changed. I still care about you. A lot. It's just been hard, with everything that's going on."

"You can say that again." I gave Mars one last look, then turned to glance over my shoulder at his face, alternating red and white in the reflections of the lights outside. "You can stay," I said, and his answering grin dwarfed all the brightness behind me.

ELEVEN

MY ALARM JERKED ME FROM A SOUND SLEEP a few hours later. I shot straight up in bed, disoriented and confused. I'd gotten out of the habit of waking to an alarm, and out of the habit of sleeping on anything soft or comfortable. I jabbed the alarm into silence and took a moment to thread my fingers through my hair, calming my racing heart. Since Sanctuary, I hadn't had a single night of dreamless sleep. I'd hoped the new setting, away from the alien presence, might help. But it hadn't. The aliens stalked me in my dreams, and as always, it ended with Matt's lifeless body at my feet, the gun trembling in my hands as creatures closed in from all directions.

Cage groaned beside me and pulled a pillow over his head. We'd fallen asleep fully clothed but close together. Sometime in the night I'd apparently piled most of the blankets and pillows between us. I hoped that wasn't a metaphor. "Get up," I muttered, shaking off the vestiges of my nightmare.

"Why?"

"Because it's time, and because I'm not waking Mia. That's why."

He clenched the pillow more tightly around his face. "Is that my life's only purpose? As a Mia buffer?"

"It is today." I nudged him until he tumbled to the floor, grumbling under his breath as he climbed awkwardly to his feet.

Something clattered outside. We both froze, staring at the door. "That was just Jasper getting up," I whispered, my heart hammering in my throat. "Right?"

"Right." But Cage whispered too. Slowly, he grabbed his shoes and tugged them on. I did the same.

We both listened intently. No further sound came from outside. If it was one of the others, surely they would have said something by now? Made some sort of noise? "Stay back," said Cage, tiptoeing toward the broad double doors.

I hesitated, but after a moment I moved out of his way. I still didn't love him telling me what to do, and there was probably nothing there. But if there was, Cage's speed gave him a much better chance of dodging bullets than my ability to understand languages.

I grimaced. Of all the powers to wind up with . . . sure, it had come in handy on the ship, but it wasn't much good in life-or-death situations, and lately, those seemed to occupy the bulk of my day. I'd never been the strongest or fastest in my classes, but I'd always been in the top five. With the other anomalies, I kept getting pushed out of the way. I remembered a gangly, sarcastic boy at a three-month training camp. He was always at the bottom of the class and just seemed to get angrier and angrier about it. At the time I'd scorned him, but now I was starting to empathize.

Cage eased the door open a crack, leaning to one side. He angled his head. "What do you see?" I asked, my voice barely loud enough to qualify as a whisper.

He held up a hand in my direction. An agonizing moment passed, every silent heartbeat an eternity. Finally, Cage turned back to me, shrugging—

And a bullet shot through the gap where he'd just been standing, cracking into the wall above the headboard.

I gaped at it in openmouthed disbelief. Cage, more accustomed to shootouts involving actual bullets, slammed the door and flew across the room, tackling me to the floor on the other side of the bed. From this vantage point, the bullet wedged in the wall jutted into my line of view. It was bigger than most bullets and had a familiar shape. "I think it's a tranquilizer," I said with some relief.

Cage's face was grim and taut above me. "If they surrender us to Omnistellar and leave that ship's signal functioning, they might as well put a bullet in our skulls. It'd be quicker." He raked his hand through his hair, his body braced above mine. No more shots came from the other room, and no more noise. "They're being quiet so they don't wake the others."

The others . . . of course. "Get off me," I muttered, shoving him so he rolled aside. As Cage rose on his elbows to peek over the bed, I activated the comm link embedded in my wrist.

Jasper answered a moment later, voice only, and a voice thick with sleep. "I'm up," he muttered in the least convincing lie I'd ever heard.

"Good," I whispered, "because there are people with tranq guns in the main room."

That got his attention. "What?"

"Shh! We need to get out of here. Can you give them something else to worry about?"

"You bet. Wait just a minute."

Across the room, the door slid open. Cage dropped to his belly and growled, "We don't have a minute!"

"Under the bed," I whispered, pulling him after me as we slid beneath the massive frame. This bought us a couple of seconds at most. There weren't a lot of hiding places in the room, and if these were security professionals, even if they weren't Omnistellar, they were bound to find us. But maybe those seconds would be enough for Jasper to take action?

I muted my comm device so Jasper wouldn't give us away if he called. Cage's broad chest pressed against my back, one of his hands cupping my arm as if he could shove me somewhere safe if we were discovered. Unbidden, my thoughts returned to Sanctuary, where Cage and I had huddled under my bed as an alien stalked through the room. He'd clutched me as if he could shield me from its claws, and we'd both trembled, white-lipped and petrified, until it clattered away. Bile rose in my throat at the memory. My breath came in short gasps, my heart racing. My God, if we couldn't stop the signal, if we couldn't—

A loud crash reverberated through the suite.

Someone bellowed. Feet stampeded. Cage and I slid from under the bed in time to see a figure in a black suit bearing the Mars Mining logo dash out the door. Cage grabbed my hand and half tossed me into the air, catching me and breaking into a run—a full-on, superpowered burst of speed that plastered my skin to my skull and left my eyes watering. A second later, we were in the corridor. "I'm going back for Rune!" he shouted, vanishing before I responded.

Damn it! I paced the hallway, searching my training for answers. What did you do when you faced an unstoppable force that outnumbered and outarmed you? Especially when you had no idea where your compatriots were. Omnistellar hadn't given me any answers. They'd always led me to assume I'd be on the unstoppable side.

A burst of flame from the suite told me Alexei was awake and moving. A second later, Cage returned, dropping Rune and Imani in front of me. Alexei, Jasper, and Reed bolted after him. "Go!" Jasper yelled. "Make for the service door at the end of the hall!" He pulled the doors shut behind us and blasted them, crumpling them against each other, effectively locking the Mars Mining goons inside for the moment.

"Wait!" Imani cried. "Mia!"

Mia shimmered into view behind her, blood dripping from her bottom lip. "I'm here."

Alexei scowled. "He hit you."

"I hit him back, and he's not getting up."

"What is wrong with you?" Reed screamed. "Run!"

The doors behind us shook. Cage blasted across the hall, Jasper racing full tilt behind him. A scan of Jasper's thumb opened the service exit. Other doors opened behind us, curious tourists glancing out and exclaiming at the commotion.

We clambered into the stairwell, Jasper in the lead. "Your family must have called them," Mia accused as we raced down the stairs.

"Never!" Jasper snarled.

"We weren't exactly subtle in getting here." I shouldered past Mia and raced after Jasper. "Now that Mars Mining knows we're alive, they've almost certainly broadcast our info to bounty hunters. We could have been spotted by just about anyone on our way to the hotel, and from there it's just a matter of getting Tourism Rouge's permission to bio scan for a big group of teens." Mars was a great place for collecting bounties, and a great place to vacation after you claimed one. I cursed myself for not considering it sooner. Mars Mining would have flagged our names, or at least those of us they knew about, the second we escaped.

In which case, Jasper's family might be in trouble. That awareness was mirrored in his face, but we couldn't help them right now. Our only hope was to make straight for Mars Mining Incorporated, find our way inside, and destroy the alien ship. With luck, they'd sent their best people after us. Maybe the headquarters was unguarded.

Jasper directed us out the service entrance and into the fake garden. He hesitated, glancing at Spring Veil Resort with an agonized expression on his face. "Jasper," said Imani softly. "Your family will be fine."

He shook his head, forcing a smile. "Right. If we stop the aliens from ripping them to shreds, you mean. Hopefully they'll see that as a good excuse for abandoning them . . . again."

"What are we going to do?" Rune demanded. "The plan . . ."

"The plan's off," I said dryly. We were going to distract the Mars Mining guards with a diversion in the tourist area and then sneak back to the ship while they were occupied. Unfortunately, that wasn't going to work any longer.

"We're heading to the ship. We have a lot of power between us. We'll blast our way in and wreak some havoc. I'm not sure what else to do at this point."

Mia spit blood on the ground and scowled. "I like havoc."

Rune shook her head furiously, but something crashed

behind us, and she gave up. "All right, already! Whatever we're doing, let's just move!"

We broke into a run. Jasper led us through Mars's side streets, avoiding attention as much as possible. It wasn't nearly as crowded as earlier, but even at four in the morning, there were plenty of people out and about. Of course, by this time many of them were too drunk to notice us rushing past.

I scrambled over a stack of crates separating tourist Mars from its shantytown cousin, Reed on my heels. That was when his steady, strong gait broke through my worry and fear. "Your ankle!" I exclaimed. "It's better! What happened?"

Reed's face broke into a broad grin. I got the sense he'd been waiting for someone to ask. "I have no idea! I went to sleep thinking about how sore it was and wishing I had some painkillers. And when I woke, *presto!* It didn't hurt at all. I healed myself!"

"That's ridiculous," said Cage sharply. "Your power doesn't work that way."

"You're telling me? God knows I've tried hard enough in the past. But *something* happened. You got a better explanation?"

From Cage's expression, it was evident he didn't. I couldn't come up with one either. "Do powers mutate?" I suggested as we threaded our way through the streets. "I've never heard of that."

"Neither have I." Rune had drawn close behind us and was examining Reed like an interesting science project. "We should test it out."

"What, by cutting me open and seeing if I heal? No thanks."

"No!" Rune was so appalled, so clearly not understanding that Reed was joking, that even in the midst of this chaos, I couldn't help laughing. Neither could Cage, apparently. For a second Rune looked angry. Then her face relaxed, and she smacked Cage in the arm. "Knock it off. I meant we should see if any of the rest of us have new powers."

"How would we do that?" I asked dubiously.

"Hey, here's a thought!" Mia popped into view in our midst, making everyone jump. "Let's worry about that later and focus on, oh, I don't know, the armed guards chasing us, or the alien ship we have to destroy. Huh? What do you think?"

I scowled at her, but she only winked in response. Danger brought Mia to life. I'd seen it before, and it never failed to creep me out.

I had to admit, though: she was good at it. Jasper and Alexei might have the most destructive powers of the group, but Mia brought a chaos all her own.

"She's right. Come over here," Jasper called, and we drew up behind him. He'd taken us on a different route, approaching Mars Mining from another angle. Massive walls surrounded the complex. "What do you think?" he asked. "Should I blow another hole in the wall?"

Silence followed, and I realized, with some horror, that he was asking *me*. I glanced around. Cage, as usual, pursed his lips in thought, considering the situation from every angle, but everyone else stared at the two of us expectantly—even Mia, who usually had an answer for everything.

Oh God. They thought I was in charge. Or me and Cage, anyway. Why did that terrify me so much? When I'd been part of Omnistellar, all I'd wanted was that sense of command. Now, with these former prisoners staring at me, the thought petrified me.

Was I a criminal mastermind now? I almost choked on the idea. I bit my tongue to stay calm, the pain focusing me as I followed Cage's gaze. This was about preventing an alien invasion. Robo Mecha Dream Girl wouldn't have hesitated to act. "No," I said slowly. "Or at least, not yet." An idea formed in my head, a glimmer of a hope with probably nothing behind it. "Mia. You heard what Reed said about healing his own ankle?"

She snorted. "*If* that's what happened, sure."

"Let's assume for a moment that it is. Just for the sake of argument, let's say something happened to us. Maybe on the alien ship. Maybe not. But for some reason, our powers are changing. Getting stronger."

Cage seemed to snap out of a trance, his focus shifting abruptly to me. "I see what you're saying," he said.

"How sweet." Reed scowled. "Want to fill the rest of us in?"

I clenched my fists to stop their trembling and managed to meet Mia's piercing gaze. "I'm wondering if Mia can make Jasper invisible."

They draw near.

Sinews curl. Tendons awaken.

Glimmering through time and space.

They cut. They drive.

They are one and many and all and few. They consume.
They harvest.

The harvest is broken.

Tendrils unfurl.

Fully.

Fully.

Awake.

TWELVE

COMPLETE SILENCE GREETED MY SUGGESTION.
Then Mia snorted loudly. "You're joking."

"Why?" Cage demanded.

"Because it doesn't work that way, genius."

"Have you tried?"

"Oh, for the love of . . ." Mia threw up her hands in disgust.
"Yes, I've *tried*. My invisibility affects me and a limited range of
things touching me. My clothes, for instance. I can make your
hand invisible if you stand close and keep it on my shoulder. Is
that useful to you, Cage?"

I glanced over my shoulder nervously. So far, I'd heard no
signs of pursuit, but Mia was really loud. And those guards had
to be back there *somewhere*. "Have you tried since we left the
alien ship?" Her silent scowl was answer enough. "Will you give
it another shot? Please? Humor me? I'll . . ." I tried to think of

something to bribe Mia. What did she like? Violence? Chaos? Guns?

Guns. My heart stuttered in my chest, but I forced the words out. "I won't say another word about that gun in your waistband ever again."

Her eyes narrowed. "That's almost worth it. *Almost.*"

Cage sighed heavily. "Mia . . ."

"Oh, fine," she said. "Sorry, Jasper." She laid her hand on his shoulder. Jasper shrugged, his dark gaze boring into me rather than her.

Mia shimmered and vanished. Her voice came from nowhere, more hollow and disembodied than usual. "See?"

"Mia," said Imani, her voice strangled, "his arm disappeared."

A long silence followed, during which we all stared at the place where Jasper's arm should be. "Weird," he said in seeming fascination, flexing the muscles in his shoulders. "I still feel it, but I don't see it. Mia, do you not see yourself when you're invisible?"

"Shut up," she replied. Another long moment passed—and then Jasper faded out of existence.

"I'll be damned," said Reed. "I did heal myself."

Alexei frowned. "Mia mine, how are you doing that?"

"How the hell should I know?" She and Jasper both reappeared, and for the first time since I'd met her, Mia didn't appear confident. Her eyes were wide, and her hands trembled. Without her characteristic brashness, years slid away. I never thought of Mia as a teenager, someone my own age, but now she looked it. I didn't even know how old she was. She could be years younger than me.

Mia turned to Alexei, her voice a bit quicker and higher than usual. "What's going on, Lex?"

He shook his head, and I frowned, working things through. "Something happened. I don't know what, but our powers are increasing." Or at least, some of our powers. What about mine? "This could be the thing that turns the tide in our favor," I continued, my excitement growing. "Increased powers that Omnistellar doesn't know about? That's exactly what we need to—"

"Oh, that's fine for you," Mia snarled with such ferocity I retreated a step. "With your month-old powers and your sheltered Omnistellar past. But it's different for us. Our abilities are part of who we are. How would you feel if you woke up and your eyes were suddenly a different color?"

I gaped at her in disbelief. "Mia, your power didn't *change*. It got stronger. How is that not a good thing, especially in this situation?" *And do you have any idea, any, what I would give to have your problem?* Not to mention the fact that, once again, Mia was setting me apart, tossing me to the side, making sure I knew she didn't fully trust me. Maybe no one did. I was still different from them, not Omnistellar, but not fully an anomaly, either, at least not in their eyes. Where did that leave me?

If she realized she'd hurt me, Mia didn't show it. "Stronger, weaker, it's still something happening to my body that I can't control. Sure, it might be useful now. But what if this is just the beginning? What if my powers keep changing? How am I supposed to predict *anything* if I can't even predict my own abilities?" Her hands clenched into fists, her arms steel bolts of tension.

Cage raked his hands through his hair, standing it on edge. "I hear you, Mia. But for now, can we focus on using the resources available to us? Please?"

She hesitated a moment, and something clattered in the distance. We all froze. It was probably nothing. "I'll be right back," said Mia, and vanished.

"Great," I snapped. Her comments strained me more than I wanted to admit. They drove home the fact that even though I'd thrown myself fully in with the others, they hadn't accepted me. I wasn't one of them, and I sure as hell wasn't Omnistellar. Tension edged along my neck, creeping up my skull and setting off a pounding headache behind my eyes.

"Give her a second," Alexei said calmly.

Of course. Mia could throw a table at a waiter in a crowded restaurant and Alexei would find a way to excuse it. My teeth clenched, and words bubbled in my throat, stumbling over one another in their rush to escape.

"It's okay," said Cage softly, and Rune took my hand, not in warning or restraint but in support. It was enough to make me swallow the words. I still didn't know where things sat between me and Cage, but we'd made some progress. He'd given me answers openly and honestly and that had to mean something. Rune, I loved without reservation. She was the sister I'd never had. I squeezed her hand gratefully and tried not to think about the fact that our entire relationship was founded on a lie. Sometime, and sometime soon, she'd learn the truth. Would she still be my friend once she did?

"Don't take it personally," Reed told me, breaking into my thoughts. "It's just Mia being Mia."

Jasper's eyes took on a calculating look. "For what it's worth, I'm very curious to see what my powers can do now."

"And another healer could be useful." Imani flashed me a smile. "With a bit of luck, maybe I'll be able to heal someone else for once."

"Mia isn't angry at you," Alexei added, leaning against the wall and folding his arms. "She doesn't like surprises. She'll be back."

Well, I could sympathize with her dislike of surprises, especially since Sanctuary. And the others' support gave me a rush of strength, one I wasn't sure I deserved. I caught Cage's eye, and he shook his head in warning. It didn't matter. As soon as we were out of danger, I was telling them the truth.

A moment later Mia did indeed return, her expression back to normal and a Mars Mining ID card clutched triumphantly between her fingers. Even in taking a moment to cope, she was working. "All right," she said. "Let's do this."

An ID card wouldn't get us into the more sensitive areas of the complex. If we'd been dealing with Omnistellar, it wouldn't have gotten us anywhere at all. We had omnicards as backups to our retinal scans, but they were smaller and more secure than ID cards, which were issued to every company employee. Mars Mining spent most of their budget on their dome tech, though, and parts of the facility were still old-fashioned. Jupiter's colonies, which had only sprung up over the last decade, used Mars Mining's proprietary tech, and my mom used to say Mars Mining was on the way up because of that. The moons had their own corporation, Phantasmatech, but they relied on Mars Mining for their very existence. As Jupiter's colonies grew, so would Mars's royalties and prestige. For now, though, they were biding their time until their big windfall. Hence the ID cards, a cheap but effective method of controlling access to your facility—as long as no one stole them.

An ID card would at least get us through the front gate.

We crouched in an alley. The shadows grew lighter, hints of illumination edging across the Martian sky, Phobos still visible above. Much longer and we'd have miners leaving their homes, heading for work. I didn't like to think what they'd do if they stumbled across us lurking outside Mars HQ. All I could do now was wait, though, until Mia and Jasper made their move.

I huddled against Cage, Reed on my left, his nervous energy infectious. He never stopped moving, always drumming his fingers against his thighs, quirking his head from side to side, or just blinking rapidly in thought. Cage, on the other hand, stayed still as a statue, his long, lean body relaxed and deceptively loose, even though I knew from experience he was coiled and ready for action.

Was his power shifting? Was *mine*? If it shifted enough, I might learn to communicate with the aliens. On Sanctuary, I'd tried to understand them and caught glimmers of meaning, and on their ship, I'd come to understand their written language with limited capacity. I imagined having the ability to talk to those things, to understand their thoughts as they flew out of the darkness and slashed us with their claws and—

Cage nudged me. "Relax," he murmured, and I realized I was breathing in short, sharp gasps, my muscles so tense they ached.

I blinked at him in the shadows. "How are you so calm?" It wasn't just what we were doing. Ever since Sanctuary, aliens snapped from the corners of my imagination.

"Experience." He shrugged, then squeezed my arm. "You'll be fine. You've got this."

His confidence gave me a burst of renewed hope. As much as I'd always tried for self-reliance, it was so good to have someone else believe in me. "Thanks," I whispered, knowing the word didn't convey the depth of my appreciation.

He leaned in so close his lips almost touched my ear. "Kenzie, I . . . about what you said earlier. About Matt. I never meant to order you around, to tell you what to do. I only—"

As if on cue, my wrist comm gave three short buzzes against my skin, the signal I'd prearranged with Jasper. "That's it,"

I announced, cursing everyone's timing. Talking with Cage would have to wait. "West wall."

We split into two groups: me, Cage, and Reed to the left, Alexei, Imani, and Rune to the right. We were going with a quick and sloppy version of our original plan, and I had no idea if it would work.

I expected the wall to blow open in shards of metal, but instead it was more of a controlled disintegration. The material collapsed softly, scraps curling and floating away like paper caught in a flame. The resulting hole in the wall revealed Mia and Jasper, posed like action movie stars around the crumpled bodies of three Mars Mining guards. "Did you kill them?" I demanded.

I earned myself two identically dirty looks. "They're unconscious," snapped Mia. "Come on. Let's move before more of them show up."

This early in the morning, Mars Mining was virtually deserted, but red lights and blaring alarms warned that Jasper's reorganization of the wall had not gone unnoticed. Rune dove for the nearest panel and jammed her hands inside. The alarms stilled, and nearby doors sprang open. "Should be clear," she announced.

We ran through several hallways, following Rune, who had memorized the headquarters layout from a computer printout earlier that night. Before long, we reached familiar territory, returning to the landing pad. We were banking on the ship being too large to move and impossible for anyone but Rune and me to pilot. I had no idea what we'd do if it wasn't where we'd left it.

It had *better* be where we'd left it. In spite of our desperation to destroy it, I thought of the alien ship as ours. We'd earned it. It was a profoundly ridiculous thought, but the idea of Mars Mining messing around inside *our* ship continued to rankle.

Two guards skidded around the corner ahead of us, weapons raised. "Hands up!" one of them bellowed.

Two sharp crackles sounded behind me, and the guards stiffened and collapsed.

I spun, mouth open, to find Imani lowering the stun gun. "Nice shot," I managed.

She flushed. "Thanks." A slight smile touched her lips. "My grandfather used to take Aliya and me hunting. I guess the principles are the same." It was the first time she'd mentioned her sister in weeks, and her voice stuttered on the name. My heart ached for her. For all the time we'd spent together, Imani and I had never discussed our shared losses. Maybe it was soon time we did.

We had the presence of mind to relieve the guards of their weapons. I took one stun gun and Reed took the other. I was surprised how much better I felt with the gun in my hands. After what had happened with Matt, I never wanted to hold a real firearm again, but the stun gun was smooth and familiar. I could defend myself without killing anyone. I was instantly less dependent on the others, more in control, more *myself*. Omnistellar might have been behind me, but I hadn't eradicated the guard from my system just yet.

Rune got us through the corridors without further incident. Relief suffused me at the sight of the ship on the tarmac. I'd forgotten how big it was, how alien. It seemed to swallow the light. A handful of guards surrounded it, but Imani, Reed, and I disabled them quickly and cleanly. I made Cage and Alexei haul them into the corridor, out of the blast range, assuming we managed to destroy the ship.

Alarms went off again. Someone had spotted us. Jasper raised his hands and wrinkled his brow, and the door crumpled in on itself. "That should buy us a few minutes. Now what?"

The original plan involved swiping explosives from the mines. Obviously, the midmorning attack on our room obliterated that idea. I'd had some vague idea of Alexei simply overheating the ship until it exploded, but standing in front of it, it was clear I'd been dreaming. It was too big, too sleek, made to withstand weapons fire in the vacuum of space. No amount of flames would damage it. "Maybe we can find where the signal is coming from?" I asked hopefully. "Destroy that instead of the entire ship?"

Rune shook her head. "I tried that when I first spotted the signal. If I'd found it, I might have been able to deactivate it."

We all stood stupidly staring at the thing, and I cursed myself. The others relied on me to come up with something.

They'd probably assumed I had a plan in mind when in truth, I hadn't been sure we'd make it this far. What were we supposed to do now?

A heavy sigh came from the other side of the tarmac. We all spun, raising our weapons and targeting the area. "You're surrounded by fuel," came an annoyed voice, and a man strode around the corner of a nearby ship. "Use it to obliterate that pain-in-the-ass ship."

We stared in silence for another moment before Cage found his voice and asked the question on everyone's mind. "Excuse me," he said, "but exactly who the hell are you?"

THIRTEEN

THE MAN STEPPED INTO THE LIGHT. HE HAD
smooth olive skin and a loose black ponytail and, disconcertingly, a patch over his left eye. He looked like someone's modern vision of a pirate, right down to the loose white shirt, tight black pants, and tall boots. A pistol and an actual sword hung at his side. All told, he could have stepped out of the pages of *Robo Mecha Dream Girl 5*, and at the sight of him I was almost overcome by longing, brief but painful in its intensity, for my old life, when evil corporations existed only in the pages of fiction.

"Does it matter who I am?" He lifted his hands in surrender, although I got a strong sense he was mocking us. "I'm giving you the answer to your problem. Fill the ship with fuel and have your fiery friend there blast it to kingdom come. Or would you prefer to stand around waiting for security to break through that door?"

We exchanged glances, but he was right. "Do it," I ordered,

without stopping to think that they might not want to obey me.

To my surprise, no one argued. Weapons were holstered, and everyone sprang into action. "Can you lift those barrels?" Cage demanded of Jasper, already on the move.

"Physically, maybe. Not with my power."

Alexei and Cage grabbed one of the containers. Their muscles stood out in sharp relief as they strained to hoist it between them. Ship fuel in barrels this size weighed a lot. I had a feeling I'd sprain my back if I even tried lifting one. At this rate, we'd be here all night—and already guards banged on the door behind us. In a few minutes they'd break through, or just start tossing smoke grenades over the walls. Reed and Jasper grabbed another barrel. They almost managed to lift it between them, but then Reed gasped and shook his head, and it clattered noisily to the ground.

Rune sighed heavily. "*Boys*," she said, breaking into a run. I exchanged mystified glances with Imani and we followed.

Rune jumped into a nearby hoverlift, closed her eyes, and melded her fingers with the control panel. It roared to life, wavering about a foot above the tarmac. She directed it with practiced ease to where Alexei and Cage shamefacedly dropped their burden.

Imani laughed. "Trust Rune," she remarked as Rune steered the lift under the platform of fuel, carefully leveraging the platform into the air.

She rose high to get it above ship level. If any of the guards had the brains to look, she was well placed for a shot above the walls. "Come on," I said to Imani. "We'd better make sure the ship is open and help guide those barrels inside." Maybe I couldn't help Rune drive, but speeding things up would minimize her exposure.

The two of us scrambled up the ship. Alexei and Cage were on our heels while Reed, Mia, and Jasper conferred with our new pirate friend on the ground. I didn't know what they were talking about, but I trusted Reed, at least, to keep the conversation in the realm of the possible. Mia you never knew about, and Jasper was still a wild card. I trusted him at least as much as Mia, but his family was involved, and I wasn't sure how far he'd go to keep them safe. Reed caught my eye over the pirate's shoulder and gave me a slight nod, and I remembered how easily he'd handled the fights and outbreaks on the ship. I nodded in return. I could leave this to him.

I outpaced the others—climbing was one thing I did a lot of in training—and reached the top of the ship just ahead of Cage and Alexei. Imani had fallen behind a bit, breathing heavily, and as Alexei passed her, he silently caught her in his massive arm and boosted her ahead of him. Imani didn't say a word, either of censure or of thanks. Alexei had a way of making you feel neither was needed. He would have done the same for Anya, or Cage. Maybe it was a side effect of growing up the size of a mountain, but Alexei treated people in need of physical assistance like it was second nature to help.

With Rune hovering nearby, I clambered onto the ship. Sure enough, the hatch was closed. I pivoted to find Cage extending a flat-head screwdriver in my direction. "I grabbed it last night," he said. "Thought we might need it."

It's amazing how grateful a life-and-death situation can make you for a little foresight. The awkwardness lingered between us, but at the sight of that screwdriver I felt like I could forgive him for anything. I jabbed it into the ship, and the door slid open. I stared into its inky depths. We'd lived on this ship for three weeks. We'd killed hundreds of sleeping aliens on it and stolen their home. And now their home was calling for help.

"Uh, guys?" called Reed. I spun to find him perched on the wall, a good fifty feet above the ground. Another hoverlift floated nearby. Either Reed was adept at hot-wiring or he'd found the keys. "We've got trouble."

Of course we did. "Go," said Alexei, cresting the ship right behind Imani. "I'll help Rune with this."

Imani groaned. "I just got up here," she complained, but the three of us slid to the ground and raced for the wall. Reed perched on top with an honest-to-God spyglass in his hands, like from some kind of old pirate movie. I glared at our new arrival suspiciously, and he gave me a smirk and folded his arms, clearly having a great time. Who the hell was this guy? And why did he look like he'd walked off the set of a Disney ride without having time to fully change his clothes?

"What's going on?" Cage demanded.

Reed gestured. "There are guards out here. A lot of them."

"How many is a lot?" asked Imani.

"At a guess? Thirty or forty?"

Mia and Jasper jogged up behind us. "That door is done for," Jasper gasped. "They're welding through it."

Fantastic. "Reed, get off the wall before they start shooting," I ordered, and he obediently dropped to the hoverlift. Sliding inside, he did something I couldn't see, and the lift descended toward us.

I looked back to the alien ship. Rune maneuvered above it, tilting the barrels toward the opening. But she couldn't just let them drop in case they missed the gap, so Alexei used his broad forearms to knock them into the hole. He wasn't getting every one, which was fine. A few scattered around the outside might help too. "Alexei!" I shouted. "How long?"

He didn't look. "A couple of minutes."

Great.

From outside came an amplified voice. "Fugitives. We know you are in the landing area preparing to take off in your stolen ship. You will not be permitted to do so. The second you clear city airspace, we will destroy you."

I laughed in spite of myself, and Reed scowled. "Those twits," he said. "They still don't get it."

"The authorities never do," said the pirate. "Not until it's too late."

We ignored him. "Well, if Alexei can't blow the thing up, I guess we have a plan B," Cage replied. Of course, plan B involved at least one of us dying with the ship. And since the only one of us who could really pilot the thing was Rune . . . My stomach clenched. Nope. Plan B was a nonstarter.

The voice continued. "We will breach the door in approximately ninety seconds. At that time, if you are not kneeling on the ground with your hands behind your heads, we will launch concussion gas grenades into the landing area. This will be your only warning."

"Nice of them to provide us with a time frame." Mia spun on her heel and shouted, "Lex! Whatever you've got will have to be enough!"

The barrels were only half gone, but the edges peeked over the ship. Not many more would fit anyway. Alexei didn't waste time arguing. He never did with Mia. He said something to Rune and jumped onto the lift with the rest of the barrels. "Take cover!" he shouted as he hoisted himself into the cockpit and Rune tilted the platform, sending the remaining barrels crashing to the ground. They surrounded the ship now, some of them cracking open and oozing their contents over it, around it.

"Cover sounds good," agreed Jasper. He spread his arms, flexed his shoulders, and a nearby wall, a few ships, and Reed's hoverlift rearranged themselves over and around us. His muscles trembled with the effort of maintaining the structure, and I gave him a worried look. I'd never seen him struggle to control his power before. "I'm anticipating some feedback," he explained, gritting his teeth. "Shelter won't do us much good if it collapses as soon as it takes a blow."

"Exactly how strong are you?" I demanded, casting a worried glance over the assorted debris.

Somehow, Jasper managed a shrug, even as sweat trickled down his brow. "Dunno. I've never pushed it. I can manipulate objects telekinetically, as long as they're inanimate, and it's never given me much trouble before. But I've never tried to hold out against an explosive force before, either."

"What about Rune and Lex?" Cage demanded.

The pirate sighed. "They'll cause the blast from above and withdraw. If they're lucky, they'll get out of the way. Most of the force should head out, not up. I'm going to cover my ears now. You might want to do the same."

"*Who are you?*" Imani demanded, but I grabbed her and pulled her to the ground. Everyone followed, and we clamped our hands over our ears—all but Jasper, standing in our midst braced against nothing, sweat pouring down his face in the dim light oozing through the cracks in his makeshift shelter.

For a second, nothing happened. Had the plan failed? Maybe Alexei hadn't managed to blow up the ship. Maybe the guards had broken through. Maybe . . .

A faint rumble in the ground was my only warning before the concussive force of the explosion struck. Jasper had no hope of standing against it; in an instant, he'd collapsed, the walls crumbling around us. The explosion rocked the air and set my ears ringing even with my hands clamped over them, and pieces of metal and rubber tumbled around me, bouncing painfully but harmlessly off my shoulders.

I winced in a sudden field of smoke and chaos. "Jasper!" I

cried, the intensity of my fear catching me off guard. How had I become so close to these people? I struggled to my feet and made my way to where he'd been standing, only to find Reed crouched at his side, jaw tense, channeling his healing power. As I watched, the wounds on Jasper's face knitted shut and he opened his eyes, groaning loudly.

My relief burst out of me in a gasp as I took stock. Cage was on his feet, holding Imani's arm. They both seemed unhurt. Mia and the pirate were already on the move. I followed them, running through the smoke to where the mangled remains of Rune's hovercraft lay crumpled on the ground. For a heartbeat everything froze, nothing but flames and twisted metal and somewhere in its depths, Alexei and Rune. "Reed!" I shouted, breaking into a sprint. *"Reed!"*

Mia beat us there and tore into the vehicle with her bare hands. She hauled Rune out first, semiconscious but apparently not seriously injured, bleeding from multiple wounds and lesions. Mia dumped her on the ground, and I grabbed her, pulling her against me. "Are you okay?" I demanded.

"Yes," she said softly. "Alexei shielded me. I think . . . Kenzie, I think he *absorbed* some of the explosion."

"Of course he did." Mia spoke in short, sharp syllables as she tugged Alexei free of the wreckage. "Everyone else has shiny new powers. Why shouldn't Lex? And also, *would somebody goddamn help me?*"

I jumped to my feet and grabbed Alexei's other arm. The

pirate caught his shoulders and together we dragged him free. Reed ran over and dropped to his knees beside him, his face pale and sweating. The fire's heat became more noticeable, moving past discomfort into tinges of pain. As Reed worked on Alexei, I risked a glance at the ship. It was a sea of flames, nothing but fire and shimmers and the occasional shadow. If that didn't block the signal, nothing would.

"Rune!" Cage caught his sister in his arms, knocking both of them to the ground. Sheer panic laced his voice. "Are you okay?"

"I'm fine, *gege*." She pulled back and caught his face between her hands, smiling at him. "Everything's fine."

Something released in me at the sight. Surrounded as we were by flames and chaos, the genuine care between the twins made things a little less horrifying. Their tension hurt me, too. I hadn't realized how much until this moment.

Alexei moaned as Imani and Jasper staggered into view, both relatively intact. "We did it," said Jasper, staring at the ship. As he spoke, something else caught and a small explosion made us wince. The heat from the flames forced us back, smoke choking us as we struggled downwind.

At last we found a reasonably safe place to stare at the growing wall of flames. "We did it," I agreed softly. "So what do we do now?"

The pirate yawned, stretching and popping the joints in his arms. "Well, that's up to you, of course," he said. "But if I were you, I'd come with me."

FOURTEEN

I CLOSED MY EYES. I WAS OUT OF PATIENCE with this guy, and so I was surprised when my voice only sounded weary. "Come with you where?"

"Does it matter? I have a ship." He arched an eyebrow. "At any rate, I'm leaving, not waiting around for Mars Mining and their buffoons to take me captive. You lot can follow or stay put." He turned and strode away from the flaming debris.

We exchanged frantic looks. Where was he going? Should we follow? What choice did we have? "Wait up!" Cage called, making the decision for us, and we broke into a run.

I skidded to a halt as we rounded a corner to find the pirate opening the hatch on a Titan 365 Racing Ship. "Whoa," I said. "That thing must cost—"

"A million credits," Reed finished. His eyes shining, he

took a step forward. "At least. With an acceleration that leaves the competition in the dust."

"Would you like to get in? Or did you want to stand there admiring it?" Mia brushed past us, and we all put on a burst of speed. We weren't out of the woods yet.

"How do you know they won't just shoot you out of the sky?" Cage demanded as we scrambled onto the ship. We found ourselves in a barren cargo hold, kind of a letdown compared to the Titan's flashy exterior. Reed, who did not appear to share my disappointment, hovered over the control board like a kid examining his Christmas gifts.

The pirate thumbed the controls, and the doors slid shut. "My ID signal is messed up and I can't seem to fix it," he sighed heavily. A chair appeared from nowhere, emerging from the cargo hold floor, and he sank into it, hauling the safety straps over his chest. Reed drew nearer, peering over his shoulder in what he probably imagined was an inconspicuous manner. "Sometimes it projects that I'm Omnistellar security. No one wants to shoot until they have the details. Risks an interstellar incident, you know? By the way, you might want to hold on to something."

Cage grabbed an overhead rack with one hand and Rune with the other, and I braced myself between him and a stack of crates. We were just in time. Reed hadn't been kidding about this thing's acceleration. I wasn't sure Mars Mining would have time to demand identification, even if they hadn't been busy dealing with the inferno Alexei had left in their docking yard. The ship's ID must have already been keyed to pass through the dome, because it didn't incinerate us. In fact, we blasted out of there so fast the gravity pinned me to the wall and Cage to me, sending the air whooshing from my lungs.

Mia shouted a few inventive curse words from across the room, where she, Alexei, and Jasper clutched at Imani, who hadn't grabbed anything in time. Reed had made no attempt to brace himself, apparently too fascinated by the controls. He was paying for it, lying on the floor clutching his head, but I didn't feel too sorry for him and his newly discovered healing abilities.

The ship's acceleration became almost painful, yanking my skin taut against my bones. The muscles in Cage's arm tensed as he pulled away from me, but it was like trying to fly. You can't fight gravity after a certain point. The pressure on my lungs increased, both from the g-force and from Cage's weight. Right when I thought I would pass out from the lack of oxygen, it released with a recoil that sent all of us spiraling into the cargo bay. Our momentum carried us upward. We were weightless.

"Whoops," said the pirate cheerfully. "Restoring artificial gravity in three . . . two . . . one . . ."

The gravity kicked in with a whoosh, and I tumbled to the floor, fortunately landing feetfirst. Cage clattered beside me, less lucky. He swore loudly as he landed on his shoulders, but he also rolled neatly to his feet and gave me a cocky grin. I shook my head in response, fighting a grin of my own.

We collected ourselves, everyone coming to terms with the last few minutes. "Did they even ask for your ID?" Imani asked at last, her voice weak. I glanced over to find her healing a cut on her arm. It looked painful, but she didn't appear fazed.

"Nope. Guess their attention was elsewhere." The pirate chuckled.

"Fantastic." Mia crossed the room in three steps, her face a barely contained explosion of rage. "Then I think it's about time you answered some questions."

He pivoted in his chair, unstrapped himself, and leaned back, folding his long, lanky legs at the ankle. "It's not enough that I just saved your lives?"

"Actually, no, it is not. So, let's start with the basics. Who are you, why did you help us, and where are we going?"

The rest of us gathered behind her. Mia might be overly aggressive, but she asked reasonable questions. For all we knew, this guy was some sort of Omnistellar bounty hunter who'd smuggled us out of Mars to turn us in. We might have leaped from the frying pan into the fire.

The man sighed and jumped to his feet. Up close, he wasn't much older than us, maybe in his early twenties. He gave Mia a mock bow. "Liam Kidd, at your service," he announced. "I helped you destroy that ship before it attracted any more of the aliens, which is a very worthy deed. And I am heading home, where, alas, we shall part ways. You're on your own once we reach Obsidian."

A resounding silence answered his pronouncements. Eyes shot open. Mouths worked furiously. For my part, I merely rolled my eyes. Obsidian was a fairy tale, a stupid story kids told when *Robo Mecha Dream Girl 5* and the other anticorporate media didn't fill their rebellion quota.

But then I caught sight of Alexei, his face twisted in a snarl. "We are *not* going to Obsidian," he said, danger in his tone.

"What do you know about the aliens?" Rune demanded at the same time. "*How* do you know about them?"

Her question echoed in the cargo bay, maybe the most important question of all.

The pirate—Liam—sighed. "Let's discuss this in a friendlier setting, shall we?"

"Oh, I don't think so." Alexei stepped forward. For the first time in a long while, I remembered him as he'd been when we first met: physically imposing, dangerous, and aggressive. His shoulders seemed to expand to fill the room, his eyes hard flecks of steel above a jaw so sharp it looked like it could draw blood. "Let's talk about Obsidian, where we are not headed."

"What's Obsidian?" Imani demanded.

"A fairy tale," I said irritably. "Alexei, you can't believe that place exists." Imani quirked an eyebrow at me, and I explained, "The story goes that Obsidian was an Omnistellar prison near Mars. It was an old one, housing dangerous criminals who didn't belong on Earth—not anomalies, but murderers and the like. The prisoners overthrew it and now they control it.

It's said to be the only criminal-run space station in the solar system, but—"

"It's real." Alexei snarled.

"It is not. Omnistellar doesn't make that sort of mistake."

"Kenzie." His voice softened. "I have been there."

That brought me up short. Alexei didn't lie. But how, why, would Omnistellar allow a place like that to continue? My former corporation might not be invulnerable as I'd once believed, but they were still the most powerful corp in the solar system, and not lacking in finances or resources. They would simply blow Obsidian out of the sky.

Unless . . . there was some reason they couldn't? Or *wouldn't*?

Alexei and Liam continued to argue, with Mia occasionally interjecting. Rune glanced back and forth between them, her mouth working as if she had something to say but couldn't quite find the words. Finally, she turned to Cage in frustration.

He rose to the occasion, obviously jumping at the chance to mend some bridges between himself and his twin. "Hey!" he shouted. The other three spun on him with identical glares, and Cage folded his arms. "We can talk about where we're going later. Right now, let's return to Rune's question: What the hell do you know about the aliens? And how do you know it?"

That got everyone's attention, even drawing Reed away from the control board where he'd been hovering. Imani and I exchanged glances. We, more than anyone, knew what the aliens meant if they arrived. But then I caught Jasper's worried expression, the way he gnawed at his lip, and remembered that his family was closest. If Liam had something to do with the aliens, if he brought them here, Jasper's family was in the most immediate danger.

I shook my head. Liam had helped us destroy the ship. Thinking he was in league with the aliens was nothing but paranoia, my lingering terror nudging the corners of my psyche. But at the same time, we knew nothing about Liam. We'd jumped on his ship because it was that or imminent arrest. No, he probably wasn't working with the aliens, but he could easily be Omnistellar. Or a bounty hunter. Or a murderer.

But one look at him brought me up short. All his forced confidence dissolved, and his face turned pale and drawn. Slowly, he sank into his chair. "I guess you have a right to know," he said quietly. "You might as well take a seat." Meeting Alexei's frustrated gaze, he sighed. "Even in this ship, it'll take us an hour to get to Obsidian. You'll have plenty of time to argue about it before then. But may I ask where else you want to go? The only other location within range of my fuel is the planet we just left, and I suspect you're about to become very unpopular there."

I glanced at my wrist monitor to check the time. I didn't know exactly when I'd spoken with my father, but I guessed about twelve hours had passed since then. Once Omnistellar arrived, "unpopular" would be an understatement.

Liam's words, or maybe the change in his demeanor, had the desired effect. Alexei sighed and retreated, taking Mia with him. Without asking, we gathered crates and boxes, anything we could find to sit on, forming a loose circle. Reed perched near the control panel, still seemingly more interested in it than in anything Liam said, but as for the rest of us, the pirate had our undivided attention.

I glanced at Liam's pallid face. We were bullying him, exactly like the anomalies had done to me when they were prisoners and I was the guard. And just like then, the reasons made sense, the ends justified the means. But I remembered how it felt, being on the receiving end of that power game. "For what it's worth," I said softly, "thank you. We never would have made it off Mars without your help."

Liam looked surprised, then gave me a grateful smile that instantly made me sure I'd said the right thing. "Thanks," he said. "But really, my motivations were selfish, at least at first. I had to make sure that ship was destroyed." His voice wavered, and he clasped his hands tightly, but not before I caught them trembling. I exchanged mystified glances with Cage. What happened to the overconfident jackass who'd mocked us into blowing up a spaceship?

Liam continued. "I picked up the ship's signal a day ago on Obsidian. At first, I thought I was imagining things. It's been years since I've heard anything on that particular frequency. I kept checking, though, every day, just in case. It became a matter of habit. When I actually heard something . . ." He focused on his shiny black boots. He sputtered a few words we couldn't catch, but no one, not even Mia, pushed him, and after a moment he seemed to get himself under control. "I'd almost convinced myself I was safe. That I'd never hear that signal again. I wasted a couple of hours telling myself it couldn't be real. By the time I came around to the truth, you were already heading for Mars, and I'd missed my chance to intercept you."

"Intercept us," said Imani softly. "Did you know who we were?"

Liam shook his head. "No, but I suspected. Earth already knew some of you had escaped Sanctuary, but they only had theories about how. When I saw that ship floundering around like a dying fish, I put it together, especially when you didn't start attacking. I mean, I heard what happened on Sanctuary. No one mentioned the . . ." His voice trailed off, his face somehow going even paler, and he clenched his hands so tightly I thought he'd draw blood. "No one knew what really happened on your prison, but the timing couldn't be coincidental. My first instinct was to try to contact you, but I reconsidered. I was pretty sure you were human, but what if I was wrong and I drew your attention? And even if you were, even if you could have been convinced of the danger of your transport, I knew the corporations couldn't. They only see in credits. And they have a blind spot to anything that might interfere with the bottom line."

"You can say that again," muttered Jasper.

The rest of us remained fixated on Liam. "None of that explains how you recognized the signal," Mia snapped. "Or what you know about the aliens."

Liam took a deep breath. It caught in his throat. He shook it off and continued as if she hadn't spoken. "And if you weren't human, well . . ." He gestured to the pistol strapped to his belt. "That's what this was for."

"You obviously haven't encountered those things," I said quietly. "If you had, you'd know guns are all but useless against them."

He stared at me for a minute. There was something strange in his eyes, something flatter, or maybe brighter, as if he had more colors than I expected to see in a human iris. "The gun wasn't for the aliens," he said at last.

His words settled over us with the weight of a shroud. Before anyone could ask any more questions, Liam rushed on. "I headed for Mars. One way or another, I had to know the truth. I called in every favor I was owed on Obsidian to hack the comms and figured out exactly who you were and what you'd gotten your hands on. The second I got the details, I knew you had the right idea: to destroy that ship. But I wasn't sure you'd be able to do it before Omnistellar showed up, so I headed to the planet to make sure. I was monitoring Mars security, so I knew when you attacked, and we arrived on the landing strip at about the same time." He gestured to a backpack at his feet. "I had some explosives with me, but you had a walking flamethrower. Once we destroyed the ship, I didn't feel like leaving you behind at corporate mercy."

I leaned forward, bracing my elbows on my knees and dragging my hands through my hair as I struggled to process this new information. It was too much to take in. Earth knew we'd survived Sanctuary? How? They should have assumed we'd all been blown up with the station. I opened my mouth to ask the question, but Liam wasn't done yet.

"As for how I knew about the aliens," he continued, glaring at Mia, who'd already opened her mouth, "I'd think that was obvious. They destroyed my planet."

Complication, Legion. I believe we'll need your involvement after all.

Well, color me shocked. I would never have guessed.

Can the mockery. Intel says the subjects are headed to Obsidian.

So, your source is working. Nice. Do they have the ship?

No. That's been destroyed.

Then how in the name of corporate bliss . . . ?

Does that really matter, Legion?

I guess not. We're on an intercept route. We have a little surprise in store for your brats.

I'm sure you do. Just try not to cause too much damage before the cavalry arrives.

Copy that, base. Legion out.

FIFTEEN

VARYING DEGREES OF SHOCK GREETED LIAM'S comment. We'd known we weren't the only ones the aliens had attacked. When I'd scanned the files on their ship, I'd found plenty of evidence that they'd done this before: injected their DNA into a planet, allowed it to fester a few generations, and then harvested the results as a sort of genetic terraforming. But that meant . . .

"You're an alien?" Jasper demanded bluntly.

Liam shrugged. "Depends on your perspective, I guess."

"How'd you get here?" I challenged.

"Not sure of that, either."

"So, you just woke up. On Mars."

"On Obsidian," he corrected. "Otherwise, that's more or less accurate. The *zemdyut* attacked our planet in force. They started small, like they did with you: a few outposts here and there, harvesting a few hundred people at a time. We'd barely start to recover from an attack and they'd return and take more. After a few generations, we were at war. My people had powerful weapons, but they weren't any use. Yours won't be either. The *zemdyut* are fast. Unpredictable. Adaptable. Much smarter than you think."

Zemdyut. I mentally repeated the unfamiliar word, committing it to memory.

Reed chewed his bottom lip. "But, dude . . . I mean, don't take this the wrong way, but you look exactly like us."

"What did you expect? Tentacles? Horns?"

"Well, the other aliens we met weren't exactly humanoid," Jasper pointed out. Mentally, I agreed, but looking at Liam, I picked up little differences I hadn't identified before. The sparks in his eyes. A pointed, defiant edge to his chin. A slight extra length in his arms. None of it screamed alien, but there were differences if you looked hard enough.

Now he chuckled. "Yeah, that's what I thought when I woke up here: that *you* looked just like *me.*"

"And your world?" Cage demanded. "Is that just like ours too?"

Liam hesitated. "I still don't know much about your solar system," he hedged, obvious deception in his voice. "I'm a stranger here, even after all this time." Prickles stood along my spine. For all his bluster, Liam was a rotten liar.

"Then tell us about yours," demanded Alexei and Mia in

unison. Reed pulled a face, but he was careful to do it out of their line of sight.

"Similar to Mars, I suppose. It's dry and dusty. Has an atmosphere without any fancy tech, but we'd managed to destroy a lot of the surface before the last century. Most of the vegetation and water are artificial. Or were. I suppose it's gone now."

He was still hiding something, but the pain in his voice rang true, and I took pity on him. "The creatures destroyed your entire planet? How did you escape?"

Liam hesitated, then shrugged again, an almost defiant look settling over his features. "I abandoned my family when the *zemdyut* came through our front door. There was nothing I could have done for them. My mother and brother were already screaming. I went out the back window, stole a ship, and called up every ounce of power I had."

Mia jumped on that. "You have powers?"

"The alien DNA has a different effect on everyone, but it always does *something*. Yeah, I have an ability. I can open portals through space . . . or at least, I used to be able to. I'd never transported anything so far before, and certainly never anything alive. I mostly used my ability to win games of *valjorvakk*."

"Of what?" Imani asked a second before I could.

Liam frowned. "A sport I played in school. Uses a *valvakk*, a big yellow ball."

"Like basketball?" I asked, ignoring that Reed was making faces at *me* now. I didn't mean to sound so eager, but it had been a while since I'd done anything normal. I missed basketball. And *Robo Mecha Dream Girl 5*. And since I was compiling a wish list, regular showers, clothes that fit, and parents who loved me.

Liam nodded. "I've seen your basketball played. It's not dissimilar. Maybe a cross between basketball and hockey. We use sticks. Anyway, prior to the alien attack, that was the most I'd ever managed. But I stole a shuttle in the chaos." He passed a hand over his face, his strange eyes flickering. "It was . . . fire and screaming and . . . the aliens had abandoned any pretense of subtlety. They attacked to harvest and kill. Everywhere you turned, there they were."

My brain rebelled at the description and the images it evoked, and Rune threaded her arm through mine, clutching me as if I was the only thing keeping her upright. Liam's words evoked every moment of the horror on Sanctuary. We all felt it. Tension settled over the room, physical in its intensity, until the slightest sound might have pushed someone over the edge.

Liam's gaze refocused, and he cleared his throat. "I stole a shuttle," he repeated with false bravado. "I got it into space, and I saw one of those ships. Just like yours. It was . . . I knew if I stayed I would die just like everything else, so I pulled every ounce of power I could manage. The doctors on Obsidian said I bit through my own tongue, I was concentrating so hard. I didn't even notice. I pushed that ship so hard and so far, I lost consciousness. When I came to, I was in the Obsidian infirmary, and I've been on the station for the last five years."

Liam sank his teeth into his lower lip. "I abused my powers that day," he said slowly. "They've never worked the same since. Not reliably. Maybe I don't want them to. I don't know. I'm scared to try. Anyway. Is that what you wanted to know?"

An uncomfortable silence followed. After a moment, Imani leaned forward and offered him a smile and a change of topic. "But you must know where you came from. I mean, after five years, you must have seen charts. You must have wondered how far you traveled."

His devil-may-care attitude settled back into place. "Far enough that I can't find it on any of your maps. You know how many stars there are, sweetheart? Lots. It's anyone's guess which one is mine. Anyone's guess for the *zemdyut*, too. We never did figure out where they'd come from. I tried to guess where my planet was, but . . . well, if I showed you a map of a random star system, do you think you could point to the pinprick that was Earth?"

Alexei's eyes narrowed. "Five years on Obsidian," he said in a conversational tone I recognized as his most dangerous. "Doing work that earned you a flashy ship and the freedom to come and go as you please. You must rank very high."

Liam scowled in response. "Yeah, I know what you're getting at, Alexei Danshov. And believe me, I damn near left you on Mars because of it."

Alexei Danshov. Did these two know each other somehow? I glanced at Mia, but she was staring at the floor. Cage, the only other person Alexei might have confided in, shook his head in confusion. Liam, meanwhile, drew himself up and faced off against Alexei, ignoring the bigger boy's clear malice.

Why had Liam pulled us off Mars? Trying to make up for abandoning his family? And where had he come from? How far away? How fast did the aliens travel? Rune and I hadn't uncovered anything faster than our typical engines on the alien ship, but that didn't mean much. We hadn't been on it long enough to decode all its secrets. "Hey," I said, before Alexei and Liam started chest thumping or something, "you still haven't explained the most important thing."

For a moment I didn't think it would work, but then Liam shook his head and broke Alexei's stare. "What's that?" he asked, gathering the remnants of his persona around him like a cloak.

"Why are you dressed like a nineteenth-century pirate?"

Liam burst into laughter. "I'm a fashion icon," he said, grinning.

"You have a cutlass," replied Imani pointedly.

"It's useful."

At that moment, Alexei shot to his feet and stomped up the staircase. Liam moved as if to follow, but Mia rose at the same time. "I wouldn't," she advised, chasing after Alexei.

Liam scowled after them. "What if they wreck something?"

"They won't," Cage assured him. "I mean, probably. Almost definitely." He hesitated, taking in our dubious expressions, and raised his hands in defeat. "All right. Maybe I'd better go too."

SIXTEEN

AN HOUR LATER, I SAT WITH RUNE, JASPER, and Imani in a lounge on the main level of the ship. Creature comforts surrounded us: VR games, prepackaged snacks, holoscreens, and just about everything else. But the closest we'd come to using any of them was grabbing a few sodas from a fridge.

Well, okay. I'd borrowed a tablet and quietly downloaded the latest issue of *Robo Mecha Dream Girl 5*. I wasn't callous enough to read it right now, but its presence in my wrist chip felt like an old friend had dropped by to say hello. Even though I much preferred reading on a tablet, I'd use the holoreader if necessary. Almost everything in my old life had gone up in a puff of smoke. Nothing I'd believed in mattered anymore. *Robo Mecha Dream Girl 5*, though, that I could hold on to. More than ever, actually, since Yumiko's battles against evil corporations now had an edge of reality.

What we mostly did was pace. Alexei, Mia, and Cage were still missing. Reed had spent so much time drooling over the ship's controls that Liam had offered him a reluctant tour. And the four of us were waiting.

I hated waiting.

Rune semi-dozed on a sofa, and Jasper and Imani stared out opposite windows. I hesitated, torn between Imani's hollow expression and the two unread episodes of *RMDG5*, but my human side won out. I dropped onto a seat by Imani. "You okay?"

She nodded without looking at me. We sat in silence for a few minutes, gazing at the stars as they slid silently away. I tugged at my braid, nostalgia surging. "I didn't realize how much I'd missed this view while we were on the alien ship."

She smiled tiredly. "Try three years in a cell."

I rested my head against the window. There hadn't been accusation in her voice, but part of me itched to apologize all the same. I resisted the urge. I'd promised myself after we escaped Sanctuary that I wasn't going to take the blame for Omnistellar's ills anymore. They'd locked my friends in cells, but they'd done the same to my mind. The chip planted in my arm without my knowledge, without my permission, left a part of me permanently behind bars. "My dad is on the Omnistellar ship," I told her now, still staring at the stars. Was Dad doing the same thing? "That's going to be an awkward reunion."

"You're not on your own there." She hesitated. "I lied, you know."

"What?"

"To my parents." She blinked heavily, holding back tears. "I was so desperate to talk to them I didn't even consider what I'd say about Aliya. When they asked me how she was, I lied. I said she was fine. I said we'd sent her to a family on Mars with another girl from the ship." She closed her eyes, and tears slid over her cheeks. "Why did I do that? I'm going to have to tell them the truth sometime. And it will be twice as painful for them now."

My heart lurched sickeningly. I relived the moment I'd found my mother's body dangling from chains . . . my desperate search for a heartbeat. I heard Rita's screams as the creatures tore her to shreds. I saw the life drain from Tyler's eyes as the aliens dragged him from our hands.

And of course, I saw Matt . . . my friend Matt, lifeless on the floor because of my misaimed bullet.

To my horror, answering tears welled in my own eyes. I swallowed them firmly and laid a hesitant hand on Imani's. Her fingers closed over mine and squeezed tightly. She tugged on her ear, gaze fixed on the window. "Sorry, Kenzie," she said after a moment. "I know you've lost a lot too. It's not only me."

"We've never talked about it." I took a deep breath of air, ignoring the tremble of my lungs around it. "Our families."

"I guess I felt everyone's awkwardness whenever they looked at me. I knew they were thinking about Aliya, even if they couldn't bring themselves to say it. When I was with you, it was different. You had your own grief, your own pain. Not like you didn't care about Aliya, but you didn't look at me and wonder what to say. It was nice to just hang out."

"I know exactly what you mean." I slid closer and tucked my arm around her shoulders. "And for what it's worth, I get why you lied. I wasn't exactly honest with my dad, either." I could have contacted him from the ship before my battery died, let him know I was okay. I'd chosen to let him suffer. Whether because, like Imani, I was afraid and didn't know what to say, or because on some level I'd *wanted* him to experience the same pain and betrayal as me, I didn't know. I didn't dare consider the question too closely. "When the time comes, we'll figure out what to tell your parents. I'll help you if I can. Okay?"

She nodded, tipped her head onto my shoulder, and then quickly wiped the tears away with her knuckles. "Okay."

Awkward silence stretched between us. "So," I said, desperate to break it. "Hunting?"

She laughed through her tears. "I know. Not what you'd expect from a belle, but . . ."

"Belle?" I stared at her, taking in her delicately shaped eyes, perfectly formed lips. "You were a beauty belle?" Conversations from the ship drifted back to me: Imani analyzing my facial structure, my skin tone, talking about beauty blogs. I'd known she followed them, but I hadn't realized she had her own.

"Top five hundred," she returned defiantly. "My beauty channel was the most watched in Egypt two years running. I was sponsored and everything."

I continued to gape, trying to imagine Imani running makeup tutorials. I mean, yeah, she was beautiful, and I'd noticed her habit of healing blemishes and hangnails, but . . . "What happened?"

"Omnistellar happened," she replied, unable to keep a bitter edge out of her voice. "They found Aliya, and I couldn't let them take her. We spent almost a year on the run before bounty hunters caught us."

"And they put you on Sanctuary?" I asked. "How did they know you were an anomaly too?" Imani's power didn't lend itself to easy notice.

"I told them," she replied, her chin jutting out in defiance. "What was I supposed to do? Let them send Aliya to that place on her own?"

I started to say something else, apology or question or I didn't know what, but a sound caught my attention. I turned to find Cage, Mia, and Alexei in the doorway, none of them looking particularly happy. "Where's Reed?" Cage asked, taking in the scene.

Jasper stretched and leaned forward. "If he got his way? Dismantling this ship piece by piece and pocketing the components. What's going on?"

Alexei rubbed his face and took Mia's hand for support. She let him. Aside from the times Mia was in danger, this was the least composed I'd ever seen him. "There are things I should explain."

A shrill screech tore through the room, jerking Rune awake with a cry and sending the rest of us cringing to the floor, hands over our ears.

"Sorry!" came Reed's voice, hollow and disembodied over the ship's loudspeaker. "Oh man. Sorry, everyone. That was too loud."

"Reed," Mia growled in the same tone she would have used if she'd spotted a cockroach scurrying under the couch.

Liam shouted something in the background, and Reed said, "Yeah, yeah, I know! Delicate machinery! Got it!" He cleared his throat. "Attention, ladies and gentlemen. We are about to dock on Obsidian. All interested parties, please report to the cargo bay. That is all. Over and out. Signing off, farewell, and—*ouch!*" A scuffle came over the loudspeaker, abruptly dying in another, mercifully less shrill, screech.

Silence.

The moment would have been comedic if not for Alexei dominating the scene, his face a mask of some unreadable emotion. I scanned Mia and Cage for clues, but no one gave anything away. "Alexei," I said, "what's going on here? If we're walking into danger, you'd better let us know."

He smiled grimly. "Oh, it's danger, all right. Obsidian is my family's station."

SEVENTEEN

ALEXEI EXPLAINED AS WE RUSHED FOR THE cargo bay. "My family is powerful in Russia. Powerful on Earth. Not corporate powerful, but the other side, the side the corporations don't touch."

Organized crime, in other words. I bit my lip to keep from judging. After all, I'd spent seventeen years blindly believing every lie Omnistellar fed me. I tried not to leap to conclusions anymore. "It wasn't a life I was interested in leading," Alexei continued, "even before my parents and my brother were killed in a . . . terrorist attack." He glanced at Mia, almost imperceptibly, and suddenly I remembered she'd been in prison for domestic terrorism.

She was framed, Cage had told me.

Was she? Unbidden, my gaze also slid to Mia.

She caught my look and muttered a curse. "Are you going to ask if I did it?"

I stared at her a moment longer. Rune, Jasper, and Cage all watched me expectantly, although I wasn't sure what they were waiting for. "I don't have to," I replied at last, realizing as I said it that it was true. Mia was violent and unpredictable and volatile. But she never meant to hurt anyone. I knew that now.

To my surprise, her mask wavered, something like vulnerability surfacing before she slammed it down. "I might disappoint you," she said, so quietly I barely heard her.

My heart skipped a beat. Beside me, Rune stopped short. "So, you did it? You killed Alexei's family?"

"They took my sister." The words spilled out of Mia in a rush, her gaze fixed on the floor, her hand lost in Alexei's grip. Imani tensed at the words. "Or he did. There was a man, someone who . . . who used me occasionally. Once he learned of my powers, he'd have me set things up for him, steal things, spy. That kind of crap. I went along with it because he paid me well, and I needed to take care of Shannon." She swallowed hard. I got the sense she hadn't said that name in years, that she hadn't meant to say it now. But as always, she recovered quickly. "And maybe because I was afraid." She met each of our stares in turn, bright, challenging, as if she expected we'd pounce on her admission of weakness.

But no one did. We all knew fear. Jasper moved toward her, but Cage gestured him back. "What happened, Mia?" he asked softly.

She sighed. "They wanted me to get my hands dirty, starting

with Alexei's family. There was a bomb. I was supposed to plant
it on the top floor of their hotel and let it go off. I refused, obviously. But when I got home . . ." She took an unconscious step
closer to Alexei, and he slid behind her, still holding her close.
"Shannon was gone. No one knew where she was. My mom was
never in any condition to notice anything. Even her youngest
daughter being kidnapped, apparently. And then he called me.
Caleb." She put so much fury and hatred into the name, I didn't
have to ask who he was.

"Caleb wanted Mia to assassinate my father." Alexei picked
up the thread of her tale. "And also, me, my mother, and my
brother. He threatened to kill Shannon if she resisted. So Mia
went to the hotel, all the way to the penthouse. But when she
saw my little brother . . ."

"I couldn't do it," Mia snapped. "All right? I didn't
want to kill anyone, even a notorious criminal like Lex's
dad. I certainly wasn't going to murder a child. But in that
moment of hesitation, I lost my invisibility, and Alexei saw
me." She glanced at him, and he slid a hand over her face.
Turning her cheek into his palm briefly, she continued,
"He followed me outside. He'd never seen another anomaly
before. He was fascinated. He . . ." She looked at him with
an expression I couldn't read, something I'd never seen on
her face before. "He knew what I'd been sent to do, and he
didn't blame me."

Alexei shrugged as if dismissing the murder plot against

his entire family. "My father was a horrible man. Many people wanted him dead. Besides, you didn't go through with it."

"No, but Caleb did. He suspected I'd fail him, so he had a backup in place. And he pinned it on me."

"My father died in that explosion," Alexei continued. "No great loss." The tendons on his neck stood out. "But so did my mother. Vitaly, my brother. And for them, I needed revenge. Unfortunately, by that point . . . Mia did too."

"Alexei's father and uncle founded Obsidian almost a decade ago," Mia broke in quickly. She obviously didn't want to discuss the vengeance they'd taken, or what had happened to her sister. She didn't need to. I remembered Alexei's words on Sanctuary: *Mia had a little sister.* "They made it the interstellar hub for black-market deals and organized crime. Kenzie, you asked why Omnistellar allowed somewhere like Obsidian to continue. The short answer is, it suits their needs. If there's something they don't want to get their hands dirty with, Alexei's uncle takes care of it. In exchange, they leave him Obsidian."

Jasper let out a slow whistle. "And that's where we're going? A hub for organized crime run by Alexei's uncle?"

Alexei nodded. "An uncle who may try to throw me out an airlock, yes. The Danshovs blame Mia for the attack. They believe the official line. And they think I am *izmennik*—a traitor. That I chose the girl who murdered my family over them."

"Fantastic." I turned to Cage. "Any bright ideas?"

"Hijack the ship?"

But even if he'd been serious, Rune was already shaking her head. "There's no way we get anywhere but Mars without refueling, and even if we did, somehow I don't think we'd be welcomed at any station with a stolen ship and warrants for our arrests. We're going to have to dock on Obsidian. Alexei, can you reason with your uncle?"

Alexei snorted eloquently.

By now we'd reached the doors to the cargo bay. Alexei hesitated. "I hate to even suggest it, Mia mine, but . . . maybe you should stay on the ship."

She shrugged. "I will if you want me to," she said, uncharacteristically agreeable. "If you think you can trust Liam not to tattle. And if you think your uncle doesn't already know I'm here. And if you think Obsidian doesn't have the technology to scan the ship and notice someone left behind, and if you're sure they're not going to kill the life support while refueling or doing maintenance or—"

"All right." Alexei scowled. "I get the point."

As we reached the door, Imani suddenly stepped in front of Mia. The girls' eyes met, and Imani seemed to falter. "Mia," she said softly, wringing her hands as if trying to break her own fingers.

Mia hesitated, not looking at her, then nodded. "Thanks," she muttered. That seemed to satisfy Imani, and we entered the cargo bay to find Liam and Reed arguing over something. Reed blocked the controls, arms spread wide, a look of terror on his face, and Liam . . .

Liam stood in front of him pointing a pistol at his chest.

I'd barely registered the pistol before Mia raced across the room, catching Liam's arm and shoving it into the air, stomping on his instep in the same movement. Alexei leaped to her assistance, but she didn't need him: by the time he arrived, Liam was on the floor with Mia's foot on his throat, the gun trained on his face. "Why don't you go ahead and move?" she suggested pleasantly. Her every limb trembled with restrained violence, as if eager to compensate for her recent disclosures.

Liam scowled and sputtered something.

"Mia," said Cage, "I think you're choking him."

She considered that for a moment, then stepped back, releasing him but keeping him in her sights. "Want to repeat yourself?"

Liam sat, gagging and choking theatrically. "Bloody hell."

"What's going on?" Imani demanded of Reed.

He scowled. "I said not to open the doors until all of you arrived. He said he was getting off this ship now. I told him to wait, and he pulled a gun on me."

Liam sniffed daintily, rubbing his throat. "Well, joke's on you, kiddo. That gun's not loaded."

Mia hesitated, then twisted her wrist to check. The second she did, Liam lunged for her. He encountered Alexei's fist halfway through his leap and collapsed to the floor, unconscious.

"It is so loaded," Mia said crossly.

Alexei sighed and glared at Liam's unconscious form. "Guess we'll have to open the doors sometime."

We quickly filled Reed in on what Alexei had told us. He responded with his characteristic optimism: "We have enough fuel to get us back to Mars," he suggested.

"And what then?"

"I don't know. Hide in the desert until we run out of life support? It's sounding like the best option at the moment."

Rune sighed and flicked her fingers toward the console. Gears shifted, and the doors slid open. The rest of us withdrew, weapons held loosely, ready for action.

The seals parted, and three uniformed security guards strode inside, looking so official that for a moment I almost could have been on a corporate station. Three more stood in the docking ring, weapons drawn. They all stared at Liam's unmoving body. The man at the front of the group scowled. "We ordered him to open the doors some time ago."

Alexei shrugged. "He fell."

The guard didn't seem amused. "You will follow us."

We exchanged unhappy glances, but there wasn't much choice. We followed them.

I craned my neck, desperate for my first glimpse of a rogue prison station. Was this what Cage had in mind when he took over Sanctuary? Another Obsidian? Or did he only mean to escape, to secure passage off the station for himself and his friends, maybe even get them to Obsidian itself? Had he known a station like this existed? Aside from Earth, Obsidian must be the only place in the solar system a criminal could disappear. Everywhere else was too small, too rigid. On Earth, you still had government-run territories, places the cunning and ruthless remained hidden.

And apparently on Obsidian, you had what was essentially a mafia-run space station. My head swam. I'd heard rumors of the place, of course, but Omnistellar had quickly dismissed them. They described Obsidian as a run-down first-generation prison. Nothing more, and nothing less. With better technology, better orbital prisons, and better security on planetside facilities, Omnistellar had made the decision to abandon Obsidian almost ten years ago, and it had sat empty ever since.

Well, that much I could declare categorically false. Sure, the station looked a bit old-fashioned, with less shiny chrome and more exposed pipework than Sanctuary. But Omnistellar's unique brand of architecture was everywhere. We emerged into a large docking ring and ascended a lift, exiting into what should have been the crew quarters. I suspected if I made a break for my right, I'd find the entrance to the prison spiraling below the domed station proper. Except who the hell knew what was down there now? I wished I'd had more time to question Alexei. I hated walking into a situation blind. If there was one thing Omnistellar had drilled into me, it was preparation. We had the Cub Scouts trounced in that area. And yet here I was, with almost no information, marching into a situation I'd considered fantasy until fifteen minutes before.

Three security guards in front, three behind, they led us through seemingly deserted halls. I scrutinized the others. Cage stared straight ahead, his dark eyes working frantically as they always did when he planned. I hoped he was coming up with something good, because right now I had nothing. Rune was on his other side, chewing her bottom lip, her hands clenched into fists. Alexei and Mia walked in front of us, their arms almost touching, both seemingly relaxed aside from the tension in their shoulders. I glanced behind me and caught Reed whispering to Jasper. He winked at me. I exchanged worried looks with Imani. Sometimes Reed's easygoing nature bordered on denial. Jasper at least seemed appropriately concerned.

The guards led us inside what should have been the commander's rooms. The quarters resembled my own back on Sanctuary so closely my heart gave a sickening lurch. The decor was different, and it was a bit bigger. But Omnistellar had clearly kept the same room model when they designed their newer stations. For a moment I pictured my parents lounging on the couch, Mom going over work schedules, Dad reading the old historical novels he loved. It even smelled the same.

I swallowed a lump in my throat. This wasn't home. My bed wasn't through that door. That room was gone forever.

And so was my mother.

The security guards withdrew, leaving us alone. Before anyone could speak, a massive, broad-shouldered man strode into the room. He was the spitting image of Alexei in thirty years, but with a mean edge Alexei lacked. Even dressed in a button-down shirt and casual pants, even without weapons, even lounging casually against the wall, he made my heart catch. Cage's arm tensed against mine and I knew he sensed danger too.

"Uncle Grigori," Alexei said coldly. He shifted subtly, pressing Mia behind him and placing himself between all of us and his uncle.

Grigori broke into a broad grin. "Lyosha," he said, stepping forward to embrace his nephew. Alexei returned the hug one-armed, his right hand remaining deceptively loose at his side, ready for action. Grigori withdrew and held Alexei at arm's length, examining his face. "Prison has been kind to you, my boy. Perhaps kinder than you deserved, huh?"

He chuckled. Alexei did not. "It seems we find ourselves in need of your assistance," he said through clenched teeth, as if every word pained him.

"Of course. Of course!" Grigori spread his arms wide, encompassing all of us in a suddenly beatific smile. I drew a step closer to Cage, who slid his hand against the small of my back, and we both moved to shield Rune from his view. "Let me see if I understand the situation. You have all escaped from prison and have Omnistellar on your tails. You staged a *second* prison break on Mars, then proceeded to blow up a valuable piece of alien technology. And now you have incapacitated the man sent to help you and left him bleeding on the deck of his own ship. Have I summarized the situation?"

"Well, when you put it that way," Jasper said dryly, "it does sound kind of bad."

"Sent to help us?" I broke in sharply. "He said he came to destroy the alien ship."

Grigori brushed that aside. "Of course, of course. I misspoke." Had he, though? Grigori didn't strike me as someone who made mistakes. Who the hell was Liam? I believed his story, as far as it went. But that lingering sense of mistrust warned me he hadn't told us everything.

Cage and I exchanged nervous glances. Grigori's genial act was somehow almost painful in its duplicitousness. You could read through every friendly glance. He was a man of pure danger, and every muscle in my body sensed it.

All at once, the mask slid away, leaving only malice in its place. Grigori switched to Russian, presumably not aware I understood him. I kept my face carefully blank as he said, "I am happy to help you, Lyosha, on two conditions. One, that you run a small errand, nothing of importance, for *me*. And two . . ." He nodded in Mia's direction. "She does not draw another breath on my station."

The signal is found. The signal alerts.

Awakens.

Unfurling.

Not one. Not the harvesters.

All.

The hunters.

Awake now, they progress.

They proceed.

Awakened.

EIGHTEEN

ALEXEI'S SHOULDERS DREW TOGETHER SO tightly they almost swallowed his spine. He, too, switched to Russian, but Mia clearly sensed trouble: her right hand rested casually on the pistol at the small of her back. "That is not negotiable," Alexei snarled.

"Your loyalty to the woman who murdered your family is commendable," Grigori replied coldly.

"She no more murdered them than I did."

"You admit your role?"

"I said no such thing."

"The courts were very clear."

"The man who murdered my parents, my brother, he is dead." Alexei clipped every word cleanly. "Whether by my hand or hers, I don't even know. Nor do I care. We both shot him, and he died. Honor is maintained. Vengeance is satisfied.

If you trust me so much as you claim, Uncle, you will take my word for it."

"What are they saying?" Cage murmured in Mandarin, so softly I barely heard him.

I shook my head, in warning, not negation. I was already scouting the room for means of escape. If Grigori insisted on killing Mia, he'd have a war on his hands. Funny to think how I'd seen Mia as my enemy. Now, in spite of the fact that Alexei had just confirmed that he and Mia had shot a man, I thought of her as family.

The realization jolted through me. These anomalies, these criminals, they *were* my family. In such a short time they'd become the most important people in my life. I'd hated my mother for choosing the corporation over me. But if I had a choice between saving Dad's life and Cage's or Rune's? I swallowed hard.

No point dwelling on imaginary what-ifs. I had a real problem on my hands, and no doubt as to where everyone in the room stood in terms of loyalty.

But what could we do? This was Grigori's station. If it had Omnistellar security, even of an obsolete variety, we'd never make it far on our own. And God help us if we killed the station commander, a criminal lord in his own territory.

Would anyone's powers help? Probably, if they knew what was going on. I nudged Alexei's ankle with my foot, hoping he'd take the hint and switch to English. He didn't.

"We have no need of your assistance." Alexei spoke in a crisp, clear voice, enunciating every syllable. The others tensed at his tone. "Simply let us go, and we'll be on our way."

Grigori threw his head back and laughed. "Go where, my boy? You have no ship. No credits. You have nothing but an Omnistellar team on your tails and warrants for your arrest. Without my help, you won't make it ten steps."

"Leave that to us."

Amusement sparkled in Grigori's blue eyes, highlighting the family resemblance. "Very well," he said, spreading his hands. "I give you free passage on my station, for as long as it lasts. For the sake of your father, I won't kill you outright. But once Omnistellar arrives, they have the same access as you. If you change your mind between now and then, my offer stands. Remove the girl, and I'll help you and your friends."

Alexei barely inclined his head in acknowledgment, pushing Mia behind him with the same movement. "Go," he muttered, backing away, never breaking eye contact with his uncle. "*Now.*"

No one argued, not even Mia. We retreated from the room, stumbling over one another in an undignified mess until we reached the corridor and the door closed in front of us. Before it even shut, Mia spun on Alexei. "What the hell was that?"

"We're on our own," he replied shortly. Mia's eyes narrowed. I wasn't surprised. Alexei never withheld information from her, and he was clearly doing so now. But he shook his head. "Trust me, Mia mine. This is a best-case scenario. We aren't bleeding, and he's letting us walk away—for now."

"He won't do anything to protect us from Omnistellar, though," I pointed out, wanting to make sure everyone had caught that essential fact.

Alexei snorted. "That's if he doesn't change his mind and have us hunted down in the next . . . what are we looking at?"

I glanced at my comm device, thumbing it so the time appeared in an offset area above my wrist. I did some mental calculation between Mars time and interstellar standard. "About eight hours."

"More to the point," Jasper interjected, "did anyone else think his comment about Liam being sent to help us was no slip?"

Rune and I nodded rapidly, although the others seemed less concerned. "I think we should watch out for Liam," I said darkly.

Imani shrugged. "He did help us."

"He also pulled a gun on us." Mia gnawed on her bottom lip in a stunningly unsexy display. "Kenzie's got a point. I don't trust him."

"Great." Reed blinked. "Let me see if I've got this straight. We have no money. No ship. No way off this station. Its owners may decide to murder us at any moment, and the one person on board who tried to help us, we don't trust. That about sum it up?"

"Let's continue this conversation elsewhere." Alexei cast a nervous glance at the closed door. I nodded in agreement. The others hadn't understood Grigori's words, but you couldn't miss the gleeful malice in his tone; no one argued.

"Where are we going, though?" I demanded as we hurried down a corridor. At any moment I expected someone to grab us, but although we saw a few uniformed officers, they ignored us completely.

This could almost have been Sanctuary—again, not as new and polished as the station I'd called home, but with the same quirks of design, the same layout. I even caught a few Omnistellar logos remaining in obscure areas. I almost expected my parents to walk around the corner, a tablet held between them, arguing over the latest command schedule.

My heart gave a sickening lurch at the thought, almost toppling me in its intensity. I had to stop remembering my mom, her limp, cold body on the alien ship.

Cage glanced at me, worry in his expression. I shook my head. In some ways I wanted his reassurance, his support. But in others I remained confused, unsure of where we stood. And more to the point, I had to return to my professional skin. It was the only way to keep my wits about me until we found a way to safety.

He did me the courtesy of accepting my rejection without question or comment. It only increased my confusion.

As we reached the gateway to what should have been the

prison, Rune spoke. "There might be a way off the station if we can find a ship," she said. "Cage? Do you think there's still a Lóng presence on Obsidian?"

Cage hesitated, his eyes sliding from left to right. We clustered around the prison entrance in a loose circle. "Almost certainly," he said at last. "But . . . do we really want to risk getting involved with them again?"

"A long presence?" Reed asked doubtfully. "Like . . . ?"

"Lóng." Cage corrected his pronunciation. "Not the English word. The name of the gang Rune and I worked with in Taipei. They might help us get back to Earth. But they'll want something in return."

We exchanged glances. "Like what?" asked Imani at last, wariness lacing her tone.

Jasper shook his head. "Does it really matter?" I blinked at him, surprised, and he shrugged. "Look. We're trapped on this station. Omnistellar's on their way. I have no idea what Mars Mining is doing to my family for sheltering us." His voice rose on the last few words, and he closed his eyes, visibly struggling for control. "I can't help them from here. I might be able to help them from Mars, or from Earth. If there's a way off Obsidian, we have to take it. We can deal with the consequences later."

"Yeah, you say that," Cage replied dryly, but when I looked at him, he sighed. "I don't see another option. I'll go to Géxià. But none of you are coming with me."

"Who's Géxià?" Jasper and I demanded at the same time.

Cage waved us off. "A contact. Someone I met long ago. Obsidian's her home."

Mia snorted. "You're not going alone."

"I have no idea what she's going to do when she sees me. She may shoot me in the face. She may serve me tea. Whatever happens, it'll be better if I don't bring guests. The rest of you can head to the lower market and look for an alternative. Maybe we can work our way off this station if Géxià won't deal."

A babble of argument rose, and I cut it off. "I'll go with him." Cage opened his mouth, but I silenced him with a glare. "I'm not leaving you to navigate this place by yourself. Rune, I'll keep him safe," I promised, noticing the tension in her posture. "We'll meet again in the . . . lower market?"

Cage sighed. "I couldn't get rid of you on Sanctuary, so I guess I'm not getting rid of you here," he said, and I punched him in the arm, making him grin. "The rest of you, find us another escape."

Alexei frowned but nodded. "If you're not there in an hour, I'm coming after you."

"If I'm not there in an hour, I'm probably dead."

"Reassuring," snapped Rune, about as angry as I'd ever heard her. Cage caught her by the arm and pulled her aside, talking quickly and softly in Mandarin. I deliberately tuned it out.

"One more thing," Imani said quietly. "The shift in our powers. I want to know what's causing it. And I want to know if it's going to continue. What if Alexei starts bursting into flames unpredictably?" She glanced at him, taking in his impassive demeanor. "No offense. But if our powers start raging out of control, you clearly represent the biggest danger."

Alexei never changed expression, but I nodded, resisting the urge to hold my head. "One thing at a time." There was only so much I could handle at the moment, and standing on Obsidian was messing with my brain. The station bore only a superficial resemblance to Sanctuary, but my last moments on the orbital prison refused to leave me. Facing the aliens there had been bad. Facing them here, with the worn-out security and the rusted grating . . . I choked on my own fear. No. We were safe now. We'd destroyed the signal, stopped the aliens. Sure, we had Omnistellar to deal with, but I could handle them. Even if I couldn't, the worst-case scenario beat a lungful of alien slime and an eternity as a mindless stalker killing and slaughtering to express my reproductive drive.

Bile touched the back of my throat, and I stared at my shoes until the sensation subsided. Every time I thought of the aliens, it left me hollowed inside. I forced myself to consider Imani's words instead. My power was useful at times, but it left me defenseless in a lot of situations. Diplomacy had never been my strong suit. What if a more useful power lurked inside me? Definitely worth exploring.

And more than a little concerning, given the destructive nature of someone like Jasper or Alexei.

So far, everyone's powers seemed to be extensions or

adaptations of the original. I probably wouldn't find myself firing force missiles or bursting into flames. But if I could do something more, I wanted to know about it. Maybe something lingered inside me that could give us an edge against Omnistellar—or the other, darker threat constantly lurking in the corners of my mind.

I just had to figure out how to trigger it.

While I considered, Alexei worked the switch that would have opened the prison on Sanctuary. It did the same here and seemed to respond to his thumbprint. "I'm keyed to all security," he said in a monotone. Something rumbled through the room, and I realized with a wince it was Mia grinding her teeth. Jasper and Reed took a casual step away from her.

We proceeded through the door, and I stopped in horror. In the decade since the criminal element had taken over the station, they'd done some substantial remodeling. Jagged edges in front of me marked a rough door, forcibly torn into the wall. The corridor was dim, illuminated by flickering fluorescents with every second bulb missing—smashed, or maybe burned out and never replaced. Rust marred exposed metal. A staircase sank ahead of me. Assuming Obsidian, like most prisons, was built on the same ice cream cone model as Sanctuary, that meant the gaping area ahead used to be prison sector 1.

I examined my surroundings more carefully. Sure enough, cells lined the walls, although the doors had been propped open, torn off, or in some cases bent in on themselves so they could never close again.

Each cell functioned as a makeshift shop or home. People glared at me from their recesses, and I realized I was staring. It reminded me powerfully of my first venture into Sanctuary's prison level, and how the prisoners gaped at me from behind their bars. The muscles in my arms spasmed instinctively, itching to defend myself from a nonexistent threat.

Cage glanced at me, but it was Imani who reached out to squeeze my hand, offering me a reassuring smile. We descended two levels, dodging people with every step. Claustrophobia seized me, but I resolutely ignored it, focusing on Cage and Imani flanking me, Rune's booted feet scrambling down the stairs ahead. After two levels, Cage and I broke off from the others, and they kept going. I swallowed hard. Somehow, we'd wound up back in prison, me and Cage, fighting for survival together. What were the odds of that?

NINETEEN

I LEANED AGAINST THE WALL FOR SUPPORT as the others retreated. "Setting foot on this station is the stupidest thing I've ever done."

Cage nodded. "Well, it's not like we had much choice. But between you and me? I don't think this is going to work. If the Lóng gang is still here, and if they're willing to help us, they're probably going to demand a price we can't pay."

"Unlike Alexei's uncle?" I couldn't help myself. I quickly summarized the conversation for Cage.

He hesitated, his face unreadable in the shadows. Far above us, something crashed. I leaped a mile, pivoting, heart in my throat, my hand flying up to shield myself from lashing claws.

A man shouted, followed by the unmistakable sounds of fists hitting flesh. I winced. Right. No aliens. Just people. "Okay," I said. "This is okay. I'm okay."

Cage leaned against the wall, arms folded over his chest. "Look, Kenz, I'm not sure how to say this without pissing you off."

I raised an eyebrow. "Well, that's a great start."

Again, that ghost smile touched his lips, there and gone almost before I glimpsed it. "I know you've been around prisons most of your life, but this . . . it's different. The kids on Sanctuary were mostly victims of circumstances. The people here are a hell of a lot more dangerous. I've dealt with them. I know how to deal with them. You . . ."

"Don't," I said, a queasy feeling in my stomach. He was right, but I hated the reminder of my helplessness. I rolled my shoulders and drew myself to my full height. "But I'm going to have to learn. I can't hide behind you forever, Cage. And I can take care of myself."

"There is not a doubt in my mind that that's true," he said with such conviction that, to my horror, tears welled behind my eyes. I forced them back, but I couldn't get rid of the pleasant warmth that came with them. I'd spent so much of the last weeks doubting myself. Cage's obvious sincerity sent a jolt right to my heart. "I just want you to be careful. There aren't any second chances here."

I nodded, steeling myself. I didn't have a lot of experiences to draw on for navigating an enclosed space full of people who would probably slit my throat as soon as look at me. But if I survived a shipful of alien creatures determined to harvest my flesh and assimilate my mind, well . . . a street gang and a Russian mob didn't seem like much of a threat.

"I can handle myself," I said firmly. I hesitated a moment, then pressed on. "But you should know I haven't changed my mind. As soon as we're out of danger, I'm telling the others the truth."

He didn't have to ask what I was talking about. "It's a bad idea," he said flatly.

"Maybe, but it's *my* bad idea." I imagined the betrayal on everyone's faces, especially Rune, my gentle, soft-spoken friend. "I can't hide this forever. I did what I did, and I have to face up to it. I mean, I feel like they're beginning to trust me, and . . ."

"And you're determined to break that trust."

My head shot up, my eyes locking with his. "No, to *earn* it. What's this really about, Cage? Are you worried about the others trusting me? Or about them finding out we lied?"

His brows knit into a solid, heavy line. "I told you I'd be honest with you," he said, his muted voice making me realize I'd almost yelled the last few words. "So yeah. I am worried about how they'll react about us lying to them. Especially Rune. She barely trusts me as it is. But that doesn't make my other objections invalid."

I closed my eyes, struggling to focus. Cage had a much more violent past than I did. He'd killed to survive, to protect his sister. He lied and gave orders with an easy grace I would never possess and wasn't sure I wanted. But I'd asked him for honesty, and he'd given it. "You started this lie for me," I told him at last. "And I know I went along with it. I'm not even sure it was wrong. But I can't live it forever. I'm sorry if that feels like a betrayal."

"It's not a *betrayal*, I just . . ." He sighed and raked his hand through his hair. "Look, let's discuss this later, all right? You can't tell them now, and Alexei gave us a time limit. I don't want him charging in here like some kind of bear protecting its cubs." He forced a grin. "My ego couldn't take the hit."

It wasn't much of a joke, but I let myself smile in return. "Okay. Let's protect your fragile male pride. So how do we go about finding . . . who is Géxià?"

He shouldered away from the wall with obvious relief. "She's a pain in the ass, but she's also the top buyer and seller on Obsidian, and the official Lóng clan representative. Or she was. She's . . ." He shook his head. "You'll see. Let's go."

I didn't resist when Cage threaded his fingers through mine, and we started through another torn-out door. The contact tingled. It wasn't the first time we'd touched since Sanctuary. He'd picked me up, shoved me out of harm's way, guided me in one direction or another. I'd tapped his shoulder to get his attention, examined a wound on his wrist. But this sort of prolonged contact was different, somehow, even if we were only holding hands to avoid getting separated. We dodged people with every step. Alexei's family might run Obsidian, but clearly other groups and organizations held sway here too.

I didn't recognize all of the symbols and colors, but there were street gangs everywhere, marked by tattoos and clothing, and lots of random criminals besides: mercenaries and pickpockets, shifty-eyed, hands spidering through the crowd.

I peered down the stairwell as we progressed. Obsidian seemed bigger than Sanctuary, with far more prison levels. Some of them were open, some still closed. I heard shouting and cheering from below, suggesting that other things might be going on in Obsidian's depths.

Or maybe it was just the sounds of people at life. Who knew? My own life was so reclusive and sheltered, lived mainly through the pages of manga and the dreams of following in my parents' footsteps. Now, with my family in tatters, what did I know about anything?

I heard the market before I saw it: a cacophony of chaos, people shouting and bellowing. A crowd lined the walls, and Cage kept a firm grasp on my hand as he pulled me in. Fingers danced over my pocket, but I ignored them. I had not one thing worth stealing besides my comm device, and Cage pressed that tightly between our wrists.

The smell of food hit me with such power my knees buckled. The feast on Mars had sated my appetite, but I was hungry again, and the spicy scent of cooking meat made my mouth water. Familiar packages of freeze-dried food littered the area, but I also caught real vegetables in the mix. There must be hydroponics somewhere on Obsidian.

I forced myself to turn away from the booths of people hawking bowls of steaming broth. We had to find a way off this station first and foremost. Besides, I doubted anyone would give me a meal out of the goodness of their hearts, and I didn't have to scan my omnicard to know Omnistellar had long since frozen my accounts.

We dodged around people, people everywhere, more than I'd ever seen in a single place. Some haggled, some hawked, some simply stretched along the ground, looking too weak and emaciated to move. If I'd thought a criminal-run space station would do better with equality than we did on Earth, I'd been mistaken. Just like everywhere, some people had power, and some had nothing. Cage ignored them all, even as my stomach twisted unpleasantly at the sight of a little girl and her mother huddled against a wall. I fumbled in my pockets, but I had nothing to offer them, not so much as an energy bar. Cage tugged me on. "Don't give anyone anything."

I blinked at him, surprised he'd caught my impulse. "That little girl—"

"Could have someone waiting around the corner to jump you." He sighed impatiently. "This isn't a corporate-run city, Kenz. The rules don't apply."

I bit my tongue to keep from arguing. He was probably right. I'd never set foot outside a corporate city except for a few months when we'd lived in a government slum, and even that had been in the transition process. My ignorance stung my pride. Another way Omnistellar had failed me.

At last we reached what, on Sanctuary, would be the work area. There was no reason to assume the same thing here, although logic dictated something similar. Two guards stood outside: a tall, lanky Chinese woman and a short, stocky man with skin and eyes so pale they almost glowed. They were a study in contrasts, except that they both held an impressive array of weaponry.

Cage inclined his head. "I have business with Géxià."

"I know." The man swept his gaze over us. "Cage, right? We heard you'd come on board."

Wow. *That* news traveled fast. I wasn't sure what else I expected on a station of criminals, though. Here, information was currency.

Cage sighed. "Do you really want to stand here and banter, or can we get to business?"

The woman shook her head. "You. Not her."

"No deal. We stay together."

She shrugged. "Then you don't go in. You're lucky Géxià is willing to see you at all. She's certainly not letting your Omnistellar plaything inside."

Cage snarled, and I shoved him between the shoulder blades. "Go," I said. "I'll be fine." I glared at him until he backed down. The woman had pissed me off too, but we needed her help. We could get mad about it later.

Cage's grip tightened around my hand. "Don't move from this spot."

Bolts of anger prickled my spine. "I'm not your sister, Cage. And neither of us needs you ordering us around."

"I know." He visibly forced himself to let go of my hand. "Sorry. I'm just . . . this place makes me nervous, that's all."

I regarded him for a moment. Some of his bravado peeled away, leaving the boy I'd gotten to know on Sanctuary. The bond between us surged suddenly, and I saw my own fear reflected in my eyes. He didn't mean the market, or Géxià. He meant Obsidian itself: its resemblance to Sanctuary, and all the memories that came with it.

It was that, more than his high-handed commandments, that made me nod. "I'll be here waiting," I told him.

He sighed in obvious relief and raised a hand toward me. It hovered between us as if he might lay it on my shoulder, maybe hug me. But then it dropped to his side. "Be careful," he said, and turned to the guards. "All right. Take me to Géxià."

Cage followed the woman through the doorway, leaving me alone with the stocky man, who promptly folded his arms over his chest and ignored me.

I shrugged and moved away. In spite of my annoyance with Cage's orders, I had no intention of wandering around by myself. This place triggered my fight-or-flight instinct on every level. I was equal parts curiosity and terror. Omnistellar hadn't prepared me for the real world in any way. Or maybe,

Omnistellar *had* been my real world, my only world, and had expected to remain so. They hadn't needed to prepare me for anything else. Even without the vivid memories of alien pursuit Obsidian conjured, it would have overwhelmed me with its sheer realness.

The marketplace was straight out of *Robo Mecha Dream Girl 5*. I mentally relived Yukiko's journeys into the slums of Nuokyo, seeking her strength and courage. Of course, she had a mech suit and a childhood of ninja training to protect her, while I had only my anonymity and background as a prison guard. That meant submission holds and ways to endure until backup arrived, not skills I thought would help me here.

But no one seemed to notice me. They went about their business buying and selling, arguing, laughing, living. These might be criminals, but they were also families, people. For a prison guard, someone who'd spent her whole life in the system, I knew very little about the illegal world. It was a sobering reflection.

A hand ghosted along my arm, barely registering in the throng of people.

But I definitely noticed the moment my wrist monitor popped out of its slot.

My eyes shot open, and I jerked upright in time to see a blur of white rags vanish between bobbing heads. "Hey!" I shouted, and without stopping to consider the wisdom of what I was doing, I plunged into the crowd in pursuit.

Arrival on schedule. Where is master ship?

Six hours behind.

Turn around and go home, base. We'll have things cleaned up by then. Legion is active.

TWENTY

"STOP!" I SHOUTED, PLUNGING INTO THE CROWD.
The wisp of white vanished into a sea of people, and I shoved
after it. That wrist communicator was my last link to home, to
my father, to my friends, to my family. I might be conflicted
about talking to my dad, afraid of what I'd discover, but I sure
as hell couldn't afford to lose it.

I stumbled over someone's feet, colliding with a decidedly
hostile group of men. One of them stepped in front of me.
Without stopping to think, I drove my elbow into his ribs. He
doubled over, grunting, and I ducked under his friend's arm,
charging past the crowd.

I put on a burst of speed, bulling my way through the market. A trail of shouted anger marked my wake until I emerged
into the stairwell.

I peered down the stairs, blinking. Hordes of faces peered

back at me, probably wondering who and what had caused all the fuss. But I didn't see the thief. Unless he'd ditched his clothing and casually blended in with the crowd below? Desperation made my head swirl. How would I ever find him?

Someone shouted behind me, and I winced. So much for keeping a low profile. I was going to have the entire marketplace on my heels in a second. I needed to get out of here and hope I found Cage later. Otherwise he'd have to rescue me from some sticky situation, assuming I survived long enough. And if that was the case, I'd have to deal with him muttering about how he'd warned me to stay put. My fists tightened involuntarily. No, I would find a way to save myself.

My gaze settled on a grated panel against the wall. Sanctuary didn't have large ventilation ducts like this, or at least I didn't think it did. But then, I'd learned that a lot of Sanctuary was hidden behind smooth walls and civilized veneers. Obsidian was an older model, with everything in the open.

The voices behind me grew louder. I risked a glance back. The man I'd elbowed pushed his way through the crowd, a sizable following behind him. I didn't have much time to make a choice.

Did the grate look askew?

If the thief hadn't gone into the vents, I at least hoped my knowledge of Sanctuary would give me an edge in dodging any pursuit. Besides, the men looked too big to crawl through ductwork. I lunged for the grate, yanked it aside easily—too easily, giving me hope I wasn't the first person to crawl through here today—and dove forward, squirming along on my elbows without bothering to pull the grate into place behind me.

And not a moment too soon. A roar erupted, and the vent shuddered as someone lunged against it. I risked a glance over my shoulder and saw a huge, leather-bound arm groping around the entrance, nowhere near my feet. Allowing myself a sigh of relief, I pressed onward. Definitely the right choice.

My satisfaction quickly faded, though. I'd plunged into a vent on an unfamiliar prison station. Who knew where it led? It could be a dead end, leaving me no choice but to shamefacedly climb back to the entrance and hope my pursuers weren't waiting on the other side.

Not to mention that the vent was pitch-black. Without my wrist monitor, I had no way to illuminate the passage. After I crept around the first corner, I was completely blind. A moment of panic assailed me, like the alien ship times a thousand: pitch-black, cramped, terrifying. For a second, I was sure I heard the soft drag of alien tails on metal.

"Damn it, Kenzie, keep it together," I whispered out loud. The aliens weren't on Obsidian. If we'd destroyed that beacon in time, they were searching for their comrades somewhere far, far away.

Of course, that didn't mean they wouldn't be back. They had to know their harvest had failed. If they didn't, they'd figure it out soon enough. The realization washed over me as I dropped my head to my clasped hands, my heartbeat echoing so loud it reverberated off the metal walls.

Destroying the beacon hadn't saved us. The aliens would be back. Was there anything we could do to stop them?

Maybe. With time, with information, we might be able to do something. And if nothing else, destroying that beacon had bought us time. How much, I didn't know. Maybe days. Maybe months. But we had time, time to plan, time to think. Omnistellar, for all their malice and apparent Machiavellian tendencies, employed some of the best scientists and researchers in the world. All I needed to do was survive the current situation long enough to get in touch with my dad, make him listen to me, make him *believe* me. And then Omnistellar could take it from there.

Omnistellar would *have* to take it from there. I wasn't a weapons specialist, just a guard. No, not even that. An anomaly. A fugitive. I had information, and I had to convince them it was real. From there I'd let the company do what they did best. And they would. We would survive. Everything would be okay in the end.

The air was cool and carried a vague scent of oil, machinery. Nothing like the warm, humid depths of the alien ship. There were no aliens here. Not yet. Hopefully not ever. I sank my fingers into the slick metal and pulled myself forward.

With each advance, I probed ahead, making sure the vent didn't suddenly drop into nothingness. I groped along the walls on either side, too, dreading the moment I'd find a branch and have to make another choice. None came, though. A new terror enveloped me: the inevitable dead end. There was no way to turn around in the close quarters, the walls brushing my arms, the roof against my head. I'd have to crawl all the way backward.

Sweat dripped from my forehead. How much time had passed? Long enough for Cage to worry? Long enough for him to follow me? He wouldn't be that dumb, would he?

Yes. Yes, he would. I stifled a curse and redoubled my efforts, my fingers sweat-slick against metal.

I rounded another corner and blinked against sudden light. Relief surged in my chest as I pulled myself forward, my bruised knees and elbows banging against the walls. A grate loomed in front of me. I threaded my fingers through it and shoved with all my might.

It didn't budge.

Of course it didn't. "Hey!" I shouted, throwing caution to the wind. I rattled the grate as hard as I could, metal clanging in echoing reverberations. "Hey!"

A face appeared in front of me—an all-too-familiar face, one I was coming to hate. "You!" I shouted.

"You," Liam groaned in response, leaning against the wall to glare at me through the grate. He was wearing a white cloak over his pirate garb. "Why won't you leave me alone?"

"Why won't I . . . ?" My brain short-circuited for a second. "You stole my comm!"

He grinned, a flash of teeth gone before I'd properly registered it. "Precisely. Fair and square. Now crawl back to your hole, little girl, and—"

I slammed my hand into the grate. Pain reverberated all the way to my elbow, but I got the satisfaction of seeing him jump in surprise. "I'm not going anywhere," I seethed. "Not without that device."

He scowled. "Well, then I hope you enjoy your new life in that vent."

We glared at each other, at an impasse. I craned my neck to see around him, revealing a tiny alcove resembling nothing so much as a maintenance shaft, but he'd clearly converted it to a home, with a crumpled pile of blankets in the corner. A crate with a fluorescent lantern illuminated the space. I couldn't see more from my position.

I regarded him a moment through the grate. "Nice place you've got here," I said at last, fishing.

He didn't respond, but his eyes narrowed. Encouraged, I pressed on. "I'm guessing this isn't exactly an official setup. I'm not sure how rent control works on Obsidian, but this looks pretty off the books." I raised my eyebrow, as if a thought had occurred to me. "Hey. Maybe I can trade the location of your little hideout for a ride off this station."

"Damn, you're an annoying piece of work."

I grinned in spite of myself. "So I've been told."

Liam hesitated, then swore and reached up, doing something

to the grate. He pried it loose, letting it dangle from a corner. Unbidden, he extended a hand.

I took it, letting him help me down from my perch. "Thank you," I said, stretching my sore back. Something popped in my spine, and I grimaced.

We stood there awkwardly a moment. I glanced around the room, a tiny space no more than five feet square, barely high enough to stand. There were two other grates in the walls, and an open maintenance hatch stretched between them. It looked like a good base from which to squirrel around the station stealing stuff. It was messy but not uncomfortably so. He'd arranged crates and blankets as rugs and furniture. It wasn't even dim, at least to my eyes. Of course, I'd spent the last month on a spaceship designed for blind aliens, so what did I know?

"This is where you live?" I asked dubiously.

Liam scowled. "If you must know, I have a lovely set of quarters very near Grigori Danshov. This is where I go to do things I don't want him to know about. And if you tell him about it, he'll kill you, then me. Now go."

"Not without my wrist monitor."

"I don't have it."

"Liar." I glared at him. "You didn't have time to get rid of it. Why'd you take it in the first place?"

"Why do you think? So I could turn you in to Omnistellar and claim the bounty."

Temper surged in my throat, but I swallowed it, forcing myself to be calm and rational. "If you wanted to do that, why not do it on Mars?"

He shrugged. "Maybe I just wanted one. It's nice tech."

I glanced at his wrist. "You're telling me you're cozy with the people who run this station and they couldn't get you a black-market comm unit?"

Something beeped from a computer at the back of the room. Liam rolled his eyes. "Fine," he sighed heavily. He crossed to the computer and deftly withdrew my comm unit, tossing it in my direction.

My heart flip-flopped right along with that shiny bit of silver, but my reflexes held true, and I snatched it out of mid-air. I closed my fingers over it, willing my breath to return to normal as Liam casually blanked his screen, but not before I got a glimpse of what it contained.

"Those are my comm logs!" I grabbed him, swung him around, and slammed him against the wall before he drew any of his fancy weapons. I'd been suspicious of Liam from the beginning, but now . . . "You're spying on me, and you're going to tell me why!"

TWENTY-ONE

LIAM SIGHED, SINKING ONTO THE CRATE. "IT'S not what it looks like."

"No?" I drew my hands into fists, shifting my weight subtly. He didn't look ready to attack, but he was strong and lithe, and he carried those weapons. If he reached for them, I had to move first. "Because what it looks like is you using my comm unit to send Omnistellar my location and collect the bounty."

His brows drew together in irritation. "They don't need my help. You said it yourself, sweetheart. Omnistellar knows where you are, and they're on their way. They don't pay for information they already have."

Right. Exhaustion catching up with me. I heaved a sigh between clenched teeth. "Then what the hell are you doing?"

He hesitated, then shrugged. "I've intercepted some of their comms. They really wanted that alien tech."

"What do you mean?"

"What do you think I mean? Omnistellar's lagging. Mars Mining is up-and-coming with the dome technology. Omnistellar is the unquestioned king of the prison yard, but that's not enough to keep them on top of the pile forever. They need new technology. New advancements. They want to focus on their interstellar travel arm, keep advancing. The alien ship provided a golden opportunity to do exactly that, reverse engineer the thing until they had a way to travel beyond our solar system. Do you know what it would be worth? Controlling that kind of technology? Being the first corp to travel beyond Jupiter?"

I did know. And I understood that Omnistellar didn't exactly have humanity's best interests at heart. I wanted to question Liam, demand more information. As if reading my mind, he held up his hands. "That's all I've got. They didn't exactly send me a briefing. Everything I learned is from intercepted comms. I'll tell you this much, though: they were banking on that alien ship. They aren't happy it got blown up, and they're willing to do whatever it takes to get it back."

I shook my head. "They can't. We destroyed it. Right?"

"Whatever it takes," he repeated, staring right at me with those strange piercing eyes. He drew the words out slowly, and I got the sense he was saying something I wasn't getting.

We gaped at each other a moment longer before it sank in. We *had* destroyed the alien ship. There was nothing left of it, or at least not enough to salvage. The only way to get their hands on alien tech was to find a way to summon the rest of the creatures. "Oh my God," I choked. "They couldn't be that stupid."

"That's not a humble company you work for."

"I don't work for them," I corrected automatically, surprised at my vehemence. Omnistellar was my entire being for so long. Now the very thought of them filled me with blind rage. "They don't really think they can take on the aliens, do they?"

"They think they have a good chance, yes. But first they need you. They need intelligence. They need information. And from there, they think they can summon the creatures, defeat them, and take their tech."

I staggered, grabbing the wall for support. Images overwhelmed me: the creatures, three of them, stalking me through the corridor, Cage slumped lifeless against the wall. Just a few of them decimated my entire station in a matter of hours. What would a whole ship do? Omnistellar thought they could stand against the aliens. They probably didn't care if they lost a handful of people in the process, not if they emerged on top. But I'd seen the aliens in action, and I knew the truth. Omnistellar didn't stand a chance against them. Not unless they blew them out of the sky, and they'd never do that. It would damage their precious alien tech. "My dad," I managed. "Does he know about this?"

"The comms didn't say one way or another. You could ask him." He gestured at the device on my wrist. "Of course, activating your comms would give him your exact position.

Speaking of which, I did intercept one thing you might find interesting. Have you ever heard of Legion?"

I searched my memory but came up empty. "No. I'm not familiar with every aspect of Omnistellar's operations, though. It's a big corporation."

"Well, whatever Legion is, it's after you. And I suspect it'll be here long before Omnistellar. You have a few hours at most."

Of course. If we meant that much to Omnistellar, they would stop at nothing to find us. "Bounty hunters. Has to be." I eyed him suspiciously. "Why are you telling me all this?"

"You have to ask?" A tremor raced through him. He pivoted to stare at the wall, his shoulders shaking with each breath, the tendons on his arms jutting out at odd angles. After a moment he spun back to me, but none of the tension had left his face; his eyes reflected my own horror. "You think I want those *things* here? They destroyed my planet. I escaped by luck and cowardice. Somehow I don't think I'll get away a second time."

I frowned. The explanation made sense. God knew I'd go to some pretty heavy extremes to avoid seeing those creatures ever again. But I still sensed there was something he wasn't telling me. "And what else?"

"That's not enough?" He bit off every word, and a wave of uncertain guilt washed over me. Maybe I was wrong. Maybe he was just a man, a slightly alien man, sure, but a man nonetheless, one living with the things he'd done to escape with his life—just like me, just like Cage.

And assuming he was at least being honest about this Legion . . . "I have to warn the others." I stared at my comm, mulling over what Liam had said. Could Omnistellar really trace me if I used it?

Liam heaved a sigh, apparently recovered from his fear. I saw through his mask now, though. It was the same one I wore, the same one we all kept on so that the raw terror lingering from the monsters stalking our steps wouldn't shine through. We all put a different tarnish on it. For me it was strength. For Mia, aggression. For Cage, authority. And for Liam, well . . . the pirate. "Oh, all right, already," he grumbled, reaching for his computer. "If it'll get you out of my house faster." His fingers flew over the screen.

Seconds later, Jasper's face materialized. "Good to hear from you," he said, making no effort to hide his relief. "Please tell me you and Cage had some luck up there, because we're getting nowhere."

"I'll have to get back to you on that. In the meantime, we have another problem."

Jasper groaned. "What now?"

"Omnistellar may have sent a bounty hunter team called Legion after us. If they're not already here, they will be soon. Get everyone hidden."

Jasper's cheerful face grew serious. "I'm guessing Omnistellar bounty hunters won't be anything to joke about."

"You guess right. Hide, Jasper. Alexei might know some

good locations. I'm going to get Cage, and then I'll find you somehow."

"I'll keep my comm active."

"Only as a last resort," I said, frowning. "Liam thinks they might be able to trace me if I use mine. It's possible they can track yours, too."

"Liam? What's he got to do with it?"

"Don't ask. Just get somewhere safe. Please?"

"Got it." Jasper narrowed his eyes. "Be careful, Kenzie. You're on your own if someone comes after you."

"Believe me, I know." Jasper cut the comm, and I turned to Liam. "Thanks," I said awkwardly.

He smiled. "Take your friend's advice. Be careful."

"I will."

Liam offered me his hand and boosted me into the grate. I glanced at him over my shoulder. "You be careful too. They know you helped us."

"Why do you think I'm hiding in this hole?" He smirked, lifting the grate into place. "But I'll take my chances with Omnistellar over the *zemdyut*. Hell, I'll take my chances with the Danshovs over the *zemdyut*, and that's saying something. There's a tight left about fifty feet down the second corridor, easy to miss. I suggest you head that way and not return to the market."

I nodded. I needed to find Cage, but I didn't want to risk running into the thugs I'd dodged earlier.

Liam touched his fingers to his forehead and vanished into his hole. I stared after him a moment, struggling to come to terms with the information he'd given me. For all of Liam's annoying qualities, he'd come in very handy so far. He'd shown up in the nick of time on Mars, and he'd just given me a heads-up about the bounty hunters.

So why did a nagging voice in the back of my mind scream not to trust him?

I sighed. Trust him or not, I had to get moving. Sitting in the ductwork didn't help anyone and wouldn't give me any clues as to Liam's motivations.

I could safely use my comm to access offline messages and functions without alerting anyone as to my location. With a thought, I triggered my wrist monitor, giving myself a beam of light to work with. Other bits of information flashed through my head: nineteen unread messages, all from my dad. I glanced at the most recent one. It was about what I expected: *Kenzie, we have to talk. If you turn yourself in, there's still a chance we can salvage this. If Omnistellar has to hunt you down, I can't imagine how I can save you. I love you, sweetheart. Please. Contact me.*

I froze, a riot of emotion tangling my thoughts and limbs. Images of my father flashed before my eyes, images of my family. Was Dad in on this plan? He couldn't be. He couldn't know Omnistellar planned to lure the aliens right to us.

Just like he couldn't know about my abilities. Or my chip.

But no. That was different. I forced myself to move again,

considering everything I knew about my father. The way he and my mom had chipped me was wrong. Or at least, not telling me about it was wrong. It cut deep, violated the security and trust I'd had in them—and in Omnistellar. But at the same time, I could sort of understand their logic. The file I'd read back on Sanctuary said as much. If they hadn't chipped me, the company would have taken me away. I still didn't like what they'd done, but they'd done it to protect me.

But Mom hadn't tried to protect me when she'd left me to die on Sanctuary. What about Dad? He couldn't know about this plan with the aliens. I had to believe that. When I found him and told him the truth, he'd be as horrified as I was. I would *make* him understand. If he still loved me, and his constant stream of messages told me he did, he would listen.

I rounded a corner and scrubbed my hands over my eyes, and in the same instant another realization occurred to me: Liam had neatly distracted me with this new information. He'd never explained why he'd stolen my comm device in the first place.

"You slippery son of a bitch," I said aloud, half in admiration, as all of my earlier guilt slid away. I *knew* he was leaving something out. I was tempted to go back and beat the answer out of him. But he'd locked the grate and probably wouldn't open it to a raging teenager, even if I felt like crawling backward through the tunnel. Besides, I had to get to Cage. Liam could wait.

I found the turn Liam mentioned and wasn't surprised I'd missed it the first time. I had to bend almost double, but if

Liam could squeeze through here, so could I. I scraped a good chunk of skin off my arms, then crawled along until I reached another grate. Peering through the tangled metal, I distinguished a few people moving in the shadows. I watched them a moment, heart racing, until the shadows settled into human forms. For just a moment, they'd looked shapeless, reptilian, cold. But no. Humans all.

I seemed to be in another section of living quarters, possibly a level down, as I'd thought the vent had sloped as I'd crawled. I threaded my fingers through the metal and pushed experimentally. Three corners popped loose. Across the room, a woman gave me a cursory glance, then returned her gaze to her tablet, clearly uninterested in why I was climbing out of a wall.

In spite of my drumming heartbeat and a frantic need to hurry, I eased the grate down carefully and with a minimum of noise. I made the short drop to the floor and pressed the grate into place. It seemed to attach magnetically at three of the corners, only the fourth fastened by an actual screw. I gave Liam credit for the arrangement. What was his relationship with the Danshovs? Why had he taken my comm? He claimed fear of the aliens motivated him. But maybe he only said that because he knew it drove *me*. For the first time, I recognized my lingering terror as a perceptible weakness, one others could exploit. I swallowed hard. This just reinforced the need to find the others. We were stronger together.

No one seemed to have noticed my appearance except the

woman with the tablet and a wide-eyed boy. He gave me a shy smile, as if people popping out of grates was normal in his world, and turned back to his mother.

I was in a small, dark room, but it didn't seem to be anyone's private quarters, more like a public gathering space. A door stood open to one side, and when I emerged, I found myself in the prison proper. I didn't know what the room had been. A server room, equipment long since stripped? Obsidian predated Sanctuary by several decades, and although it seemed familiar at first, I was quickly realizing that I couldn't rely on my memories of Sanctuary, or of any Omnistellar facility, to navigate.

I pressed through the prison. Families and individuals inhabited some of the cells, but no one gave me a second glance as I passed, emerging at last into the stairwell. The buzz of the market reached me from above. I was right, I'd descended a level at some point. At least now, I had a minute to breathe.

So . . . what next? The most sensible thing was to head upstairs. That was where I'd last seen Cage. I drew my hood over my face, enclosing myself in safety and anonymity. I'd caused some commotion, but with my hood I was nothing but another grubby teenager on a crowded criminal hideout. The sheer indifference of the place sheltered me.

"Kenzie!"

I winced at the shout from below. So much for anonymity.

Mia grabbed my arm and shoved me forward. "Don't look!" she bellowed. "Just run!"

Alexei seized my other arm, and they tore up the stairs, dragging me between them. "What's going on?" I cried.

At that moment, a stun gun blast erupted behind me, narrowly missing us. "Does that answer your question?" Mia shouted.

"No!"

We shot into the marketplace, diving into the crowd. I fought a surge of panic. Who the hell was chasing us now?

The signal is gone, but the draw remains. The pull. The strength is weakened but present. There is connection. They are growing. They are expanding. They are increasing.

Prepare.

Draw.

Contain.

TWENTY-TWO

MIA AND ALEXEI DRAGGED ME INTO THE UPPER market. I caught a glimpse of familiar leather jackets in the distance and pulled my hood farther over my face. "Where's Cage?" Mia demanded.

"The person he needed to talk to wouldn't see me. Who's chasing you?"

"Bounty hunters," said Alexei grimly. "Apparently Earth knows we survived Sanctuary."

"Yeah, I know," I said, and told them as briefly as possible what had happened to me. "Didn't Jasper warn you?"

"We got separated."

The three of us ducked behind a stall selling some sort of broth, and my stomach rumbled again in response. The bounty hunters would no doubt follow us into the marketplace, but they'd have a hard time locating us. "Why'd Liam take your comm device?" Mia asked abruptly.

"He, um . . ." I cleared my throat in embarrassment. "He didn't say."

"And you just let him walk away?" An edge of disbelief laced her anger.

I ground my teeth and forced my voice calm. "No, *I* walked away, because I wanted to warn all of you before some team of bounty hunters caught up to us." And because Liam had manipulated me, using my fear of the aliens to stop me from asking too many questions. I didn't add that part.

"I don't suppose you had the common sense to demand to see the contract? Or ask who it's for? Is it all of us? Do they know who lived? Is it a blanket call for the survivors of Sanctuary?" My face must have answered her question, because Mia scowled in disgust. She might like me better now, but a few weeks of living in close quarters hadn't increased her patience any. "All right. Lex? We're going to have to nab one of the bounty hunters and get a look at that contract."

He grinned. "That, I can do."

"Yeah, but we're going to have to do it quiet. That, *I* can do." She smiled grimly. "You two wait here." The air shimmered, and Mia disappeared.

I swore internally. Once again, my training failed me. Seventeen damn years of training camps and sweating and studying and never having friends and all for what? I didn't know how to do anything but parrot company propaganda and dodge semi-incapacitated prisoners. "What's she doing?" I demanded, leaning around the booth and trying to spot evidence of Mia's passage. She might be invisible, but she still *existed*.

"Mia's a thief from long ago. She'll be fine."

I glanced at Alexei. "How'd you spot the bounty hunters, anyway?"

"It was fairly simple once they captured us."

I blinked. "They . . . *captured* you? How?"

"By sticking a gun in our backs and dragging us into a control room. Then they stuck more guns in our faces and demanded to know where you were."

"How'd you escape?"

He grinned. "I set the control room on fire."

Yup. That would do it. I wasn't thrilled about the idea of Alexei using his pyrokinetics in an enclosed environment like a space station, but there wasn't much to say now that it was done. Obsidian was still here. I'd call that a win. "I don't suppose Mia got to keep her gun?" Never thought I'd be rooting for that.

"Unfortunately, no. It is now the proud possession of some bounty hunter with an ugly mask." Suddenly, Alexei's face paled. He caught my elbow and jerked me back. "*That* ugly mask."

I shrugged free of him to lean around the corner, more carefully this time. A sleek figure in black strode through the market, the crowds parting as he passed. Something about his presence made even the burliest criminals dart aside. As he drew closer, I realized he wore a silvery mask drawn over his face, reminding me of a villain from *Robo Mecha Dream Girl 5*.

I looked closer. "Son of a bitch," I said out loud. It *was* a villain from *Robo Mecha Dream Girl 5*. A perfect reproduction of the mask worn by the Silver Oni, and not a cheap Halloween copy, either. "Where did he *get* it?"

"What?" Alexei stared at me like I'd lost my mind.

"Alexei, that mask is a freaking collector's item. I wanted one last year and they were selling for five *thousand* credits on—"

"Are you kidding right now?" he demanded, incredulity lacing his voice.

I swallowed my annoyance. Somehow seeing that mask, the mask that should have been *mine*, on a bounty hunter's face was simply the last straw. We had to do something. I stalked him with my gaze, ignoring Alexei tugging at my elbow. There was a familiarity to his movements, like a panther prowling his territory. *Robo Mecha Dream Girl 5* had been the place I retreated for so long that seeing the Silver Oni stomping around like he owned the place rattled me more than I cared to admit.

Mia popped up between us, and we both cursed louder than we'd intended. "Hush," she said, waving a tablet. "Now. Let's see what we're dealing with."

I cast a nervous glance around, watching the Silver Oni vanish into the crowds opposite us. Our hiding place wasn't particularly secure. "How many hunters are we talking about here? Should we find someplace safer?"

"This will only take a minute." Alexei took the tablet from Mia and thumbed something with practiced ease. I arched an eyebrow. Exactly how involved had Alexei been with his family's criminal endeavors before his arrest? Within a few seconds, he had a projection on the wall. I recognized my face immediately, along with Cage's, Rune's, Alexei's, Jasper's, and Mia's. Imani and Reed were conspicuously absent, maybe because their powers were less destructive, maybe because they'd made less of a scene on Mars.

"Are those the specific contracts?" I asked.

"Yes. It's a capture order, if you're wondering. Not a kill. There's also a blanket order for any other survivors of Sanctuary, but we're the ones named." Alexei snapped the holo shut before I could get a closer look at the specifics.

That was probably for the best. We needed to get somewhere safe. "Let's find Cage."

"I'm not worried about Cage's ability to outrun anyone stupid enough to chase him," Mia replied dryly. "I'm a lot more concerned about Rune, Reed, and Imani. None of them has a power that's going to help them if Jasper isn't—"

"Shh," Alexei cautioned suddenly. He caught us by the shoulders and pulled us into the shadows.

I let him tug me back but craned my neck to peer over the stall. In front of the woman serving soup, who seemed to take no notice of us whatsoever, a man and a woman in black clothes were conferring, sidearms in their hands. Anywhere else in the galaxy, that would have brought security down on them in seconds, but on Obsidian, no one even looked twice.

I edged closer, trying to hear their conversation. They seemed to be arguing, the woman gesticulating wildly while the man shook his head in frustration.

"Kenzie," Alexei hissed.

I shoved his hand away. "We need to know what they're planning," I whispered, moving in a fast half crouch toward the booth. But my focus was on Alexei, and I stumbled over a loose panel in the floor. For a second my arms pinwheeled and I almost caught myself, but then I plunged forward and crashed into the makeshift wooden stall with a resounding thud that echoed over the market noise.

For a moment everything froze. Then Alexei seized me and physically hauled me against him and Mia. I risked a glance at the stall. Both hunters moved in our direction, eyes narrowed in suspicion. Alexei scowled and raised his hand, sparks leaping.

"No!" I snapped. He absolutely could not start slinging flames in the middle of a crowded marketplace filled with flammable materials.

Of course, letting ourselves get arrested wasn't a great choice either.

Mia cursed and threw her arms around both of us, catching me off guard. She wasn't exactly the affectionate type. She shimmered and vanished . . .

And so did we.

I blinked at the spot where Alexei had stood a moment ago. A glance at my own arm revealed nothing, although when I tensed my muscles, everything felt normal. I didn't dare move more than that, for fear of disrupting Mia's concentration.

We stayed frozen and silent as the bounty hunters rounded the stall. Our eyes locked, and for a second I was sure they saw us. Then the woman threw her hands up. "They've got to be here somewhere."

The man shrugged, holstering his weapon. "It's a closed station, Priya. They can't get off without clearance. Obsidian's cooperating. We'll run 'em down. Let's go find the others."

The woman, Priya, hesitated, staring right at me. My heart seized in my chest. She couldn't see me, I *knew* she couldn't see me, but it felt like she was about to step forward and shove that gun in my face.

After a moment, though, she tucked it into her holster and followed her partner into the crowd.

Mia's and Alexei's arms relaxed under my hands. A moment later, all three of us flickered into view, Alexei's face a mirror of my own astonishment. "So that's three," he said. "Exactly how powerful are you now?"

Mia shrugged, averting her gaze. "I guess we'll find out when we need to."

Great, another thing to worry about, on top of the bounty hunters chasing us, the aliens possibly coming to kill everyone for venting their friends into space, the weird guy who lived in the vents tracking my comms . . . the list went on and on. You'd think that after escaping a station full of murderous aliens, things would get *easier*, not the other way around.

Then again, if your life is easy, you're probably not running from space monsters. So there was that. *Fall down seven times, get up eight*, I reminded myself. Except I thought I'd probably stumbled at least a dozen. "Okay," I said, my mind racing, searching for something to grab on to. "I take your point about Rune needing us more than Cage, but he might be in the marketplace right now." *And so is the Silver Oni*. Even though I knew I should avoid him at all costs, something drew me toward that mask. Longing for my past life, maybe, but it felt like something more. Shouldn't we at least look for him? "Where is Rune, anyway?"

"Probably in the docking ring," said Alexei. "Kenzie, you can contact Jasper, can't you?"

"Not unless it's an absolute emergency. Liam figures my dad is watching for my signal to activate. If he's in touch with those hunters, they'll know our exact location if I use my comm."

"That's problematic," Mia agreed grimly. "You two stay here. I'll do a fast sweep for Cage. If I don't see him, we'll head to the docking ring."

Before we could argue, Mia disappeared. I sighed in exasperation. "Yup," said Alexei.

I fixed him with a glare. "She's not the only one with secrets," I said, dropping my voice to a whisper in case she was still in hearing range. "Why didn't you tell Mia your uncle wanted her dead?"

Alexei sighed. "It's not a secret, just not something I want to advertise. Mia already knows my uncle blames her for my family's deaths. And since I have no intention of giving Grigori what he wants, why worry her?"

I opened my mouth to ask more questions, but at that moment the tablet in Alexei's hands vibrated. We stared at it. "Is it the hunters?" I asked. "Maybe they realized Mia lifted their device."

"No." He frowned, perplexed. "It's a general call. Targeting the whole station. It keeps cutting out and repeating."

"Don't answer. It could be a trap to get us to pick up. I'm sure they can track their own devices."

Alexei shrugged. "I live dangerously," he said, and before I could stop him, he activated the link. "Allo?" he said.

"Alexei!" Rune shouted. "Finally!"

"Rune, you're broadcasting to the entire—"

"I know!" Her voice became shrill, tinged with hysteria. "It was tell everyone or tell no one. They have comms locked down, and I couldn't access anything but whole-station comms. Come quick! We're in—"

Her voice cut off with a burst of static.

TWENTY-THREE

ALEXEI WAS ALREADY ON HIS FEET. "FIND Mia," he snapped.

Mia popped into view a few feet away. "Right here. What's going on?"

"Rune just contacted me. She didn't say much before the signal cut out."

Mia swore creatively and at some length. "I knew it! What did I tell you?"

"Yes, that's very helpful." Alexei stormed into the crowd, catching our elbows to pull us along with him, apparently not at all concerned about the bounty hunters as he dragged us into the marketplace. I stumbled after him, my gaze fixed on the crowd, watching for a flash of silver.

Mia glared at him and shook loose. "Did Rune give you any idea where she was?"

"The comms cut out too quickly. Probably good, because wherever she is, the whole station heard her."

I tugged free of Alexei and found myself running to keep up. "I guess we start in the docking ring, assuming you know where that is."

"I do."

"How many bounty hunters are there?" I asked as the three of us pushed our way through the crowds. I caught a glimpse of the men I'd elbowed earlier, thankfully on the other side of the market, and pulled my hood more closely around my face. Still no sign of the Silver Oni, or of his two partners.

"Five I've seen," said Mia.

"Teams of four or five are standard," I confirmed.

"But I didn't see any of them in the market while I searched for Cage, who I didn't find, obviously. I think they've withdrawn."

Great. We were probably going to walk into a situation where as many as five trained bounty hunters, *armed* bounty hunters, held Rune captive. I didn't think it was pushing things to guess they had Imani, Reed, and Jasper as well. And we had what to fight them? Fire, which would hurt our friends as badly as anyone else. I could speak to them in different languages, which was awesomely useless. Mia, though . . . could she slip in, vanquish them, and sneak out again? "No one knows you can share your invisibility. It's not listed in your file," I thought out loud as we emerged from the marketplace, unmolested. "That might work to our advantage."

"Maybe." Mia set her face in determination. We took the stairs at a run, Alexei's bulk clearing a path through the crowds. We drew a lot of unnecessary attention, but did it really matter at this point? I wished we could get a message to Cage. I wished Mia had found him in the marketplace. His speed would definitely come in handy in this situation, and I knew how he'd react once he realized Rune was in danger and he wasn't here to protect her. I'd simply have to stand in as best I could.

Mia vanished at will. Cage moved at the speed of light. Alexei made fire. Jasper dismantled buildings. Back home, I'd always been top of my class, working myself into exhaustion to master every skill. Here, no matter what I did or how hard I tried, I was never anything but a burden. The realization struck me with the force of a physical blow. Maybe the best thing I could do was surrender myself and give my friends a chance to escape.

With that unpleasant thought in mind, I followed Alexei to the very bottom of the stairs and into the docking ring. This must have been an addition to Obsidian after the criminal element took over, because it definitely didn't resemble any Omnistellar design I'd ever seen. We emerged through what I thought would be the emergency airlock on Sanctuary into a large, donut-shaped area reminiscent of the alien ship.

Doors spaced at intervals along the walls marked berthed ships. We'd seen it before for all of twelve seconds. Now I took a good look and confirmed my first instinct. This was a hasty but well-built affair, tacked on sometime after the criminals seized Obsidian.

For now, all seemed quiet. People milled about, working and talking and laughing. No one shouted or screamed. "Bounty hunters can't be popular on Obsidian," I said nervously. "Maybe we can convince someone to help us."

"They aren't, but my uncle also has an unofficial agreement with Omnistellar," Alexei replied grimly. "Remember, this station is illegal salvage. It's technically Omnistellar's property. They ignore the fact that a gang of criminals has taken over their prison and turned it into a hub of illegal commerce, so if they demand the return of a few particularly dangerous criminals, Obsidian isn't going to do much about it." He hesitated. "That's the people running the place, of course. Individuals might feel differently."

"We don't have time to make new friends." Tension radiated from the corded muscles on Mia's bare arms. "We need to find the others before they get themselves killed."

"Can you make us invisible?"

She hesitated, then shook her head. "I don't think so. First of all, I'm not sure it's a great idea to vanish where everyone can see us. But it also took a lot of focus to hold all three of us in the market. I don't think I can maintain it with everyone moving around."

The very fact that Mia was admitting she couldn't do something made me accept her statement without question. "Then let's just start searching." It wasn't my best plan, but I didn't have anything better.

We set off through the docking ring. It was less busy than the rest of the station, but enough people lingered that we didn't stand out. Some of them looked like workers you'd see at any spaceport, wearing overalls, fixing things, munching on sandwiches, once again reminding me of how powerfully hungry I was. I resolutely pushed that thought away. We had friends to save. I was not going to start lusting over reprocessed cheese.

But we clearly remained in a criminal hub. People huddled in groups, marked as gangs by clothing or tattoos or other distinguishing features. Someone shouted in the distance, but it was only two men arguing. They shoved each other, and we quickly moved on before we got caught up in something new.

We made it halfway around the docking ring before a glint of silver caught my eye. I threw out my hands, arresting Mia and Alexei midstep. "Wait," I said. "Ahead of us and to the right. See that?"

They followed my gaze, and Alexei instantly drew both of us into a more sheltered area, assuming a casual position leaning against the wall. I saw the wisdom at once: standing in the middle of the room staring would only attract unwanted attention. I angled myself, blocking his very recognizable bulk.

Mia glanced both ways and, satisfied no one was watching, shimmered into invisibility.

About fifty feet ahead, five bounty hunters gathered outside a door. Of course, the Silver Oni instantly drew my eye, making me bite my lip in annoyance. I also recognized Priya and her partner from the market. There were two others, a man and a woman, all clad in black, all armed. They seemed to be, if not arguing, at least intensely discussing something.

"Mia," I said. She didn't answer. I reached for her and, not to my surprise, came up empty. "She's gone," I said in disgust.

"She does that."

"I wish she'd let us know now and then."

"Not her way." Alexei flashed me a grin. I smiled in spite of myself. Over the last few weeks Alexei had revealed himself to be a surprisingly gentle, kind, and even humorous person. You only had to look at his relationship with the little girl Anya to see it.

Which was why I didn't understand his obsessive attraction to Mia, the virtual epitome of selfish aggression. But to each their own, I supposed.

Mia alerted us to her return by jabbing us in the ribs. I jumped and swore softly, glaring in what I thought was her direction. "They've got them on their ship," she said without preamble. "They're talking about who's going to stand guard while they go and look for us. I don't know how these people function. They've been arguing forever."

I shrugged. Bounty hunter interpersonal relationships were

neither my specialty nor my concern. "Okay, we wait until some of them leave. Then with a bit of luck we eliminate whoever's left and free our friends. Simple."

"Sure, simple. They'll probably leave the door unlocked for us too." Mia brushed past me, sending chills down my spine. "Okay, they're on their way," she said. "Lie low."

I turned, although I positioned myself to watch their passage. Four of the hunters stalked past us. I didn't see the Silver Oni among them, meaning that, by process of elimination, he'd stayed behind to guard the ship.

That was good. He would be armed and well trained, but there were three of us and only one of him. Even if there was somehow a sixth hunter, we held the advantage, at least in numbers. And we had our powers. Against their weapons and training, well . . . I still liked our odds.

We waited until they passed, and the Silver Oni retreated into the ship. All we had to do was get inside without him knowing, incapacitate him, save our friends, and escape before the other bounty hunters returned.

And just maybe, we would finally get a stroke of luck. "If we get on that ship and eliminate the hunter," I said, "and if we find Cage, I bet Rune can hack the system, no matter what kind of security they have."

Alexei stared at me in confusion for a moment before his jaw dropped, realization dawning in his eyes. "You're not suggesting . . . ?"

"Sure. Why not? We need a way off this station. And there's a perfectly good ship behind that door."

Mia materialized, something like admiration in her expression. "Well, well, well. Look at Ms. Omnistellar Guard. No qualms about stealing an entire spaceship?"

"From people sent to capture us so they can summon those *things* back to Earth? No. Definitely not." And to my surprise, it was true. I didn't feel even an inkling of guilt at the idea. If it meant protecting humanity from aliens, I wasn't about to balk at stealing a ship.

Alexei buried his face in his hands like he was in pain, but when he raised his head, he smiled. "All right," he said. "What the hell? If we're going to do this, let's go big."

Grand theft starship it was.

TWENTY-FOUR

THE DOOR TO THE SHIP WAS, OF COURSE, LOCKED.
Mia took one look at it and shook her head. "I can't pick this."

"It's an airlock," Alexei snorted. "How the hell would you pick it? We'd need Rune to hack the door panel."

I pressed my hands to the door as if I could borrow a bit of Mia's power, make it invisible, and see what was on the other side. "We could trick them?" I suggested dubiously. "Alexei, you know the station. Can you sound official? Convince them to open up?"

"Maybe." Doubt laced his tone, and Mia promptly made an alternate suggestion. I barely heard it, though. Energy thrummed through my fingers, keeping all my attention on the door. I leaned against it, and the sensation grew stronger. Obsidian's electronics at work, maybe? Probably. So why couldn't I step away?

The buzzing grew almost painful. I recoiled, but something held my fingers fast, like I'd inadvertently glued them in place. "Hey, guys?" I said, but my voice sounded far away to my own ears, and if Mia or Alexei replied, I didn't hear it. I stared at my fingers, expecting to see them sink into the metal. They rested there, looking entirely normal, but I still couldn't move.

My throat clenched. My entire world narrowed to the door in front of me. The buzzing increased, and my vision tunneled. A flare of light shot across my vision. I squeezed my eyes shut, and . . .

Suddenly I was on the other side of the door.

I gaped in disbelief. There was no mistaking what had happened. This was clearly the airlock leading to the ship.

I spun, every muscle trembling, and slammed my hand on the release for the airlock. The seal hissed, opening to reveal Alexei and Mia, their jaws hanging somewhere around their knees. "*How* . . . ?" Mia demanded.

I shook my head and the trembling grew stronger. The world gave a sickening lurch. A moment later Alexei had me in his big hands, easing me down against the wall. "Breathe," he ordered.

I sucked in a gasp of air. "Sorry," I whispered. "I just . . . I don't know how I . . ." I squeezed Alexei's wrists, their solid steadiness reassuring in the void of confusion. "What happened?"

"We don't know, *dorogaya moya*. You were leaning against the door when light spread from your fingertips. It happened quickly. The light enveloped the door and you fell through, and it vanished."

"Like I walked through the wall?" I managed.

"More like you opened a doorway through a door," he corrected.

"But I don't know how I did it. I didn't even try. I didn't . . ."

"Our powers are changing, and it's freaky," Mia agreed, sliding the door shut. "But pull yourself together. We don't have time to come apart right now."

That was usually my line. Blood surged to my cheeks. After all, wasn't this what I'd hoped for? A more dramatic power, something more useful? "I'm fine," I insisted, struggling to my feet. Alexei kept his hands on my shoulders, but I gently shrugged them off. "I'm fine," I repeated with more confidence than I felt.

What the hell had just happened? My ability let me understand languages, not create portals through walls. How were those things even related? So far everyone's new abilities seemed like extensions of their old ones. I didn't see the connection here.

I'd wanted a better power, sure . . . but I hadn't stopped to think about what that might look like. Understanding languages didn't make me feel so much like an anomaly, maybe because it wasn't a visible thing.

Creating portals, though . . . No one would dismiss this power. My new ability would raise alarms. And so far, I'd only discovered that I could port through a single wall. That didn't mean I wouldn't expand my ability later, maybe even be able to leap to places some distance away. My earlier powers hadn't represented much threat. Maybe that was why my parents were allowed to keep me, to chip me instead of surrendering me to Omnistellar's custody. But now, what stopped me from walking into bank vaults—or into Omnistellar's secure facilities? I was no longer Kenzie, a former prison guard with an innocuous power.

I was an anomaly. I was *dangerous*.

I managed to pull myself together enough to walk in a straight line, avoiding Mia's gaze, very conscious of Alexei hovering behind me, ready to catch me if I collapsed. I forced steel into my spine. There was no way I was going to fall down again. For one, Rune needed me. For another, if Mia managed her powers' morphing and changing, I could damn well do it too.

We came to the ship's exterior door and found the airlock standing open. That wasn't totally outside the realm of possibility. Typically, you didn't expect someone to breach the outer airlock to your ship in the first place. Still, I'd thought a team of bounty hunters might be a little more careful.

We let Mia scout ahead, invisible, in case the Silver Oni waited on the other side of the door with his gun drawn. But she returned after a few minutes, shaking her head. "I don't see anyone, and it's a pretty linear design. You guys might as well come along. Hang back and let me take the lead."

She didn't give us time to argue, disappearing again before

I opened my mouth to protest. "Well," I sighed, "I guess we're going that way."

"So it seems." Alexei gestured for me to precede him. I wasn't sure if he brought up the rear to protect me or monitor me. Either way, I wasn't thrilled with the development.

And yet, a tiny part of me appreciated having him at my back. I'd never had anyone stand behind me, not ever. My parents were firm believers in the sink-or-swim philosophy.

I stopped short at the revelation. I might have lost my family, but for the first time in my life, I wasn't on my own.

"Kenzie?" Worry laced Alexei's voice.

I shook my head. "It's nothing." Nothing I wanted to talk about, at least not here or now.

The ship was small and dim, utilitarian, with lots of exposed ductwork and grating. There were signs that the people who inhabited it might be more professional than their prolonged argument indicated. Omnistellar would have approved of the neat racks of weapons storage, all carefully locked, unlike the ship, wrecking my ideas of appropriating a gun or two. The living quarters might be another story, but we hadn't made it that far.

How did bounty hunters live, anyway? My parents had always treated them with distant scorn. They served the corporations but lived outside them. Even though any bounty hunters working for Omnistellar were on exclusive contract with my old corp, they weren't citizens. They didn't have the rights and benefits of everyone else. My parents said that was because most bounty hunters were ex-cons: dangerous people who should be grateful for the opportunity to serve a purpose. I pictured the Silver Oni, and a chill raced down my spine. Who was that guy? And why did he have to wear that mask? Bounty hunters were frightening enough on their own. I'd never heard of one running around masked before.

I kept my eyes peeled for security cameras, but either they didn't have them—unlikely, especially on a ship like this—or they were very well hidden. I only hoped the hunter was too busy with his captives to monitor them, or that if he did notice us, it would be after Mia noticed him.

A couple of seconds later, Mia appeared, her fist raised to halt us. She hesitated at a branch in the corridor, then consulted a nearby panel. "I think this leads to the holding cells," she said.

A single glance at the display told me she was right. "Yeah." I indicated the correct spot. "This is the ship map. We're here. Holding cells this way. And at a guess, that's where we'll find the Silver Oni."

"The silver *what*?"

"Kenzie has a cosplay fetish," said Alexei dryly.

"I don't . . . Never mind. The guy in the mask."

"I'll see him before he sees me," Mia replied grimly. "Let's get moving."

She vanished again, and we resumed our trek, slightly faster now that we knew where we were going. I kept expecting shouts from ahead as Mia stumbled over the hunter, but nothing came. Worry kept my shoulders as stiff as boards. Where the hell was he? Flashes of silver kept catching my eyes, but they always turned out to be innocuous. Maybe the mask didn't mean anything. Maybe it was a coincidence. After all, *Robo Mecha Dream Girl 5* had lots of fans. It made sense some of them would be bounty hunters. Right?

We emerged into the holding cells, still with no sign of our silver-masked antagonist. A shimmer marked Mia's return. A trio of reasonably large holding cells stood in front of us, each maybe twice the size of the cells on Sanctuary, with a single bench at the back and an actual private space I assumed contained a toilet. Rune stretched out on a bench with her head on Reed's lap, Imani holding her hand. Jasper stalked across the cell, his arms taut bands of tension.

Reed's face lit up when he saw us. "Oh, hey," he said. "Nice of you to stop by."

Jasper spun so fast he almost fell on his face. "Mia, thank God," he said. I arched an eyebrow. *Mia?* But he was already gesturing to Rune. "They must have known her power. They zapped her with something. Reed and Imani are trying to heal her, but . . ."

"They didn't zap her with anything," I said irritably. Honestly. If you want to know about prisons, go to the former prison guard, not the invisible thief. "Or they might have, but it's not inhibiting her abilities. See the cuff on her wrist?"

"It's different from the ones we're wearing. They slapped it on her when . . ."

"Uh-huh." I crossed to a terminal, releasing a sigh of relief at the familiar visual programming. I called the prison controls, made sure there were no monitors, and shifted things around to open the door. At the same time, I deactivated all cuffs.

The force field between us and the prisoners vanished with a flash, and the cuffs popped off Rune's wrist. A second later she sat up, moaning and clutching her head. "Ow."

"Rune," Reed gasped in relief, holding her arms and keeping her steady. "Are you okay?"

Her gaze flickered over the three of us, and worry crossed her face, hidden so quickly I barely caught it. "Where's Cage?"

"He's fine. His contact wouldn't see us together, and we got separated." At least, I hoped he was fine. Mia was right, though: there wasn't much Cage couldn't outrun. "What happened?"

Jasper slammed his fist into the wall, then stared at it as if he'd surprised himself. He said: "We went to the lower market and told people we wanted to work our way off the station, but everyone we approached stared at Alexei like he was the Grim Reaper. We split up so he'd stop scaring our contacts. I figured I could keep everyone safe, but the first person we talked to pulled a gun on us, and I realized it might be a bad idea to start rearranging matter on a space station." He grimaced. "Bounty hunters?"

"Bounty hunters," I confirmed. "Who will return any

second. Do you know where the Silver—the jerk in the silver mask is?"

"No idea. Haven't seen him in a while. Is he the only one on the ship?"

I nodded. "Rune, can you stand?"

She started to rise and staggered, wincing. Reed was at her side in an instant. "Here," he said, pressing his hands to either side of her forehead.

Nothing happened visibly, but Rune instantly relaxed. "Oh, much better," she sighed. "Thank you."

"What did they do to her?" Alexei asked, frowning.

I retrieved the cuff from where it had fallen on the floor and turned it over in my hands. A tiny needle, almost invisible and completely painless when you inserted it, just like the inhibitor cuffs on Mars. "It releases a sedative. Either they didn't have enough power-inhibiting cuffs and figured it was the best way to keep her powers quiet, or they thought she was the most dangerous of anyone."

Rune laughed, but no one else did. She arched an eyebrow. "Me? Dangerous?"

"Your ability is the only thing that allowed anyone to escape Sanctuary in the first place," I pointed out. "No one else can cause the havoc you can when you get going. If I were a bounty hunter, you'd be damn high on my list of people to keep under control."

Her eyes lit up, and a smile touched her lips. "Thanks!"

Reed laughed. "Only you would take that as a compliment. Now let's get the hell off this ship."

"Well, that's not *quite* the plan," I replied. "Rune, are you well enough to hack the system?"

It took her about five seconds to realize what I was asking, and five more to understand the implication. A glimmer of interest lit her eyes as she advanced to the console.

"Hack it why?" Imani demanded, adjusting her hijab. She stretched until her shoulders popped and came to join us, watching Rune sink her hands into the console.

I shrugged. "Well, we need a way off this station."

"Without Cage?"

"Of course not without Cage." I heard the defensive irritation in my voice and cut off the rest of the sentence. It might feel like we'd abandoned him, but he could take care of himself, and he was fine. "We'll get him first. But that will be easier if Rune can hack the system and make the ship ours."

As if on cue, Rune stepped back from the panel with a gasp. "I can do it," she said. "But I'll need to be in the command center or engineering. Everything is on separate and localized systems."

Alexei nodded. "It's not a big ship. We can find engineering easily enough."

"Let's go quickly," I added. We still hadn't seen the Silver Oni, and it made me nervous.

We retraced our steps with Mia once more in the lead,

Alexei and Jasper bringing up the rear, and me shepherding our three more nervous charges. I kept glancing over my shoulder. Where the hell was the Silver Oni? The bounty hunters couldn't be this incompetent, could they? An unlocked door? One guard left behind, and that guard nowhere to be seen? Not to mention how easily I'd unlocked their cell.

My stomach plummeted into my feet as I took in the ship's careful organization, its meticulous order.

No. They weren't this inept.

"Wait!" I said, at the same instant as Mia shouted from ahead.

We broke into a run, rounding a corner to find ourselves facing the Silver Oni and all four of his companions, weapons drawn, arrayed around the airlock. Mia knelt on the floor, breathing heavily, completely visible.

The hunter I'd seen with Priya in the marketplace grinned. "Welcome aboard," he said. "Hope you enjoy your stay. It's gonna be a long one."

TWENTY-FIVE

I RAISED MY HANDS IN THE UNIVERSAL GESTURE of surrender. "Let's talk about this."

"Let's not." Priya gestured for the others to follow my lead. They did: Rune, Reed, and Imani immediately, Mia, Jasper, and Alexei more slowly. "We figured you'd be here for your friends. How many more of you are there?"

One of the men smirked, revealing a cracked front tooth. "Now that we've got this crew, I say we sit back and wait. We're not gonna run down the speedster. Let him come to us, and any others with him."

That was . . . exactly what would happen. My heart stuttered. If we let them take us prisoner now, we were finished, all of us. But what options did we have? Alexei couldn't set fire to an airlock. That was a colossally bad idea, even if we hadn't been standing in it. Mia might slip away, but the rest of us were pretty much screwed.

"We are not on different sides, you and I," said Alexei conversationally. I glanced at him. Where was he going with this? He took a few steps, placing himself between us and the hunters. At the same moment, Mia shifted ever so slightly toward us.

Oh no. What did these two have in mind? It was super charming that they knew each other so well, but I wasn't following the plan.

The man with the cracked tooth chuckled. "Really, boy? This is your strategy? Tell the big bad bounty hunters we have more in common than we think?"

"We have plenty in common." Alexei spread his hands, as nonthreatening as someone well over six feet and composed of pure muscle could make himself. "For instance, money. You like it. I have it. My uncle . . ."

Priya snorted and mimicked his tone. "We have a contract. We fulfill the contract. It's how this works."

The rest of us were within Mia's reach. She glanced at me. "Portal," she mouthed.

My heart sank. *That* was their plan? I didn't even know how I'd opened the door the first time! I shook my head frantically, and Mia nodded, equally urgent, her brows drawn together.

Oh my God. I bit my tongue. What choice did I have?

And then everything happened at once.

Alexei seemed to flash and a steady stream of flame, more concentrated and powerful than I'd realized he could produce, emitted from his cupped hands like a laser beam directed straight at Priya. She shrieked and dove aside. The other hunters opened fire on Alexei with their stun guns, but he'd already thrown himself straight backward, landing on top of Reed and toppling him to the floor. In the same moment, Mia's eyes narrowed, and everyone vanished—or at least it looked that way. We were still there, and completely vulnerable.

Fortunately, the hunters didn't seem to catch on. "Find them!" Priya shrieked, and they fanned across the hall, blocking our access.

Mia gasped beside me, and something shifted in my vision: my own arm, rematerializing. *No no no*, I screamed inwardly. Not now. I willed us invisible, *intangible*, urging Mia's power to work.

My arm vanished again, almost too quickly to be coincidence, and Mia's breathing steadied beside me. I blinked. I hadn't really helped her, had I?

The hunters advanced steadily. They had the sense not to start shooting blindly, but they also weren't about to let us slip by. At this rate, they'd be on us in seconds.

Unless I saved us. I didn't know how the portal I'd created worked. I'd only made one once, more or less by accident, and it had only moved me through a thin barrier. But then, that was all I had to do now. I had access to an exterior wall, one I knew led to Obsidian's docking ring and not into space. *Just do what you did before, Kenzie. Somehow. With a whole bunch more people. And try to make sure no one gets stuck halfway between the ship and the station.*

I drew my shoulders down my back, laying my hands on the wall and ignoring the voice screaming at me to stop trying the impossible. The first time I'd done this, there was an actual door. What if my portals only worked when I had an opening available? Maybe I couldn't open space between walls. Or maybe I couldn't yet, maybe the power was still developing, maybe . . .

But we were out of options. My mind raced, exploring other ideas even as I pressed against the wall and screwed my eyes shut. What if we tripped one of them, got our hands on their stun gun, took them hostage? Except I had the sense that these bounty hunters would cheerfully shoot one of their own along with us. Not a fatal blow, just enough to put us all down temporarily. We'd obviously underestimated both their competence and their dedication.

I ground my teeth, Mia's hand tense on my ankle. I didn't dare open my eyes to see how close the hunters were. Instead I pictured the docking bay, focused on the sensation I got when another language became clear to me, trying to imagine the bay in that same vivid detail and draw it toward me, rather than myself toward it.

The wall gave way beneath my hands. My eyes flew open in surprise and the metal shimmered in front of me, but my broken concentration quickly solidified it. Footsteps pounded nearby. I ground my teeth together, shut my eyes, and forced myself to concentrate. I knew I could do it now. All I had to do was *reach*.

The hunters shouted in surprise. Someone shoved me, and I flew through the blinding portal, landing on my knees and elbows on the docking bay floor. More shouts of surprise greeted us. Apparently even on Obsidian, it wasn't normal to see people dive through bright circles of light in walls.

I twisted to see the rest of the crew stumble through seconds before the portal resealed itself, much like the entrances on the alien ship. They stared at me in amazement. "I didn't know you did that," Rune gasped.

"Talk later," ordered Mia, scrambling to her feet. She looked sallow, and she staggered on her bad leg, as if the escape had exhausted her. "They'll be right behind us. Get moving!"

As if on cue, the airlock door hissed. Alexei hauled Reed and Rune to their feet. Mia and I caught Imani between us and took off with Jasper on our tails, not sure of where we were heading, only knowing we needed to escape the hunters. "Make for a crowd!" Mia shouted. "They won't risk shooting into it!"

"You sure about that?" I demanded. We rounded a corner, shouts behind us.

We couldn't outrun trained bounty hunters. Alexei, Mia, Jasper, and I might have managed it, even with Mia's limp, but we couldn't abandon the other three. Still, I didn't have a better plan. If we escaped the docking ring and reached the station proper, it might buy us time to come up with something.

A blur of motion in front of us and the man with the cracked tooth landed in a crouch, dropping straight out of the air, his stun gun aimed in my direction. I skidded to a halt before I crashed into him, my eyebrows shooting up my forehead. "How . . . ?" I whispered.

He grinned. "Did you think you were Earth's only anomalies?" He targeted me. "Let's make this easy. Stop where you are."

Another blur of motion and Priya landed beside him, pivoting with the grace of a dancer. Her legs barely buckled under the impact as she vaulted over us. "Show-off," she said.

The man laughed. "We were going to catch them anyway. I simply expedited it a bit."

"What part of *inconspicuous* do you fail to grasp, Hallam?"

He flipped the gun in his hand, leveling it in our direction. "Oh, relax. We're legal."

None of this made a damn bit of sense to me, and I really didn't care at the moment. I glanced at Mia and saw frustrated defeat in her expression. We had powers, sure, but they were useless against bounty hunters who could leap ten feet straight into the air. Alexei might have fried them, but the mere fact of being on a space station kneecapped his abilities. "You're anomalies?" I asked.

Hallam shook his head. "We're so much more. I'll tell you

all about it on the ship. Come on, little girl. It's time to go home. Your daddy's worried about you."

The mention of my father tensed every muscle in my body, my jaw locking too tightly to even reply to the taunt. My own frustrated defeat was mirrored in my friends' expressions—and I glimpsed something like panic in Mia's. I glanced at Alexei, hoping if she charged, he would catch her. Mia more than anyone hated confinement. I wasn't at all sure she wouldn't choose death over imprisonment, and if that meant taking the rest of us with her, well . . .

But before anyone could do anything, Hallam jerked as if someone had shoved an electric rod down his spine. He shot straight as a bar of steel, his body spasming, and then collapsed to the ground.

Priya spun. "Reinforcement!" she yelled. "We need—" Her voice cut off as she, too, went numb from an electrical burst and tumbled on top of Hallam.

Cage stood behind her, a powerful Omnistellar-grade stun baton in his hand. "This way!" he snapped. "Hurry, before they catch up!"

I didn't wait to be told twice. He opened a nearby grate in the wall and the others dove through it. Panic drove me forward and I lunged. Everything vanished in a flash, a blur of motion and wind just like when Cage had carried me. I slammed hard against the grate's opening, stilling my motion, and launched myself forward without thought, blind panic driving me. I scurried along so fast I jammed my elbows into the walls, drawing blood with every movement, leaving the others behind. The scent of the aliens filled my nostrils as every memory of pursuit swallowed me, blinding me and making me rush for any sort of freedom. Ghost claws tore at my flesh as I lurched farther into the darkness, bile teasing the back of my tongue and the sick, clattering hiss of their breath echoing in my ears . . .

"Kenzie!" called Cage. "Wait up!"

The panic dulled at the sound of his voice, although it didn't abate. *Obsidian. You're on Obsidian. Running from bounty hunters, not aliens.* I dug my fingers into the grating, forcing my heartbeat to return to normal. Bounty hunters. Dangerous, yes. But not aliens. Would these glimmers of terror haunt the rest of my life?

It was that stupid silver mask, I realized in irritation. It had unsettled me. Primed me to panic. "Up here," I called, my voice echoing in the darkness but seeming quiet over the sound of my racing heart. I clenched my hands into fists, letting the pain of my nails biting my palms return me to the moment.

The last few minutes came back to me in a rush, and my mouth went dry. The blur of motion reaching the shaft . . . Had Cage picked me up? No. He'd been by the opening. Somehow, I'd propelled *myself* forward.

Just like I'd opened the portal.

And . . . maybe . . . helped Mia keep us invisible?

My heart stuttered. No. Not now. I couldn't deal with this now. We had to escape. All the weirdness could come after.

I activated the light on my wrist monitor, and half the terror left me. I forced myself to be calm, to take command of the other half. "Alexei," I called, "any idea which direction I should go?"

"None. But if there's a way in, there's a way out. I suggest we find it before the hunters find us."

I swore softly. I did not want to think of the hunters on our tails in this tiny place. I got myself moving again, scrambling forward on my elbows and knees. No one seemed to be pursuing us through the vents so far. Maybe they wouldn't fit. I pictured Priya next to Alexei and scratched that idea. They'd fit if they wanted to. If they weren't in here, it meant they didn't follow. And *that* was a worry of its own. Did they have some other way of tracking us? Or were they so confident in their ability to find us that they didn't even bother giving chase?

I came to a branch in the vents and crawled left at random. About fifty feet farther along the tunnel, I opened a service hatch to find an emergency ladder. It stretched above us into darkness, dim lights embedded into the walls, presumably heading all the way up.

It was a relief to straighten, even if it meant a long climb ahead. I deliberately angled my light downward, providing illumination for the others as I climbed. I hauled myself hand over hand to what I thought was probably the third floor of the station, then clambered off the ladder and aimed my light down the shaft. My friends had staggered themselves with Cage and

Alexei at the bottom, presumably ready to catch anyone who fell. Cage had some sort of light, maybe from the stun baton. Mia was almost by my side already, Rune surprisingly close behind her, and Jasper a few feet below. Imani and Reed made slower progress near the bottom.

Mia appeared on my tail. "Go on," she said. "Cage has a light. He'll bring up the rear."

"Are you sure?"

"Well, I suppose you could hang out in the shaft and block anyone else from climbing the ladder," she replied dryly. I scowled at her, flipped over, and resumed crawling.

I found an exit vent in short order. Like the others, it was magnetically attached on three corners and came away easily in my hands. Was that a station quirk, or had Liam casually fixed all the vents to his own specifications? I dropped into a surprisingly comfortable area, resembling my own quarters on Sanctuary, a small but well-furnished living room done in shades of gray, with a leather couch facing a holoscreen on the far wall. I had no idea where we were, but it beat the ventilation system. It almost felt nice enough to be the upper levels. No way we'd climbed that far, though.

I moved away to let the others drop behind me. As soon as Cage hit the floor, I grabbed his arm. Guilt over leaving him behind gnawed at my chest, and now here he was rescuing us. "Are you okay?" I demanded. "What happened?"

"What *happened*?" he repeated, his eyes so wide I could see the red rimming them. "Kenzie, how the hell did you move so fast back there?"

I sagged against the back of the couch as my last doubts vanished. "I don't know," I whispered, acutely conscious of the others listening. "I opened a portal, and . . . and I think I might have helped Mia keep us invisible on the hunter ship."

"You did." There was no hostility in Mia's voice, only frank curiosity as she draped herself across an armchair, examining me with interest. "Or someone did. I was losing my grip, and then it got much easier. I didn't know what had happened at the time. You say it was you?"

"But *how*?" The words exploded from me in a panic, and I finally understood why Mia had been so upset on Mars. Having something inside you that you didn't understand, no matter how useful, was terrifying. Goose bumps prickled over my skin and my stomach flip-flopped. "What else can I do? Where are these powers coming from?"

"I don't even dare guess," said Cage, exhaustion seeping through his voice.

Jasper and Reed flanked Imani, who had dropped into another chair. All three seemed deep in thought. "Invisibility, speed, portals," said Jasper slowly. "Mia has invisibility and Cage speed. Your original power is picking up other people's languages. Maybe now you're somehow picking up other people's abilities?"

"What about the portals?" Reed demanded. "We don't know anyone who can do that."

"Yes, we do," Rune interrupted so quickly she almost tripped over the tail end of his sentence. "Liam. Remember? He said he opened a portal to Obsidian."

She was right. I exchanged glances with Cage and shook my head. "I can't deal with this right now," I whispered. "I just can't. I know it's important and we need to figure it out, but please, *please*, can we talk about something else? Just for a minute?" I needed time and space to process this, to come to terms with what was happening to me, whatever it was.

Alexei nodded, and I gave him a grateful look as he shifted his attention to Cage. "What happened with your contact?"

Cage stared at me a moment longer, worry and fear creasing his brow, but then he allowed his calm, carefree mask to surface. "Short version, Géxià was willing to help. She gave me the baton and told me where to find you."

"She didn't want anything in return?"

Cage shook his head, clearly frustrated. "She wasn't willing to help us off the station, and she was short on details. It sounds like Omnistellar is putting Obsidian in danger. This is her home. She doesn't want it destroyed. She also implied that if we save Obsidian, she'd be willing to talk again. I guess our goals happened to align, which is very fortunate for us."

"Well, only kind of," I replied, and quickly explained Liam's theory: Omnistellar was working on summoning the damn aliens to steal their tech.

He took it about as well as could be expected, shaking his

head, his eyes wide in disbelief. "No offense, but your company is short a few brain cells."

I scowled. "It's not *my* company, not anymore. And we'd better get out of here. This is someone's home, and from the looks of it, someone important."

"Can we stop for just one minute?" Imani sounded on the verge of hysterics. I blinked. I'd never heard her speak with anything but perfect calm. Even when she'd been on the edge of tears, her control remained in place. Now she trembled, her hands clenched into fists. The encounter with the bounty hunters had shaken her. "We haven't rested in hours. We're exhausted. We're going to start making stupid decisions very soon. In fact, we already are."

Jasper laid a gentle hand on her arm, and she peered at him through a veil of unshed tears. He said, "We do need to rest. But this is not the place to do it. We might still have hunters on our tails, and Kenzie's right: whoever lives here isn't going to be happy to see us. Okay? Let's keep moving. We'll find someplace safe soon."

"Will we? Where on this station is safe?" Imani shook him off and stomped her foot. "Where in this *solar system* is safe for us now? I wish I'd stayed on Mars with the others."

Mia scowled. "If that's what you want, we'll find a way to get you back there. And if you want to stay here while the rest of us move on, that's fine too."

"Take it easy, Mia," said Jasper quietly. Her eyes narrowed, but she didn't tear into him. "Imani. We're all scared. It's going to be okay. Keep moving a bit longer, all right?" I wasn't sure anyone but me caught his next words, spoken so softly I barely heard him. "I know you're thinking about Aliya. About who's going to tell your parents what happened. I'm thinking about my family too. It'll be okay. I promise."

So, he'd been listening to us back on the ship. Imani didn't seem to catch that detail. She laughed shakily and wiped her eyes. "Sorry," she said. "Sorry. I'm tired. I'm . . ."

Cage was already on the move, checking other rooms. "No one's here," he reported. "We can stop for a few moments, Imani. Okay?"

She nodded gratefully and sank onto the leather couch, Jasper beside her, keeping his hand on her arm and speaking softly. Our eyes met, and he nodded. A wave of some unrecognizable emotion surged over me, concern and love and gratitude and fear and sadness somehow all bundled into the pit of my stomach. Jasper understood family. He, more than anyone except me, knew what Imani was going through.

Cage and Rune drew to the side a bit, Rune recounting their capture in hushed tones, and Mia and Alexei sat on either side of the door, their hands joined across it. That left Reed and me as an awkward duo near the holoscreen. Was he going to ask about my powers? What was happening to me? Was my ability to understand languages somehow becoming an ability to translate powers? I squeezed my fists to hide my shaking hands and pushed it to the back of my mind. Practical concerns. Something, anything to distract me.

I glanced at the stun baton in Cage's hands. It was the only weapon we had. If someone came through that door, we might need it. But I didn't want to interrupt him to say anything. Besides, Alexei and Mia wouldn't let anyone in. They hadn't chosen their position by coincidence.

Reed had vanished while I considered this, but now he reappeared with his arms full of bottled water and a bag of dried fruit dangling from his hand. "I raided the kitchen," he said around a mouthful of apples, passing the bag to me.

I only hesitated a second before helping myself. We were so far beyond breaking the law that a handful of rations probably didn't matter. I passed the bag to Jasper on the couch and bit back a moan as the sweet tang of dried peaches burst over my tongue.

Reed and I leaned against the wall, sipping from water bottles. He gulped down his food and said, "Hey, Kenzie. I've been thinking a lot about what you said about Liam earlier. Doesn't he seem like he knows a little too much?"

I frowned. "What do you mean?"

"I'm not sure, exactly." Reed shook his head and drained half his water in a gulp, crumpling the bottle in what seemed entirely too noisy a fashion. "I just . . . watch out for that guy, all right? I mean, he can decode transmissions, he monitors alien frequencies, he has powers but he can't use them, he works for the Danshovs but also against them . . . Whose side is he on?"

"I really don't know. His own, I think." I considered Liam for a minute, the terror in his eyes when he mentioned the . . . what did he call them? The *zemdyut*. "I believe this much: he is genuinely afraid of the aliens. He'd do anything to keep from facing them again. Other than that, you don't have to worry. I don't trust him at all." And I still didn't know what he'd wanted with my comm device. I ran my fingers over the sleek metal. Part of me really wanted to run into the guy again and get some answers. Part of me hoped he just stayed in his hole so we didn't have to deal with him.

On the couch, Imani raised her head, apparently calmer now. "I'm with him on that. Whatever it takes to keep those *things* from coming back here, I'll do it. Whatever it costs. We have to stop Omnistellar, Kenz. You know that, right?"

"I do," I told her, and a sudden burst of warmth surged in my chest. For a moment, just a moment, I felt like I had at Omnistellar training camps. Part of something. Like I belonged, knew my place, knew my heart. I risked a smile and Imani returned it—determined and grim but a smile nonetheless.

Cage scraped the last of the raisins out of the bag of fruit, then set the empty container and his water bottle on a nearby shelf. "Everyone okay? I really think we should get out of here. We don't know how far the hunters are behind us."

The question was really for Imani, who sighed but nodded.

Jasper squeezed her arm once more as they got off the couch and we reassembled at the door, Cage and me in the lead. Having him by my side reassured me. Somehow, no matter what happened, the two of us kept winding up together. We had problems to work out, but in terms of survival, we were at our best side by side, and I knew everything would be all right as long as we stayed together.

At least until we opened the door to find the Silver Oni lurking in the corridor.

TWENTY-SIX

"YOU!" I CRIED. CAGE, REED, AND I ALL SKIDDED to a halt simultaneously, crashing into one another and almost toppling to the floor. We struggled for footing as the bounty hunter pivoted on us. He was of average height and build, but something about his posture combined with the mask gave him a distinctly threatening look.

He raised his weapons: a stun gun in his left hand and, no lie, a shiny silver sword in his right. I knew enough about Japanese weaponry from my obsession with *RMDG5* to know it wasn't a katana or a *wakizashi*, but it was a reasonable replica—with some modern upgrades, as I realized when electricity arced along the blade.

Something brushed against me: Mia slipping past, positioning herself more strategically. Cage made a show of folding his arms, keeping the hunter's attention on him. "You really think you're going to take us all on by yourself?" he demanded.

At last, the Silver Oni spoke. "Hold still, Mia," he said, his voice tinged with amused malice. "Or I shoot Alexei in the head."

I blinked. Something about his voice was familiar. Was he copying the Silver Oni's tone from the films too? But no, that wasn't it. *Everything* about this guy was familiar. I'd known it from the moment that mask glimmered in the marketplace. Who was he?

Beside me, Cage had gone ramrod straight. "Take off your mask," he said, his voice barely a whisper.

"Let's see you, Mia," the Oni continued. "Right now. If you're not standing in front of me in three seconds, I'll kill Alexei. I don't care about the bounty. I have this thing set to full power."

I got to two counts in my head before Mia shimmered into view between us and the hunter. I couldn't see her face, but her posture told me she was furious. The Oni gestured. "Back up," he said, and Mia complied, retreating until she hit Alexei, who quietly pulled her behind him.

I looked to Cage. Obviously, I wasn't the only one who'd noticed something strange about this guy. But whatever I'd hoped to find in his expression: reassurance, confusion, just that moment of shared camaraderie—it wasn't there. Instead, Cage had focused all of his attention on our adversary. "Take off your mask," he repeated, his voice stronger, carrying a ring of authority.

"You sure that's what you want?" The Oni laughed, although there was no humor in it; more like bitterness. "Is that what everyone wants, or is Cage making decisions on the group's behalf again?"

Rune pushed through us, dodging Cage's attempt to grab her. She stood directly between her brother and the Oni, her eyes even wider than usual, her hands clenched into fists. She opened her mouth to speak but seemed to trip over her words and just stood there, staring, her entire body trembling.

Silence settled over the group. We all felt it now. Something was wrong. This wasn't your typical bounty hunter. He knew us too well. And we . . .

The Silver Oni hesitated. Slowly, he returned his sword to its sheath at his side. Then, keeping the stun gun trained on us, he reached up and slid the mask aside.

A collective gasp echoed through the hallway. "Matt?" asked Cage, his doubt and fear so strong they echoed through my own terrified heart.

My knees gave way. I dropped to the floor, gaping up at him as disbelief warred with terror and elation. Seeing Matt standing here, alive and . . . well, *alive*, brought back every second of that moment on Sanctuary. The alien scream. The tearing claws. The gun bucking in my hands.

I'd killed him.

But here he was. Glaring at me with barely contained fury. Drawing breath.

Alive.

"Impossible," Rune whispered. She caught Cage's arm to steady herself but couldn't seem to tear her eyes from the newly unmasked hunter. "Even if the aliens hadn't killed you . . . we left you on that station."

Matt—because it was Matt, no doubt about it—laughed coldly. "Yeah, that about sums it up. Except, of course, for the part where Kenzie shot me."

The shocked silence greeting his pronouncement was of a different variety. I felt five pairs of eyes glued to my back, and Rune twisted in Cage's arms to stare at me, bewilderment in her face. "Kenzie what?" she demanded.

"Oh." Matt laughed again. I was starting to hate his laugh, even as I fought to process the sight of him. "Did you forget that little detail when you told them I died, Kenzie?"

Rune shook her head, frantic. "It's not *true*. It wasn't only Kenzie. Cage said it too. The aliens got you." She pulled away from Cage and turned to him, but he wouldn't meet her eyes. "Cage?" Then, almost hysterically: "Cage? Kenzie? It's not true."

I swallowed hard. "It's true," I said, forcing the words around the icy hand clenching my throat. I grabbed the wall and leveraged myself to my feet, clutching it for support. My legs still didn't want to hold me up, but I couldn't kneel there in the middle of the hallway.

I opened my mouth to explain further, but before I managed another word, Mia slammed me against the wall. She jammed her forearm under my throat, not quite choking me, but clearly meaning business. "What the hell, Cord?" she snarled. "You and Cage told us the aliens killed Matt."

"And they did," Cage interjected from behind her. "Kenzie tried to shoot them." He met my eyes over Mia's head, and I couldn't quite read his expression. "She missed."

"*She missed?*" Mia shouted so loudly I winced. "What do you mean, *she missed?*"

"Mia!" Jasper grabbed her and tried to pull her away, but Mia shoved him aside. I looked frantically to the others. No one moved to help. Alexei stared at me with the same raw fury I saw in Mia's face. Tears slid down Rune's cheeks, betrayal and fear and an awful, heart-wrenching sadness mingled in her eyes. Imani and Reed stood very close together, both looking confused. Imani hadn't known Matt, and Reed hadn't been there when we'd lied about his death. But they knew what his death meant to us, and they knew I was a liar. A murderer. Except . . .

My eyes met Matt's over Mia's shoulder. *Not* a murderer, then. Somehow, Matt had survived. To my horror, tears spilled over my lashes. But I'd been holding in this secret for so long, living with this guilt, knowing that no matter how many people I saved, I'd always carry Matt's blood on my hands. I swallowed as best I could with Mia's arm wedged against my throat. "I'm so sorry," I said. In some ways it was a relief to get it out. My secret was a wall between me and my shipmates. It was a wall instigated by Cage, who'd believed they would turn on me if they learned the truth, but a wall nonetheless, and one I'd helped him build. "Mia," I pleaded, turning to the personification of fury in front of me. "I didn't want to kill him. You know I didn't. I saved your lives on that ship. I would have given anything, *anything*, to save Matt, too."

She shook her head and dropped her voice, speaking just for me. For once her tone wasn't enraged. It was flat and cold and something underlaced it, maybe hurt or betrayal, and that was somehow even worse than rage. "You lied about it, Kenzie. You and Cage both."

"Yeah." I forced myself to meet her gaze. "Yeah, we did." I could have pointed out that they didn't know me as well back then, that they would have greeted the truth with suspicion and anger. I could have told them how it had torn me apart, carrying this secret. I could have made excuses. But I didn't. Because when you came down to it, Mia was right: I'd killed Matt, and Cage and I had covered it up.

Or so I'd thought. But here stood Matt, glowering at me, a stun gun trained on his former friends.

Mia must have had the same thought. Slowly, as if it hurt her to do so, she released me. She took a step back, her arms tightly corded bars of steel at her sides. Squaring her shoulders, she faced Matt. "Your ability is to sense life, not heal. So what the hell happened to you?"

Matt seemed disappointed she hadn't killed me on the spot, but he only shrugged. It might have been a casual gesture if not for the stun gun still pointed in our direction. "I died," he said bluntly. "Kenzie shot me, and I died. And then . . . I got better."

"How?" demanded Rune, her voice little more than a tremor.

I watched to see how Matt would respond. He and Rune had been close not so long ago. They'd stolen moments and gazes and maybe even the odd kiss. Now, though, he resolutely avoided her eyes. "Beats the hell out of me. I hoped one of you might know."

"The mask," I said dully. "Did you wear that just to mess with me?"

Matt shrugged. "I needed to hide my identity." A slight grin touched his lips, nothing humorous about it. "But I guess messing with you was a secondary motive."

"How did you know?"

"You're also not the only one who can read a file, Kenzie." He tossed me a disdainful glare, one I wouldn't have thought the old Matt capable of. "And your fanfiction sucks, by the way."

Blood rushed to my cheeks, and I struggled for words, but before I found them, Reed literally shouted. "Your powers!" he exploded, answering Matt's earlier wonderings. "It has to be." We all turned to him, and he waved his hands excitedly. "Our powers have changed. I can suddenly heal myself, and Kenzie

291

can do whatever the hell she's doing, and Mia can—" But Mia stomped on his foot hard enough to make him swear and hop up and down, glaring at her.

"Mutated powers?" Matt arched an eyebrow. "Don't quite see how that's possible, or what coming back from the dead has to do with my abilities. But you might be right, because somehow, I woke up. I dragged myself to the airlock just in time to see you escape in the shuttle, taking the aliens with you. Not to mention Tyler's dead body. Did you accidentally kill him, too?"

Cage moved to take my hand, but I pulled away. He had barely managed a syllable in my defense this whole time. Maybe for once he was merely at a loss for words. Or maybe he wasn't used to getting caught in his lies. All of my earlier doubts about him surged to life, the pain and frustration and betrayal simmering just below the surface. I closed my eyes. "That was the aliens," I said to Matt. I remembered Matt and Tyler had been friends, cellmates. Another reason for him to hate me.

"That's what you said about me," he pointed out, eyes narrow. "Right before you left me to die. It's a good thing I remembered something Kenzie told me about an escape pod."

My eyebrows shot up so far, I saw my own hairline. "That's why Sanctuary blew up. You activated the self-destruct and took the capsule."

"And arrived on Earth to find a not-so-friendly squad of Omnistellar soldiers waiting for me. They were *very* interested in my story, though. Interested enough to cut me a deal. Work for them, sign on as a bounty hunter, and they'd clear my criminal record, provide for my family, and give me a chance to take out the people who killed me in the first place." A sneer touched his face. "How could I refuse? It was a good thing I already had some training. All that remained was an expedited surgical process. A very painful process, but at least it was fast. And look at me now: an honest-to-God Omnistellar metal soldier."

Mia scowled, sagging against the wall. "How fast? You've been gone less than a month, Matt."

"Legion had an idea where you might be heading. They set me up on their ship. I spent most of the journey here"—a shadow crossed his face, a glimmer of remembered pain—"being *rebuilt*. I lay in their med bay and screamed while machines shoved steel into my spine and reconstructed organs. My healing ability helped with that, or I'd still be on bed rest. No one had time to ask too many questions about what that ability was or where it came from. They just wanted me on my feet and ready to fight." He glared at each of us in turn. "Priya promised me vengeance. Every time I woke up screaming, she was there, her face inches from mine, whispering promises of strength and power and a future, a future where my murderers would face the justice we deserved, and I'd have a place with the hunters. And here we are."

Rune's fists spasmed at her sides. She took a step forward,

scowling up at him. "Your *murderers?*" she whispered, disbelief lacing her tone. "Is that how you think of us? Think of me?"

For the first time, a shadow of doubt crossed his face. "Rune, I . . . It's more than just vengeance. It's better this way. I need to get you off this ship."

"And into prison."

He shrugged. "You *are* criminals."

She moved so fast I didn't see it coming, her fist flying at his face.

In the same heartbeat, Matt caught her hand in his. She trembled, arm extended, fist enclosed in his grasp, their faces inches apart. For a long moment they just stared at each other. Then Rune jerked away, shaking her hand as if he'd contaminated it with his touch. For just a second Matt stared at her with something like regret in his eyes, but it vanished so quickly I might have imagined it.

Reed reached out to Rune, pulling her back to join him and Imani. They flanked her, staying close, glaring at Matt with more fury than I'd thought either of them possessed.

"Matt," Cage said, "come on. We never would have left you if we'd thought you were alive. *Never.* You know that. You know us."

"It doesn't matter." He leveled the gun in our direction. "This is my life now. Even if I wanted to turn my back on Omnistellar, I couldn't. You have no idea, *no* idea, what I owe them. So you're all coming with me."

Jasper's eyes narrowed. "From what I've gathered, your power is sensing people. That, your sword, and your gun against the whole lot of us? I don't envy your chances, even with some new fun healing abilities thrown in."

"Did you think I told you my story for fun?" Matt arched an eyebrow, and for a moment I saw the old him in his face: determined, dryly amused, kind. Then it vanished. "I was waiting."

"Waiting for what?" I demanded.

But as soon as I said it, footsteps echoed behind us. We spun to find Priya and the man with the chipped tooth, Hallam, advancing, a small Asian woman at their side. Spinning, we saw another hunter behind Matt, a man in his forties with a shaved head. He, too, had a stun gun aimed right at us.

In the narrow corridor with hunters on either side, we were completely and utterly trapped.

Arrival. Imminence. Completion of one thread only to unravel it and follow it back in on itself. One thread becomes many.

Voices.

Sound.

Cacophony.

Silence.

They do not drift.

They hunt.

TWENTY-SEVEN

AGAINST MATT, WE'D STOOD A CHANCE.
Against all five bounty hunters, clearly anomalies themselves,
we were helpless. It took us about thirty seconds to arrive at
that conclusion before we surrendered.

They snapped cuffs on us to inhibit our powers and
marched us through Obsidian, past the curious and hostile
glares of the criminals assembled in the halls, back to the docking ring, back to their ship. Alexei's uncle Grigori waited by the
airlock, and Alexei lunged at him so hard it took Hallam and
Matt together to restrain him, even with his arms cuffed behind
his back. "You said we had twelve hours until Omnistellar
arrived," he seethed in Russian.

Grigori's impassive features distorted into a rage to match
his nephew's. "And *you* betrayed your family," he spit in English,
making sure we all understood. "Besides, I didn't lie. Omnistellar

is still several hours away." He inclined his head to Priya. "Legion finds their quarry again."

She snorted. "Don't bandy words with me, old man. I work for Omnistellar. I'm not interested in friendly chitchat with criminals." She spun to the others. As she did, the sleeve of her jacket pulled back, revealing a glint of metal. My mouth dropped open. She followed my gaze and smiled faintly. "What, you thought we were just anomalies? Omnistellar doesn't take risks. Legion is the best of the best." She pushed up her sleeve, revealing a glistening cybernetic arm. I hadn't ever seen tech like that before; hadn't even been aware it existed. But now Matt's words echoed in my mind: *steel into my spine. An Omnistellar metal soldier.* Not hyperbole, then.

Priya snapped her fingers to get our attention. "Take it as a sign, huh? There's no point fighting us, and no point resisting. Be good boys and girls and relax in your cells until we rendezvous with Omnistellar."

The docking ring lurched to the side so hard I staggered, barely catching myself before I went over. Imani crashed into me, and I steadied her as best I could without hands. A hint of a gasp escaped her before she clenched her lips, obviously determined to stay strong in front of our captors.

"What the hell was that?" I demanded.

Grigori must have had the same question, because he was already striding away from us, one hand raised to his face as he snarled into his wrist comm. Over the nervous babble in the docking ring, I couldn't hear anything he said.

Priya shrugged. "Doesn't matter to us. We're out of here as soon as we're cleared for takeoff. Stow the baggage and let's get moving."

My mind raced frantically as they shoved us into their ship, leading us toward the holding cells. "Bian, Finn," Priya said, addressing the Asian woman and the bald man, "ready the ship and get clearance from Obsidian."

"Understood," Finn replied in a gruff voice tinged with a British accent. Bian only nodded.

"Contact Omnistellar and let them know we're en route. Hallam and Matt will take care of the prisoners."

Priya didn't say what she was going to do, and no one asked. My mother would have garnered the same respect from her crew. I looked at Priya with new eyes, seeing not a bloodthirsty bounty hunter, but a woman fiercely dedicated to her job and her corporation.

Which meant, *maybe*, she could be reasoned with.

Or maybe she had the same undying loyalty to Omnistellar as my family.

I wouldn't get a chance to find out now, though. Hallam and Matt took us to the brig, shoving Imani, Rune, and me into the first cell. "Listen," I pleaded. "*Matt*. You've seen the aliens. You know what they're like, what they can do. Omnistellar is luring them in, using them to get new tech. If those things show up here—"

Hallam rapped on the bars of my cell, a smirk on his face. "I think the entire combined might of Earth's corporations might have a little more success against your aliens than a station full of unarmed teenagers, sweetheart. No offense."

But something flickered on Matt's face, something like terror. Then he glared at me like I was responsible for the feeling, shook his head, and loaded the others into the remaining cells: Cage and Alexei in the second, Mia, Jasper, and Reed in the third. Mia hissed and snapped her teeth at Matt, aiming for his jugular, but he sidestepped her easily and shoved her into the cell with such force she bounced off the rear wall.

"Easy, brother," said Hallam, clearly surprised.

Alexei's face settled into a neutral, almost pleasant expression. "You will pay for that," he promised.

Matt snorted. "Take your best shot," he invited. "My teeth are reinforced steel. So is my spine. I have a crew of superpowered bounty hunters behind me. And apparently, I'm immortal. What do you think you're going to do against that?"

"Matt, please." I approached the bars. He spun on me, his expression anything but friendly, but I didn't let myself back down. This mess was my fault. I was the one who'd pulled the trigger. If I could only make him understand . . . "Please," I repeated. "You have to listen. You can't really think I wanted to kill you."

For a split second, his face gentled before returning to its now-characteristic scowl. "I know you didn't. I don't even blame you for that, Kenzie. What I blame you for, what I blame *Cage* for, is leaving me behind. Leaving me to face Omnistellar by myself."

"We thought you were dead!"

"You saw Sanctuary explode!" he shouted, inches from my face. Instinctively, I recoiled. Imani was at my side in a heartbeat, grabbing my shoulders and pulling me back. "You knew damn well what caused that to happen! You were the one who told me about it, Kenzie. One escape pod, triggering the self-destruct mechanism. You saw it, and you didn't come back for me."

"Matt!" Rune's volume matched his, making everyone jump. *"We didn't know.* It didn't even occur to us! We thought the station took too much damage, maybe the aliens caused irreparable harm. We never even suspected—"

"Of course *you* didn't." Was it my imagination, or did his voice soften just the tiniest bit when he turned to her? "As far as you knew, I'd been torn to shreds by alien monsters. And you didn't know anything about the escape pod. Kenzie and Cage, on the other hand . . ."

Hallam cleared his throat. "All right, brother. This is all well and good and fascinating, but we have other jobs to do." He pointed a finger in our direction. "If you're smart, you'll settle in. This ship's a bit bouncy on takeoff."

For a moment I thought Matt would argue. But then he shook his head as if we weren't worth it, and the two men left us alone in the cells.

Silence reigned. I risked raising my head. Rune and Imani had retreated and sat on the bench on the far side of the cell, staring at me. Alexei glared at Cage. Reed and Jasper only looked confused, but Mia glowered at me with intense hatred. I was suddenly very, very glad she wasn't in my cell.

Slowly, Cage rose from where he'd slumped against the wall. "All right. We'd better talk about this."

"About what?" Mia demanded. "About how Kenzie killed Matt and lied to cover it up? Exactly what is there to say?"

Cage sighed, raking his fingers through his hair. "It was my call, Mia. I was the one who suggested we hide what happened."

I cast him a look of gratitude. I still hadn't forgiven him for leaving me twisting on the end of my hook earlier. We were supposed to be in this together. We'd lied together. We'd hidden the truth. And then when they called us on it, he'd abandoned me.

But he was back now. Maybe it had just been the shock of discovery, of Matt being alive? My relationship with Cage, if you could even call it that, was so new. We'd only known each other a few weeks. How could I anticipate what he'd do? Did I even really know who he was?

I examined him, looking for signs of manipulation, of lies. But all I saw was the same Cage I'd known on Sanctuary: tough, charismatic, a bit weary. He raised his hand, forestalling Mia's objection. "If it happened yesterday, we would have told you the truth," he said, biting off every word. "But back then, not one of you trusted Kenzie, especially you, Mia. If I'd told you what happened, you'd have gone for her throat, just like you did in the hallway."

"What did happen?" Rune asked softly. All the anger seemed to drain out of her and she slumped over her knees, looking more exhausted than I'd ever seen her, even on the alien ship when we'd spent full nights fighting the AI to direct it where we chose.

Our eyes met, and I winced. Rune was angry. She was every bit as angry as I'd feared she would be; she was just showing it in a different manner. But I knew her well enough by now to read her emotions, to see the betrayal in her gaze. Next to her, Imani watched me with suspicion. She hadn't known Matt, though, and couldn't have the same investment in the situation as the others. I drew a deep breath. "The alien jumped down the stairwell," I said. As the words passed my lips, I relived every horrifying moment: the creature's scream as it lunged, Matt's answering yell, the clatter of claws, Cage's panicked calls for me to shoot. "I . . . I've never been much of a shot, but it was hurting Matt. Killing him, I thought." Unless I was wrong? Was it merely paralyzing him, planning to put him in stasis with the others? "I had the gun," I said, and my voice locked in my throat. My mouth formed words, but no sound emerged, my vocal cords catching and tangling into knots.

"I yelled for her to shoot," Cage filled in quietly, his gaze locked on Mia's. "Before that thing tore Matt to pieces."

I drew strength from the support, from the reminder I wasn't alone in this. "I pulled the trigger," I managed, struggling to keep my voice steady. "I still don't know what happened next, whether it moved at the last second or I just missed. But Matt went down, and the alien chased us." I nodded at Rune. "Then you electrified the floor and killed it. When we returned to Matt, we realized what had happened."

"And I pulled him into sector four and told Kenzie to lie about it," Cage interrupted, his voice strong and clear. How did he sound so confident in this situation?

Jasper scowled. "The worst thing about all of this is you're not even sorry, are you? You'd do it again in a heartbeat."

We all turned to Cage, even me. I had no idea how he'd answer.

For a moment he seemed to consider it, meeting each of our eyes in turn. Then: "Yes," he said. "You're right. If it meant saving Kenzie's life, and maybe all of yours, if it meant stopping you from killing each other when we had a horde of alien creatures on our tails, then yes. I would tell you a thousand lies if it meant getting you to safety." He sighed, some of his confidence draining away. "But that doesn't mean I'm not sorry."

Silence met his pronouncement. I risked glancing at the others. Rune closed her eyes and clenched her hands at her sides. Imani and Reed looked somewhat sympathetic, and even Alexei, Jasper, and Mia's hostility deflated a bit. I examined Cage again, torn between admiration and fear. I'd noticed on Sanctuary how

305

easily he manipulated a crowd. It was only recently that it had occurred to me to wonder if he did the same to me.

But he gave me a tired smile, and all the artifice I'd seen in him slid away, leaving only the boy who'd fought by my side against the aliens. "Hate me if you must," he said. "But leave Kenzie out of it. You don't know what she's put herself through since she pulled that trigger, how many times she's tried to convince me we should tell you the truth. This is on me."

Alexei laughed humorlessly. "But that's the problem," he said, his accent a bit thicker than usual. "Do you not understand that? The lying is the problem."

"Lex," I pleaded, "I wanted to tell you the truth. I did. But I couldn't know how you'd react."

"You mean you didn't trust me." He gave me a sad smile and I opened my mouth to argue, but then shut it again. Because he was right. I hadn't trusted them. Cage had started the lie, and I'd tried to convince him to tell the truth a few times. But had I really wanted to succeed? Or did I just want Cage to talk me out of it? The reality was, I hadn't trusted the others. I thought I knew what was best for them. But now, staring at Alexei, I realized what a high-handed and presumptuous choice that had been.

Alexei heaved a sigh. "Cage," he said quietly. "Three years together in that cell, and you still lied to me."

"Yes, I did." Cage glanced at each of us in turn. "Maybe I underestimated you. Maybe the stress of the situation got to me. I just knew we couldn't afford any more conflict, not when we'd barely escaped Sanctuary. I made the best decision I could at the time, and I won't apologize for it."

Rune drew close to the bars, slumped in sadness. "You always do this, *gege*," she said, not at all unkindly. "You take the weight of the world on your shoulders and make decisions for everyone else. Don't you think it's time you trusted all of us, trusted Kenzie, a little bit more? We can make our own choices. We don't need you to do it for us."

Cage's eyes flew open in surprise. I didn't think his sister had ever spoken to him like that before. For once, he was at a loss for words.

And before he could find them, alarms rocked the ship.

TWENTY-EIGHT

WE SHOT TO THE FRONTS OF OUR CELLS, arguments forgotten. The alarm was deafening for the thirty seconds it echoed through the enclosed space. When it finally stilled, I didn't know whether I should be terrified or relieved. "Did something go wrong?" I asked.

Beside me, Imani murmured a prayer and drew herself to her feet, her eyes flashing as she scanned the room. "They said it'd be a rough takeoff, but the ship hasn't moved. Has it?"

We all glanced at Reed, who shook his head. "No," he said. "I know ships. This one is still docked. There wasn't any of the drift that comes with takeoff on a model like this."

A long silence lingered, and then Mia cursed loudly. "All right," she said. "Imani. You got a safety pin in that hijab of yours?"

"What? Yes, I—"

"I need it."

Imani's eyes narrowed. "For what?"

"To pick the lock on these cuffs." She rattled her hands. "They're an older model. Actual locks. With my hands in front of me, I could do it no problem. With my hands behind my back, it might be more of a challenge. Just be glad they're not the mitten models they used on Mars."

"And then what?" Imani demanded. "You'll still be trapped in these cells."

"Yes, but they didn't turn on the power dampeners when they brought us in. Don't want to affect their own abilities, I'm guessing. That means the only thing inhibiting our powers is these cuffs, and I'm not going to pick my own," Mia explained patiently. "I'm going to free Jasper."

It took a second for us to catch her meaning, but when we did, a collective gasp went around the room. Without another word, Imani dropped to her knees. "See if you can get the pin free," she instructed.

"I'll do my best." I turned my back to her and stretched out my fingers. Imani wiggled into place, settling her chin in my hands. I winced, groping for the pin, terrified I was going to jab her in the eye or something. But it went smoothly, the pin popping open in my hands. I even managed to leave her hijab relatively undisturbed.

We passed the pin through the bars, and Mia and Jasper knelt back to back. Her face screwed up in concentration, she set to work. She faced me, sweat beading on her forehead, her eyes squeezed into creases. None of us spoke. I don't think anyone even exhaled. I certainly didn't. One wrong move and Mia might not only blow our only chance of escape but electrocute Jasper in the process. These cuffs might have actual locks, but they also contained electronic components to power the inhibitors.

After what felt like an hour but was probably only a few minutes, Mia gave a gasp of relief and Jasper's cuffs clattered to the floor. She drooped against the wall as Jasper flexed his arms and rose smoothly to his feet. Two seconds later, the molecules of his cell door rearranged themselves, leaving a hole large enough to walk through as alarms once more shot through the ship. A heartbeat later, we were all free. Or at least, we were free of our cells. "Can you get these off?" I raised my cuffs.

Jasper shook his head. "I don't dare mess around with something right against your skin like that."

"Don't look at me," said Mia. "I broke the pin in Jasper's cuffs."

We all blinked. "You did?" asked Jasper.

"Yeah, and somehow picked the cuffs anyway, if you missed that feat of prowess." She glanced at Imani. "Sorry."

Imani shrugged, pulling off her scarf and folding it into her waistband. "It's all right. I don't always wear the hijab. I just feel safer with it than without." She smoothed her hair into place, curling it behind her ears with the practiced ease of a beauty belle. Now that I knew, I couldn't believe I'd missed the signs earlier. Did anyone else know they had an online sensation in their midst?

I offered her a smile, but she only half returned it. Everyone was too concerned with escape to target me at the moment, but I knew I hadn't heard the last about our lies. And I deserved it. Yes, Cage had led the charge to lie, but I went along with it.

I needed to prove myself to them again, and even without powers, I wasn't useless. "Could you come here, Jasper?" I asked, shouldering my way to the panel. He was the one who seemed the least hostile at the moment. In fact, when he joined me, he even gave me a gentle nudge, although he kept it out of sight of the others.

"What do you need?"

"The code. Maybe we can find something useful. And since you're the only one with hands . . ."

He nodded, understanding, and I directed him to unlock the console, searching for visual code. If I could only find something to release the cuffs, or at least learn what had triggered the alarms . . .

Unfortunately, I couldn't find anything quite that easily, not like before. The hunters had made their system harder to navigate. It was also incredibly frustrating describing things to Jasper when my own fingers would have flown through the commands. Rune fairly jumped up and down with impatience, and I didn't blame her. Without her powers inhibited, it took her mere seconds to hack a system.

At last we gave up in frustration and stood in a rough semi-circle, staring at one another. "What now?" Reed asked dryly.

"Jasper," said Imani, "come over here, would you?"

Cage and I ignored her, searching each other's expressions for answers. "I don't know why no one's come for us yet," I said, half to myself. "But whatever the reason, we can't have much longer."

He frowned, pacing in a tight circle. "You couldn't find anything in the system?"

"Not trying to direct Jasper. Maybe if my hands were free . . ."

Someone cleared their throat behind me. I ignored it at first, and then Imani was there, jabbing me in the side with her elbow. "Hey," she said, brandishing what looked like a computer chip.

"What is that?"

"The key," she said dryly. "This isn't my first run-in with bounty hunters. I found it over there in a lockbox."

"How'd you open the lockbox?"

"Hello?" Jasper wiggled his fingers.

Imani grinned. "Hold still and let me uncuff you."

Sure enough, within minutes she had us all free. Rune lunged directly for the console, sinking her hands into it, and the alarm vanished.

The sudden silence echoed, almost as deafening as the klaxon. I held my breath, every muscle poised for action. My mind created footsteps echoing in the corridors. What would we do when the hunters came charging into the cells? And seriously, *why* hadn't they come already? The alarm had been going for at least a minute or two. No matter how distracted they were, they couldn't have missed it.

The others must have followed my train of thought. Mia

vanished. Alexei and Cage took positions on either side of the door, poised for action, and Jasper retreated to the rear wall, his fingers twitching, ready to use his power. The rest of us huddled out of harm's way.

Seconds passed, then a minute. Cage and I exchanged glances. Was nobody coming? Why? Either the alarm hadn't activated outside the cellblock, which seemed like a pretty stupid setup, or the hunters were deliberately not responding. Because something else had their attention? It would have to be something pretty major. Or because they'd secured us with some other method?

Either way, it gave us a few minutes of breathing room. If the hunters had planned to rush in, they'd have done so by now. Everyone relaxed imperceptibly, although Mia didn't reappear and the boys stayed in their positions, and I glanced at Imani in admiration.

"How'd you know that was the key?" asked Reed, cracking his knuckles. The echo made me wince, but I wasn't in a position to criticize. "Or where to find it?"

"There's always a key in the prison sector in case of emergencies. Medical, evacuation, stuff like that. I told you, I've encountered bounty hunters before. They arrested me and Aliya after we'd been in hiding for a month." Her face crumpled slightly at her sister's name, but her voice remained steady as she carefully tied her hijab around her arm, fashioning it into a bracelet. "We passed through three of their ships. I got good at spotting their hiding places." She didn't quite meet my eyes, but I couldn't tell whether it was because of Aliya . . . or Matt.

"Rune." Cage tugged at her shoulder, then growled in frustration. "She's in deep. We need to get moving. I can't figure out why no one's come already. That alarm was ringing for too long."

I didn't echo the scariest thought I came up with: something was going on that took precedence over even an escaped bounty. I didn't want to consider what that might be.

"I'll watch the corridors with Mia." Alexei shouldered off the wall and into the hall. After a moment, Jasper followed, leaving Rune buried in the console and Reed, Imani, Cage, and me staring at one another in frustration.

"Kenz," said Cage slowly. "I hate to ask. But . . ."

"Can I detach Rune from the console?" I walked around her, examining the computer dubiously. I ran my fingers over it. It felt solid and strong, but something shimmered beneath my fingertips, something I'd never felt from electronics before. My heart stuttered into overdrive and I forced it still. "Maybe," I managed around my tongue, which seemed to have swollen to twice its normal size. "But maybe I shouldn't. She might be onto something. Let's give her another minute before I . . . before I try."

The awkward silence descended again, and it felt like everyone was staring at me, questioning the extent of my abilities. "How does this happen, exactly?" Imani demanded. "So you're a copycat now? Kenzie, you might be the most powerful of us all."

I shook my head. I wanted to be offended by her harsh

tone, but I had to take responsibility for lying to her. She deserved to be hurt. And worse, she wasn't wrong. "I honestly don't know," I told her, letting some of my exhaustion seep into my voice. "I'm not even sure how this works. So far I've copied Cage's power, and Mia's . . . and maybe Liam's."

"Liam's?" Cage said thoughtfully. "You mean the portals?"

"Unless one of you has an ability you're not telling me about."

Imani chewed her lip. "I didn't mean to sound like I was attacking you. I'm just . . . well, I'm scared. Exactly what can you do, Kenzie? Or more accurately, what can't you do? Can you heal us? Make fire like Alexei? Maybe even copy some of the abilities of the prisoners who didn't make it off Sanctuary?"

"I don't know," I repeated, struggling to catch my breath. Their eyes fixed me in place, not hostile, but not exactly friendly, either. I was glad Mia wasn't here for this conversation. "I'd love to find out, believe me."

For a moment no one responded, and I wondered if that was enough. Were they scared of me, scared of these powers even I didn't understand? This ability that had come out of nowhere with no warning? I swallowed, waiting for the next barrage of questioning.

But then Reed shook his head. "I can't believe Matt threw in with these jerks. I mean, I never knew him that well, but he seemed like a decent guy." He gave me a slight smile of acknowledgment as he deliberately changed the subject, and a rush of gratitude raced through me, even if I didn't like this topic much better.

"He *is* a decent guy," Cage interjected sharply. "I betrayed him. That takes a toll."

There was so much self-loathing in his tone that it broke through my haze of anger and confusion. A part of me wanted to reach out to him, but there was still too much lingering unsaid between us. "We both betrayed him," I said, my voice unsteady.

Cage shook his head, running his hands through his hair and standing it on edge in a familiar nervous gesture. "I appreciate the sentiment. But I'm the one who convinced you to lie about things. You were ready to tell the truth."

I really hoped Mia believed that, because I had a sense she'd forgive Cage more readily than me. Instantly guilt suffused me. Here I was worrying about whether my newfound friends would be pissed off at me instead of about Cage, about Matt, about my approaching father, about any of the myriad of things that took precedence.

Friends. I paused at the word. Were these *really* my friends? We'd been thrown together by circumstance more than anything. Three weeks ago, we'd been enemies. They'd taken me hostage and threatened me, threatened my family. But then, my family had betrayed me too.

Friends. I'd never had friends before, not like this. Not people you loved and would die for. I glanced behind me at Reed and Imani, standing close together, their faces taut with worry, and almost choked on the desire to make that worry go away, to keep them safe. It clenched around my heart, sending blood to my cheeks and tremors to my hands, giving me both vulnerability and strength.

Friends.

"You all right?" Cage asked.

I'd never been much with words, especially when I had to speak them out loud. But . . . "Cage," I said, staring at his chest under its flat green T-shirt, "I want you to know, whatever happens here . . ."

"Nothing's going to happen to you," he replied, his voice calm and assured, *too* calm and assured. It was the same tone he'd used to soothe the prisoners on Sanctuary. I was close enough to see through him now. "To any of us. We got off Sanctuary, and we'll get through this."

He'd misunderstood. I didn't want reassurance. I wanted *him*: his fears and his lies and his truth and just all of him, every breath, every sigh. I wanted to surmount the obstacles between us, the lies and the death and the betrayal. He examined me, and something slipped in his confident mask, his exhaustion breaking through and giving me a glimpse of the heart of him. I lowered my eyes, searching for words. Somehow, I knew there was something I could say, now, in this moment, that would undo all the hurt, that would set things back to the way they used to be. I just had to find the words and the courage to speak them.

Suddenly Rune broke away from the console with a gasp.

Her eyes fluttered open, and Cage flashed across the room to catch her before she fell. "You all right, *meimei*?"

The unspoken words, still unformed, shattered on the edge of my psyche and disappeared. I didn't resent Cage for running to his sister, not for a second.

But God, did her timing suck.

Rune blinked as if returning to reality, seeming to take a moment to focus. Then she said, "You'd better listen to this. I tapped into the ship's comms."

A second later, Priya's furious shout filled the room. ". . . docking ring, do you understand me?"

The answering voice was female, cold and impassive, lightly tinged with a Russian accent. "*You* understand *me*, Legion. We have an unexplained hull breach and no contact with the residents of that sector. No one is leaving this station until we know what happened."

"You're going to have to answer to Omnistellar if they don't get their prisoners."

The other woman chuckled. "Right now, that is the least of my problems. Obsidian out."

Reed and Imani gasped as one, the sound echoing through the enclosed space. My knees weakened, and Cage and I turned to each other, our faces identical masks of horror. My mouth went dry. *Hull breach.*

This was exactly how the alien attack had started on Sanctuary.

TWENTY-NINE

"MOVE." AS USUAL, CAGE WAS THE FIRST TO find his voice. "Move. Now. Rune. Come on."

Rune released the console and Priya's furious cursing faded into oblivion. At the same moment, Mia, Jasper, and Alexei appeared in the doorway, their drawn faces reflections of my own. "Hull breach?" Mia demanded.

"We were too late," Imani whispered. Her eyes were pools of terror. "They killed my sister, and now they're back. We didn't destroy the ship quickly enough. We were too late."

The room erupted into a babble of chatter, but Cage's powerful voice cut through everyone else's: "All right, calm down! So far, all we know is that there's a hull breach. Don't go jumping to conclusions. Let's get off this ship and take it from there."

"Off this ship?" Reed shrieked. "Dude, if there are aliens on

Obsidian, then *off this ship* is the exact opposite of the direction we should be going! No wonder the hunters didn't come for us! They don't think we're stupid enough to run *toward* the danger. We should be booking it to the other side of the solar system."

"With the bounty hunters?" Cage demanded. "The ones determined to hand us over to Omnistellar, who plan to attack the aliens for their tech? Great plan."

"Don't be a jerk," I muttered. He spun on me, his jaw dropping in surprise, but I ignored him. So much for that moment. Aloud, I said, "Whatever we're going to do, we can't do it here. Let's move." Without waiting for the others, I strode into the hallway—

And crashed right into Matt, with the Asian woman, Bian, at his back.

Instinctively, Matt steadied me, then shoved me away as if realizing what he'd done. In the blink of an eye he drew his gun and aimed it at my chest. "Goddamn it!" I shouted without even thinking. Matt blinked, and I jabbed a finger in his direction. "Enough of this, already! What's happening on Obsidian?"

He hesitated only a fraction of a second, but I saw it. "Get in your cells," he said coldly.

"We're not doing that." Cage took half a step in front of me, his arms spread wide. I withdrew. Usually that kind of protective gesture annoyed me, but in this case, Cage knew Matt better than I did. And also, Cage hadn't shot him to death. So there was that.

Bian snapped, "Get moving or I'll shoot." It was the first time I'd heard her speak.

We didn't even look at her. Cage focused on Matt, and the rest of us focused on them. "If you want to take us captive again, you'll *have* to shoot us," Cage said. "All of us. You okay with that? Because if not, we'd better have a conversation."

"Stun them," said Bian coldly. "Or I will."

Matt's eyes narrowed. "What do you mean, what's happening on Obsidian?" he asked me, deigning to meet my gaze over Cage's shoulder.

My heart skipped a beat. "You don't know? Matt. There's been a hull breach. A big one they can't explain. Ring any bells?"

For a split second my own terror reflected in his eyes, and then he shook his head. "No. There's no way. The aliens aren't anywhere near here. We'd have picked them up before now."

"Sure about that? Because Sanctuary didn't."

"Matt. Dude." Reed held up his hands placatingly. "Why'd it take you so long to respond to the alarm?"

He hesitated, glancing at Bian, who frowned. "Priya wouldn't let anyone leave command," he said slowly.

"Because of an emergency, right? An emergency so serious it mattered more than escaped bounties? Think about what Kenzie's saying. We can stand together against this. We have to. Otherwise . . ."

My peripheral vision reflected movement an instant before Cage slammed against me. He swept me off my feet, pulling Rune and me out of the way as walls and ceilings suddenly collapsed. We hit the floor, Cage hurling his arms around us and taking the brunt of the force on his back. For a moment I didn't know what was happening. There were sound and vibration and impact, but nothing that made sense.

And then it ended. Cage released us and stood, wincing as he stretched his arms. I pulled Rune to her feet along with me and staggered in a sudden pile of debris. She yanked out of my hands, but I barely had time to register a tinge of hurt before I noticed Jasper standing with his arms outstretched. Matt and Bian both slumped unconscious on the floor.

"What the hell was that?" I demanded.

Jasper shrugged. "Bian was about to shoot us."

Imani stomped her foot. "How do you possibly know that?"

"Because while all of you were watching Matt, I was watching her." He cocked an arrogant eyebrow in challenge. "Either way, now we have a clear path off this ship."

"And weapons," agreed Mia cheerfully, helping herself to Bian's stun gun.

After a moment's hesitation, I picked my way to Matt and took his stun gun before Alexei or Jasper did it. At least one person who would think before pulling the trigger should have a weapon. I checked the setting three times, compulsively making sure it was set to stun. I wouldn't risk killing someone, not ever again. The relief of knowing I hadn't murdered Matt was so intense that I wouldn't trade it, not even for my own life.

But I wasn't stupid, and if it came down to stunning someone or getting captured, the choice was clear.

"I didn't kill them," Jasper announced. I glanced over my shoulder to find Imani crouched over Bian, checking for a pulse, a slight tic working in her eyebrow. "We'd better run before they wake up."

I hated to agree, but I nodded. Matt's chest rose and fell, so I knew he'd be all right too. And if something was wrong on Obsidian, I had no intention of letting anyone lock me in a cell until we uncovered the truth.

"I'll scout ahead," Mia announced.

"Wait." I held up a hand. "I'll come with you."

"What the hell for?"

I glared at her, resenting the unabashed anger in her voice even as I knew I deserved it. "I can turn invisible too, remember? If we're together, I'll be able to back you up, report back to the others."

"Right. I forgot you stole powers now too. No thanks. I work better on my own." She vanished while I was still fumbling for a response. *Stole powers?* I wasn't . . . I didn't . . .

Far too conscious of everyone's eyes on me, I scowled and set off after her at a jog.

"Take it easy," Cage murmured, catching up to me, and I realized I was using his speed again, not at full power, but definitely moving faster than normal. I forced myself to slow to a fast walk. He shoved his hands in his pockets and adopted an air of nonchalance I could only marvel at. "We have no idea what's happening on Obsidian. It might be anything. A malfunction. Omnistellar arriving and getting mad. There are lots of nonalien explanations."

I risked a glance behind me, but he spoke too low to be overheard. If any of the others didn't share my fears, I wanted to keep things that way awhile longer. "I know," I returned. "But it's too close for comfort."

Cage hesitated. "Kenz. If it *is* aliens . . . what are we going to do?"

I didn't have an answer for that. I didn't dare even consider one. Obsidian was far bigger than Sanctuary. If aliens got loose on this station, I trembled to think of the devastation. And it wasn't like we could just destroy the station with everyone on it, even if we had a ship. "One problem at a time," I sighed at last. "Let's find out what's actually happening." But even as I said it, something broke loose in my chest. Cage confiding in me, not hiding behind his bluster, even if it was just for a moment: that was what I needed to give me courage, more than anything else he could ever say.

Courage or not, every step, I expected to encounter one of the three remaining bounty hunters. But they apparently had their hands full and trusted Matt and Bian to take care of us. Exactly what was Matt's relationship with these people? We'd only been separated for a little under a month. By the time they debriefed him and fused a bunch of metal to his spine, convinced him to join Legion, he couldn't have known these hunters for more than a few days. How did they claim his loyalty over people he'd known for years?

With a rush of embarrassment, I realized the same question applied to me. Was my dad wondering that himself, sitting on an Omnistellar ship, desperately trying to figure out what had happened to his dutiful, rule-abiding daughter? Or was his only concern *recapturing* me? Or worse yet, alien tech?

One problem at a time, I reminded myself. Fall down seven times, get up eight.

We reached the docking ring without incident. We found it completely deserted. Red lights illuminated the space in periodic bursts, but no alarms sounded. We stepped off the ship hesitantly, Mia still invisible in front of us somewhere, me with my stun gun drawn, Alexei, Cage, and Jasper poised and ready for action.

But there was no one there. It was like one of those horror movies where a disaster sweeps through a bustling area and suddenly it's a graveyard. The formerly busy, crowded docking area stood completely empty.

There was no sign of attack, though. Aside from a few hastily dropped tools against one wall and the creepy red mood lighting, everything seemed to be in order. All docking doors were sealed, but most of them still had the green light illuminated overhead, meaning no one was cleared to depart.

I advanced barely a step into the docking ring. Something about the silence, the red lights, the emptiness, set off warning bells in my head. The air seemed thicker, saturated with tension. I swallowed hard. "Mia?" I whispered.

She shimmered into view barely a foot in front of me. Her shoulders drew together so tightly my neck ached in sympathy. "What the hell is going on?" she demanded.

We'd all frozen where we entered, as if no one dared take another step. And we should be moving. We had Bian and Matt breathing down our necks, not to mention the rest of Legion. But somehow no one seemed able to do more than stand and stare.

This was ridiculous. I closed my eyes and slowly lowered my neck, stretching the taut muscles. It helped. I did it a few more times and, when I trusted my voice, I said, "Okay. Let's go."

"Where?" demanded Reed, but I didn't answer, only set off toward the exit from the docking ring. *Where* didn't matter so much right now. What mattered was action.

Because if we stood there a moment longer, I had a feeling we'd never leave.

THIRTY

RED ALARM LIGHTS CONTINUED TO ILLUMINATE us in bursts as we approached the stairwell. Not a single sound came from above as I stared up the first of twelve flights. That in itself was terrifying. Obsidian was a crowded, busy place, throbbing with life. Now it seemed utterly deserted.

Reed gave voice to my thoughts. "This can't be good."

"Where is everyone?" Jasper demanded.

"It might be okay," said Alexei, although doubt echoed in his voice. "Obsidian has procedures in place in the event of a station raid. We haven't needed them, not in a long time. But people may be gathered in bunkers, in safe zones."

"I swear to God," Mia muttered, "if anyone says anything about it being *too quiet*, I open fire."

That at least had the effect of shutting all of *us* up, and we proceeded up the stairs in silence. I hoped I looked calm and collected on the surface, but my insides were roiling in fear. I barely kept my feet, my sweat-slick hands shaking around the stun gun. *Get a grip, Kenzie. Before you accidentally shoot someone.*

Someone else.

I winced at the memory. Somehow, I didn't think I'd heard the last of that conversation, either. Our escape pushed pause on the argument but didn't resolve it.

Still. I wasn't a murderer. This last month of hell, living with Matt's blood on my hands . . . maybe I could finally release that now. And with a bit of luck, I might be able to convince Matt to let go too. I didn't know what exactly Omnistellar had done to him, but the Matt I knew was still in there. I'd seen glimpses of him beneath the facade. I looked to Rune, a few steps ahead of me, seeming small and ghostly in the flickering lights. If anyone could reach him, it was her.

We came to the first level of what used to be cells, now living quarters. The door was closed. I searched my memory. Had I seen a single closed door in all of my travels through Obsidian? "Alexei?" I asked softly.

Before I got any farther, he shook his head. "I thought they'd welded these doors open."

We exchanged glances. "Rune?" I asked at last.

She slid past me, strangely hesitant, still refusing to meet my eyes. Rune was always slow to act, except where computers were involved. There, she dove in with, if anything, an overabundance of enthusiasm.

Now she paused by the panel, running her fingers over it as if stroking a timid puppy. Cage laid his hand on her shoulder and spoke to her in Mandarin. I felt like I was intruding on their conversation, but I couldn't help overhearing: "It's okay, *meimei*," he said softly. "Whatever's back there, we'll handle it."

She swallowed hard. "Cage, you don't think . . . It can't be *them*, can it?"

"Of course not," he said, too quickly. "I'm sure the residents closed the door themselves when the alarms sounded."

That didn't seem to comfort her. "Then they may not take too kindly to us barging in."

It was a good point, and it brought me up short. But Cage continued without missing a beat: "Alexei's a Danshov. No one's going to mess with him. We'll be fine."

Alexei's eyes slid in Cage's direction at the sound of his name, and then toward me, but I only shook my head. I couldn't begin to imagine how I'd explain the gist of the conversation, and it felt like a betrayal to try.

At last, reluctantly, Rune slid her fingers into the panel, and the door shuddered open.

We stared into a prison larger than any of the ones on Sanctuary. We couldn't see beyond the corridor's dim depths, but I guessed where we'd find work spaces, entertainment areas, and the server room. If we got there, Rune might bond with the computer, ascertain what was going on? Cage nodded, my idea mirrored in his eyes. It was worth a shot.

We entered the hall, staying close together, even Mia within a few steps. Rune left the door open behind us. Part of me wanted her to close it, wanted the security of the metal at my back. But if we encountered something in the prison, we might have to make a quick escape.

I peeked into the first cell on our left. Ugly stained cloth draped the bars, providing the illusion of privacy. Some sort of antique hot plate stood in a corner, and a few cushions piled along a wall made a rough bed, complete with a tattered blanket. A few pieces of clothing hung along the walls, some of them a woman's, some of them a child's. A dirty teddy bear lay beside the cushions. Immediately, Anya came to mind. Where was she? Somewhere safe and warm on Mars, I hoped, far from the notice or attention of Omnistellar or Mars Mining or whatever horror stalked us next.

I must have stood there staring for a while, because Cage came up behind me and touched my arm. "We should get moving," he said, barely loud enough for me to hear.

His voice startled me out of my stupor. I glanced over my shoulder to find the others watching me with varying levels of concern and suspicion. There wasn't much room for doubt in their expressions. Imani and Reed hoped I'd take the lead, Mia, Alexei, and Jasper questioned my stability, and Rune, well . . . she was every bit as hurt and angry as I'd known she would be. At least part of it, I knew, was because I'd lied to her. But maybe some of it was because I'd shot her . . . whatever Matt was to her.

Maybe Cage's instincts weren't so far gone. Regardless, standing and staring with tear-filled eyes at a teddy bear wasn't going to gain me any goodwill.

I nodded, forcing a confidence I didn't feel. "Sorry. I was just thinking. Let's move."

Cage pulled me along with him, slightly ahead of the others. Still in that quiet voice, he said, "All that stuff back there? That's a good sign. If there'd been a hull breach on this level, nothing would be in its proper place like that. It'd be sucked into space, or at least thrown around."

I nodded, accepting the wisdom of his words. His touch on my arm sent warmth arcing through me. "I know. But where are they? All the people who live here? *Where are they?*" Panic clawed its way into my voice, and I resolutely shoved it down.

An idea struck me. "Matt's power. Maybe I can use it. Maybe I can sense them."

Cage hesitated, then shrugged. "Worth a try."

I closed my eyes. How did I go about this? Anytime I'd used someone else's ability, it had been almost instinctual. I braced my feet against the floor, clenched my teeth, and reached out the way I would if I were trying to understand a language. I listened with my ears and my mind and my heart and searched for anything, any little anomaly that might mean life.

At last I gave up in frustration. "Nothing."

"That doesn't mean much. Remember, the aliens always messed with Matt's ability."

"Then we're trapped," I replied, my voice rising an octave. "All these people. There's no way to help them."

Cage shook his head. "They could be anywhere. In a shelter, maybe. We don't know Obsidian's emergency procedures." His gaze traveled to the stun gun in my shaking hand and he asked, a little too casually, "Did you want me to take that?"

My head snapped up, steel spiking my spine. "I'm capable of handling a stun gun, Cage. Or did you think I . . . ?" I trailed off, catching the barely suppressed grin. "You're a jerk."

"Yeah, well, at least that's you again," he said, no longer trying to hide his smile.

I elbowed him in the ribs, but in only a few weeks, Cage had come to know me all too well. The challenge to my competence reawakened my drive, suppressing even my fear of the . . . of whatever stalked this station. I refused to think the word "aliens." Not yet. Hopefully not ever.

Of course, an army of Omnistellar soldiers wasn't necessarily *better*.

We reached the server room without incident. Everything was just where I'd predicted, but there were no people, no sign of anyone. "Where the hell did they go?" Mia demanded, picking up a tin cup from a nearby metal crate serving as a table. She sniffed it, then touched her tongue to it. I made a face, but she set it down and explained, "Still warm. Whatever happened here, it was recent."

And she couldn't have tested the temperature with her finger? "Rune?" I gestured to the server room.

This time she nodded and stepped forward with determination, sweeping her braid over her shoulder. The server used archaic technology, and it was even smaller than the ones on Sanctuary, more a closet than a room. None of us went in with her, arranging ourselves outside. Cage and I leaned against the wall by the door, ready in case she needed us. Mia, of course, disappeared. Alexei paced, muttering to himself, while Jasper, Reed, and Imani perched on crates in various poses of discouragement and fear. I wished I had words to make them feel better. I glanced hopefully to Cage, but he was staring at his folded arms, apparently deep in thought. If anyone was going to speak, it would have to be me.

"Whatever's happening here," I offered at last, "we'll deal with it. I mean, we beat those assholes on Sanctuary, and that was a handful of us with no weapons, no training."

Reed glanced at me, bleak amusement in his face. "And without Omnistellar trying to summon the damn things," he pointed out.

"Not to mention recapture us," added Imani.

Jasper sighed, leaning back and folding his arms behind his head, propping his feet on another crate. "You two are real rays of sunshine."

"And you're in such a great mood? I thought you were worried about your family," Imani snapped. It was a cheap shot and not like her, and I read the regret in her face the instant the words left her mouth.

It had its desired effect, though. Jasper abandoned his casual pose, his mouth drawing into a tight line, his fists tightening. But his anger wasn't directed toward her. "Yeah," he said at last. "Yeah, I am. If anything's happening to them, it's my fault. I dragged them into this, and I can't even call to check on them. You're right. I should be sinking into a pit of nerves." Suddenly he leaned forward, bracing both arms on his thighs and staring Imani right in the face. She recoiled, startled. "But I'm not," he said. "And you want to know why? Because it doesn't accomplish anything. All those feelings just get in the way of what needs to be done. They slow me down, and they might get me, or one of you, hurt. So I'm going to ignore them for now, and when I have time, *then* I'll deal with my guilt and my fear and my anger." He gave her a slight smile.

I closed my eyes, hearing my own thoughts so clearly echoed at me. Everything I struggled with—Mom's death; my parents' betrayal; Dad working with Omnistellar, the corporation I'd trusted above all, to lure in terrifying monsters out of my nightmares—none of it had a place right now.

I looked up to see Imani nodding, a hard edge in her eyes. "You're right," she said quietly. And then: "I'm sorry I said that. About your family."

Jasper sank into his seat, once more the picture of a man at rest. "Don't worry about it. We're all on edge."

"You can say that again," Reed muttered, shifting from foot to foot as if expecting an alien to fall from the sky. Not that we hadn't seen that before. I glanced at the ceiling nervously. Something else to worry about.

"For many reasons," agreed Alexei, staring at his feet. "Not least because someone we thought was dead is alive." He raised his head and pinned me with his cold gray gaze.

I winced, but before I could answer, Rune's scream echoed through the room.

THIRTY-ONE

CAGE AND I STUMBLED OVER EACH OTHER IN our rush to reach her side. My heart jackhammered into my throat as images assaulted my mind: Rune bleeding, everyone torn to shreds on the floor, bounty hunters holding them at gunpoint . . .

But she was alone, on her knees, clutching her head. Cage dropped and caught her face in his hands, turning it, apparently searching for damage. "Are you hurt?" he demanded in Mandarin, the words stumbling over themselves. "What happened?"

Rune shook her head, although tears streaked her face. "I found . . ." She choked on the words, her entire body trembling. I exchanged mystified glances with Imani. I'd seen Rune panic before, but not like this. What had she found?

"She was looking for the source of the hull breach," Reed pointed out quietly. "Rune? Did you find it?"

She nodded. "I . . ." She dragged a hand across her face, then pushed Cage away. "You . . . well, you better see for yourself." Shrugging free of her brother, she returned to the control panel. "Go back to the other room." An eerie flatness settled into her tone, as if she was afraid to let even a hint of emotion break through. "Please. It's too crowded in here, too . . ." Her voice almost broke on the last word, and we scrambled to retreat. I knew exactly what she meant, though. Too claustrophobic. Too reminiscent of the alien ship, of a cell, of hiding from aliens on Sanctuary.

Back in the main room, a dark foreboding settled over us. "Where's Mia?" I asked Alexei, my voice hushed, as if frightened to disturb the tension.

"Here." Her response floated from nearby, disembodied and ridiculously creepy.

For some reason, it made every muscle in my body tense. "Do you have to do that?"

She shimmered into view, her face a furious scowl. "Oh, I'm sorry. Do you find it unnerving? Does it make you uncomfortable when you can't see me, Kenzie? Maybe I'm a harder target to shoot?"

A wave of cold rushed over my body. I knew she hadn't forgotten. "Mia, it was an accident."

"Maybe it was," she returned, her entire body taut, ready for action. "But you're still holding that gun. How long before you *accidentally* shoot one of us, too?"

Cage's arms constricted around me. "Mia, enough. For one thing, it's a stun gun. For another—"

"You shut up." Mia stabbed a finger in his direction. "You lied to me, Cage. To all of us. I trusted you, I actually trusted you, and look where it got me."

"Off Sanctuary," he replied coldly.

I drew the stun gun and raised it, careful not to point it in anyone's direction. "You all feel that way?" I looked at the others in turn. Imani met my gaze, her eyes warm and steady. Reed stared at me in confusion, as if he still wasn't sure what was going on. Jasper and Alexei seemed to hover on the edge of forgiveness, but I still got nothing but icy hostility from Mia. Her words echoed in my mind: *I actually trusted you, and look where it got me.* Was she angry, or hurt? I didn't think she really thought I'd target her. She was scapegoating me, using that as an excuse for dealing with her own emotional conflict. Well, I was no stranger to that myself, and I knew how to play along. "Okay," I said. "Imani."

Her head shot up, confusion in her face. "But . . ."

"You're a good shot, and you're just as defenseless as me without a weapon. And I trust you," I said, glaring at Mia. What stung the most? She was right. I had lied. I'd shot Matt. Sure, Cage had swept me into his plan, but I was an independent functioning human being, and I could have told the truth at any time. I'd lied because I hadn't trusted them. What right did I have to get angry when they didn't trust me in return?

And yet . . . somehow . . . I was angry. It stung. After everything, I still wasn't one of them.

Slowly, Imani took the stun gun. She'd fired it on Mars; I knew she knew how to use it. Sure enough, after examining it a moment, she tucked it into her waistband. "Thanks, Kenzie," she said quietly.

Cage gave me an encouraging smile, and so did Reed. Mia didn't soften any, but at least I'd gained some ground with the others.

"Stop arguing." Rune appeared in the doorway. Her voice was so soft we barely heard it, but it cut through us all the same, drawing every eye in her direction. She'd stopped crying but stared at us, her gaze dull and listless until it settled on her brother. "I loaded the feed."

"*Meimei*, what's on it?"

"I told you, you should see for yourself." She tilted her head and a hologram shimmered to life in our midst. Had she activated this holo without even touching the computers?

I jumped as a dozen heavily armored men stampeded straight through me. Those weren't stun guns in their hands, either. I'd seen huge rifles like that. Omnistellar manufactured some, in fact, but my parents never let me fire one. I didn't even want to consider how Obsidian got their hands on that sort of weaponry.

The security feed showed the view from someone's helmet cam, giving the whole thing a surreal look, as if we were inside a VR game. The guards took up positions outside a sealed door. "Everything looks clear," someone announced from ahead. "But we can't get in."

Over comms came a voice laden with frustration. "I know. I'm not having any luck unlocking the system."

The woman who spoke first had even less patience than Mia. "Blow it, then. Or I will."

After a moment's hesitation, the reply: "Copy that, Alpha Two. Stand clear."

The suited figure, who I now realized was the commander, gestured everyone back. The view lurched as the owner of the camera slid around the corner. A muffled explosion reached my ears, and the commander barked, "Let's move!"

The guards charged through the smoking remains of the door into a prison sector similar to the one we were in, but much cleaner and nicer, better maintained. Some sort of foam block surrounded most of the cells. I recognized it as a cheap soundproofing material. My dad used it to cover the basement walls on Earth when he and Mom set up a weekend shooting gallery. Here, it provided privacy for apartments.

I barely had time to register this, though, as the guards charged through. They kicked open doors. My camera view illuminated a nicely appointed apartment. It was tiny, being a cell, but it contained decent furniture, some framed pictures, and a plush carpet.

"Alpha One!" a voice barked. I jumped. It sounded like it

was in the room with us—because, I realized, it was the voice of our camera's owner. "You'd better see this."

The camera angled to reveal a long bloody streak marring the cream-colored carpet.

The commander drew near, and I made out her worried expression behind her faceplate. "Similar situation in the other apartments," she said shortly. "Let's keep moving. We haven't found any bodies yet. Whatever happened here, there has to be evidence."

My knees grew weak. No. No, there didn't. Not if the bodies were taken. The aliens had taken everyone on Sanctuary, even my mom, even Rita, even though they weren't anomalies. They might do the same thing here.

A sudden scream sent me shooting to my feet, my heart pounding. For a moment I thought it came from directly behind me, but after a second, I realized it was part of the recording. I wasn't the only one, either: everyone was either on their feet or sitting as tense as a steel bar.

The hologram vid jerked shakily, as if the camera owner had experienced the same reaction as me. "Did you see that?" he barked. "Alpha One! Respond, please!"

The commander's voice echoed through the comms: "All units! All units! Report to—" Her voice cut off in a strangled scream.

"Go!" someone shouted. The camera lurched forward, black-suited security guards in front of it, the feed a jumble of feet and arms and guns until it made me sick to watch, but I didn't dare look away.

Someone else screamed, a high, shrill wail that went on and on. My nails dug into the flesh of my palms. It was a human sound, not the aliens' cry. We hadn't heard the aliens yet. This might be anything. A rebellion. A gang war. Anything.

A jumble of shouting filled the room, gaining in volume, in panic, in desperation. The camera swiveled left, then right, pitching like the nose of a shuttle on reentry. A blur of motion passed in front of us, and Imani shrieked, jumping and pressing her hand to her chest.

"What was that?" screamed the man. "What the bloody hell was that?"

"Retreat!" someone shouted. "Everyone! Get out of here!"

"What was it? What was it? Did you see it? What was it?"

A black-visored face filled our vision a second before its arm blocked the camera. "Get a grip!" its owner shouted. "And go! Move! Go, goddamn it!"

The hologram shimmered into place and tottered as the guards flew down the hall at a dead run, back the way they'd come. Suddenly a claw shot into our realm of vision.

This time, no one screamed.

The reality of the situation settled with the weight of a death sentence.

I sank to the floor, my knees giving way even as Cage

fumbled to catch me, missing because his eyes remained glued to the hologram.

We'd seen those claws before. Cutting into our own flesh. We'd pulled one from Mia's side.

"You see?" Rune said, her voice nearly a sob. "They're here."

Now Cage reached for her, but Alexei arrived first, laying steadying hands on her arms. Mia appeared beside him, for once stunned into silence, her face as pale and drawn as mine.

The angle of the hologram changed as the guard stared at the claw protruding at least six inches from his chest. I reeled. "That's too long," I whispered. "Their claws weren't so long." I remembered every second on Sanctuary, every vivid, gory detail. I'd held one of their claws in my hand after it snapped off inside Mia's abdomen.

"Maybe they're mutating too," said Reed grimly.

"Maybe." Cage raked his hands through his hair. "Or maybe they're different. A different species, or even . . . I don't know. I need to think about it."

"You're saying these things might be even worse than the ones on Sanctuary?" Jasper's voice held an edge of hysteria. Something cracked, making us all jump. Jasper stared blankly at the arm of his chair, which he'd just snapped off in his hand.

The feed fizzled and went blank.

That left us staring at one another in the recesses of a new prison, surrounded by more alarm lights, and under the apparent threat of a new alien attack.

One with the potential to be even worse than before.

THIRTY-TWO

"I CAN'T DO THIS," REED WHISPERED, BURYING his face in his hands. "Not again."

I bit my tongue to keep from snapping at him. Mia didn't bother. "You never even saw the aliens on Sanctuary. It was me who fought them, me and Cage and Alexei and . . ." Her voice trailed off, and she glared at me, Matt's name dying on her lips.

I swallowed hard. "And . . . Matt," I finished for her, meeting Mia's gaze defiantly. "And Tyler. And my mother. And Rita. And a hundred other people we'll never see again—"

"And Kenzie," interrupted Cage, his voice a dagger, his stare targeting Mia as if he could lock her in place. "Kenzie fought those things as hard as you did, Mia. Maybe harder. All of you seem to be forgetting that."

To my amazement, Mia broke eye contact, as if she'd realized she'd edited me out of her own traumatic memories. But although Reed ducked his head in embarrassment, I didn't blame him. He had heard and seen enough to scare him. The same with Jasper.

And Imani . . . Imani had choked on the slime they'd used in an attempt to mutate her, and her sister had died from the same process. But she wasn't crying or screaming, only staring ahead with a horribly blank expression. "Imani?" I whispered, crouching in front of her.

Her head shot up, and I recoiled in shock. It wasn't fear or anxiety in her expression, but raw, utter fury. "They're here," she said, her voice steady. She drew the stun gun and considered it. "We're going to need better weaponry. Something more than the security team had. Something with a hope of destroying those things."

"Imani?" I repeated.

She met my gaze straight-on. "Those things killed my sister. They sure as hell aren't going to kill anyone else if I can stop them."

Our eyes met and understanding passed between us. "No one else," I agreed, and she nodded. Imani, at least, didn't hate me. My heart rate slowed a few beats per minute.

She rolled her shoulders and got to her feet. "We should move if we're going to stop those things."

Well, if nothing else, you had to admire her courage. Part of me wanted nothing more than to crawl into one of these cells and hide. I swallowed that down and glanced at the others.

"Can we work together on this? Or do I have to worry about getting stabbed in the back?"

Alexei arched an eyebrow. "Do *you* have to worry? I think that should be our question."

"Lex, stop," said Cage, exhaustion seeping into his voice. "We've been through this over and over. I'm not going to apologize for hiding what happened on Sanctuary. As for later, well . . . maybe we should have told you. It's too late to do anything about it now."

"He's right." To my surprise, it was Reed who spoke up. He met my eyes and gave me a quick wink. "Kenzie's proved herself more than once. So has Cage. They're allowed to make a stupid decision." He sighed when Mia shifted her glare in his direction. "Come on. Does anyone actually think Kenzie shot Matt on purpose?"

Even Mia glanced down at that. An uncomfortable silence settled over us. I could almost see their minds racing, and I clenched my fists at the sense of judgment, at being on trial. This was what Cage had wanted to avoid. But ironically enough, it seemed like they were willing to forgive me for shooting Matt. Only Rune and Mia still seemed angry enough to shove me out of an airlock. Mia, I could take. Rune, though . . .

If I'd followed my instincts and told them the truth as soon as we had escaped Sanctuary, maybe we wouldn't be in this situation? There was no way to tell. I had made a choice. Who knew how people would have reacted in the moment: knowing me less, trusting me less? Cage and I couldn't change what we'd done. All we could do was try to make amends and keep moving forward.

Mia examined me a moment, then sighed. "We don't have much choice but to keep going together if we're going to survive. We can argue about this later."

I heaved a sigh of relief. Mia might not have forgiven me, but if she said she was putting things aside for now, then she was.

The others nodded as if that settled things, and Rune swallowed hard. She'd been cringing against the wall with her arms wrapped around herself, but now, with a visible effort, she stood and clenched her hands into fists. "If we want better weapons, we'll have to get them from security," she announced, her voice steady and strong and much more like herself. "That's on the main level, where we met Grigori Danshov the first time."

"Can we get there?" Alexei demanded.

"They're under lockdown." She flashed a tight smile. "Fortunately, that doesn't mean much when you have me."

"Yeah," Jasper agreed. "And apparently not when you have Kenzie, either."

I blinked. I'd been trying not to think about my powers. But maybe I should start. If we were going to survive this, we needed as many advantages as possible.

"I want to help," I said at last. I glanced to the others for support. To my horror, a veil of tears misted over my eyes. I blinked them away, but not before people saw them. Surprisingly, though, expressions of anger and frustration melted into sympathy at the sight. Slightly encouraged, I pressed on. "I just don't know how. I don't know how to control these new abilities, or how to . . . how to . . ."

"Kenzie," said Imani softly, "it's okay. When we need you, you'll pull through. You always have before." The others nodded, even, after a moment's hesitation, Mia.

I squashed my weakness and forced my spine straight. "Thank you," I whispered. Whatever I could do now, I was going to figure it out. But in the meantime, Imani was right: In times of stress, when I needed my powers most, they were there for me. I had to trust that. For now, it was all I could do.

We hesitated, looking at one another across the room. "No one has to come," I said at last. "Some of us are better suited to fighting than others. If you want to stay here, it's fine."

Imani shook her head. "We're not safe here, either. If those things are on Obsidian, we're not safe anywhere."

"But once they'd done their initial sweep on Sanctuary, they seemed to prefer picking us off one by one to attacking in a big group," Alexei pointed out. "Safety in numbers." The others nodded, although no one moved, trapped in their own fear.

I hadn't planned on staying behind anyway. I'd merely wanted to give everyone else a chance. "All right. Then no sense delaying."

But still no one moved, as if to take a step would be to

irrevocably commit to reentering the nightmare we'd so recently escaped.

At last Mia heaved a sigh of dramatic exasperation. She cursed under her breath and, with no further ceremony, stalked toward the door. Alexei shot after her. Cage and I exchanged a glance, then ran to catch up. The others followed on our heels.

Mia poked her head into the corridor, stun gun in her hand. I missed the heavy weight of my own, but I trusted Imani to take a shot if she needed to. Between Mia and Imani with stun guns, Alexei's fireworks and Jasper's ability to rearrange matter, and our foreknowledge of the aliens' tactics, maybe we had an edge this time. Maybe we had a hope.

Mia must not have seen anything, because she proceeded into the corridor and climbed the stairs. Our footsteps echoed in the uncanny silence. I glanced into the next prison area as we passed. It looked exactly like the one we'd just vacated. Where was everyone? Were we the last people alive on Obsidian? No. Impossible. The aliens had taken hours to work their way through Sanctuary, and this station was at least three times bigger. The survivors were probably locked away on the main floor with every weapon they could find. Alexei had theorized that they'd barricaded themselves somewhere. Maybe they were safe.

Or maybe the aliens had killed them and left their bodies stacked where they fell.

Or kidnapped them, taking them back to their ship. I didn't know. I couldn't know . . . at least, not yet.

Which led to another problem: Grigori Danshov, who might shoot us himself. Or some of us. I glanced at Mia, wondering if there was a polite way to ask her to vanish without triggering her rage. The girl spent three-quarters of her time invisible anyway. Trust her to suddenly discover the joys of putting herself on display at the exact moment we most needed her imperceptible.

We clambered up two more staircases and found more of the same. There could have been people in the farther cells, but we didn't check. In fact, Mia moved so quickly we were almost running. Fear seemed to edge out her caution.

I couldn't blame her for being afraid, though. My legs and lungs burned, and adrenaline was about the only thing keeping me on my feet. We'd been awake for nearly twelve hours, running on almost no food or water, constantly fighting for our lives. Aliens or not, we couldn't keep going much longer.

A vent caught the corner of my eye, and I stopped short. Cage grabbed my arms to steady himself as he crashed into me. "What's up?"

"Liam," I said, staring at the vents. "This is his worst nightmare, the thing he tried to avoid at all costs. Where do you think he is?" *And what is he doing?* Liam's fear of the aliens was very real, but his motivation . . . that was something else. Was he huddled in a bunker with Grigori Danshov? Searching for weapons like us? Or something else, something more sinister? Preparing to vent the entire station and save his own life? I wouldn't put it past him, not for a heartbeat. After all, he'd abandoned his own family to escape the creatures before.

"Hey!" Mia snapped from ahead. "What the hell's going on back there?"

"Good question," muttered Jasper from behind me, and I realized I was blocking the staircase.

I shook my head and got my feet moving. My suspicions about Liam had to wait. I had no evidence of any kind, and no idea where he was or what he might be doing. I couldn't divert us from our mission to go on a wild-goose chase. "Sorry!" I called, keeping my voice light. I would regain their trust, I vowed to myself. Because I suddenly knew that if I was in the same situation again, I wouldn't lie to them. I trusted these people, even Mia, as unpredictable and violent as she could be. And I wanted them to trust me. I glanced up to where she and Alexei leaned over the railing, looking at me, and opened my mouth to tell them so. At some point, you had to take a risk. I'd never been good at talking about my feelings or being vulnerable, but what the hell. I'd fired the shot. I'd lied about it. I couldn't change it, but I could own it.

But before I could say anything, Matt appeared behind them, his face caked in blood and glowering in fury.

I screamed a warning, but a bolt of electricity struck Mia. She jerked ramrod straight, her body spasming, and slumped to the floor against the railing.

At almost the same instant, Alexei spun and dove into Matt.

They collided and crashed, rolling out of sight. I raced ahead to help Alexei, although I don't know what I thought I was going to do. But Cage grabbed my elbow and yanked me backward. I stumbled, smashing my ankle on the stairs as he jerked me to the previous level faster than a human eye could follow. A blast of electricity erupted where I'd just stood. "Bian," he shouted. "Everybody run!"

We spun and bolted down the stairs, but Jasper, now in the lead, threw out his arms, smacking me in the face. "They're ahead of us too!"

With no other options, we ran into the nearest prison sector. Stun guns crackled behind me—the other hunters, presumably, targeting us from below. I shot forward with a burst of speed I didn't intend, stumbling around the corner into a commons area and plastering myself to the wall. Cage, Rune, and Imani followed. There was a server room here, but it was bolted shut. I didn't see anywhere else to hide, anywhere to run.

I'd used the portals a few times now, but they still scared me. I'd only managed to move us to something right on the other side of a wall, and being in space made that dangerous if I didn't know our exact location. But there had to be something I could do. My mind raced, searching our list of powers. Alexei's fire? Jasper's telekinesis?

"Where are Jasper and Reed?" Cage demanded.

Rune shook her head, gasping for air. "Hit. They went

down." She closed her eyes, sweat beading on her forehead, and the hall door rumbled shut. We all froze. Had she closed it in time? Why hadn't I even tried to do that? Keeping track of all these powers was a nuisance.

Priya's voice echoed from the hallway. "They're in the commons room. Keep moving!"

"Stop!" I shouted in response, as Imani clutched her stun gun and crouched behind a box, her eyes wide and panicked. "Priya, listen to me!"

She laughed, the sound sharp and humorless and much too close. "The only thing I'm interested in hearing is your surrender."

"Are you that single-minded?" I screamed, hysteria finally gaining the upper hand. "Goddamn it! Didn't you notice there aren't any other people on this whole station? What is here is much, *much* worse than anything you can imagine, and it's coming for us!"

Her voice turned dark and dangerous. "The only thing I'm concerned about right now is my contract."

Something shimmered, and Hallam appeared in a flash of light, crouched in our midst. The son of a bitch was a teleporter, too. How many powers did these guys have? Were they like me? Or was something else going on here?

Imani opened fire, catching him with a stun gun blast. He froze, shock registering in his expression before he dropped to his hands and knees, still struggling to get up. Imani hit him again and he collapsed. Our eyes met, wild and frightened. Even on the stun gun's lowest setting, it shouldn't have taken two shots to drop someone like that.

"We have to find an escape," Rune gasped.

Cage was already moving, wrenching a grate loose. I shook my head at him wildly. "What if the creatures are in there?"

"We don't have much choice," he pointed out. "You three go. I'll follow."

"I have the gun!" Imani replied.

"And I can run faster!"

She leaned around the box and fired a shot at someone advancing. "There's nowhere to run, Cage. Go!"

Cage hesitated a second longer, swore, and dove into the vent. "Come on!" he urged Rune, taking her hand and dragging her after him.

I followed, squeezing my shoulders through the narrow opening. This was a much smaller shaft than the one we'd used before. As soon as my feet cleared the grate, I twisted to shout to Imani, "Okay, we're in. Hurry!"

She scrambled along the floor, firing over her shoulder. At the same moment, the bald man with the British accent—Finn, I remembered—burst onto the scene, rolling beneath her stun gun blast. He stretched his hand in her direction, brushing her ankle, and she froze.

Our eyes met, and I read her fear, her confusion, her desperation. But she clearly couldn't move a muscle. Somehow,

Finn had manifested yet another power. He could freeze people in place.

Priya appeared in a burst of wind, much like Cage (and now, I guessed, me) when we moved at top speed. "Imani!" I shouted, shoving myself backward. I could reach her, I knew I could. My fingers caught in the metal and then Cage's hand closed over my wrist.

"We can't help her!" He dragged me forward. In the same instant, Finn lunged at the vent. His fingers grazed my shoe, but Cage yanked me out of his grip just in time.

Finn and I faced each other, me staring over my shoulder, him half hunched in the grate, his lips twisted in a sneer. His brow lowered as he calculated, no doubt debating whether he'd fit into the vent.

Cage's grip on my wrist became painful as he wrenched me along. "Imani," I repeated, almost in a whisper, but I was scrambling after him already. I didn't have more time to think before Cage dragged us forward with phenomenal speed, bashing our elbows and shins as he accelerated in bursts, putting distance between us and the hunters.

At last, after what felt like an hour of twisting and turning, we stopped, collapsing against a dead end. Our breath echoed in the tiny space. I couldn't see anything in the shadows. My joints ached where Cage had slammed me against the walls in our hurried flight, and his body trembled with the effort of carrying us.

In a matter of seconds, Matt and his new friends had reduced our group of frightened but capable anomalies to three terrified teenagers huddling in a vent on an alien-infested space station. And just like we'd abandoned Matt, even without meaning to, we'd left our friends behind at the hunters' mercy. Imani, Alexei, Jasper, Mia, Reed. All of them gone in less than five minutes. How long before the hunters caught up with us, too? I dropped my head to my folded arms and faced the truth. One way or another, we were going to die on Obsidian.

THIRTY-THREE

"KENZIE," CAGE SAID GENTLY, AND I BECAME aware that he'd been calling my name for a while. I'd heard it without really registering what the word meant.

"Yeah," I said. My voice sounded listless and dull, almost unrecognizable to my own ears.

"Kenzie. We need you to get us out of this vent."

I laughed. I meant it to be a quick snort of derision, but it got out of control, gaining a life of its own and becoming a hysterical giggle.

"Kenzie!" Cage and Rune chorused.

I choked back my agitation, still fighting the odd hiccup of mirth. "Sorry," I said. "I'll get right on that. What do you want me to do?"

Cage's voice remained somehow calm and steady. "Open a portal."

I glared in the direction I thought he was. "*I. Don't. Know. How.*" I made every word a snarl, knowing he didn't deserve it, but channeling all of my hatred and energy in his direction. "I've done it twice. Both times, magic portal through a wall. Fantastic. I barely know what I'm doing. I couldn't use Matt's power before, and I didn't do anything to help us when the hunters attacked. I'm not your secret weapon!"

"Then what?" Rune cut in, her voice sharper than I'd ever heard it. "We die in this vent because you're too scared to try?"

I closed my eyes and leaned my head against the wall, letting her anger wash over me. I deserved it. I deserved every drop of it. Rune had been so upset that Cage had betrayed her, and I'd listened and talked and commiserated and the whole time I'd been guilty of something worse. "Rune." What could I say? What could I possibly say that would make things better? That Matt was still alive after all? Small comfort when he was trying to capture us. That I'd lied to her because we'd been lying to everyone else and, well, she'd gotten caught in the crossfire? "I know how you felt about Matt. And I know I betrayed your trust. I'm sorry, I'm just so sorry . . ."

Irritation edged Cage's voice. "Why doesn't anyone see that we didn't have a choice? You're all acting like everyone embraced Kenzie with open arms when they first met her."

"Oh my God, *báichī*! Both of you, just . . . is that really what you think I am?" Rune slammed her fist into the wall hard enough to rattle the vent, and Cage and I both jerked upright. My heart pounded as I waited for the telltale skittering that meant the aliens had heard us, but Rune pressed on as if she'd completely forgotten the danger. "I'm not mad at you for shooting Matt, Kenzie. I know what an accident is. You were trying to protect him. I get it. And I even sort of understand why you didn't tell the others about it, at least right away. But *me*? After three weeks on that ship from hell, you didn't trust *me* enough to tell me the truth! And *you*, Cage. After everything we've been through, you still think I'm a bloody child!" Her voice caught on the edge of tears. "If I can't trust the two of you, who am I supposed to trust, huh? If my twin brother and my best friend are lying to me, where does that leave me?" She took a moment to gather herself, lowering her voice, as her words washed over me. *Best friend*. Was that really how she saw me? "Lying about it on Sanctuary, sure, I get that. But we had almost a month on that ship. Weeks of working side by side. Of talking and trading stories and jokes. And in all that time that I thought we were becoming friends, you were hiding something from me. Something that tore you up inside. You didn't trust me with it, no matter how much I trusted you."

I pressed my palm to my face to hide the sting of tears as her words washed over me. I'd spent all those nights terrified. What would Rune do, what would she say when she found out? And here she brushed it off with nothing but understanding.

Silence echoed, more deafening than her yells, and her words echoed in my mind. *Best. Friend.* I realized suddenly that, like me, she hadn't exactly had a lot of opportunities to form friendships. She'd grown up on the streets of Taipei, committing corporate espionage to stay alive, no one but Cage to rely on.

Before I could think too hard about what I was doing, I fumbled in the darkness until I found her hand. She recoiled, but I squeezed hard and didn't let go. "You're my best friend too," I said quietly. It sounded stupid once the words left my lips, but I pressed on. "And, Rune, I'm so sorry. If I could go back, I would tell you the truth. If there were any way to undo the lies, I would take it. Please believe me."

Cage sighed heavily. "You're right, *meimei*. You're always right," he added with the air of making a huge concession, and Rune snorted. "Even if we didn't trust anyone else, we should have trusted you. I just . . . I get carried away sometimes. I start plotting and planning and I'm so worried about keeping everyone safe and alive that I forget we're still human. It scares me."

His words sent a chill down my spine. "Cage," I said softly. What he said made sense. Had my parents thought the same way? When they'd chipped me, had they only been thinking of my survival? And when they hadn't told me, well . . . I had my own experiences with lies now. Once they started, they snowballed. It was hard to escape an avalanche.

I closed my eyes against the bitter press of tears, and Rune's hand tightened around mine. Mom was gone, but maybe Dad and I could still work things out. I finally understood. Dad was trying to protect me. Cage and I had been trying to do the same thing. We'd all gone about it the wrong way, but everyone deserved forgiveness. We all needed second chances.

Rune tugged me forward to lean against her shoulder. Her arm slid around me, and I heard her pulling Cage close on her other side. "All right," she said, her voice muffled. Cage's hand brushed my face as he cupped the back of her head, leaving tremors in its wake. Would I ever fully know or understand Cage? The things he'd done to survive?

Did it matter? Couldn't we all be forgiven?

I caught Rune's hand in mine and squeezed it again. "Okay," I whispered, my heart thrumming into my throat, panic fluttering in my belly. "We have to get out of this vent. I can do it. I can open a portal."

"I know you can." Rune gave me a final hug and let me go. "Come on, Kenz. Get us out of here."

Cage stayed strangely silent, just when I most wanted his voice. I nodded, running my fingers over the metal wall. "I don't suppose you two have noticed we're on a space station? If I open a door, it might lead outside."

Now Cage spoke, calmer and more controlled than I'd expected. "It might, but I don't think so, not if you open it against the side of the vent. The last two portals you opened led straight through the surface you touched. The side of the vent isn't an exterior wall. And going back isn't really an option. Even if we managed it, we don't know how close behind us the hunters are."

"I hate it when you're reasonable," I grumbled, but his calmness restored some of my own. "All right. Here goes nothing." Unbidden, my mind sought Liam's little nook in the ventilation system. Somewhere like that. Somewhere safe and protected to plan what the hell we did next, somewhere *not* in the vacuum of space. A place like that on the other side of this wall. That was all I needed.

I closed my eyes, prayed very hard we weren't about to die, and reached.

The door opened so close beside me I tumbled out of it, Cage and Rune landing heavily on top of me. A flash of light illuminated over my head, and I got a quick glimpse of the portal I had opened before it faded back to metal. There was a lot of cursing and apologizing as we untangled ourselves and scrambled to our feet to find ourselves exactly where I'd envisioned: right in the middle of Liam's den, complete with Liam himself, gaping at us.

My insides surged with conflicting emotion: relief that I hadn't blasted us into space, fury at the sight of Liam, confusion about where we'd landed. Had we coincidentally been right beside his nook? Maybe I'd subconsciously led us here. . . . In any case, I was coming to terms with the idea of my new status as a chameleon. The thought of regaining some agency, of serving a purpose, revitalized my very core. But I needed time: time to think, to practice, to see what I could do. And that was a luxury we couldn't afford.

"Um," said Liam, "you came out of the wall."

"Yeah, apparently we do that now." I sank onto a nearby crate, too exhausted to argue. "I see you managed to get to safety."

To his credit, he didn't play dumb. He only nodded and gestured toward his computer setup. "I saw what's going on," he said, all the blood draining from his face. He played with the hilt of his stupid sword and shuffled his feet. "They're back, aren't they?"

"It sure looks that way."

Liam laughed shortly. "Fantastic."

Cage and Rune sank down beside me and we all stared at one another bleakly. "The rest of our friends were captured by Legion bounty hunters," I told him. "It's just the three of us now."

"And me, I guess."

My head shot up, my eyes narrowing in suspicion. "I mean, it's not that I don't appreciate the offer. But you never did tell me what you were doing with my comm unit." Fury surged in my chest, and I knew all of it wasn't directed at him. It was all the stress and fear and hurt and anger of the last few hours clawing inside me, desperate to escape. If I let it now, I'd punch Liam in the face before he could explain, so I forced my voice to be calmer, closing my eyes to avoid his strange gaze. "Until you explain that, you aren't going anywhere."

"You aren't in a position to refuse the help, sweetheart."

"Oh, I think we are," said Cage calmly. "Especially if you plan to stab us in the back."

Liam groaned theatrically. "Why the hell would I do that? What would it gain me? Look, I took your comm unit because I was looking for records of the *zemdyut*. Okay? That's all there was to it. I didn't want to say anything earlier because frankly, I don't really like talking about them."

He was still lying. I knew it. Cage and Rune knew it too, judging by the way they glared at him. Did we have time to fight this particular battle? And could we afford to turn down allies right now, no matter how suspect?

Something clattered in the vents, and all four of us froze, sparks of terror reflecting in our eyes. But no one reacted more strongly than Liam. He jerked upright, still as a statue, his jaw gaping in unabashed horror.

That, more than anything, made my decision. I didn't trust Liam. Not for a second. But he sure as hell wasn't working with the aliens. "You're actually going to stand with us?" I demanded.

He laughed shortly. "Hell, no. If I see one of those things, I'm running like hell."

Well, that at least read honestly. "Then why should we take you along?"

"Because at least until I run, you get another gun. If we're closed in, you'd better believe I'll do whatever it takes to get us out of there. And for me, it's try to escape with you or hide in here until the *zemdyut* find me or I starve to death." My stomach rumbled loudly at the mention of food, and he gestured to a nearby shelf. "Help yourselves. It's not enough to last much longer anyway."

Barely daring to hope, I lunged for the cupboard to find an assortment of protein bars and bottled water. I handed them to the others and tore into a bar myself, still crouched on the floor beside the cupboard. It was chalky and overly sweet, but it tasted amazing at that moment. The offer of food went a long way toward making me trust Liam. Of course, I would probably have trusted Priya by this point if she'd handed me a candy bar.

Something at the rear of the cupboard caught my eye. I reached out and examined it. "Liam. Are these . . . ?"

"Stay-awake pills," he said. "Uppers. Barely even illegal."

I hesitated, meeting Cage's eyes over my shoulder. He gestured, and I passed them over. "We've used these before," he said, examining the bottle and showing it to Rune. "There didn't seem to be any long-lasting effects."

"No, but they made us jumpy," Rune pointed out. "Given the current situation . . ."

I shrugged. "Can we take them?" I asked Liam.

"I'm not planning on coming back here."

I nodded at his weaponry, the cutlass and the musket. "Do those actually work?"

"Naturally." He sniffed, apparently deeply offended, and drew the musket to give me a closer look. It was a high-powered laser rifle, one probably costing hundreds of thousands of credits, cleverly designed to look like an antique. I had no idea why anyone would do something like that to a perfectly good rifle.

"Okay, once and for all," said Rune. "Why does it look like that? And why do you, for that matter?"

Liam grinned, back to his cocky self. "When I first came here, I flipped through some books without understanding how historical they were," he explained. "By the time I realized the pirate look was outdated, I'd decided I liked it."

Of course he had. I sighed. "Can Cage take your cutlass?"

Cage blinked. "I've never used a sword, Kenzie."

"No, but with your speed, that could be a pretty deadly weapon in your hands, even against the aliens." And with mine, I reminded myself. But I still wasn't sure how to trigger my new abilities. For Cage, his speed was second nature. For me, it only seemed to appear when I panicked. And if I lost control with that blade in my hand . . . I squared my shoulders. No more accidents.

Slowly he nodded, accepting my logic, and Liam passed him the cutlass without argument. Cage tested the edge with his thumb, wincing as he drew a drop of blood. "Why'd you do that?" Liam demanded.

Cage shrugged, sucking on the wound. "It's what they do in the movies."

Somehow that struck me as incredibly funny, and I had to purse my lips against another hysterical bout of laughter. "Okay," I managed. "We rescue our friends, find a way off

Obsidian, and avoid getting killed by aliens. Anything else?"

"That's not enough?" Liam asked dryly. "My advice, forget your friends. You can't take on the *zemdyut* and Legion."

"We're not abandoning them," said Rune sharply.

Cage laid a soothing hand on her shoulder. "Of course we're not." He gestured to Liam. "You can stay here, if you want. We'll come back for you."

He laughed scornfully, apparently attributing the same lack of honor to us that he'd displayed. "No thanks. I'll tag along. Safety in numbers and all that." He hesitated. "But let's be clear. Once the *zemdyut* show up, it's everyone for themselves. Don't expect me to sacrifice myself to save you."

"I appreciate the honesty." I shoved a few more protein bars into my pockets and stared at the wall. "I wonder if I can open a door anywhere on the station," I said slowly. With a glance over my shoulder at Liam, I added, "Or if you can."

"I told you on my ship. I seem to have burnt out my powers getting here. Or maybe it's a mental block. I don't know. I've tried using them since and nothing happened." He looked very young and tired all of a sudden and scrubbed his fingers over his face. "You have the same power as me?"

"I didn't," I said. "Not until recently. Our powers seem to be changing."

He shrugged. "Yeah, the same thing happened on my planet."

"What?" All three of us spun on him.

"How?" Rune demanded, at the same time that I said, "Explain." We drew forward, fists taut at our sides, our shoulders squared, and faced him down.

Liam seemed taken aback. "How much do you know? Did you figure out where your powers originated?"

I nodded. "Alien genetic manipulation to prep us for harvest, yeah. We've got all that."

"So prolonged exposure to the aliens mutates and shifts those powers. We discovered it ourselves after the first few attacks. It doesn't happen to everyone, and the closer you are in proximity to *zemdyut*, the stronger the effects. Since you lot spent a bunch of time in their alien goop, hanging out on their ship, I'm not surprised your powers are changing."

I frowned. Liam seemed very well informed, and I couldn't remember how much of our story we'd shared with him. But like he said, he knew everything that happened on Obsidian. And he'd shed some light on our situation. "Then the aliens cause the increase in powers?" I asked. "How? And why?"

He shrugged. "I'm not a scientist. I don't know the details. My . . ." He hesitated, his face going strangely pale, highlighting the slight differences, the hints of not-quite-human around his eyes. "My mother studied them. I never listened much. All I wanted to know was how to kill them, how to evade them. She said they emit a low-level radiation that interacts with the powers we already possess. The gunk they soak their victims in amplifies it. She said it wasn't so much that the aliens gave us powers as it was that the aliens *were* the powers."

I reeled. "Are you saying the aliens have powers too?"

"I don't know. They never needed them, not on my planet, at least."

I closed my eyes, coming to terms with this new information. At least I knew what was happening to me. Hopefully it wasn't the first step in transforming into an alien myself. "How did *your* powers change?"

"Honestly, I didn't stick around long enough to find out. But I'm guessing the change is what powered me across the universe." He swallowed hard. "I haven't used my powers since, though. I . . . I can't. Maybe I exhausted them, or maybe I . . . anyway. If you want to get us out of here, you're going to have to open the door." He flashed me a grin. "So where are you taking us?"

"Our original plan was to hit the command deck and get better weapons," Rune offered.

Cage stood up, tucking a protein bar wrapper into his pocket. "Rune? Liam? Any chance you can use the computers to find out where Legion is holding its prisoners?"

Liam shook his head, but Rune closed her eyes. Her lashes fluttered like she was in REM sleep. "Rune?" I asked hesitantly.

She slumped, and Cage caught her, panic written across his face. "Rune. Rune!"

Oh, what now? Terror surged in my chest. If something happened to Rune, too . . . But then she opened her eyes and smiled weakly. "I'm okay. I was just checking to see if I could do it."

"Do what?"

"Access the computer without ever having been in direct contact."

"And?"

"I can." She gave herself a shake. "It was pretty exhausting, and I'd rather not do it too often, but it's good to know it works. Legion is on the command deck, arguing with Grigori Danshov. I don't know what about. I only got glimpses." She gave us a tired smile. "The good news is, they have all the others with them. Everyone looks okay."

We exchanged unhappy glances. "Well," I said, "guess that's where we're going."

THIRTY-FOUR

I GAWKED AT THE PILLS CAGE SHOOK INTO MY hand. "You're *sure* these won't hurt me?" I demanded. My parents and Omnistellar had drilled me on the dangers of drug use from a very young age. I rarely took so much as a painkiller, and here I was staring at a fistful of illegal uppers.

Sorry. *Barely* illegal uppers.

In answer, he popped two pills into his own mouth and swallowed them with half a bottle of water. He leaned against the wall as if bracing himself, eyes closed. A moment later his eyes popped open, his pupils dilated slightly, and he grinned, blinking rapidly. "There we go," he said, and spread his arms. "See? No problem."

Except for the slight tremor in his fingers. I glanced at Rune and she went through the same routine, offering me a reassuring smile. "Prolonged use can be addictive," she said, "but it's not like street drugs, where one dose can kill you. It'll just wake you up. Promise."

Well, it wasn't like I had much choice. The fastest way to the command level was to use my power, and I was too tired to try it again without help. I stared at the pills. They were small and white and completely nonthreatening, and yet somehow the sight of them sent anxiety ramping through my brain.

Cage stepped in front of me, filling my vision, so close he swallowed the oxygen from my lungs. "I promise you'll be okay," he said, cupping my face in his hand and letting me examine him closely. "I wouldn't give you anything that would hurt you."

I tilted my face into his hand, appreciating the reassurance, knowing I was being ridiculous. I wished I had time to talk with him. I hadn't been ready to understand, to forgive, before. Now I thought I could, but now we didn't have the time, or the privacy.

Before I could think any harder, I popped the pills into my mouth, swallowed, and waited.

It didn't take long. For a few seconds nothing happened, and then a rush of energy shot through me, not unpleasant, exactly, but not fun, either. It was a jolt on the edge of pain. I straightened, alertness flowing through my body as my exhaustion faded, and a smile ghosted over my lips. I felt like I could do anything: run a mile or open a portal or even take on the alien creatures. "Oh," I gasped.

Cage's touch against my face suddenly burned, pinpricks of energy that made me want to yank free of him but also to pull him closer. He grinned. "There we go. You ready?"

"I'm ready," I said, and for once I meant it. He leaned toward me, and for a moment I was sure he would kiss me, or I would kiss him. But Rune shuffled her feet impatiently behind him, and Liam coughed, and Cage released me and stepped away.

Not knowing the station made it hard to picture the command level, and Liam's explanations did nothing to help. At last I simply imagined Sanctuary. As soon as I did, the entire layout leaped into my mind with such crystal clarity it almost brought a tear to my eye. I knew Sanctuary was, in many ways, an awful place, imprisoning anomalies for no reason other than their existence, Omnistellar's crown jewel in a collection of lies. But it was still my home, still the last place I'd lived with my family before everything fell apart. Maybe the pills were working on my emotions. I didn't want to think about that too hard.

Focus. Get us out of here. Where could I take us safely? Obsidian's layout wasn't exactly the same as Sanctuary's, but the general design was similar, and I bet some places were exactly the same—like the med bay. Med bays hadn't changed in decades. I visualized Sanctuary's med bay in excruciating detail and extended my mind.

At the last second a frantic fear seized me. What if, instead of taking us to Obsidian's med bay, I opened a door to the hollow where Sanctuary's actual med bay used to be? I pulled, pushed, stumbled over my own adrenaline, and eventually just swore and yanked on the door. The pills both stoked and dulled my fears. They were probably to blame for the sudden terror, but they also made me throw caution to the wind. A flash of light indicated a portal. I opened my eyes, for the first time maintaining it long enough to study it: nothing but a flare of light in the wall, about the size of a door. I glanced at Cage, nodded, and stepped through.

We stumbled into an empty med facility. At first it looked exactly like Sanctuary's, and again I found myself disoriented. After all, the last time I'd stood in that med bay, Cage had ripped a chip out of my arm, I'd learned the bizarre history of my own abilities, and a horde of aliens had torn Rita to shreds. As usual when I thought of Rita, suppressed tears stung my eyelids. Rita was the one person I mourned without any other mixed-up emotions. She hadn't lied to me or betrayed me, and she'd deserved more than death at alien hands.

But quickly I noticed tiny differences. For one, this facility was larger; for another, it wasn't as modern, not as well equipped. The machinery was old, but in excellent repair. Some of the beds were stitched where they'd torn. "There must be medical staff on duty," I murmured. "You'd think there'd be injuries from the aliens."

Liam sniffed. "The *zemdyut* don't injure. They assimilate, and they destroy."

Cage and Liam carried weapons, so they took positions on either side of the door while Rune and I hovered in the background. It made sense for Cage to have the cutlass. It was my idea, after all. And I could hardly demand that Liam hand over his gun. I still wasn't sure I *wanted* a gun. The relief of knowing I hadn't killed Matt didn't change the fact that my shot had gone astray. I *should* have killed him. I thought now I could probably pick up a lethal weapon if I had to, as long as I didn't fire it anywhere with a chance to hit a person. But that didn't make me feel any better about the possibility.

Of course, I wasn't sure I was thrilled with Liam having the gun, either. He'd already admitted he'd throw us into space to save himself, and I suspected there was more to his story, more he wasn't telling us. But taking the gun by force would create a problem, so there we were.

Still, I wasn't quite willing to play the damsel in distress, so I located two scalpels in a nearby supply locker and passed one to Rune. She nodded her thanks. The scalpels probably didn't serve much purpose, but anything made me feel a bit better.

Cage beckoned, and we crept into the deserted corridors: Cage, Rune, and me, Liam bringing up the rear. "Where is everyone?" I whispered. "I thought they evacuated here."

Rune shook her head. "Do you want me to initiate a scan for life signs?"

"No," said Cage. "We don't have time, and we can't risk alerting anyone monitoring the system. We're almost at

Grigori's apartment. Let's just go there, take those bastards by surprise, and hopefully get our friends."

By surprise . . . "Hang on a second," I said. I closed my eyes, focusing on that moment back on the hunter ship when my arm had shimmered into view and I'd reached out to Mia. I expended all of my mental energy, imagining us vanishing, disappearing.

A moment passed. "Um, Kenz," said Cage gently, "what are you doing?"

I gasped and opened my eyes, reeling with the effort. "Trying to make us invisible. Did it work?"

"Not even a little bit," said Liam dryly.

Did that mean I couldn't use powers if the people who possessed them weren't nearby? But wait, that didn't make sense. I frowned. The first two times I'd used the portal-opening ability had been on the hunter ship. And Liam should have been squirreled away in his hole. Unless he'd been closer? I opened my mouth to ask.

At that second, a horrifying scream split the air.

Not a human scream.

One we'd heard before.

My knees gave way and I collapsed to the floor, jamming my fist into my mouth to keep from screaming myself. I'd known they were here, but the shriek was so close, so intense, that it brought back every single memory from Sanctuary, all of the fear and terror and horror, my mother's lifeless body, Rita, the gun bucking as I pulled the trigger. I stared at my hands and found blood suddenly coating them, black and alien, seeping into my skin . . .

Then Cage had me, turning my body, not making a sound as he pulled me against him, his arms tight. "Breathe," he whispered, his voice barely discernible.

The world swam. I focused on Cage, the solidity of his chest against my shoulder, the warmth of his breath against my ear. Staring at the tattoo on his neck, I forced my vision to settle. My heart still raced, my stomach flip-flopping. I risked a glance behind me. Rune clamped her hands over her mouth, leaving her face nothing but wide eyes, and Liam's entire body looked like he'd been hit with a stun blast.

But they'd kept their feet. The only one on the floor shaking like an infant was me. What the hell was wrong with me? I'd faced these things before. I'd beaten them!

Barely. And at the cost of so many lives.

I closed my eyes, clenching my hands into fists. Pills. It had to be the pills. I found my heartbeat and forced it to slow, and then I opened my eyes and nodded at Cage.

Pills. It was only the pills causing this mind-disintegrating terror. And thank God I had them to blame.

Liam drew his gun and Cage his cutlass, and the four of us advanced to the corner. *They can't see you*, I reminded myself. It was so tempting to tell myself to stay back, to let the people with the weapons go first. But if I started doing that, I might never stop. I pressed myself against the wall, clenched my teeth to stay silent, and leaned around the corner.

A tail whipped across the floor as an alien stalked toward the curve in the corridor, its claws clicking almost imperceptibly. It hesitated, sniffing the air, and gave another of those piercing cries.

Another alien emerged from around the corner, hissing and leaning toward the first. I blinked, almost too taken aback for fear. These aliens looked different from the ones on Sanctuary. I mean, not totally different. They were obviously the same kind of creatures. But they were larger, paler in color, with thinner tails and longer claws, claws extending at least six inches beyond what passed for fingers and curving in talons. Everything else was the same: the mottled coloring, the glistening skin, the hunched walk, the shrill cries—and, thank God, the milky-white eyes. It never even occurred to me to look for variations in aliens, or that some of them might have *sight*.

The aliens shrilled to each other, and I closed my own eyes, absorbing the sounds. On Sanctuary, I'd briefly understood bits and pieces of their language, and I'd read it on the ship, at least to a certain degree. If I managed the same thing here . . .

As always, the alien language was impossible to translate, because they didn't speak the way humans did. I got the sense it was only a little bit like a conversation, and also a bit like animals communicating through tone and inflection. Still, I got a sliver here and there. I bit into my tongue, tasting blood and using the pain to refocus, to draw myself further into the alien voices.

At last they quieted. My eyes flew open in time to see a long, slithering tail lash around the corner, and I released a shaky breath. "They're going to the command center," I whispered, glancing to Cage. "At least, I think they are. They're searching for something, or someone. I'm not sure what." I scowled in frustration. "Sorry. I'm not much help."

"That's help," Rune said firmly.

Cage nodded his agreement. "At least we know where they're headed. Let's get into Grigori's apartment and—"

Another scream shattered the air, this one human. We hesitated for a split second before we broke into a run. No matter who it was, we couldn't leave them to the aliens.

We'd only gone a few steps before I realized Liam wasn't behind us. I spun. "Come on!"

He scowled and shook his head. "You three do what you want. I'm not going anywhere."

I hesitated, but we didn't have time to argue. "Give me your gun!" I snapped. "Coward!"

He shrugged and tossed it to me. "It's not going to do much good against those things."

I ignored his comment and snagged it out of midair. My hands trembled around the weapon as I steadied it. This was not a stun gun. It wasn't a pistol like the one I'd fired at Matt, but if I missed with this, whoever I hit wouldn't get up again.

I'd demanded it without thinking and now I almost tossed it aside. The memory of that tail stopped me. I wouldn't shoot, not unless I had a clear shot, not unless I had to. But I also wouldn't be defenseless against those things.

We raced around the corner and found two aliens flanking Bian and Priya, both bounty hunters with their weapons drawn, not seeming to know what to target. Bian bled heavily from claw marks in her arm, and her weapon kept drooping even as Priya barked orders.

Cage swung into action, blasting across the room in a flash of silver and black. He skidded to a halt on the other side of the corridor, poised with his arm stretched behind him, his blade glinting with the fluid from the alien's body.

The alien, its head now separated from its torso, crashed into the floor with a thud. Its body thrashed a moment longer before going still.

The other alien released a scream of utter rage, as if even without sight it knew exactly what had happened. It leaped for Cage with unerring accuracy, and he barely managed to propel himself out of the way. He must have swung his sword as he did so, because a moment later he tumbled to the floor, leaving the cutlass buried in the alien's arm.

He'd missed.

Cage flipped onto his elbows and froze as the creature screamed again. It ignored the sword protruding from its arm, pivoting back and forth in search of him.

Somewhere in the distance, another alien howled.

"What are you waiting for?" I shouted at the hunters. "Kill it!" I raised Liam's musket and targeted as best I could. I knew how to operate a laser rifle, but Omnistellar didn't use them much; traditional weapons and stun guns were more effective. The weird design of the weapon didn't help my limited experience, either. And then of course there were my trembling hands. I hesitated too long, making sure I had a clear shot before I pulled the trigger. By then the alien had slid out of my way.

Rune hovered helplessly behind me as Bian and Priya opened fire on the creature. I lowered the gun, more than happy to leave the shooting to them. The alien moved with bizarre speed and elegance, faster than I remembered the creatures on Sanctuary, its claws slashing for anyone within reach. I lunged out of its way, grabbing Rune and tucking her beneath me, rolling to my side and sheltering us against the wall.

Priya and Bian dove too, but Bian was too slow, and the alien caught her again. She screamed in agony as its claws tore through her neck. "Bian!" Priya roared, and the two women collided on the floor in a messy, bloody heap as she fumbled at Bian's throat, trying to stanch the blood.

The creature targeted them, but Cage launched to his feet, whipping past it. He grabbed the cutlass as he passed and wrenched it free, and the alien gave another shrill scream.

Two more answered.

Close.

Very close.

"We have to get out of here!" I shouted.

Priya straightened, her face pale, and Bian stopped choking, stopped moving. Slowly, Priya passed her hands over the other woman's eyes. Then she raised her arm and fired.

The bullet caught the alien in its left eye. Its head jerked, and its howl echoed through the halls. "Move!" she ordered.

None of us argued. I grabbed Rune, dragged her to her feet, and hauled her the way we'd come. Cage followed at a regular speed, and Priya brought up the rear, running backward with her weapon aimed at the hall behind us.

We returned to where we'd left Liam only to find, unsurprisingly, that he'd vanished. "I thought he'd at least wait for his weapons," I said in disgust.

"Who?" Priya demanded sharply.

I shook my head. "Never mind. You don't . . ."

My voice trailed off, because all at once Priya's posture registered. She'd turned her back to the aliens and now had her gun trained on us. "Sorry," she said. "But in the name of Omnistellar Concepts, the three of you are under arrest."

THIRTY-FIVE

"ARE YOU GODDAMN KIDDING ME?" CAGE demanded. "Didn't you see what happened there? This is survival, not a political battlefield!"

"Survival or not, I always fulfill my contracts." Priya's face was set, unshed tears almost completely hidden. "Drop your weapons and kick them over here or I'll open fire. And I'm not holding a stun gun. I'll aim to incapacitate, not kill, but I can't make any promises."

And who knew what the sound of her weapon might summon? We'd already stayed here too long. I hadn't exactly had time to focus on the alien cries, but the meaning was clear. The creatures were calling reinforcements.

Cage and I exchanged glances over Rune's head. Was drug-fueled adrenaline racing through him the way it was me, urging him to fight, to run? I had to resist it. I was stronger than some drug. I shook my head, and Cage nodded. As one, we dropped our weapons and kicked them to Priya.

She left them where they were, instead removing a pair of cuffs and tossing them to me. "Cuff the boy," she said. I glanced at him. I could see him calculating, but she added, "If you take off, I'll shoot anyone you leave behind."

Cage's expression darkened. He extended his hands in front of him, and I reluctantly slid the cuffs into place. They tightened automatically, blocking his powers and restraining him.

Priya tossed another pair of cuffs in my direction. "Now the girl."

I glanced at Rune, who shook her head, her face despondent. "We always seem to wind up in this situation," she said, offering me her arms.

I resisted the urge to hug her and cuffed her instead.

Priya carefully extended a third set of cuffs, keeping them in her right hand, her left still aiming the gun in our direction. "Now you," she said. "Come over here."

With every step I searched for escape. Maybe Liam would come bursting out of a vent. Maybe something would distract Priya. If she got those cuffs on all three of us, we'd be sitting ducks if the aliens attacked.

But there was nowhere to run, no last-minute rescue on the way, and before I knew it, all three of us were cuffed and shoved against the wall. "Now walk," she said, gesturing toward the staircase.

I opened my mouth to argue, but a shuffling sound in the distance got my feet moving as quickly and quietly as possible. We could escape Priya later. Cage had told me once that prison was better than being eaten by space monsters. I finally understood what he meant.

The door slid open at our approach, and we all hustled through it, even Priya, although she obviously struggled to maintain a steady demeanor. When it closed behind us, we heaved a collective sigh of relief.

If we'd thought that would make Priya drop her guard, though, we were mistaken. She hustled us down the stairs, keeping us at exactly the right distance, her weapon drawn and ready. Cage and I exchanged helpless glances. With our wrists cuffed, our powers disabled, and our friends captured, we had no weapons left . . .

Except words.

"Is this really what you want?" I demanded as Priya herded us into the docking ring. "You saw what the creatures did to your teammate."

"Turn left."

I spun on her instead. "Are you that cold? That *foolish*? You'll let Omnistellar get away with summoning those *things* that murdered your friend just so they can get their hands on some alien tech?"

All at once, Priya's steely demeanor disappeared, and she

jerked herself ramrod straight, a flash of fire igniting her eyes. She lurched forward with such violence I thought she'd swing the butt of her gun right into my face, and I recoiled.

Cage and Rune tucked me behind them. They closed ranks in front of me, shoulder to shoulder. In spite of the situation, a shiver of warmth ran through me. My parents had never stepped between me and danger. No one had. It wasn't the Omnistellar way.

Priya stopped a few feet away, her shoulders locked in a hard line. "I am a professional," she said coldly. "So was Bian. We knew the risks. And don't you dare lecture me, little girl, because I've lost more friends than you can ever imagine."

I pictured everyone on Sanctuary and thought about arguing but dismissed the idea. The steel and resolve in her face rendered any discussion useless.

"Wait," said Rune as we walked. "This isn't the way to your ship."

"No kidding, genius." Priya gestured us against a wall and scanned her thumb at a different berth than the one she'd docked at before. I frowned. Had Legion moved their ship? That seemed unlikely considering they hadn't obtained permission to leave Obsidian earlier. Why would anyone let them hop to another location? And why would they want to?

I got my answer thirty seconds later as we entered the airlock. This wasn't Priya's ship. It wasn't any ship I recognized—

and, at the same time, it was. Even though I'd never been on this particular vessel before, the clean lines, sleek white design, and soft lighting were unmistakable.

I stopped short. "This is an Omnistellar ship."

"What clued you in?" Priya nodded at the giant Omnistellar Concepts logo on the far wall. At the same time, two men advanced along the hall: Matt and the bald man, Finn.

"Where's Bian?" Matt demanded.

Priya shook her head. Matt froze, his eyes meeting mine and asking questions he dared not voice, but Finn showed no visible reaction. He grabbed Cage and hauled him away from me, and I had to physically resist the urge to leap after them.

Matt sighed, rubbing the back of his neck and shuffling his feet. For a moment I almost thought he might say something to Priya, but instead he muttered, "Come on, Rune."

She glared at him, utter fury and hatred transforming her face into something twisted. "Make me." I'd never heard so much rage and betrayal in her voice, not even when she'd yelled at me and Cage for lying to her.

Priya shoved her from behind. "If she resists, toss her over your shoulder and carry her. Just get those two locked up with the others."

With the others. Tension I hadn't realized I was holding relaxed. They must have returned our friends to the ship after Rune spotted them, which meant they hadn't been slaughtered and devoured.

"And me?" I demanded, my chest sinking.

"You're wanted elsewhere."

Rune, Cage, and I looked at one another. I desperately hoped one of them had a brilliant idea, and they probably prayed for the same from me. But nothing was forthcoming, and a moment later Finn and Matt led the twins away. Rune opted against physical force, instead spewing an onslaught of vitriol like I'd never heard in Matt's direction. He pretended impassivity, but the tension in his shoulders stood out in sharp relief beneath his armor, and I derived at least a little satisfaction from the sight.

But not much, because Priya dragged me down another corridor and shoved me into a conference room of sorts. "What am I—?" I began, but she closed the door in my face.

I yanked on the handle and found that, of course, she'd locked it. I examined my surroundings: a small office with a table and five chairs. A tray of glasses and a pitcher of water rested on a shelf on the far wall, and a recessed holoscreen sat above it. That was it, no windows, no interactive screens, nothing, only a man staring out the window, his hands clasped behind his back. I took a shaky step in his direction and his shoulders tightened before he turned.

"Oh my God," I whispered. "Dad?"

He smiled uncertainly. "Hi, Kenzie."

"Dad!" I repeated, and launched myself into his arms. It was really him. I hadn't believed, not for one second, that

Omnistellar would let him come to me, but here he was, flesh and muscle and the rough half beard he always grew in space. He clasped me tightly against his chest, my hands sandwiched between us, and rocked me, almost like a child. We pulled apart, his eyes large and bright with unshed tears. "Oh, my baby girl," he murmured, cupping my face in his hands. "I was so scared. I thought I'd never see you again."

"Dad," I whispered. It seemed to be the only thing I could say. I stared into his dark eyes. He was as neat and tidy as ever, his uniform pristine, but he looked a bit thinner, a bit paler. Had it really only been a few weeks since I'd seen him?

"It's me, Kenz." He hugged me again, and for a moment I forgot everything: the bounty hunters and the aliens and Matt and my friends and the chip, and I trembled with relief that I still had a parent, and one who loved me. "Kenz," he murmured. "I'm so sorry. I . . ."

"Don't apologize." I buried my head in his shoulder and tried to channel everything I couldn't say into my voice. "I know why you chipped me. I understand, and Dad, I don't . . . I can't . . ."

"Oh, honey." He pulled me closer, and I let him cradle me like a child. Relief flooded me. For the first time since Cage and Alexei had taken me hostage, someone older and stronger was in charge, someone who would listen. He just needed to know the whole story, understand what he was facing.

But that meant I had to detail what had happened to Mom,

and the words stuck in my throat like molasses. "Dad," I managed at last, "Mom, she . . ."

"I know, honey. Matt told us everything."

"He couldn't have told you everything. Not how vicious those things are, how single-minded. They came to kill and harvest and nothing else." I searched for a way to make myself clear. This was my last chance. I had to get through to him. "There's no reasoning with them, no fighting them, no resistance. They'll just kill and slash until they get what they want."

"Kenzie," he said, very softly. "*I know.*"

I closed my eyes against a sudden rush of terror. Dad's words made it impossible to stay in my happy bubble. I couldn't pretend he was ignorant. "If you know everything, why are you going along with this plan? Those things *killed Mom*. They killed *Rita*. They tried to *harvest* me. And you, what, opened the door and invited them in?"

Dad sighed heavily. "Sweetheart. You're not seeing the big picture."

I withdrew a few steps, examining my father. He was so familiar to me and yet so strange, too, like someone else wearing my dad's face. "What happened to you?" I whispered.

All at once his lips drew together, his jaw tightening, his eyes narrow. "What happened to me? You're the one running around the solar system with escaped criminals! Blowing up spaceships! Ignoring company laws!"

"Because I'm one of them," I said slowly, watching his reaction. "I'm an anomaly too."

"It's not the same."

"No, because I had parents who could help me." I started to reach for him, but the cuffs caught my wrist again. I waved my bound hands impatiently. "You and Mom loved me enough to chip me. You lied to me because you thought I'd be better off not knowing. I get that now." His expression melted, the hard lines of his Omnistellar mask melting into the father who loved me, but I pressed on before he could interrupt. "Now I need that same trust from you. Dad, you haven't encountered these things. I have. You can't go along with Omnistellar's plan."

"I don't have a choice."

"Of course you do." I swallowed, reminding myself that only a few weeks ago, I might have said the same thing. "Things aren't what they seem. If you just give me and my friends a chance, we can explain everything."

He frowned, shaking his head. "Lives and futures depend on that alien technology. I know how scary they were. But we're not going to let them hurt anyone. Especially not you."

My hands trembled. I clenched them into fists. "So, all the work we did to destroy the ship was pointless. Omnistellar summoned the aliens. And why? To get their hands on alien tech?"

"There's more going on than you realize. If you'll just calm down and trust me . . ."

"No." I repeated myself, staring deep into Dad's eyes. "You

trust me, Dad. Come with me. Talk to my friends. Give us a chance."

"It's against—"

I groaned. "If you say the word 'regulations,' I swear to God, I will start throwing things." It unsettled me how much I sounded like Mia. It unsettled me more that I didn't mind.

Dad's eyebrows shot up. "We live by regulations."

"Mom lived by regulations. She was willing to kill me because of regulations. And she died because of them." I tried to jerk my thumb over my shoulder, forgetting again that I was cuffed, and almost wrenched my arm out of its socket. "All those people on Obsidian are dying because of regulations. Was that part of the plan?"

Dad's silence spoke volumes, and the floor seemed to give way beneath me. I staggered to a chair and sank into it, still staring at Dad the whole time. "My God. It *was* the plan."

"We needed a quiet way to eliminate Obsidian without inflaming their contacts on Earth. The underworld is an unfortunate reality, and we have to deal with it. The inhabitants of Obsidian, though . . . they're criminals, Kenzie, every single one of them. Criminals who'd started to think they were in control of us instead of the other way around. And not just pickpockets and scumbags. Mobsters. Assassins. They live outside the reach of the law. Do you know how many people they kill every year? The solar system is safer without them."

"I was on that station!" I shouted, the words exploding with

such rage they almost took on physical force. It wasn't enough that my own mother was willing to kill me. My dad, too?

He staggered a step, eyes flashing with rare anger. "And you're here now, aren't you? You and your hooligan friends. Why do you think I sent the hunters after you? It was to get you off Obsidian before the aliens arrived! Legion had strict orders not to harm you in any way, you or any of your friends." He smiled faintly. "It's not my fault you turned out to be rather skilled at evading them."

"Don't you dare try to make this a joke." I glared at him. "What about the kids on the station, huh? The ones born there, who didn't do anything at all. Is it okay to kill them, too?"

A glimmer of something human passed over his expression again. Hope surged inside me. Maybe I could reach him after all. But his next words could have come from the Omnistellar training manual. "If there had been a way to help them, we would have. But it's too late. They've grown up in that place, surrounded by criminals, and . . . well, every war has some casualties, sweetheart." He spoke that last part in barely a whisper, not daring to meet my eyes.

I reeled. "Is that what you believe? Or what Omnistellar told you?"

"There's no difference. You knew that once."

He'd dug in to the Omnistellar line. I changed tactics. "Since when do you have the authority to order teams of hunters, anyway?"

Dad shrugged. "As the only ranking individual who'd had contact with the fugitives—which includes you now, by the way—who else would they put in charge of this mission?"

I felt like I was going to be sick. "You have *no idea* what you've unleashed."

"Of course we do. The aliens cleared out Obsidian, or most of it, anyway. We're going to flood the station with powerful gas. Hopefully we can reclaim Obsidian, but if not, we'll destroy the place. There will be no one to blame once news of the alien attack leaks. You don't have to worry. We're perfectly safe. Omnistellar won't let those things near Earth, near any human settlement. After that, we take their ship, just like you did." He sighed and turned his back to me, his shoulders taut beneath his uniform. "Look, I get how this sounds. But that's why you were a junior guard. You're not old enough to understand the complexities of how corporations work, of the sacrifices we sometimes need to make for the greater good. I need you to trust me here. That's all I'm asking."

I shook my head, betrayal warring with the need to speak, to reach him. "Trust you? This is the most ridiculous idea I've ever heard. You are connected to Obsidian. Those things rip through the hulls of spaceships. Nothing is going to stop them."

"We learned from what Matt told us, Kenzie. This ship was originally designed for high-security covert operations. The entire hull is outfitted with triple-reinforced steel and electric shields. Nothing gets through here without a blowtorch. It's—"

The ship heaved violently, and the chair lurched beneath me, throwing me to the floor. My bound elbows hit the carpet, skidding and shredding skin on the industrial fibers until I smashed into the side of the table. The world spun, and the room plunged into darkness.

THIRTY-SIX

"DAD!" I SHOUTED. "DAD, ARE YOU THERE?"

No response. I fumbled in the dark, dragging myself along the floor, groping with my bound hands. The emergency lights flickered to life. I scrambled to where my father lay slumped on the floor and struggled with his weight, heaving him onto his side. I found his pulse, fast and uneven. Blood smeared the side of his head.

"Come on, Dad," I muttered, shaking his uniform jacket. Sure enough, I found the chip that unlocked my cuffs in his breast pocket. Awkwardly, I angled my hands to scan it over the cuffs, and they dropped away. I kicked them for good measure and pocketed the chip. I never wanted to wear any kind of restraints again. Was this what had made Cage so desperate to escape Sanctuary? The prisoners spent their lives chipped and monitored. I'd long since stopped being angry with them for taking me hostage, but now I understood their motivations on a deeper level.

I had to learn what was happening on the ship. On the off chance they'd left Jasper his communicator, I triggered my own with a thought.

A wave of agonizing pain overwhelmed me. I screamed, pitching to the floor and clawing at my head as if I could scrape the shards of torment from behind my eyes.

The pain faded, leaving me gasping at my comm device in astonishment. I stroked my finger over it. What had just happened? I'd had my comm device since I was fifteen. I'd never gotten this kind of feedback before.

Did I dare retry? I hesitated. My heart clamored at the thought of more pain, but on the other hand, the comm unit was my only hope of contacting the others. Staring at my distorted reflection in its surface, I ground my teeth and triggered it again.

The agony was even worse this time. I tasted blood as I bit through my own lip. I signaled the comm device to deactivate, but the pain distracted me, shoving my effort aside and doubling me over in torment. I used the pain to narrow my thoughts, deactivating the damn thing on the third attempt.

If that first attack was a warning, this was the real thing. I yanked the comm out of its slot, leaving a metal hollow in my arm, and gaped at it in disbelief, this thin metal circle that was so much a part of my life. Having it turn against me felt like almost as much of a betrayal as my parents siding with the company.

Part of me wanted to throw it away, but I couldn't quite bring myself to do it. Still, I sure as hell didn't want it connected to my body, so I tucked it into my pocket.

Only one person other than me had touched that device. Liam.

It had to be him. He'd done this. But how? And *why*?

It didn't matter. If I ever saw Liam again, we'd be having a very serious conversation, one that just might end with me using my newfound abilities to open a hole inside *him*.

Nanakorobi yaoki . . . fall down seven times, get up eight. Except I'd lost count. I was probably on nineteen or twenty by now. What wisdom would *Robo Mecha Dream Girl 5* contain about *that*?

Dad was alive, but I couldn't wake him, and I didn't know how badly he was injured. I hesitated. Dad's omnicard allowed me to access almost anything on the ship. Only a few very sensitive systems actually required biometric scans, which were too complicated for a secure area like a spaceship. The smartest thing for me, for my friends, was to focus on escape.

I looked at Dad lying on the floor, fresh blood oozing from where he'd hit his head, but otherwise so peaceful, like he was napping on our couch at home. And I remembered going to my first Knicks game when I was nine years old, and eating popcorn for supper when Mom left town, and the absolute devastation when he'd told me he and Mom were splitting up.

And naturally I remembered Mom, her eyes sightless and staring, those white alien cataracts like a film trapping her soul.

My friends needed me.

Dad needed me more.

I hesitated, hovering over him. My powers were changing. Growing. Maybe I'd adopted Imani's or Reed's healing abilities. Even as I thought it, though, I remembered my inability to turn invisible in the corridor. Still, it was worth a try. I pressed my hands against Dad's wounds and willed every ounce of healing energy I could summon into his body.

Nothing. At least, no change I could see. And I didn't have time to mess around any longer. Maybe my friends were out of range, or maybe if I tried a bit harder, a bit longer, I'd find a connection to that healing ability. But I didn't know how long Dad had, and I couldn't afford to wait.

Grinding my teeth, I reached for the comm device embedded in the wall. Dad had his own wrist comm, of course, but they were attuned to individual brain waves and DNA; his would be of no use to me. I swiped his card to activate the comms and said, "Medical. Come in, please."

No answer, not even a faint buzz to indicate a connection.

I frowned. Medical should never be deserted, not ever. The light on the touchscreen was green, so I knew the problem wasn't on my end. "Medical?" I repeated. "This is an emergency. Come in, please."

Nobody answered. I closed my eyes, braced myself, and said, "Security. Come in, please."

Nothing.

Okay, now I was worried. This was Omnistellar we were talking about, the most paranoid corporation in the entire solar system. There was no way, *none*, they didn't have an alert security force with their comms active.

Unless security was too busy responding to another threat to deal with random calls?

I threw caution to the wind. "This is Kenzie Cord, Omnistellar security clearance 3524-89A," I said, although I was sure they'd have blanked my code. Maybe it would catch someone's attention. "If anyone can hear me, please respond. I have an emergency situation."

No answer. I slammed my fist into the wall in frustration. "This is Kenzie Cord. I'm a wanted criminal and I'm holding your commanding officer at gunpoint. If someone doesn't answer me this second, I'll pull the trigger."

Silence.

I sank to my knees, monitoring my father's chest as it rose and fell. Either comms had failed throughout the ship, an unheard-of situation for Omnistellar, or . . .

Or there was no one to answer them.

I sat another minute with my legs curled beneath me, staring at Dad, running through options in my head and rejecting them. I had no idea where anyone was, if anyone was left, no idea if I was alone or if aliens had overrun the ship or if my friends were alive.

The rush from the pills I'd taken earlier had worn off. I wished for another dose. One more, ten more, I didn't care at this point. I needed something to get me through this situation. Dad's blood coated my hands. They'd been wet with Mom's once before, with Rita's before that. I'd soaked my hands in Matt's blood, in Tyler's, in Mia's and Cage's.

It seemed like ever since the aliens had shown up, the people I was closest to kept winding up dead. That didn't bode well for my friends.

I didn't know how long I sat there, but eventually I realized I had to do something. I went through Dad's pockets again, hoping for a weapon. No such luck. Either he'd been suspicious enough to disarm himself before coming to visit, or someone had insisted. In spite of myself, I hoped it was the latter.

I considered pulling him under the table to hide him, but I wasn't sure how badly he was injured, or if I'd hurt him worse by moving him. I reached for the lights but stopped myself. The aliens didn't rely on sight. We did. If a medical or security team happened along, I wanted him found; if it was something else, darkness wouldn't shield him.

I did lock the door behind me, though, scanning Dad's omnicard to do so.

I found myself in a familiar Omnistellar corridor. Doors lined the walls, leading, I guessed, to more conference rooms and offices. At least that would be the case if this ship functioned anything like Omnistellar's usual design. I went in the opposite direction and rounded a corner. Only two doors graced this corridor, one on either side: ENGINEERING and COMMAND LEVEL 1.

Steadying myself, I scanned Dad's omnicard and entered the command center.

Half of me expected to find myself facing a horde of startled Omnistellar pilots and ship's crew in a split-second face-off before they drew their weapons. The other half expected to find nothing at all, more empty stillness—just like Obsidian.

I did not expect to find a slaughter.

The smell hit me first, copper and decay and something hard and astringent. At first, I didn't even know what I was looking at. My eyes took in the sight, but my brain struggled to catch up, to process the pools of drying blood, the sightless stares of a dozen Omnistellar crew members draped around the room. Some lay where they'd fallen on the floor. Some slumped in chairs. Lots of them had run for the exit and had died where they fell.

I took a hesitant step forward, then another. I followed the fingers of an arm to its shoulder. It had been torn right off the body that owned it.

In the same instant my brain finally processed the reality of the situation. Bile surged in my throat and I spun, spewing vomit over the floor, further desecrating this killing ground. As I straightened and wiped my mouth on my sleeve, I found myself eye to eye with a woman. She'd died against the wall, propped against a console, her mouth stretched wide in a mask of terror. Her face was inches from my own. We stared at each other, and I realized I was waiting for her to blink first.

I staggered back, almost slipping in a puddle of blood but managing to catch myself against the wall as I fumbled for the door. My feet teetered on the edge of a massive, gaping hole. I threw myself aside, landing in something wet and crying out in spite of my resolve to stay silent. The hole was at least six feet wide with jagged, sharp edges. I couldn't see below and didn't want to. Instead, I struggled to my feet, slipping once more in blood, finding the wall and spinning. With Dad's omnicard clenched hard enough to leave grooves in my hands, I slashed it past the card reader again and again, screwing up the reading so badly I had to stop, close my eyes to calm down, and give it one steady pass.

The door beeped and opened, and I ran into the hall. As it slid shut behind me, I drew great gasps of air, cleansing the stench of the command center from my lungs. My hands shook around the omnicard, and it clattered to the floor. I dropped beside it, still sucking in air until my lungs burned with the effort. One of my cousins had asthma, and I'd seen her gasping for breath before she was treated. This felt the same as she'd looked, like someone was closing a hand over my throat, leaving me less than a straw's width to breathe through. I hunched my shoulder forward, gasping, choking.

I'd seen death before but, for the most part, it was . . . *clean.* The kids who'd died on Sanctuary mostly died in the clear goop the aliens used to preserve them, no signs of visible injury. I'd seen the result of my own gunshot at Matt, and I'd seen what the aliens did to Tyler, but that was nothing, *nothing,* to an entire room of eviscerated people. And I'd never been great with even small amounts of blood. The carnage behind me . . . I was amazed I was still conscious.

I sat against the wall, staring at the closed door to the command center. I should go back in there. Search the bodies for weapons. Access the computer system and try to learn what had happened. Find the holding cells. Something.

But I couldn't move. I couldn't return. I simply couldn't. After all, it wasn't like their weapons did the ship's crew much good. If I survived, it probably wouldn't be because I'd shot my way out of the situation. And I'd hesitated on Obsidian. I wasn't the same with guns, not anymore. Maybe not ever again.

I swallowed hard, glancing down the hall to where Dad rested behind a door: my last link to a normal life, to my family. The last person from Omnistellar I'd thought I trusted. If I left him alone here and the aliens returned . . .

But if I stayed with him, I had no hope of protecting him. At least unconscious, he'd be silent. His only hope was if I found him help.

Where else could I go? I glanced behind me, at the big door indicating the entrance to engineering. I could access the computer system there. But what if I found another massacre?

I dropped my head to my hands and forced myself not to hyperventilate. Those people were dead. I couldn't help them. But my father and, I hoped, my friends were still alive. If the aliens had killed those people, and I had to assume that was the case, even though I'd never seen them attack like that before, then they were cleaning house, and I didn't have much time. And on the off chance that it *wasn't* the aliens, I had even less. It put a time limit on the driving need to figure out what was going on and who was responsible.

Either way, I couldn't keep sitting here.

I willed my legs to move. At last I managed to stagger to my knees. That seemed to give me some strength. Gripping the wall, I pulled myself to my feet and then, much more cautiously than before, I opened the door to engineering.

THIRTY-SEVEN

I PLASTERED MYSELF AGAINST THE WALL and held as still and silent as possible. The room lacked windows. A solid wall ran the length of the corridor, so I couldn't even peek inside. But when nothing screamed or lunged or attacked, I risked peering around the corner.

Engineering, thank God, was not the slaughterhouse I'd seen in the command center. Instead it was totally empty.

I ran through a list of my friends' powers, but it seemed like they had to be close enough for me to use them, and I didn't know where anyone was. I didn't even know my own range. As a test, I stared at my own hand and willed it invisible. It remained stubbornly perceptible. I *had* opened doors without Liam around, though. Why? Because he'd been closer than I realized, or because something about his power specifically connected to me? I chewed on my lip as I considered that, but in the end, I dismissed the idea. For one, I didn't see why Liam's ability should be different from anyone else's, which meant he'd probably been closer than I'd realized when I used his abilities before. Why, I didn't know. I didn't understand anything about the guy and wasn't likely to start now.

But I had another reason not to start throwing portals around the spaceship: I didn't dare open a door if I didn't know where I was going. On Obsidian, I'd started to suspect my portals did more than reach through walls, that they crossed space. But anytime I'd opened one before, I'd visualized where I was going. I couldn't do that on this ship, and I didn't want to risk winding up inside the engine or something, so I stepped into engineering the old-fashioned way and took in the lay of the room. It was a typical engineering department for an Omnistellar ship. I'd spent a bit of time in them before, not enough to learn much, but enough to know how things were arranged. If I was right, the computer core should be in the opposite corner.

Sure enough, I found it, an unassuming small box that definitely didn't look like it should run the entire ship. I called up an interface, but I was scared to mess with it too much. If I accidentally deactivated life support or something, we'd have a much bigger problem than aliens. And I wasn't sure how far the system would let me go without a biometric scan, anyway.

Still, I found a rough map of the ship. It wasn't as big as I'd suspected, and the layout was pretty standard Omnistellar. The command center was fore. Unlike Sanctuary, this ship had two command centers, the main one upstairs for command and security, and a secondary center for navigation below. Was the lower level a monsters' killing field too? Shoving the thought aside, I scanned for the holding cells and found them aft, one level below. At least I had a destination.

Still, it took a few minutes to convince myself to leave engineering. It was quiet and reassuring in there, between the hum of the engine, the computer whirring to itself, and the total absence of dead bodies. I suddenly realized this was the first time I'd been alone, really alone, in weeks. Before Sanctuary, I'd considered myself a solitary, introverted person. I'd never had many close friends. My parents were busy with work. I'd been okay with that. Sure, I went out now and then, and I played on local basketball teams whenever the opportunity presented itself. But I was just as happy curled up in bed with the latest issue of *Robo Mecha Dream Girl 5* and a cup of chai as I was surrounded by other kids.

But the last week or two, almost without knowing it, I'd come to depend on my friends. Cage, always ready with a grin and a quip. Imani, her quiet strength and intelligence. Rune, her gentle kindness, yet with a core of fierce determination. Even Mia. She might be a powder keg, but I knew that whatever happened, she'd have my back. It felt like years since I'd faced anything alone, not a matter of weeks.

You don't have a choice, I reminded myself. I clenched my hands into fists, wishing for a weapon, even if it wouldn't do much good. Something to hold on to. My thumb brushed the ring on my right hand, a sixteenth-birthday present from my parents, and Dad's face flashed through my mind, bloody and yet somehow tranquil as he lay on the office floor.

Somehow, that calmed me, strengthening my resolve. With steady hands, I scanned Dad's omnicard to leave engineering. Mom might have given up on me. Dad might have let Omnistellar suck him into their plan. But what set me apart from them was my choices, and I chose to save my dad, to go after my friends.

The hall remained eerily empty and silent. How many people staffed this ship? Where were they? Was the entire crew dead in the command center? I cast a quick glance toward the conference room where I'd left Dad, reassuring myself it remained safe and secure, resisting the urge to check on him again. Staring at his limp body wouldn't help him. But finding my friends, especially the ones with the power to heal, might.

According to my map, the lift to the lower level was on my right. I crept that way, ears perked for any sound of movement. I saw nothing. I heard nothing. It was driving me up the wall. I would have almost preferred a glimpse of the aliens at this point. The constant waiting, the fear, the gnawing panic in my heart: none of them offered anything to grab on to, only a constant gaping void of terror.

I reached the lift without incident: a large black circle on the floor. I stepped onto it and passed Dad's omnicard by the

screen on the wall. The circle descended, another instantly sliding into place above my head. I plummeted through a solid
tube, track lighting crossing the walls, clear plexiglass preventing me from touching anything on my sides. I closed my eyes
against a burst of claustrophobia. I used to like tube lifts. Now
they felt like a prison.

The ride wasn't long, though, and a moment later, a rush
of cool air told me I'd left the tube behind. I opened my eyes
as the disc lowered into place on the floor below. When I was a
kid, my parents were stationed on a prison with a tube lift, and
two other girls and I used to make a game of jumping off the
disc at increasing heights, until we got caught and grounded.
Now I found myself afraid to leave the disc at all.

The computer chimed, and its pleasant androgynous voice
advised me to vacate the space. I leaped into action, my heart
thrumming. *Stupid, stupid, stupid.* I waited with bated breath
for a shrill alien scream to respond to the computer.

Nothing.

I stood in another empty, sterile hallway. Medical was
ahead on my left, the command center's lower domain on my
right. According to the map, most of this level contained dor-
mitories and living quarters, but I was willing to bet my friends
were here too, in the holding cells at the rear of the ship.

Assuming they still lived.

I took three steps toward the stern of the ship, and the
emergency lights vanished, plunging me into darkness.

Half a scream escaped me before I clamped my lips together. Sheer terror overwhelmed me. I scrambled in the blackness until my hand reached the wall. I clung to it like a lifeline, cringing, making myself as small as possible. My heart drummed in my ears, impossibly loud, as I waited for sight to return the way it does when the lights go out.

But that was on Earth, where your eyes only needed to adjust to a lower level of illumination. This was space. There was not even a glimmer or gleam, and my eyes had no way to adjust. I was completely blind.

The reassuring thrum of the ship's systems continued in the background, telling me the life support still functioned. But why had the lights gone off? And how?

Did I dare risk reconnecting my wrist comm, or would the command to trigger its luminous function send agony tearing through my brain? I'd definitely used it after leaving Liam's hideout, but he could have triggered a virus remotely. Either way, I didn't want to try it. The pain had been worse the second time I'd triggered my comms. If I activated it a third time, it might very well knock me out, leaving me lying unconscious on the floor for whoever—or *what*ever—happened along.

Medical always stored emergency flashlights. I groped along the wall the way I'd come, reaching the corner. I was glad I'd taken the time to examine the map, to note my surroundings. This would have been a lot harder if I'd been blind *and* lost. As it was, every step sent panic racing through me. At least I didn't have to leave the wall. I clutched it, letting it lead me on until my fingers brushed the edge of the door.

I wasn't a hundred percent sure Dad's omnicard still worked given the power outage, but when my outstretched grip found the scanner, I swiped it anyway. Sure enough, a soft whoosh and the scent of astringent and cleanser indicated the doors opening. I slid my hand over the entrance, unwilling to lose the edge of the space, and entered.

As the door slid shut behind me, I realized things had gotten a lot dicier. In the halls I'd known that as long as I stuck to the walls, I'd have a clear path to retreat. But I'd never seen these med facilities before. They could, and probably did, have items around the perimeter. So where would the flashlights be? With the emergency supplies, obviously, but where were they? I had no choice but to delve around in the dark until I found them.

I took a hesitant step forward, my left hand glued to the wall, my right waving gently in front of me. When I didn't encounter anything, I took another step, and another. My fingers brushed something. I risked running my hands over it. A medical scanner, by the shape of it. I kept contact, easing myself around its edge and back to the wall, where I resumed my agonizing progress.

It seemed to take forever to cover the maybe twenty feet from the door to the corner. I encountered a cupboard along the way and carefully slid it open, rummaging through it as silently and carefully as I dared, but I didn't feel anything like an emergency supply box. On Sanctuary, on every Omnistellar facility I'd ever seen, we stored the emergency supplies in command centers, medical, and engineering in a large plastic crate with the word EMERGENCY stamped on all sides. I was pretty sure I'd know it when I found it.

I resumed my careful trek on the long second wall. I encountered more obstacles now: a bed, a desk, another cupboard. I checked under the bed and desk and in the cupboard but found them all empty save for the standard medical supplies. For a moment my hand ghosted over something in the desk that felt like a tablet, and hope soared. Even a glimmer of light would be welcome. But when I punched the keys, nothing happened. Someone had let their battery run down to nothing.

My knees gave way, and I knelt there in the black, my hand pressed over my own mouth. The darkness, the silence, were getting to me. I was imagining sounds. Imagining the sensation of ghostly hands brushing my face. I reached out, trying for Rune's powers, searching for a connection with the computer. Nothing. Either I couldn't access her powers at all, or I was still out of range. Regardless, I was on my own.

You're probably a quarter of the way through the room, Kenzie. You can do it. Come on.

I forced myself to my feet. Once I'd done that, it became easier to keep moving. I really hoped to find the emergency supplies along a wall. But if I reached the exit without finding them,

I'd have to face the possibility that they were somewhere in the middle of the room. That meant stumbling through the dark without even the wall to guide me. Panic threatened to choke me, and I forced it down resolutely. One problem at a time.

I reached the med facility's alternate entrance on the far wall. My heart beating a little faster, I pressed on. A few minutes later, I found a whole row of cupboards. I pulled the first one open and rummaged through it. Bandages. Small containers of medication. Sealed plastic crates, but none of them big enough to hold emergency supplies. At least, I didn't think they were, and I didn't want to mess with them in the darkness. What if they contained syringes or scalpels?

The second cupboard held more of the same, but in the third I found a large plastic crate on the bottom shelf. I eased the lid open and searched inside, my body sagging with relief as my fingers closed over exactly what I wanted: a light box with an elastic strap to fit over my wrist or skull.

But as I went to turn it on, a sound I *hadn't* imagined reached my ears: the long, slow drag of something over the floor, followed by an extended hiss.

I wasn't alone in this room.

THIRTY-EIGHT

I FROZE, CLUTCHING THE FLASHLIGHT, MY heart seeming to stop altogether. Maybe the sound wouldn't come again. But it did: the unmistakable drag of a tail over the floor.

My fingers fumbled on the flashlight. I pressed the button and light flooded the cupboard in front of me, so bright it stung my eyes and set my teeth on edge. Slowly, I released the button, not allowing it to make even the hint of a click. Just as slowly, I maneuvered into a kneeling position and turned around.

The creature stood on the other side of the med facility. It resembled the ones I'd seen on Obsidian, bigger and more menacing than the aliens we'd encountered on Sanctuary. Had they sent something stronger, darker, to hunt the monsters who stole their ship and killed the harvesters? The possibility sent chills down my spine.

Fortunately, it seemed as blind as the monsters on Sanctuary,

shifting from side to side. Did it hear me? Just in case, I slid farther along the wall, away from the cupboard I'd pulled open in
the dark.

As I moved, something caught my peripheral vision. I
angled the flashlight to my right in time to see another of the
creatures stalk past the alternate exit. My blood ran cold. Mere
minutes ago, I'd crept along that wall, using it as guidance in
my progress around the room. How close had I come to touching one of those things? I hadn't heard a sound from them,
not a click of claws, nothing. Had they only recently arrived?
How? From where? Did they open portals like me? Or were
they hunting me, waiting, tracking my movements in complete
and utter silence?

I cast the light the way I'd come. I'd planned to leave
through the far door, but that escape route was no longer an
option. My only hope was to retreat and make my way to the
holding cells in the corridor outside. I stayed low, crawling at a
snail's pace. The creatures didn't do anything, simply hovering
in what almost looked like suspended animation except for the
occasional quirk of their heads. I was afraid to even breathe too
deeply. Aside from the occasional flicker of my flashlight over
my left shoulder to make sure there weren't more of the things,
I kept them in my spotlight.

It was the closest I'd seen them. The bright light did nothing to make them less horrifying, bringing them into sharp
relief: glistening skin, curved fangs, sinewed limbs. Every

instinct screamed at me to run, but I didn't dare. I moved as slowly as my racing heart allowed, my soft-soled shoes nearly noiseless against the floor. After every halting step, I paused, waiting to see if they'd noticed.

I'd made it about halfway across the room when something changed. My heart stuttered as the alien by the far door jerked its chin up, sniffing the air. It tilted its head and screeched to its partner. The other creature slapped its tail against the wall and howled in response. I froze in utter terror. I'd understood just enough of those cries to catch the sense of prey, a call to hunt.

A surge of adrenaline burned through my caution, and I bolted for the exit. The monster behind me screamed, and I barely had time to register surprise in its tone. They hadn't been reacting to me after all.

They were now, though.

I was still ten feet from the door when one of the aliens vaulted into the air. Its mottled head grazed the ceiling panel, but it must have somehow sensed the proximity, controlling its height to land directly in front of me. It hunched on its hind legs, a long, pointed black tongue protruding from its mouth, tasting the air like a snake. I skidded to a halt. A clatter from behind warned me just in time, and I threw myself to the side as the other creature landed directly where I'd been standing.

Forcing my heart to beat through my panic, I belly-crawled along the floor, the flashlight clutched in one hand. I dragged myself toward a nearby bed and wiggled into the space beneath it. The aliens screamed their horrible shrill cry. *Hunt it. Contain it. Kill it.*

I was pretty sure I'd liked it better when I didn't understand them at all.

I sank my teeth into my lip and drew myself into a tight ball, folding my limbs in on each other, clutching the flashlight to my chest with trembling hands. I shook so hard the light cast the recesses of my hasty hiding place into sickly shadows, but I stayed completely still otherwise, even holding my breath as long as possible before drawing slow, silent gasps.

A tail swished past me. Then one on the other side. Their cries grew more agitated. They knew where I'd been, where I'd vanished, but they couldn't find me. Not yet.

But they would. Sooner or later, I'd have to move, and these things were relentless. . . .

There was a soft swish. It took me a moment to register it as the sound of the door sliding open. Both creatures froze, their muscles tensing in anticipation, and an even brighter light than my own cut through the darkness. "Hey!" a man called. "Over here!"

The creatures screamed and leaped into the light. Gunfire ricocheted, so loud I dropped the flashlight and clamped my hands over my ears. That wasn't a single gunshot. It was the sound of automatic fire, and maybe a laser blast mixed in for good measure.

It lasted less than a minute. Everything went quiet, and the light flickered around the room. "Come on out," he called. "They're dead."

I closed my eyes. I recognized the voice now. My mind raced, searching for an alternative method of escape. I almost preferred the aliens.

"Keeeenzieeeeee," Hallam sang, his voice teasing. "I know it's you. Come on, girl. You really want to face more of those things on your own?"

"Don't make us come after you." That was Priya, clipped and tense.

I hesitated another moment, then shrugged. I didn't really have another exit. If they came in here, they'd find me and arrest me. "Okay," I said, surprising myself with a reasonably solid voice. "I'm coming. Just don't shoot me."

Hallam chortled. "Wouldn't dream of it."

I didn't take a lot of reassurance from that, but nonetheless, I rolled the flashlight onto the floor so I could keep my hands visible and crawled out after it. Arms spread, I picked up the flashlight and got to unsteady feet.

Hallam and Priya stood shadowed in the doorway, both wearing bright lights clipped to their shoulders, almost blinding me until they angled them away. Hallam held the biggest gun I'd ever seen. It looked like a rocket launcher, but something resembling ammunition dangled below it. Priya held a laser rifle. That I *did* recognize. It was one of the newer and deadlier models. Two other people hovered behind them in the hall. Finn and Matt, I guessed.

On the floor between us lay the smoking pile of fleshy chunks that used to be the aliens. There was no blood, only the strange fluid we'd seen them use on their own ship, but my stomach still lurched at the sight. I forced myself to look at the hunters instead. "What's going on?" I managed.

"We hoped you'd tell us," Hallam drawled.

I risked a few steps toward them. "Omnistellar lured those monsters here to steal their tech, as you probably know by now. They thought they'd reinforced this ship enough to keep the creatures out, but they were wrong. Maybe they made a mistake, or maybe these aliens are stronger than the ones on Sanctuary. Either way, they're here." I swallowed hard. "Have you seen the command center?"

"Yeah," said Priya softly. The muscles in her neck clenched. "Yeah, we saw it."

"Then you have to know we're on the same side now." Déjà vu swirled around my head. A few weeks ago, I'd made this same speech to Cage, and later to Rita. "These things don't care who's Omnistellar and who's not. They might care who's an anomaly, but only because they want to soak you in slime and turn you into one of them." I risked a glance at the floor. My boot was inches away from a curved talon, at least a foot in length, protruding from a gory arm. "And that's if you're lucky—and you count turning into one of these things *lucky*.

But I get the sense these ones aren't here to harvest. They're here to kill."

Priya hesitated. She glanced over her shoulder, but I couldn't see or hear what the others said to her. "Come on out," she said at last. "We'll talk about it."

Well, that was something, at least. If she wanted to arrest me, she wouldn't beat around the bush. She didn't have to. I stepped gingerly around the mess on the floor and made myself walk with measured, normal steps rather than breaking into a run. Still, I couldn't help a sigh of relief as I exited the med facility, even if I was now surrounded by cybernetic anomalies sent to hunt me down.

I glanced at Matt, but he didn't meet my eyes. Instead he stared at the floor, an expression of barely suppressed horror on his face. I resisted the urge to reach for him. Did he wake to the same nightmares I did, to visions of the creatures tearing through his flesh?

I had new nightmares to replace those now. So that was fun.

Finn, as usual, remained silent, leaning against the wall and watching me with a carefully calculating expression. I looked from one to another. "Is anyone else alive on this ship?"

"We don't know," Priya replied. "We were in the holding cells with your friends when we felt the attack. We headed to the command center to see what was going on and found it the same way you did."

"Wait." I bit my lip, not wanting to ask, not wanting to

know. "The command center. Do you mean the one on the first level or the second?"

"Down here. We were about to head upstairs when the power went out. We doubled back to security for lights. We haven't seen or heard anyone else."

I nodded, swallowing hard. "Don't bother checking level one. Everyone in the command center is dead. My dad was alive, though. I left him in an office."

"Cord is alive?" Hallam asked sharply.

How did they know my . . . of course. They worked for Omnistellar. I closed my eyes, exhausted. "Yeah. We were talking during the attack. He hit his head, and I couldn't wake him up, so I went looking for help. Do you think . . . ?" I trailed off. It was their job to capture and imprison me. They were probably about to laugh in my face. My pride warred with the image of my father lying in a pool of his own blood until I whispered, "Do you think we could go get him?"

Priya and Hallam exchanged speaking looks. "I think we're all on the same team," Priya said at last. "For now."

A burst of hope surged in my heart, so strong it almost hurt. "Then can you let the others go? The more of us, the better our chances. And . . . Reed can help Dad. Unless one of you is secretly a doctor, he might be the only one who can."

She hesitated a moment, then turned. "Matt? You know them best. What do you think?"

My eyes locked with his, and suddenly he was once again

the boy I'd known: tired, frightened, a little lost, but kind when it mattered. Then the hunter flickered back into place. "Keep your eye on Cage," he said at last. "But . . . yeah. These things, they . . ." He swallowed hard. "We need all the help we can get."

Priya nodded, accepting that. "All right. Then let's—"

She never finished her sentence. As she turned toward the opposite end of the hall, a shriek pierced the corridor. Priya jerked her rifle up, but she was a fraction of a second too slow. The alien collided with her and tore her to the floor in a jumble of limbs and screams.

THIRTY-NINE

"PRIYA!" HALLAM SHOUTED, RAISING HIS massive gun.

"No!" Finn bellowed. "You'll hit her!" He raised his own laser rifle and squeezed off a shot. It caught the alien in the shoulder, and the alien lurched aside with a screech.

Another scream answered nearby. More of them approached. I shrank against the wall. Without a weapon, I was worse than useless. Maybe with one too. I glanced at Matt out of the corner of my eye. Even now I didn't think I could pull the trigger with him in my path.

Priya groaned and staggered to her feet. She swung her rifle against her shoulder and took a shot at the alien, but it vanished around the corner. "Quick," she managed. Matt moved to help her, but she brushed him off, swaying a bit as she steadied herself against the wall. "Into the holding cells! The door might slow them down."

That I could help with. The cells wouldn't block the aliens long, but anything beat standing here while they tore us to shreds. I lunged for the panel behind us and swiped Dad's omnicard. The door slid aside with agonizing slowness. Behind me, someone fired another shot, and Priya shouted commands. "Come on!" I yelled, shouldering through the gap as soon as there was enough room.

I pivoted in time to see an alien lunge at Matt. He jerked his gun up—too slow, anyone could see it was too slow—and before my horrified eyes, the alien's claws extended, going from three-inch curls into foot-long spears aimed straight at his heart.

At the last second, Finn tackled Matt around the waist, bearing both of them to the floor right below the monster's attack. Finn angled the rifle against the creature and fired twice. The alien screamed, staggered, but didn't go down. It lunged again. Finn and Matt rolled aside, and its claws stabbed the floor.

"Come on!" I screamed.

"Go!" Priya ordered. She fired two blasts at the alien. It collapsed on the floor, but it kept moving. I reeled. Hadn't laser blasts killed the aliens before? Were they somehow evolving? A shiver raced down my spine as I remembered Mia's theory on Sanctuary: that the aliens absorbed our powers somehow, maybe even developing the ability to use her invisibility. What if they adapted to the laser blasts? How long until they became invulnerable?

The hunters responded to Priya's command without hesitation. Matt dove through the door, Priya on his heels, and Hallam stationed himself to my right with his massive gun braced. "Come on, Finn! Move your ass!"

Finn withdrew, his gun trained on the struggling alien. Suddenly it reared up. Finn and Hallam both squeezed off a shot, but it leaped over both of them, once more grazing the ceiling, driving itself at Finn. I screamed as claws ripped through his back. Finn slumped, his eyes open and startled as his head rolled, staring at me with desperate incomprehension. His lips moved, and blood bubbled from his mouth.

The alien met my eyes with its unseeing glare and unleashed a short, shrill scream. I didn't need my power to hear its triumph.

Hallam retreated, shoving me along with him, and the door slid shut in front of us. After a second of silence, I lunged forward to stab at the lock. I didn't know if it would do any good, if the creatures used doors or unlocked them or what. But I had to do something.

Matt wore a shocked, shattered expression, like someone who'd come through a war zone. Priya, as always, was calm and professional. Only the slight tremor in her hands betrayed her.

"We're down to three," Hallam snapped behind me. "Do we call this contract officially botched or what?"

"That's one word for it." Priya passed her hand over her face. "So, Kenzie. Where the hell are your friends?"

It took a moment to process her question, but once I'd grasped the meaning, terror sent my heart into overdrive. Four holding cells filled the room, two on either side. And they were all empty. "They were here?" I managed. "I mean . . . ?"

"Yeah. This is where we left them thirty minutes ago."

A slight smile touched Matt's face. "I told you not to leave them on their own." An undercurrent of something almost like pride ran through his voice.

Our eyes met, and he quickly looked away, his hands trembling around his weapon. "I thought you hated guns," I said softly. Back on Sanctuary, Matt had been reluctant to even take a stun gun. Cage had mentioned something about a school shooting in his past.

Matt scowled. "They fried that section of my brain. Right, Priya?"

She arched an eyebrow. "Eliminating past trauma was part of the mental conditioning, yes. You think you would have been useful to me quivering in fear?"

Blood rushed to his cheeks, and he glanced away. "Sorry," he muttered.

She nodded. "We're all on edge. Get yourself together."

I blinked. *Mental conditioning?* Omnistellar had only had Matt for three weeks. They must have dumped him on one of Legion's superfast ships, blasted him into space, and set every medical nanobot they owned to work on his mental and physical refinement. How much had they changed his mind? Was he still himself? Sometimes he seemed to hate me and sometimes he didn't. As for me, my emotions tangled in a knot of confusion: guilt over shooting him, anger over his betrayal, fear over his new cybernetic implants and what they might have done to his psyche. I took refuge in the fact that Legion seemed pretty stable, more so maybe than most of Omnistellar. I still wasn't sure if they'd turn on me the second we escaped the aliens, but at this point I was willing to take that chance.

Hallam slapped his palm against the wall. "Finn's dead, right?"

Priya nodded. "You saw what happened. No way he survived that."

"How many of those things are in the hallway?" I demanded. An edge of hysteria tinged my voice, and I forced myself to close my eyes, count to five, bobbing my head along with the count. Slightly more controlled, I turned to Matt. "These aren't the same creatures we saw on Sanctuary."

Anger and fear warred in his expression when he looked at me, but the fear won out. "No," he muttered, staring somewhere over my shoulder. "They're . . . bigger. Longer claws. Faster, I think. And they were already plenty fast."

"Great." Priya frowned at the ceiling. "How do we get out of here?"

"We have to find my friends. And my dad." I pictured

him lying on the office floor and my heart skipped a beat. If the aliens discovered him, he'd be completely helpless. Everyone else on the ship was clearly dead. It was only dumb luck that saw him with me at the moment the creatures breached Omnistellar's supposedly impenetrable security. Sudden rage surged in my chest. I glared at each of them in turn, my gaze lingering on Matt. "You *went along with this*? You, of all people, knowing what they were, what Omnistellar might unleash—"

Matt jerked forward so quickly I instinctively recoiled. "They said they had it under control!" he shouted. "This ship was supposed to be impenetrable! You were all supposed to be safe!"

"Safe? You planned to *arrest us*!"

"Yeah, so you wouldn't be devoured by aliens. I figured it was the lesser of two evils."

"Oh, so all of this is what, your misguided attempt to protect us?"

Matt sneered. "Don't get confused, Kenzie. After you killed me and abandoned me on Sanctuary, I didn't have many choices left. I joined forces with Omnistellar and the Legion to protect *myself*." He raised an arm, the light glinting off the metal of his cybernetic implants. "It was this or a prison mining camp, or worse. I don't have any illusions about honorable motives. But yeah. In a way, I was looking out for everyone. I figured Legion was coming after you whether I cooperated or not. At least this way, you'd be off the station when the aliens showed up."

"That's enough," Priya interjected sharply, stepping between us. The wall of tension we'd built shattered in her wake, rebounding against us. "What the hell is wrong with you? Do you want every alien on this station converging on this room?"

Scowling at them, I approached a nearby security monitor and swiped Dad's omnicard.

"What are you doing?" Hallam demanded.

"Looking for my friends," I returned shortly. Sure enough, a quick search of the code brought up the security feeds. Familiarity and something almost like peace washed over me as I scanned through the system. This was so close to what I'd done on Sanctuary. I didn't miss the naïveté or the ignorance of my old life, but sometimes I missed its complacency, its single-minded rightness. Playing with the visual code, finding the security feeds, brought all of those memories rushing back—and with them, a powerful longing for my parents.

Even if we couldn't find Reed, we had to get Dad out of that office. I didn't know how we were going to move him if he remained unconscious, or if it was safe to do so. But it had to be safer than leaving him there.

"Here," I said, pulling up the display and jerking it loose of its console so the image hovered in the air between us. Cage, Alexei, and Imani shared a cell. Cage and Alexei were cuffed. Imani wasn't. In the neighboring cell, Reed was similarly uncuffed, but Mia, Jasper, and Rune were bound.

"We ran out of inhibitor needles." Priya answered my unspoken question as she came to stand behind me. "We didn't anticipate having to cuff and recuff you people so many damn times. We had to prioritize the most dangerous powers."

I got that. I would have left the healers free too. But as we stared at the video feed, Imani passed her hands over Alexei's hands, and his cuffs fell away.

"How . . . ?" Hallam snarled.

I reversed the feed without being asked and slowed it down, but it didn't give me any further answers. As near as I could tell from the video, she just . . . slid them off. "Did you leave them loose?" I asked, knowing the answer.

Hallam snorted. "They're self-adjusting."

As we watched, Imani crossed to Cage. They spoke in hushed tones for a moment, and then she touched his arms, and his cuffs fell away too.

"It's her upgraded power," I realized. The others stared at me, and I hurried to explain. "We think contact with the aliens did something to our abilities. To Matt's, too. That's probably how you survived after I . . ." I couldn't say *shot you*.

But he was already nodding. "The doctors theorized I wasn't really dead, only badly injured."

"You were dead," I replied sharply. "Believe me, we checked. We would never, *never*, have left you if you weren't."

He stared at me for a long moment. "But that means . . ."

"Liam said it was something about the aliens. He called

them the source of the powers. Being around them seems to extend our abilities. Sometimes it's easy to see how our new ability relates to the old one. Reed healed others, and now he can heal himself. Rune can connect with computers without being in physical contact with them. Other times, the connection is less obvious." I swallowed. These people could still turn on me, and I was giving away too much. I pressed on, hoping they wouldn't notice I was suddenly short on examples. "In Matt's case, he went from sensing life to creating it."

"That's impossible." He looked to Priya, shaking his head frantically.

"I don't know." She leaned against the wall, inspecting him, her hand stroking her chin. "I always thought you woke up too . . . too healthy for someone who'd been injured to the point of death."

"But that means . . ." Matt's gaze flickered between us.

"It means what we've been telling you." Anger surged in my voice, and I quickly reined it in. I couldn't blame Matt for assuming the worst. I would have done the same in his situation. "Your new abilities are more than a healing factor. You were dead, Matt. There was absolutely no doubt. Even if you don't trust me, do you really think Cage would have abandoned you like that?" Cage might not always make the best choices, but he was doing what he had to do to keep the people he cared about alive. Just like I'd been doing when I pulled that trigger. Resolve shot through my spine, and I met Matt's eyes straight-on. "I was trying to save your life. I screwed up. I shot you. And that has haunted me every second of every day since."

"Yeah, haunted you so much that you—"

"That I lied about it. Yeah. I've apologized for that to everyone else. I'll say it once more to you: I'm sorry. But I'm *not* sorry I took that shot." As the words tumbled from my mouth, their truth echoed through me, and I almost wept in relief. I finally got what Cage meant when he talked about the choices he'd made. We all did what we could to survive, the best we could in the moment. "Should I have stood by while that thing ripped you to shreds? It was the only choice I had."

He continued to stare at me, but I no longer read fury in his expression. He didn't exactly look ready to embrace me with open arms, but I'd take confusion over blind hatred any day.

Hallam cleared his throat. "Matt's abilities are expanding. Fantastic. Are the two of you done with your cathartic moment here, or should I open the door and invite the aliens in to observe?"

He was right. But I didn't regret the moment either. I was done with regrets, done with apologies.

I returned my attention to the screen and reversed it, since it had continued to play while Matt and I argued. I didn't know how Imani's powers suddenly included the ability to release cuffs, but that was obviously what she'd done.

On the feed, Alexei glanced directly at the camera, and a slow, unpleasant grin crossed his face. A moment later, flames engulfed the screen, so vivid and distinct we all jumped. The rest of the vid was a mess of static.

Priya approached the cells. "The lock's melted on this one," she announced grimly.

Great. The others were wandering around the ship somewhere. "We have to reach them." And not just because I needed Reed to help Dad. If they didn't realize what they were dealing with . . . My friends had powers, courage, but these aliens were stronger and more terrifying than the ones on Sanctuary.

"No argument here. Where do you suggest we start looking?"

Matt and I exchanged careful glances. "Rune can access the system," I said at last. "I think they'd head straight for the armory."

"Then we'd better find them," Hallam replied grimly. "Because that's on the first floor, where you think the attacks originated. And there's a hallway of aliens between us and them."

The four of us hesitated momentarily, none of us in a hurry to move despite the need for haste. Were the aliens lingering outside? I wondered if I could use my new powers to help us. The others seemed to be out of range, but Priya, Matt, Hallam—they had abilities too.

Priya's words echoed in my head: *for now.* I sized her up, debating how far to trust her. She'd turned on me before, the second we escaped the aliens. Chances were she'd do it again. I set my jaw. If it became a matter of life and death, I'd reveal that my powers were changing too. Until then, the less they knew about my abilities, the better.

Priya sighed and nodded to Hallam, who withdrew a laser rifle from its holster across his back. "Ever fired one of these?" he asked me.

I stared at it for a moment, then set my jaw and took it, my hands only trembling a bit. *No more regrets*, I reminded myself. Make your choices and move on. "I can manage," I said, carefully avoiding Matt's gaze even as it burned into my neck. I didn't need telepathy to know where his thoughts must have traveled.

He nodded. "Shoot at one of us, even by *accident*, and I will kill you." The emphasis on "accident" made it clear it wasn't a casual reference. "You got it?"

A thousand replies sprang to mind, but I settled for, "Yeah, I hear you."

"Good."

We turned to face the door, and Priya grinned unpleasantly. "Then let's kick some alien ass."

FORTY

I LET LEGION TAKE THE LEAD AS WE STEPPED into the hall. Say what you wanted about them, they were good. Professional. They'd lost two teammates in as many hours, but you'd never know it by Priya's and Hallam's expressions. Matt hadn't quite mastered their inhumanity, and twitches of emotion kept clawing their way into his eyes, but he resolutely stanched them. *Trying to live up to his new friends*, muttered a sarcastic voice inside my head.

Hallam crept into the hall first, big gun at the ready. He glanced both ways. "Clear," he whispered.

We followed. Finn's body was nowhere to be seen, but a massive splotch of red marked where he'd fallen. I tried not to stare.

The aliens had left the bodies where they'd dropped in the command center. Why drag Finn away? He was an anomaly, of course. Maybe they continued to harvest after all? But even as the thought occurred to me, I dismissed it. Anomaly or not, no way Finn had survived four sharp blades through the chest. His lungs, his heart, all must have punctured instantly. They'd taken the body for some other reason, even if only to mess with us. Had they done the same to the bodies on Obsidian? Or were they piled together somewhere like the command center, someplace they'd thought was safe and gathered for protection? I shuddered at the thought.

Priya and Hallam ducked into the medical center we'd recently cleared, swinging their lights around before leading us in. The alien bodies remained motionless on the floor. "Looks clear," Priya whispered. "But no guarantee it'll stay that way. Keep close. Hallam, grab a med kit from the cupboard, just in case we need it before we find the healer."

Hallam had given me a shoulder light like the ones Legion wore. Strapping it to my body left my hands free to hold the laser rifle. I gripped it tightly, terrified of dropping it. More terrified of having to use it, in spite of my new resolve. Matt lingered behind me, and I was very conscious of his gaze.

We advanced carefully through the facility, no aliens in sight. Where were they? They must have known we'd gone into the holding cells, but they hadn't followed us. Because the holding cells were reinforced more strongly than the rest of the ship? Because we didn't represent enough of a threat? Or because something had distracted them?

My feet itched to run, but I let Hallam and Priya set the pace. They moved as silently as Mia, their training impeccable and absolute. I glanced at Matt. "Hey," I whispered, barely more than a breath. It was still enough to earn me a glare from Hallam.

Matt hesitated, then drew a bit closer. "What?" he mouthed, his expression not inviting confidence.

I lowered my voice even further. "I'm starting to understand things a bit better. None of us are in normal circumstances. So, whatever Legion did to you, whatever Omnistellar did to you, I just want you to know that I forgive you for turning on us."

He gaped at me in disbelief. "*You* . . . forgive *me*?"

"Yup." I forced a smile. "I'm not blaming you or saying we didn't deserve it. I'm just saying that I get it. You made a choice. You protected your family. You survived."

Matt scrubbed a hand over his face. "They ripped me apart, Kenzie," he said quietly. "In just a few weeks they dismantled my body and my mind. I was unconscious until a day before we arrived at Obsidian. I hardly know what happened. But when I woke up, all I could remember was that sense of betrayal . . . and Legion. Somehow, they'd been fused in my head. I know it's not real. I know I've only known them for a few hours. But . . ."

I nodded. "That's how Omnistellar works. They need you loyal, so they go into your brain and make you that way. Just be glad they didn't make you loyal to them."

He met my gaze, his eyes wide and wounded, for the first time without even a trace of anger. "Why didn't they?"

"I don't know. Not enough time, maybe? Too much of a stretch? They needed the others physically present to bind you? We can ask Priya about it later."

"We?"

I shrugged. "If you want. You're not on your own, Matt. You don't have to forgive us. You don't even have to like us. But if you need us, we'll be here for you."

"Look, let's just . . . let's get through this, okay?" He bit his lip, clearly shaken, and something in me jostled loose. Whatever Omnistellar had done to him, they hadn't destroyed him. And that meant that neither had I. "We can talk about it on the other side."

I appreciated his confidence that there would *be* another side. "Deal."

"Will you two *shut up?*" hissed Priya over her shoulder.

We shut up. But I felt better. Whatever happened, whatever he'd been through, the Matt I knew lingered beneath the new facade. It gave me hope that everything would be okay, that we'd find the others, save my dad, get off this ship alive. How, I didn't know. There had to be shuttles. Where had the aliens come in? Maybe we could escape the same way.

We reached the opposite side of the med facility without incident. Priya and Hallam carefully eased the door open and, finding the hall empty, beckoned us through. All four of us crowded onto the circular lift, although Hallam had to lean against Priya and angle his gun upward to make it fit inside the tube. We ascended in the same total silence, even without risk of the aliens hearing us. In the enclosed space, our lights seemed intensely bright. I closed my eyes against them, not wanting to have to readjust to the darkness when we arrived at the top.

The disc settled into place, and I opened my eyes. The upper corridor looked exactly as I'd left it. "Where's the armory?" Priya murmured.

"Opposite corner." As far from us as possible. "My dad's in an office right down the hall." I knew we needed to get to Reed fast, but it had been a long time since I'd left Dad. I kept seeing him in vivid detail, limp against the carpet. "Can we check on him? Make sure he's stable before we find the others?"

Priya hesitated, exchanging glances with Hallam, then nodded to me to take the lead. She stayed right on my heels, and for once I appreciated her presence. Legion had an imposing, competent air that made me feel we might have a chance.

Of course, they'd already lost two of their members. That was worth remembering. Who else was dead? I spared a thought for Obsidian. Alexei's uncle Grigori, Cage's contact and her people, the little girl I'd seen in the marketplace, Liam . . . was everyone on the station gone? Horror raced through me as I imagined their last moments, especially Liam's. I'd never figured out who he was or what he wanted, but the aliens were his worst nightmare come to life. If he had died, I hoped it was quick. If he hadn't, I hoped he'd escaped, no matter what he'd done to us.

My skin crawled as we passed the closed command center. I suspected other areas of this ship, areas with large concentrations of people like the downstairs dormitory, were equally gory. I had no desire to find out firsthand.

We reached the office without incident. I swiped Dad's omnicard, stepped inside, and stopped short.

Dad was gone.

"I left him here," I said, panic lending volume to my voice. "*Right here*. He was hurt. He couldn't have moved far, not by himself."

Matt gently pushed me aside and crouched where I pointed. "There's blood on the carpet," he said to Priya. "No trail or anything, though."

"He couldn't have moved without help," I repeated, staring at the empty space as if I might will him into existence. "I never should have left him. I should have . . ."

"What?" Priya demanded, her tone gentler than I expected. "Sat here with him in the dark and waited for a monster to attack you?"

"I don't . . ."

"If the aliens got him, there'd be more blood. He probably woke up and dragged himself to a more secure location." She glanced around the room. "Nowhere to hide in here. Our best bet is to stick to our original plan. Find your friends. The girl who talks to computers can locate your father."

My head jerked up. "Matt," I said. I hated to ask him for

any favors, but . . . "Does your power still work the way it used to? I mean . . ."

"I know what you mean," he said softly. "I've been looking for other human life off and on since we discovered the command center. That's how we found you."

"And? Do you sense anything now?"

He frowned. "Yes. Something. Someone. Farther along this corridor. I can't tell how many or who, though. The aliens always messed with my abilities."

"That's it?"

"No," he replied, but very slowly. "Kenzie, I really can't say for sure. I think . . . there's someone in engineering."

Hope sparked in my chest. "It was empty when I checked earlier."

"And now it maybe isn't. I don't know."

Something clattered in the hall, and we all jumped to attention. Hallam jerked his heavy gun toward the exit and scowled. "This is getting us nowhere. Priya, what are your orders?"

She glanced at me, at the closed door, at Matt, but her expression never changed. "Engineering is right across the hall, but it's big and full of hiding places. It's safer once we have reinforcements. We'll stick to our original plan and check the armory. If nothing else, we can upgrade our weapons." She raised a hand, forestalling my objection before my lips even formed the words. "We'll head to engineering after."

It looked like she expected me to argue, but she wasn't

wrong. Part of me didn't know where I wanted to head first, anyway. My father seemed like my last link to my old life, but my friends were my family in so many ways now. It was almost a relief to have the decision about who to save first taken from my hands. "All right," I said. "But let's hurry."

No sooner did the words leave my mouth than a shriek filled the air. The floor exploded into jagged metal and, not ten feet in front of me, an alien leaped into the room.

FORTY-ONE

IT CLAWED ITS WAY THROUGH THE SCATTERED remnants of the floor and vaulted easily into the office, howling and snorting. In the same instant, Hallam opened fire. Bullets tore past me and I instinctively dove to the side. Matt must have done the same because we wound up lying on the floor shoulder to shoulder, arms thrown over our heads.

The bullets tore through the creature in a messy, horrific display. It screeched at the top of its lungs, flying against the wall, a mess of holes and goo and sinew, before crumpling in a heap.

"Almost out!" Hallam shouted, checking his ammo count.

Alien screams echoed below. "Run!" Priya ordered.

The door wasn't locked, and I didn't need to scan the card to open it. We bolted, Matt in the lead, me on his heels, Priya and Hallam bringing up the rear. I heard her squeeze off a few shots and an answering scream. More of the creatures must have attacked. They weren't even bothering with subtlety now. They were literally tearing the ship apart in an effort to destroy every last one of us. And from there—what? Mars was closest. But Earth was undoubtably next. I pictured everyone I'd left behind, Anya and my cousins and Jasper's family, and my blood ran cold.

It wasn't enough to survive this. We had to *stop* them.

"Kenzie, come on!" Matt grabbed my arm and dragged me after him, and I realized I'd slowed, turned toward the creatures. Three of them stalked into the hallway. Priya and Hallam weren't firing, only running, and they shouted for us to do the same. But where were we going? What could we do? What possible hope did we have?

The answer appeared in a blast of flame and light as someone shimmered into view right in our path. "Get down!" Alexei roared. We threw ourselves forward, and a burst of fire lanced over our heads. An alien yelp answered.

Wind rushed past me: Cage. I twisted just in time to see one of the aliens' heads fall from its body, and Cage appeared on its far side, now with a long, sparking ionic blade in his hand.

The other two aliens were badly burned but still standing. They shrieked, and Cage burst into action again, but this time when his blade struck home, the alien braced its arms, shielding itself somehow. The blade clattered from his hand and Cage, with nothing to check his speed, smashed to the floor and skidded at least twenty feet. Alien claws clashed down behind him, missing him by inches.

Mia and Jasper appeared in front of Alexei. The sudden illumination from the emergency lights strapped to their shoulders almost blinded me. Mia held a laser cannon almost as big as Hallam's gun, and her eyes narrowed in intense concentration. Jasper raised his hands and chunks of wall came loose. The light spaceship material wasn't enough to damage the aliens, but he swept it around them, striking them, knocking them off balance, interfering with their senses. At the same instant, Mia opened fire. The force of the recoil knocked her off her feet into Alexei's arms, but her aim was true. Both aliens screamed as the laser roasted their flesh and shriveled their bones.

And then, as suddenly as it had started, it was over. We were alone. I was on my feet before I'd even fully registered that the aliens were dead; I raced down the hall and collapsed at Cage's side, rolling him onto his back. "Cage!" I shouted. "Cage!" Memories assaulted me: Cage, bleeding and unconscious on the floor of Sanctuary, the gashes in his stomach angry and red, and the utter terror of facing the creatures without him.

He moaned and opened his eyes. A strangled sob escaped my lips, and I collapsed against his chest. His arms surrounded me, hesitant and weak but gaining in strength every second. I pulled him to a sitting position and cradled him against my shoulder, and he cupped the back of my head. Every second we'd wasted flooded back to me. Why had I doubted him, doubted myself? "This whole thing has been so stupid," I whispered, pulling away to stare into his dark eyes. "Cage, I'm so sorry. I never—"

He cut me off by kissing me, apparently indifferent to our audience. His hand was firm against my neck, and I dragged him forward, returning his kiss with every ounce of passion and strength inside me. After weeks of near touches and awkward silences, the walls crashed down between us, a crescendo of something I'd never felt sweeping me against him with almost terrifying power, as if we were one person clamoring to rejoin our shattered halves.

"Oh God," announced Mia loudly. "You two realize you're making out in a pool of alien goo, right?"

We broke apart and grinned at each other, but a veil of tears blurred my vision. I blinked them back. An encounter with death has a way of prioritizing matters. "I'm sorry," I repeated.

"You have nothing to apologize for." He brushed my hair behind my ear where it had come loose from its braid. "If anyone's to blame, it's me. I owe you explanations. I—"

I kissed him again, just once, quickly. "Let's do this later."

"That might be a plan," he agreed, and I helped him to his feet. As we rose, he snatched the ionic blade from the batch of alien goo and swept it into a sheath along his back.

We turned to face the others. Priya, Matt, and Hallam had picked themselves off the floor and faced off against Alexei,

Mia, and Jasper. No one lowered their weapons—or, in the case of Alexei and Jasper, their hands, which shimmered with energy. Flames sparked at the edges of Alexei's fingertips. Rune, Imani, and Reed stood behind them, their relief palpable. Seeing everyone again brought home how desperately I needed them. I'd always thought I could do everything on my own. Not anymore. And the weird thing was that I didn't even care.

Of course, before I could fall over myself and tell them I loved them, I had to stop everyone from killing one another. "All right, children," I announced loudly, forcing my unfamiliar rush of emotion beneath my more characteristic Omnistellar mask. "You want to put the guns down before someone gets hurt?"

Matt, Hallam, and Priya barely glanced at me, keeping their gazes focused on their opponents. "Sure," said Priya. "Just as soon as they do."

I took in the three faces opposite and ventured for the most reasonable option. "Alexei, you know we need to work together right now. Remember? Survival and all that. These three helped me. Let's escape the aliens before we deal with grudges, okay?"

He grunted in reply, his eyes narrowed. Then, abruptly, he dropped his hands, the shimmer of heat fading away.

Matt responded by lowering his rifle. Within seconds, everyone stood down, and Rune flew across the hallway, taking a second to elbow past Matt and glare at him on the way. She hugged me tightly. "We were worried," she explained in

Mandarin. "We didn't know what those creeps might have been doing to you."

"Taking me to my father," I replied in the same language. I glanced over my shoulder at Cage and added, "Who's missing. Matt thinks there's someone in engineering."

Cage frowned. It didn't take powers to follow his thoughts. We'd been here before, on Sanctuary with my mother. It hadn't ended well. My hands trembled, and I clenched them into fists at the thought of Sanctuary, its familiar halls and corridors turning into deathtraps as we searched for my mother.

Things with Dad would not end the same way. I would find him, and not dead and shackled to a wall. Whatever happened between us, I couldn't let him die like Mom.

Imani and Reed drifted to our sides, Reed keeping a careful eye on Matt. Imani squeezed my arm, and I squeezed back. Relief passed between us without words.

Before I could speak to either of them, Priya started barking orders. "We need to get out of this hallway," she said. "The aliens are just tearing through chunks of the ship. We have three priorities right now: recover Kenzie's father, find a way off this ship, and destroy it, Obsidian, and the alien vessel before those things set off for Earth."

Well, hard to argue with any of that. I shouldered my laser rifle and chimed in. "Also, the aliens seem to be adapting. The first time we shot them with laser rifles, they went to pieces.

Now they have some sort of shielding against it. Same with Cage attacking them a moment ago."

"Kind of like us," said Alexei thoughtfully.

I blinked. He was right. Kind of like us . . . and especially, kind of like *me*. A shudder ran through me, and Cage's hand drifted to the small of my back, steady and reassuring. "We have a few other weapons. Rune got us into the armory. We'll fight as long as we can. The shuttle bay is at the rear of this level, and Rune says the manifest lists at least five shuttles. Once we get your dad, escaping shouldn't be too difficult. Actually destroying this ship, or anything else, with the weaponry we find on a shuttle, though . . ."

"Let's cross that bridge when we come to it." Priya marched forward, ignoring how Alexei and Mia refused to part for her, shouldering her way past Jasper and into the lead. "Engineering's next. Hallam and Matt, take the rear. The rest of you, keep your eyes peeled."

Mia's face twisted into a snarl of rage, but Alexei caught her arm and pulled her along, murmuring to her under his breath.

Imani offered me a shaky smile as we followed. "I'm glad you're okay," she whispered.

"You too." I examined her. "You doing all right? With the aliens?"

Some of the blood drained from her face, but she nodded. "I thought once I saw them again, I'd either be furious or too terrified to move. Turns out, I'm neither. I mean, I am scared, and I am angry. But mostly I just want to go home. Tell my family the truth about Aliya. I want to survive, and I'll do what it takes to make that happen." She smiled faintly. "Ideally without losing any of you."

"Speaking of which," said Reed, "do I dare ask where the other bounty hunter is?"

"Dead," I replied quietly. "And the aliens took his body. I don't know why." I glanced between him and Imani. "My dad . . . he was injured in the attack. If—*when* we find him . . ."

"You don't even have to ask," Reed replied gently, and Imani nodded.

I blinked back tears. I'd never doubted them, but their words reassured me, gave me hope. Could I have healed Dad myself? Maybe. Who knew with the way things were going? But between the three of us, I knew he'd be okay . . . as long as he survived until I found him.

Cage's hand tightened against my back, lending me unspoken support. "That reminds me, Priya's hurt," I managed, turning to Reed. "Can you maybe heal her before we go into engineering?"

"I will if she'll let me." Reed jogged ahead and caught up to Priya. They engaged in a quick conversation, and then she reluctantly lowered her weapon, allowing him to lay his hand on her arm.

"Speaking of powers," I said to Imani, "how the hell did you get everyone out of their cells?"

"Oh, that."

"Yes, *that*. I saw the security feed. It looked like you slipped the cuffs right off."

"Apparently I can move through pieces of solid material now." She shrugged, as if this were no big deal. "Only small ones. I tried getting through the bars earlier, and it didn't work. But I can sort of make things intangible if they're small and I don't make it last too long."

Imani made things intangible. Mia made people invisible. Matt resurrected. And me . . . I did everything, or seemed to. Was this a good thing? Were our powers increasing, or was our DNA shifting? Were we becoming aliens ourselves? That thought almost knocked me off my feet, but I forced myself steady. None of us showed any physical changes, and Liam hadn't mentioned anything of the sort happening on his own planet. I clung to that hope.

Cage also seemed worried, or maybe only thoughtful. He caught me staring and smiled. Somehow that helped. Whatever changes the aliens might work on our DNA, we were still ourselves. We were in another alien-infested ship, seconds away from a grisly death, and once again trying to rescue one of my parents, but having Cage at my side made all the difference.

Part of me wanted to feel guilty over wasted time, over the tension between us, but I smacked that part of me down. I might have started building walls, but my suspicion of him was in some ways justified. We'd both kept secrets. Both clung to lies. Both let fear and anxiety drive us. Feeling bad didn't make things better. It was time to let all of that go.

Ahead of us, Priya, now healed, beckoned me forward. Without being asked, Mia took a position on the other side of the door, the big laser cannon at the ready. We stationed ourselves around the corridor. Priya gave me a short nod. I swiped Dad's omnicard, then jumped aside.

Nothing leaped out of engineering to greet us, so we advanced cautiously. With everyone wearing emergency lights, engineering stood out in sharp angles and shadows, fully illuminated. Priya, Alexei, and Mia blocked my view, though, so I didn't see Dad until I'd taken a few steps inside.

He stood with his back to us, bent over a console. Blood still oozed from the wound on his head, but he was conscious and working. He must have heard us come in, must have seen the lights, but he didn't look up from his task. "Dad!" I cried, half in relief, half in terror.

That made him hesitate a second. Then he continued plugging away at the console. "Dad," I repeated, more fear in my voice. Cage's arm tightened around my waist.

"Commander Cord," Priya called, her voice loud and clear. The phrase made me reel. For a moment I looked for my mother, and then I realized: Dad had been promoted. "Please stop what you're doing and turn around."

"He can't do that," said another voice. We spun to find Liam lounging against the wall, his arms folded over his chest.

"You!" I exploded. I lunged in his direction. Cage's other arm circled me, dragging me against him, so I targeted Liam with the laser rifle instead, even if I surreptitiously thumbed the safety first. I wasn't about to shoot anyone, not even him. "What are you doing here? And what the hell did you do to my comm device?"

"What they told me to." He passed a hand over his head, his face drawn, frightened and exhausted. "Sabotaged the damn thing so it wouldn't work if you managed to evade capture a bit longer. Did you call him?" He nodded at Jasper. "If so, his is infected too."

I glanced at Jasper, but there was only an empty slot in his arm where his device should have gleamed. They must have taken it from him when he was arrested. I returned my attention to Liam. "*Why?* Why would you do that?" Realization dawned, slow and painful. "You've been working with Omnistellar all along," I said. "That's why I could open portals on the bounty hunter ship. You were there."

"I was . . . nearby," he replied reluctantly. "But I wasn't working for Omnistellar. Your father contacted me directly, Kenzie."

Dad didn't even glance up from the console, but his voice was shaky when he answered. "I didn't trust the bounty hunters not to kill you when they found you. Liam was . . . a backup. I had to make sure you were safe, and that you got off Obsidian. His job was to protect you, even if he went about it in a strange way."

"I did what you asked," Liam cut in, annoyance tingeing his voice. "Keep an eye on the hunt. Sabotage her comm device so you could make sure you were the only one to contact her if she escaped. All of that. I upheld my end of the bargain, so make sure you keep yours."

"And what is that, exactly?" I demanded.

"Sanctuary from those things. Omnistellar is too powerful, Kenzie. The *zemdyut* were coming no matter what, and I didn't want to get caught in the crossfire." He met my gaze, his face so pale he resembled a ghost in the shadows. "It's not personal. I just . . . I couldn't face them again."

"Yeah well, Omnistellar isn't so great at providing sanctuary," I replied, unable to keep the sarcasm from my voice. "Their last one blew up. And now here you are, in the same spot."

"Not quite." Dad straightened up, turning from the console, his face heavy. "Liam's coming with me. And so are you, Kenz. We're getting off this ship."

FORTY-TWO

I STARED AT DAD. IT DIDN'T TAKE LONG TO absorb what he hadn't said. "We're getting off this ship," I repeated dully. "You, and me, and Liam. What about everyone else?"

"We won't be able to take them." He hesitated. "I'm sorry, sweetheart. I know how that must seem. And I meant to save them, I really did. Criminals or not, they helped you off Sanctuary. But it's too late now. We have to escape, and this is the only way left."

"And us?" asked Hallam dryly.

Dad winced. "Criminals who let the corporations tamper with their bodies in exchange for amnesty," he said at last, but he sounded tired, not accusatory. "Omnistellar handed you a lot of power. You've been abusing it."

Hallam snorted and jerked the gun more solidly against his shoulder, targeting Dad. "Really."

"Legion got too powerful, Hallam. You had to know Omnistellar wouldn't let you keep going forever." He gave Priya a pointed look. "The real mistake was enhancing your own cybernetic implants."

Priya laughed shortly. "You knew about that?"

"It's Omnistellar. They know everything. You were slated for elimination a few months ago, but they wanted the opportunity to use your powers one last time. You were meant to die on Obsidian." He turned to Hallam. "I wouldn't pull that trigger. Not unless you want to kill everyone on this ship."

I reeled. "Wait. You led Legion here to die?" I asked in disbelief. "Fully intending to lure the aliens to our solar system, to kill my friends?"

"If things went according to plan, I would have saved your . . . friends. That's no longer an option. There's an Omnistellar warship nearby. It only has room for two passengers, but they've agreed to take on a third." He glanced nervously at Hallam, although like me, his training masked the worst of his fear. Hallam, apparently as familiar with Omnistellar tactics as me, ground his teeth, held his target, but didn't fire. Dad must have had something up his sleeve.

Priya snorted. "Well, that explains why Omnistellar was willing to rush Matt's implantation. They didn't care if everything took properly." She gave Matt a rueful smile. "Sorry, kid. You were supposed to die with us."

Dad nodded reluctantly. "For what it's worth, I made sure

they kept their promises," he said. "Your family is safe."

Relief passed over Matt's face, and he shrugged. "For what it's worth," he replied, "I appreciate it."

Rune moved as if to take his hand, then withdrew. Her natural compassion shining through? Or did some of her feelings for Matt linger?

Everyone else hovered in a loose clump, staring at my father and Liam, who refused to meet anyone's eyes. He was doing the same thing he'd done on his own planet. "I shouldn't be surprised," I said coldly. "My mom was willing to let me die. Liam let his family die. And now my father turns out to be a corporate drone. The aliens just bring out the best in people, don't they?"

Dad ground his teeth, his gaze taking in each of us in turn until it rested on me. His expression softened, the shadows of the man I knew peering through. "I refused to cooperate unless they let me bring you home," he said. He took a half step toward me, then stopped as Hallam jerked his gun more firmly against his shoulder. "Kenzie, Matt told me everything. I know what happened on Sanctuary, what your mother did. I can't imagine how much that must have hurt you. I hope you know I would never have pressed that button. No matter what company regulations I was breaking, I would have brought you home safe."

Tears began to blur my vision. I closed my eyes until they passed and managed to say in a steady voice, "But here you are, Dad. Doing the same thing as Mom."

"It's not the same. Kenzie, she tried to *kill* you." Sudden fury underlaced his tone, his eyes wide with disbelief. How many nights had Dad lain awake piecing together events on Sanctuary? What had really motivated his coming here? Maybe . . . just maybe . . . he had come for me after all. His actions were twisted and wrong, but unlike my mom, his motivations might be a little bit purer. "I almost couldn't believe it at first," he continued, a strain of disgust entering his tone. "But your mother . . . she was always Omnistellar to her core. Even above her own family."

He wasn't wrong. And yet a protective impulse shot through me, a deep-seated need to defend my mother . . . and maybe even Omnistellar. I swallowed it down. This was still my father. There was a chance to reach him. "You're not her. I know that. There's got to be another way. Dad, work with us here. We can all get off this ship, stop the aliens together."

"Kenzie, I tried. This is the best I could do. And even this nearly cost me my career. I had to make sacrifices you can't imagine to save you."

His voice had gone solid again, the uncertainty fleeing. I'd missed my chance, if it had ever existed. Whatever Dad's plan, he was going through with it. I grabbed on to Cage for support as Priya raised her rifle. "Just one problem, Commander," she said coldly. "We're not going to let you kill us and walk away."

At the same instant, a pleasant voice announced, "Self-destruct sequence has been activated. Five minutes remain until detonation."

Dad gestured at the computer. "If you'd prefer, we can all die here together," he said.

"And Obsidian?" I demanded. "What's going to happen to all the people over there?"

For a moment, something like guilt washed over my father's expression, quickly smothered in the company mask. "Kenzie, they were . . . criminals. Murderers. Evil people. They . . ."

I heard my own voice as if from a distance, cold and terribly quiet. "Are you saying that everyone on Obsidian is dead?"

"Dead where they fell," said Liam softly. "You saw the bodies on this ship. The *zemdyut* did the same thing on Obsidian. The residents made it easy for them, grouping in bunkers and safe zones." He passed a hand over his face, looking much older now. "I always knew that was a bad idea. But no one listens to me."

Dead. Every one of them dead, just like the people in the command center. I actually staggered, only Cage's arm keeping me upright. I looked from Dad's trembling resolve to Liam's wilting defeat to Priya's set jaw. "Dad, what are you doing?" I tried desperately. "You can't mean this. You can't—"

"Kenzie, do you have any idea what that alien tech means to Omnistellar?"

I saw red. "You are doing this for tech?"

"I'm doing it for Omnistellar! For the corporation that sheltered me, that sheltered *you*. Sweetheart, we hid how much trouble the company is in. *We need this.* Without some sort

461

of advance, Omnistellar has maybe two, three years before the other corporations start to catch us. And what happens then? To me, to you, to the millions of people who depend on Omnistellar for their lives and well-being? Is that really what you want?"

"What about the people on Obsidian?"

"Your mother *died* for Omnistellar!" he snapped, then blinked, as if taken aback by his own reaction. Dad had left us before the alien attack. On some level I'd blamed him for that. Maybe he blamed himself too. Did that explain his renewed vigor for the company? "She died," he repeated softly. "I thought you did too. It made me realize that without Omnistellar, I would never have had either of you at all. We owe the company everything, Kenz. Never forget that."

"You can't be serious," I whispered. But then, my own mother was willing to kill me herself if it meant holding to Omnistellar regulations. At least my father had tried to save me, however misguided his methods. "Dad, please. Think about what you're doing. That alien ship . . ."

"I know. It's just like Matt told us. The other aliens are sleeping. All we have to do is get rid of them and their vessel is ours for the taking." Like Liam, he avoided my eyes. "That's what you did, isn't it? We destroy this ship and its occupants, we destroy Obsidian, we take the alien tech."

"You can't fly it without Rune," I replied stubbornly.

He shook his head. "Do you really think that girl is the

only one of her kind? Omnistellar has many anomalies willing to work for them if it means a pardon."

"Yeah," said Mia dryly. "Until Omnistellar turns on them because they outlived their usefulness."

"Forget that for now. These aren't the same aliens," Cage interjected as the computer announced we had four minutes to live. I glanced around, hoping someone had a brilliant idea. But no one moved. Everyone kept their weapons trained on Dad and Liam, but no one opened fire. Cage continued, his voice calm and cool and persuasive as always: "Hasn't anyone told you? The aliens we encountered on Sanctuary were harvesting. These ones are killing. They're not here to collect us, they're here to contain us." His eyes flickered toward me and Rune. "Maybe it's our fault. We killed hundreds of them back on the ship. Maybe that brought them here with murder on their minds. But whatever their motives, there's no reason to assume any of them are sleeping."

"We'll take care of it." Dad glanced at the red countdown on the console. "You need to understand that this isn't my choice. Omnistellar is tired of Legion, tired of anomalies. It took everything I had to convince them to save Kenzie and honor their agreement with Legion. Even if I tried to take you along, or if you killed me and took the shuttles, Sabre would destroy you on sight."

"Sabre," Priya repeated. "That's a high-powered warship. You did come prepared."

He sagged against the wall, clasping the back of his head and wincing in pain. "You have a choice to make. We can all die here together, along with the aliens, and Omnistellar will try to take the ship anyway. They might fail, with Obsidian still standing and all of its creatures alive. If they do, the aliens will be free to advance throughout the solar system. Or you can let me, Liam, and Kenzie go. You'll die, but humanity will survive. I suggest you choose fast."

"You've thought of everything, haven't you?" Fury surged in my chest. Once again Cage's arm turned restraining as I lunged at my father. "You arrogant, selfish bastard."

Dad recoiled, his mouth dropping as genuine anger and hurt spread across his face. "I could have escaped this ship an hour ago," he pointed out. "I delayed the self-destruct mechanism. I stayed and risked my life for *you*, Kenzie."

"You were inputting the self-destruct when I came in! You were going to kill me!"

"Don't be ridiculous," he snapped. "I saw you coming on the reactivated security feeds. I'm not . . ." He swallowed hard. "I'm not your mother, Kenzie. I would *never* hurt you."

"And you expect me to be *grateful*?" I was shouting now, heedless of the noise, even with Imani and Rune frantically shushing me. "To leave my friends, the people who saved my life when Mom abandoned me? Is that really what you think of me?"

"Please," whispered Liam, looking around in frantic terror.

"You have to stop. Listen, I don't like this any more than you do. I *don't*. But it's about survival, you know? I've seen what those things can do to a planet. You don't want them on yours."

He shot to his feet, but before he took a single step, he jerked upright, eyes going wide as a stun gun blast rippled through him. I spun to find Imani, arm extended. "That's enough out of you," she snarled as Liam dropped to the floor. "It was on stun," she added unnecessarily. His chest rose and fell visibly.

I'd be lying if I said I wasted a moment worrying about him. I turned on Dad instead. "You keep saying you're different from Mom," I said, forcing my voice to be calm and steady. I'd thought I'd lost any hope of reaching Dad, but now I could see the father I knew again, the kindness and good humor and logic. Maybe my last chance hadn't vanished after all. "Dad, please. If you love me at all, listen. We have to find another way."

He hesitated. "Omnistellar—"

"Forget Omnistellar!" The words were almost a shout. I clenched my fists and lowered my voice. "This isn't about them. It's about you and me, and whether you trust me. Dad, I've come this far. I've escaped these things and the bounty hunters and every obstacle you've thrown in my way. I think I've earned at least the chance to prove myself."

Once more he hesitated. "Kenzie," he whispered. He glanced at the others behind me, and a familiar bewilderment suffused his expression. I understood. It was the same expression I'd worn when I first questioned Omnistellar. Hope exploded in my chest. I was reaching him. If I could just have a few more minutes, show him that the anomalies weren't dangerous criminals, I knew I could convince him of the truth. We could escape together. I just needed to hold his attention a little while longer.

But I never got the chance.

With a shriek of rending metal, a claw ripped through the door behind him. It raked through the triple-reinforced, shielded metal like it was nothing, disintegrating it in two swipes. Mia and Hallam opened fire, but the alien was too fast. It lunged through the door, screaming and trembling with effort.

And launched itself at my father.

My mouth opened in a silent scream as the world slowed down around me. I felt like I was moving in slow motion as I lunged for my father. I had time to register every movement, every nuance of his facial expression: the shock, the horror, the fear, all of it dissolving into pain as the monster stabbed its claws into Dad. They tore through his body. I reached for him, searching for someone's power, *anyone's* power, some way to stop this thing.

And then the world jerked back to normal speed. The alien swiveled Dad into the line of fire. His body jerked as bullets and laser blasts raked it, and I screamed, running for him.

I only made it a few steps before Cage tackled me to the floor. I fought against him, clawing at his face until he caught my wrists and pinned me. "Kenzie, stop!" he shouted. "It's too late!"

The alien screamed again, and someone opened fire. The noise faded into the background as I struggled against Cage, shouts and orders and claws and bullets. But I only had eyes for Dad. "No. No. There's something. Someone. Me! I can use my powers, Cage. I can help him!"

"You can't resurrect people," he whispered, pulling me into his arms.

"Matt. Matt can. Matt!"

Matt shook his head, his face ashen. "I can't help anyone but myself. I'm not even sure how I do that." Behind him, Imani clutched Jasper's arm, their faces twin masks of horror.

"Get out of the way!" Priya shoved all three of them aside and jumped between us and the alien. It leaped at her and she targeted it, her expression cool and calm and professional as she squeezed off a series of shots. The alien howled in agony and slumped against the wall.

For a moment, all was silent. I twisted in Cage's arms, reaching for Matt, blinded by a veil of tears. I could only think of finding something, *anything* to save my father. "I'm sorry for Sanctuary," I whispered, my fingers straining for his. If I could only make him understand, make him forgive me, make him turn to Dad and work his magic. "*Please*. Please help me."

Matt's expression crumpled. For a moment he looked like he might cry, and that more than anything broke through my agony. "Kenzie, I can't," he said, so softly I barely heard him.

I can't.

Not *I won't.*

I can't. The words shattered my shields and left me limp, my entire body shaking and exhausted and fighting to resist the knowledge that my father was gone, my parents, were gone.

A horrifying silence filled the room. Over Cage's shoulder I saw Mia's face, ashen and more frightened than ever before. She met my eyes, and her lips moved as if to say something. Then she turned away.

An alien scream broke the silence. Another answered nearby.

Something struck the wall across from me. Long, claw-shaped indents appeared along the wiring. It wouldn't take more than a few strikes for them to break through. I stared at them numbly, still unable to absorb anything happening around me. Dad couldn't be dead. The man who'd introduced me to Omnistellar, who'd lectured me on company regulations, who'd placed my first basketball in my hands, who'd bought me ice cream when we walked by the beach visiting his sister . . . I remembered Mom and Dad laughing together, my cousins running around their feet, Mom watching with a tolerant smile as I raced over with my arms full of seashells. Dad had scooped me into his arms. I couldn't remember what he'd said. Why couldn't I remember? It was one of the last vacations we all took together, before the promotions and the work and the company claimed everything else. Why couldn't I remember his words? Why was it so important?

I suddenly became aware of Cage babbling to me, cupping my face in his hands, trying to make me meet his eyes. "Kenzie, please," he said, his words a mixture of Mandarin and English and something in between. "Please. Don't do this, not now. I need you. I'm sorry, but I do. Look at me. Please."

I drew a deep breath, forcing myself to meet his gaze. Relief surged through him, so powerful and profound I almost cried. "Is he dead?" I whispered.

"Yeah. I'm sorry. But if we don't get moving, we're going to be dead too."

I knew. I knew that. I knew both of those things. I simply couldn't make myself believe them.

The alien shrieks tripled in volume and another creature leaped over my dad, ignoring the other alien crumpled beside him. I threw up a hand to shield my eyes as Hallam opened fire. The alien shrieked, recoiled, but shook off the gunfire, shifting on unsteady feet before seeming to recover.

"I'm out!" Hallam shouted, throwing the big gun aside. He yanked a second laser rifle off his back and braced it against his shoulder. "You, girl! Whatcha at?"

If Mia bristled at being called 'girl,' she didn't show it. "Quarter charge," she replied as she opened fire. Jasper lunged into action at the same time, jerking an entire console free of the wall and slamming it into the creature. "Eighth charge," Mia amended as the alien slumped.

"Self-destruct in three minutes," announced the computer.

"Let's move," Priya ordered.

"What about the other ship—Sabre?" Reed demanded. "If he was telling the truth . . ."

"You want to stay here? Be my guest! Everyone else, go!" Priya spun for the door behind us. At the same moment, claws slashed through it. Alexei and Mia attacked in the same instant, and the alien released a shrill scream.

Mia pivoted and fired another shot at the far door, where a creature struggled past Dad's body. It howled in pain but didn't drop. Mia threw the weapon aside. "I'm out!" she shouted.

Another strike on the far wall. This time, the tips of claws emerged through the shielding. Shrieks came from all directions. Three of the aliens charged through the gaping hole behind Dad and paused, sniffing the air, calling to one another. More claws burst through the door behind us. And at last, the aliens tore through the wall.

We all stood frozen, silent. For a heartbeat I wondered if the aliens knew where we were. Maybe they thought we were all dead. If we stayed very still, didn't even breathe, then maybe . . .

An alien charged through the door behind us, flailing wildly. Alexei and Jasper dove to either side just in time, but they collided with the floor in a giant racket, and every one of the creatures—five in the room, and two more tearing through the walls—spun in our direction and screamed. They leaped, and we scattered. Cage swept me out of harm's way. But there was no escape, not anymore. The creatures closed in.

"Two minutes to self-destruct."

And we were out of time.

"Kenzie," shouted Mia suddenly. "You have to open a door!"

"What?" I yelped. My voice cut off as Cage yanked me twenty feet across the room, avoiding another alien attack. We landed by Mia, all of us clumped together. Priya and Hallam continued shooting, but their laser blasts didn't seem to have any effect anymore. The same went for Alexei's fire. Reed, Rune, and Imani weren't even attempting to use their weapons, simply cringing on the floor, despair in their expressions. Jasper waved his hands and pieces of engineering flew toward us, building a sort of circular wall. It wasn't much, but it might protect us for a minute.

Of course, we didn't have much more than that to live, anyway.

"Open a door," Mia repeated, twisting from one direction to another as if she could anticipate the next attack and somehow stop it.

"A door to *where*? This time there really is a good chance I'll launch us into space! We have nowhere to go!"

"As far away as you can," said Cage grimly, his hands firm on my arms. "It's our only hope."

"He's right," Alexei said. He crouched on the floor, very close to Mia, watching Jasper's shield of rubble shake and tremble under the force of alien attacks. "It's a chance, Kenzie. Not a good one. But even if you dump us into space somewhere, at least we'll have tried. It's better than being killed by those things or blown up with the ship."

I looked from one face to another: Rune and Cage, Mia and Alexei, Priya, Hallam, Jasper, Imani, Reed, Matt. Somewhere beyond our protective shelter lay my dad's body, dead and torn, and Liam. And I couldn't help Liam now, even if I wanted to.

But maybe, just maybe, I could save the rest of us.

I swallowed a whimper. "I'll probably kill us," I whispered.

With impeccable timing, the computer replied, "One minute to self-destruct."

No one answered. There was no answer. There was no choice.

I closed my eyes and focused on getting away from here, as far away as possible, somewhere we maybe even had a hope in hell of beating these things, of saving humanity. Why not get greedy, since I was already pushing my boundaries?

I didn't know where in the system I could take us, but I fixed the idea firmly in my mind: someplace we could survive, someplace we could help, someplace we weren't about to die.

And I opened the door.

FORTY-THREE

I CAME TO IN A BLUR OF NOISE AND MOTION.

Confusion surrounded me. I stared up a long tube, sounds echoing without meaning, everything a nonsensical swirl of light.

And then, as if a camera zoomed in on the action, the end of the tube rushed toward me. Everything came into sharp clarity. Sounds became almost too clear, piercing my brain like spikes. I howled, clamping my hands over my ears, closing my eyes against the onrush of images.

Hands grabbed me, almost painful in their intensity, and I cringed away. They released me. I tumbled onto something that felt like sandpaper and screeched as it scraped my back.

The hands had me again, less violent than before, lifting me off the sandpaper and propping me up. Sounds slowly coalesced into voices. I focused on the most familiar, which turned out to be Rune: "What's wrong with her?"

"Give her a minute." That was Cage, close by.

Hands ran over my skin, and they weren't violent at all. Something had oversensitized me to every little sound and sensation. It faded now, but for a moment it had overwhelmed me with pain and intensity like I'd never known, not even when Cage cut the chip from my arm.

I forced my eyes open, blinking against what I now realized was dim, shattered sunlight. I slumped in a pile of sand with Rune and Cage crouched nearby. Imani and Reed knelt behind me, Imani holding me up while Reed used his power on me. The sensation on my back—Reed's hands, touching, channeling, healing. Strength and cooling seemed to flow from him, and I closed my eyes, embracing the awareness.

After a moment the pain receded, the world coming into sharper focus. But with the physical pain receding, my grief surged inside me. I dropped my head to my hands to hide my tears. I couldn't cry in front of them, not now, not here, wherever *here* was.

But Dad . . . I could have convinced him. I was so close. He'd been opening up, ready to listen. We could have escaped together. And instead I'd left him lying on the floor of an Omnistellar ship, soaked in blood, killed by the aliens he'd summoned and entombed by his own corporation.

Cage slid a hand over my arm as if he knew what was going through my mind. I bit hard on my lip, so hard I tasted blood and saw stars, and between that and the warmth of his hand I managed to choke back the tears. Dad, my dad . . . but no. Not now. I almost laughed. It seemed like I never had time to grieve anyone properly.

But Dad would want me to survive. He'd want me to fight. And to do that, I needed to get myself together. I closed my eyes until the urge to cry passed, surreptitiously wiping a few stray tears away as I got to my feet. I tried to pass the effects off as the lingering consequences of the healing. "Thanks," I managed. Cage cast me a knowing look but kept his mouth shut. His hand lingered on my arm, and I leaned against him gratefully even as I squared my shoulders and found what remained of my training, becoming Omnistellar strong. "What happened?"

"We don't know." Imani regarded me carefully, as if wondering if I'd break. I forced a little more steel into my spine. "You pulled us through the portal and instantly collapsed. When you woke, you were screaming. We didn't know what happened, so Reed tried healing you."

I rested my hand on Cage's and took in my surroundings. We stood in a dimly lit desert, but I didn't get the sense that it was night. Instead the sun itself seemed dull. Its reddish tinge reminded me of my night on Mars, even though the sand looked more like Earth. Memories flooded me, summers spent with my cousins at their beach house before we'd started moving all over the planet. This had the same white, soft quality, and it was almost comforting.

In most directions, an endless sea of sand rose and fell in

wavelike dunes. Toward the sun, though, buildings shadowed against the light. It looked like a city, but something—the angles of the buildings, maybe, or the way it leaned into the horizon—didn't fit. I couldn't quite put my finger on what was wrong, but I got a distinct feeling we weren't on Earth.

As far away as we can get, I'd told my power.

And . . . it looked like it had obliged.

"We're on another planet," I whispered, almost to myself. The others stared at me, their expressions glassy, and I realized that my revelation trailed theirs. "That's impossible. Isn't it?"

Reed laughed shortly. "Kenz, I'm not sure the word 'impossible' is in my vocabulary anymore. Aliens, shifting powers, livable planets we've never heard of. Sure. Why not?" He laughed again, but without humor, his fists clamped at his sides and his arms ramrod straight.

I shook my head, my senses returning, and as they did, I took in something I'd missed before. Cage, and Rune, and Imani, and Reed . . . "Where's everyone else?" I demanded.

Reed and Imani stared at their feet. Cage and Rune met my eyes, their faces hesitantly sympathetic, and that was somehow worse. "Where are they?" I repeated hoarsely. I stumbled a few feet toward the city, spinning frantically in place, searching for them in the vast open desert. "Cage, where are they?"

"We don't know," he replied, very gently, taking me in his arms and running his hands over my shoulders. "We landed here, the five of us."

I yanked free, stumbling and landing in the sand. Puffs of dust flew around me. "Are you telling me I somehow *lost everyone else?*"

"We don't know that. They might be nearby . . ."

"Nearby where?" I gestured frantically. "They're *nowhere*, Cage! Either I left them behind, or I lost them along the way."

"*We don't know that,*" he insisted sharply, but I shook my head, dropping my face to my hands.

A moment later, Rune crouched beside me. "Kenz," she said softly. "I don't think that happened. You know why? Because you're you. You would have fought tooth and nail to hold on to all of us, whether you were aware of it or not."

"She's right," said Reed unexpectedly. He flashed me a quick smile. "You saved us on Sanctuary. You got us off the ship. And now you want me to believe you accidentally lost your friends on something as minor as a magical journey through space? Nah."

"Here's what happened," said Rune with more confidence than I thought was justified. "You pulled all of us through, but when we came out the other side, you lost your grip. We scattered. They can't be far."

As if timed by her statement, a flash lit up the sky toward the city. My head flew up, dried tears staining my cheeks as hope surged in my heart. "Was that a laser?"

"Just might be," agreed Cage. His tone was light, but I read the relief under his voice. "I'm going to go out on a limb and say it's Mia signaling us."

"Why Mia?"

"Because she's the one who'd be angriest about being dumped on some barren patch of alien desert." He flashed me a quick smile. "And because in spite of what you think of her, she's the one who'd be the most worried about getting everyone together."

What *did* I think of Mia? After everything, I cared about her, *trusted* her, and I wanted her to trust me. And maybe the first step to gaining her trust was telling her that, telling her the truth. I really hoped I'd get the chance to see her again and work it out. "All right," I said, letting Cage help me to my feet. We squared off, the five of us, facing the strange city outlined in the distance. "Let's say you're right. Let's say our friends are over there. What next?"

Rune slid her arm through mine. "We go find them, of course."

The simplicity of her answer made me smile, nearly laugh. I was pretty sure I'd trapped us on some sort of alien planet and damn near killed myself in the process. I'd split us from our friends, and I had no idea where we were or if I could get us home. But to Rune, the answer was obvious. Fall down forty-nine times, get up fifty. One problem at a time. We were separated; now to get back together. "Then what are we waiting for?" I asked as Cage's fingers threaded through my free hand. Reed and Imani drew together beside us, and we stood a moment silhouetted against the red-tinged sun, staring into the distance.

The alien landscape seemed to open up and swallow me whole. In such a short time, my life had flipped upside down. I'd lost everything: my family, my corporation, my future. I'd lost my faith in my mother when she pushed the button that she thought would kill me, and then I'd lost the chance to ever reconcile with her when she died. I'd found my father again, and then I'd lost him, too. The same grief swelled in my heart. Dad. He'd never been the most hands-on parent, always toed the company line. But with him far more than Mom, I had memories that *weren't* Omnistellar-related. Basketball games and ice cream and breaking the rules when Mom went away.

He'd listened to me at the end. I knew he had. And I couldn't blame him for what he'd done under Omnistellar's influence, not really. They'd controlled me for enough of my life. Dad had been willing to open his eyes. But now he'd never get that chance. Guilt twisted my stomach. I should have done more. Should have protected him. I had all these powers, and I couldn't even save my own father.

"Kenz," said Reed softly.

I glanced at him and realized the others were waiting on me. I took in their expressions, their trust, their quiet courage and strength, Cage's hand firm against mine. The guilt inside me twisted into something new: resolve, purpose. My parents might be gone, but I still had family. And I would not let anything happen to them.

"All right," I said. "Let's get going." We started forward

together, shoulder to shoulder, a force of determination against the dangers ahead. Maybe we'd find our friends over this hill. Or maybe we'd find nothing but blood and death and destruction. But whatever awaited us, we'd deal with it. Because whatever it was, well, we'd been there before.

ACKNOWLEDGMENTS

ACKNOWLEDGMENTS ARE AMAZING. THEY'RE A great way to make sure you offend a lot of people who helped you along your journey and then slipped your mind when it came to the all-important public part of saying thank you.

But that said, there are so many people who affect an author's book. *Containment* would not exist without them, and I would be remiss not to thank them.

First of all, to everyone who read and reviewed *Sanctuary*: *Containment* exists because of you. Thank you for your kind words, for your support, for your enthusiasm. Young adult readers are the best community in the world, and it's an amazing privilege and joy to be part of it. I would particularly like to thank the members of reading groups such as TBR and Beyond, as well as the amazing bookstagrammers whose beautiful photos of *Sanctuary* filled my heart with joy.

As always, my family plays a critical role in supporting me: my husband, Dan, who let me drag him to Tokyo for a year just because; my parents, Audrey and Lanny; my siblings, Chris and Kim; and my nephew, Emmett. I'm also blessed with an amazing family by marriage: Liz, Brian, and Erin, you are incredible people.

And my cousin Sarah. She gets grouchy when she's not included.

On the writing side of things, my agent, Caitie Flum, is one of the best people I know, and has been beyond supportive no matter what problems we encounter. Liza Dawson and all of the people at Liza Dawson Associates deserve a share of the praise as well! My editor at Simon Pulse, Sarah McCabe, is not only a fantastic editor but an incredible human being. And there are so many others who bring a book to life: Tricia Lin (special thanks for your editorial input and help with the Mandarin!), Mara Anastas, Chriscynethia Floyd, Rebecca Vitkus, Sara Berko, Sarah Creech, Caitlin Sweeny, Alissa Nigro, Anna Jarzab, Lauren Hoffman, Nicole Russo, Samantha Benson, and Christina Pecorale and her sales team.

I was also so lucky to have phenomenal support from other authors: the Class of 2K18, Timanda Wertz, Danika Stone, and all of #TeamCaitie. The team at Simon & Schuster Canada was similarly wonderful in supporting *Sanctuary*, especially my Canadian publicist, Mackenzie Croft, who put up with A LOT of questions. The University of Lethbridge and Chapters Indigo, the staff and students of both St. Patrick Fine Arts in Lethbridge and the Canadian International School in Tokyo—all of you, thank you from the bottom of my heart.

As always, I've almost certainly missed some people. Does it help if I say that I thank you most of all? You may have slipped my mind, but you are never far from my heart.

ABOUT THE AUTHOR

CARYN LIX is a sixth-grade teacher with a master's degree in English literature, specializing in children's literature and fantasy. She and her husband are proud Canadian nerds and live with their annoying (but lovable) dogs.